URBAN
SHAMAN

C.E. MURPHY

URBAN SHAMAN

LUNA™

www.LUNA-Books.com

LUNA™

First edition June 2005

URBAN SHAMAN

ISBN 0-373-09072-2

This edition published by arrangement with Harlequin Books S.A.

® and TM are trademarks of Harlequin Books S.A., used under license.
Trademarks indicated with ® are registered in the United States Patent
and Trademark Office, the Canadian Trade Marks Office and in other
countries.

www.LUNA-Books.com

Printed in U.S.A.

This book is for my grandfather,
Francis John Joseph McNally Malone,
who would have been proud of me.

Acknowledgment:

I hardly know where to begin saying thank-you.
Starting at the end and working my way backward
seems appropriate.

First: my editor, Mary-Theresa Hussey,
for taking a chance on a brand-new author;
my agent, Jennifer Jackson, for her enthusiasm;
and cover artist Hugh Syme, whose work
I'm delighted to have my book judged by.

Second: Trip, for pointing out the glaring error in the rough
draft and thereby making this a *much* better book; Silkie,
for demanding the next chapter every time she saw me; and
Sarah, my critique partner extraordinaire.

Third: my family, who never once doubted they'd be holding
one of my books in their hands one day...

And most of all, Ted,
who looked out the airplane window in the first place.

CHAPTER ONE

Tuesday, January 4th, 6:45 a.m.

There's nothing worse than a red-eye flight.

Well, all right, that's wildly untrue. There are lots of things worse than red-eye flights. There are starving children in Africa, hate crimes and Austin Powers's teeth. That's just off the top of my head.

But I was crammed into an airplane seat that wouldn't comfortably hold a four-year-old child, and had been for so many hours I was no longer certain what species I belonged to. I hadn't slept in over a day. I was convinced that if someone didn't stay awake, the airplane would fall out of the sky, and I couldn't trust anyone else to do the job.

My stomach was alternating between nausea from the airline meal I'd eaten hours earlier, and hunger from not eating another revolting meal more recently. I'd forgotten to take my contact lens case with me in my carry-on, and my eyes were burning. My spine was so bent out of shape I'd have to visit a chiropractor for a week to stand up straight again. I was flying back from a funeral to be fired.

Overall, starving children in Africa were taking a distant second to my own misery and discomfort. Shallow, but true.

A very small part of my mind was convinced that if the flight attendants would just let me into the unpressurized luggage compartment to find my contact case, everything would miraculously be right with the world. None of them would let me, so my contacts were welded to my eyes. Every several minutes I decided it wasn't worth it and started to take them out. Every time, I remembered that they were my last pair and I'd have to suffer with glasses until I made an eye appointment.

I might have succumbed, but the glasses in question were also with my luggage. The idea of navigating a soft-focus world full of featureless faces gave me a headache.

Not that I didn't have one anyway.

I climbed over the round man sleeping peacefully beside me and went to the bathroom. At least I could take the contacts out and stew them in tap water for a few minutes. Anything would be better than keeping them in my eyes.

Anything except my reflection. Have you ever noticed that the mirror is by far the largest object in those tiny airplane restrooms? I was a sick pasty color under the flickering florescent light, my eyes much too green against a network of bloodshot vessels. I looked like a walking advertisement for one of those "wow" eyedrop commercials. Second runner-up for Least Attractive Feature on an International Flight was my hair. I put my contacts in two little paper cups and set them ostentatiously on the appropriate sides of the sink, then rubbed water through my hair to give it some life again.

Now I looked like a bloodshot porcupine. Big improvement.

The only thing on my person that didn't look slimy was the brand-new silver choker necklace my mother'd given me just before she died. A Celtic cross pendant sat in the hollow of my throat. I wasn't used to jewelry, and now that I'd been reminded it was there, it felt mildly horrible, like someone was gently pushing his thumb against the delicate flesh. I shuddered and put my contacts back in before weaving my way back down the aisles to my seat. The flight attendants avoided me. I couldn't blame them.

I rested my forehead on a grease spot I'd left on the window earlier. The airlines, I thought, must have custodians who clean the windows, or there'd be an inches-thick layer of goo on them from people like me.

That thought was proof positive that I shouldn't be allowed to stay up for more than eighteen hours at a time. I have a bad habit of following every thought to its miserable, pathetic little end when I'm tired. I don't mean to. It's just that my brain and my tongue get unhinged. Though some of my less charitable acquaintances would say this condition didn't require sleep deprivation.

The plane had been descending for a while now, and I squinted at my heavy black wristwatch. The bright orange button for changing the time had become permanently depressed in Moscow, or maybe Venice. Probably Moscow; I'd found Moscow depressing, and saw no reason why the watch shouldn't. It claimed it was 5:50 p.m., which meant it was almost seven in the morning. I frowned out the window, trying to find the horizon. The sky wasn't turning gray yet, not flying into Seattle three days after New Year's. I blinked at the darkness, trying to unglue my contacts again.

My eyes teared up and I spent a few minutes with my hands over them, hoping perversely that I didn't blink the contacts out. By the time I could see again, the captain had announced the final descent into Seattle. Couldn't they find a less ominous phrase for

it? I don't like flying as it is, even without the implication that before landing I might want to have all my worldly and spiritual affairs in order. I pressed my head against the window so I could see
the ground when it came into view. Maybe I could convince it to
let us land without it being our real final descent.

Or maybe not. The plane banked abruptly and began to climb
again. A moment or two later the captain's voice crackled over
the intercom.

"Sorry about that, folks. Little disagreement over who got to
land next. We're going to take another spin around the Emerald
City and then we'll have you at the gate right on time."

Why do airline pilots always call passengers "folks"? I don't usually take umbrage at generic terminology—I'm one of those for-
ward-thinkers who believes that "man" encompasses the whole
darned race—but at whatever o'clock in the morning, I thought
it would be nice to be called something that suggested unwashed
masses a little less. Ladies and gentlemen, for example. Nevermind that, being an almost six-foot-tall mechanic, I had a hard
time passing for a lady on a good day, which this wasn't.

I watched lights slip away beneath us as we circled. If I have to
fly, I like flying into cities in the dark of morning. There's something reassuring and likable about the purposeful skim of vehicles, zooming along to their destinations. The whisk of cars meant
that the people driving them had a goal, somewhere to be, something to do. That was a hell of a lot more than I had.

I stared down at the moving lights. Maybe I didn't like them
after all.

The plane dropped the distance that made me an active voyeur
in people's lives, instead of a distant watcher. I could see individ-
uals under the streetlights. Trees became sets of branches instead
of blurry masses of brown.

A school went by below us, swingsets empty. The neighborhood was full of tidy, ordered streets. Carefully tended trees, bereft of leaves, lined uniformly trimmed lawns. Well-washed cars reflected the streetlights. Even from the air well before sunrise, it screamed out, This Is A Good Place To Live.

The next neighborhood over didn't look as posh. Wrong side of the metaphysical tracks. Cars were older, had duller paint and no wax jobs to make them gleam in the streetlights. Mismatched shingles on patched roofs stood out; lawns were overgrown. It wasn't that the owners didn't care. It was that the price of a lawn-mower or a matched roof patch could be the difference between Christmas or no Christmas that year.

Not that I knew anything about it.

A whole street went by, lightless except for one amber-colored lamp, the kind that's supposed to cut through fog. It made the street seem unnaturally vivid, details coming into sharp-edged focus below me.

A modern church, an A-frame with a sharp, nasty spire, was lit by the edges of the lone amber light. Its parking lot was abandoned except for one car, parked at an angle across two spaces, one of its doors hanging open. I wondered if it closed at all. Probably: it was a behemoth from the seventies, the kind of car that will last forever. I grew up with that kind of car. Air bags or no, the little crumply things they make today don't seem as safe.

Someone tall and lean got out of the car, draping himself over the door as he looked down the street toward the functional light. Even from above I could see the glitter of light on the butterfly knife he played with, comfortable and familiar. Watching, I knew that he could play knife games in the dark and blindfolded, and he'd never stab a finger.

A woman broke into the amber light, running down the center of the street. She took incredibly long strides, eating a huge amount of distance with each step, but her head was down and her steps swerved, like she wasn't used to running. Her hair was very long, and swung loose, flaring out as she whipped her head back to look behind her.

I twisted in my seat as the plane left the subdivision behind, trying to see.

A pack of dogs leaked out of the darkness. Their coats were pale gold under the amber light, and they loped with the casual confidence of a hunting pack following easy prey.

The woman stumbled, the pack gained and the plane took me away from them.

"You don't understand. There is a woman in trouble out there." It was the fourth time I'd said it, and the pilot kept looking at me like I was on drugs. Well, maybe I was. Lack of sleep has the same effect as certain narcotics. I was lodged in the door of the cockpit, other passengers pushing out behind me. Fourteen minutes had passed since I saw the woman. There was a knot of discomfort in my stomach, like I'd throw up if I didn't find a way to help her. I kept hoping I'd burp and it would go away, but I didn't, and the pilot was still eyeing me.

"And you saw this from the plane," he said, also for the fourth time. He had that bright lilting sound to his voice that first grade teachers use to mask irritation. "There are lots of people in trouble, ma'am."

I closed my eyes. They screamed with pain, tears flooding as I opened them again. Through the upwell, I saw an expression of dismayed horror cross the pilot's face.

Well, if he was going to fall for it, I might as well milk it. "It was five minutes before we landed," I quavered. "We circled around and came in from the northwest." I lifted my wrist to show him the compass on my watch band, although I hoped that, being the pilot, he knew we'd approached from the northwest. "I was looking out the window. I saw a woman running down the street. There was a pack of dogs after her and a guy with a switch-blade down the street in the direction she was running."

"Ma'am," he said, still very patiently. I reached out and took a fistful of his shirt. Actually, at the last moment, I grabbed the air in front of his shirt. I didn't think security could throw me out of the airport for grabbing air in a threatening fashion, not even in this post-9/11 age.

"Don't ma'am me…" I stared at his chest until my eyes focused enough to read his name badge. "Steve. Is that your name? Steve. Don't ma'am me, Captain Steve. I just need to know our rate of descent. Humor me, Captain Steve. I work for the police depart-ment. You don't want me to go to the six o'clock news after a murder's been discovered and tell them all about how the airline wouldn't lift a finger to help the woman who died."

I didn't know why I bothered. The woman was probably dead by now. Still, Captain Steve blanched and looked back over his shoulder at his instruments. I retrieved my hand and smiled at him. He blanched again. I guess my smile wasn't any better than my hair or eyes just now.

"Hurry," I said. "Once the sun comes up the streetlights will go off and I don't know if I'll be able to find her then."

I left my luggage in the airport and climbed into a cab, trying to work out the triangulation of height, speed and distance. "Drive," I said, without looking up.

"Where to, lady?"

"I don't know. Northwest."

"The airline? It's just a couple feet down the term—"

"*To* the northwest," I snarled. The cabby gave me an unfriendly look and drove. "Do you have a map?" I demanded a minute later.

"What for?"

"So I can figure out where we're going."

He turned around and stared at me.

"Watch the *road!*" I braced myself for impact. Somehow—without looking—he twitched the steering wheel and avoided the collision. I collapsed back into the seat, wide-eyed. "Map?" I asked, somewhat more politely.

"Yeah, here." He threw a city guide into my lap. I thumbed it open to find the airport.

Airplanes go fast. I realize this isn't a revelation to stun the world, but it was a little distressing to realize how far we'd flown in five minutes, and how long it would take to drive that. "All right, we're going northwest of the lake." I remembered seeing its off-colored shadow making a black mark below the plane as we'd left the subdivision behind. "Somewhere in Aurora."

"Think? That ain't such a good neighborhood, lady. You sure you wanna go there?"

"Yeah, yeah, I know. I'm trying to find somebody who's in trouble."

The cabby eyed me in the rearview. "That's the right place to look."

I glared at him through my eyebrows. He smiled, a thin I've-seen-it-all grin that didn't really have any humor in it. He had gray eyes under equally gray, bushy eyebrows. He had a thick neck and looked like he'd be at home chewing on a stogie. I asked if he had a cigarette. He turned around and looked at me again.

"Those things'll kill you, lady."

His voice was rough and deep like a lifetime smoker's. Surprise showed on my face and he gave me another soulless smile, reflected in the mirror. "My wife died of emphysema three years ago on our forty-eighth wedding anniversary. You want a smoke, kid, find it somewhere else."

Sometimes I wonder if I have a big old neon sign stamped on

my forehead, flashing Asshole. I retaliated with stunning wit: "I'm not a kid."

Gray eyes darted to the mirror again, and back to the road. "You're what, twenty-six?"

Nobody ever guessed my age right. Since I was eleven, people have misguessed my age anywhere from three to seven years in one direction or the other. I felt my jaw drop.

"It's a gift," the cabby said. "A totally useless gift. I can tell how old people are."

I blinked at him.

"Great way to get good tips," he went on. "I go into this long explanation of how I always get ages right, and then I lie. Works like a charm."

"So why'd you guess my age right?" The question came out of my mouth without consulting my brain first. I didn't want to have a conversation with the cabby.

"Never met anybody who didn't want to be in their twenties, so what's the point? Why you going out there, lady? Lotta trouble out that way, and you don't look like the type."

I glanced sideways at the window. A faint reflection looked back at me. He was right. I looked tired, hopeless and worn-out, but not like trouble. "Looks can be deceiving." His eyes slid off the rearview mirror like he was too polite to disbelieve aloud. "It's somebody else who's in trouble," I said. "I saw her from the plane."

He twisted around yet again. "You're trying to rescue somebody you saw from an *airplane?*"

"Yeah." I flinched as he twitched the steering wheel to keep in our lane, again without looking. "What do you do, use the Force?"

He glanced at the road and shrugged before turning around again. "So, what, you've got a hero complex? How the hell are you gonna find one dame you saw from the air?"

"I passed a couple basic math classes in college," I muttered.

"Look, I got the approximate height and speed we were traveling from the pilot, so figuring out the distance wasn't that hard. I mean, adjusting for the change in speed is kind of a pain in the ass, but—" I set my teeth together to keep myself from rattling on. It was a moment before I was sure I had enough control over my brain to continue without babbling. "Someplace in that vicinity there's a modern church on a street with only one amber streetlight. If I can find it before the lights go out—"

"Then you'll be the first one on a murder scene. You're nuts, lady. You must be desperate for thrills."

"Like it could possibly be any of your business," I snapped.

"Touchy, too. Pretty girl like you oughta be on her way home to her sweetie, not chasin—"

"I don't have one." I admit it. I snarled again.

"With your personality, I can't figure why not, lady."

I leaned forward and rubbed my eyes with my fingertips, elbows on my knees. The knot of unpleasantness in my stomach felt like it was trying to push its way out through my sternum, pressuring me to act whether I liked it or not. The idea that it would go away if I could just find the woman was settled into my bones, logic be damned. "Haven't you ever just really felt like you had to do something?"

"Sure. I felt like I really had to marry my old lady when she got knocked up."

I was in a cab with Plato. His depth overwhelmed me. I lifted my head enough to stare over the back of the seat at his shoulder. He grinned. He had good teeth, clean and white and strong, like he hadn't ever smoked. They were probably false.

"Never felt like I had to go chasing down some dame I saw from an airplane, nope. Guess I figured I had enough troubles of my own without adding on somebody else's."

I leaned against the window, eyes closed. "Maybe I've got

enough that I need somebody else's to make the load seem lighter."

I could feel his gaze on me in the rearview mirror again. Then he grunted, a sort of satisfied noise. "All right, lady. Let's go find your corpse."

CHAPTER TWO

"Thanks for the vote of confidence." I glowered out the window. I wouldn't have been so annoyed if I'd felt more confident myself. The cabby—whose name was Gary, according to the posted driver's license, and whose seventy-third birthday had been three days ago—drove like the proverbial bat out of hell, while I clung to the seat and tried not to gasp too audibly.

The streetlights were still on when we got to Aurora, and I wasn't actually dead, so I felt like I shouldn't complain. Gary pulled into a gas station. I squinted tiredly at the back of his head. "What are you doing?"

"Go ask if anybody knows where that church of yours is."

My squint turned into lifted eyebrows. "I thought men couldn't ask for directions."

"I ain't askin'," Gary said with aplomb. "You are. Go on."

I got.

The pimply kid behind the counter didn't look happy to see me. Judging from his thrust-out lip and down-drawn eyebrows, I figured he wasn't happy to see anybody, and didn't take it personally. He smirked at me when I asked about the church. Smirking is not a nice expression. The only person in the history of mankind who'd been able to make smirking look good was James Dean, and this kid, forgive me Senator Bentsen, was no James Dean.

I tried, briefly, to remember if I'd been that sullen and stupid when I was sixteen. I figured the fact that I couldn't remember didn't bode well, and went straight for the thing I knew would have gotten my attention at that age: cash. I wasn't usually prone to bribing people, but I was too tired to think of anything else and I was in a hurry. I dug my wallet out and waved a bill at the kid. His eyes widened. I looked at it. It was a fifty.

Shit.

"You better walk me to the church for this, kid."

He didn't take his eyes from the bill. "There's two A-frames I can think of. One's about five blocks from here. The other is a couple miles away."

"Which direction? For both of them." He told me, still watching the fifty like it was a talisman. I sighed, dropped it on the counter, and muttered, "Thanks," as I pushed my way out of the gas station. He snatched it up, hardly believing I was really handing it over. Great. I'd just turned a kid onto the lifetime role of snitch.

Worse, I'd given away a quarter of the meager cash I had on hand, and cabs from SeaTac were damned expensive. I climbed back into the car. "East a few blocks, and if that's not it, there's another one to the southwest. Hurry, it's getting light out."

"What, you want to get your fingers in the blood while it's still warm? You need help, lady."

"Joanne." Having a nosy cabby know my name had to be better than being called "lady" for another half hour. "And you're the one hung up on corpses. I'm hoping she's still alive." I tugged on my seat belt, scowling again. It was starting to feel like a permanent fixture on my face.

"You always an optimist, or just dumb?"

A shock of real hurt, palpable and cold, tightened itself around my throat and heart. I fumbled the seat belt. It took effort to force the words out: "You have no right to call me dumb." I stared out the window, seat belt in one numb hand, trying furiously to blink tears away. Gary looked at me in the rearview, then twisted around.

"Hey, hey, hey. Look, lady. Joanne. I didn't mean nothin' by it."

"Sure." My voice was harsh and tight, almost too quiet to be heard. "Just drive." I got the seat belt on this time. Gary turned around and drove, quiet for the first time since I'd gotten in the cab.

I watched streetlights go by in the hazy gold of sunrise, trying to get myself under control. I didn't generally cry easily and I didn't generally get hurt by casual comments from strangers. But it had been a long day. More than a long day. A long week, a long month, a long year, nevermind that it was only the fourth of January. And the day was only going to get longer. I still had to stop by my job and get fired.

The streetlights abruptly winked out as we turned down another street, and with them, my chance to find the runner. A small voice said, "Fuck." After a moment I realized it was me.

"That one's still on," Gary said, subdued. I looked up, keeping my jaw tight to deny tired, disappointed tears. A bastion of amber stood against the dawn, one single light shining on the entire street. I watched it go by without comprehension, then jerked around so fast I hurt my neck. "That's it!"

Gary hit the brakes hard enough to make my neck crunch again. I winced, clutching at it as I pressed my nose against the window. "That's it, that's it!" I shrieked. "Look, there's the church!

Stop! Stop!" The car was gone from the parking lot, but there was no mistaking the vicious spire stabbing the morning air. "Holy shit, we found it!"

Gary accelerated again, grinning, and pulled into the church parking lot. "Maybe you're not dumb. Maybe you're lucky."

"Yeah, well, God watches over fools and little children, right?" I tumbled out of the cab, getting my feet tangled in the floor mat and catching myself on the door just before I fell. "Well?" I demanded. "Aren't you coming?"

His eyebrows elevated before he shrugged and swung his own door open. "Sure, what the hell. I never saw a fresh murdered body before."

I closed my door. "Have you seen stale ones?" I decided I didn't want to know the answer, and strode away. Gary kept up, which surprised me. He was so broad-shouldered I expected him to be short, but he stood a good two inches taller than me. In fact, he looked like a linebacker.

"You look like a linebacker."

"College ball," he said, disparaging enough that it was obvious he was pleased. "Before it turned into a media fest. It's all about money and glory now."

"It didn't used to be?"

He flashed me his white-toothed grin. "It used to be about glory and girls."

I laughed, stopping at the church door, fingertips dragging over the handle. They were big and brass and twice as wide as my own hands. You could pull them down together and throw the doors open in a very impressive fashion. I wasn't sure I wanted to.

"You sure your broad is gonna be in here, lady?"

"Yeah," I said, then wondered why that was. It made me hesitate and turn back to the parking lot. Except for Gary's cab, it was empty. There was no reason the woman couldn't have gotten into the car with the man with the butterfly knife, no real reason to think she'd even made it as far as the parking lot, much less the church.

"Yeah," I said again, but trotted back down the steps. Gary stayed by the door, watching me. The car'd been on the south end of the parking lot, between the woman and the church. I jogged over there, eyes on the ground. I heard Gary come down the steps, rattling scattered gravel as he followed me.

"What're you looking for? I thought you said the broad was in the church."

I shrugged, slowing to a walk and frowning at the cement. "Yeah, but that's probably just wishful thinking. I was wondering if there'd been a fight. If the guy with the knife was after her, she'd have had to have gotten thr—"

"*What* guy with a knife?" Gary's voice rose as I crouched to squint at the ground. I looked over my shoulder at him.

"Didn't I mention that?"

"No," he said emphatically, "you didn't."

"Oh. There was a guy with a knife. He was good, too."

"You saw this from a *plane?*"

I puffed out my cheeks. "You ever seen somebody who's good with a knife? Street-good, I mean?"

"Yeah."

"Okay. So have I. It looks a certain way. Graceful. This guy looked that way, yeah, even from a plane."

"Lady, you better have like twenty-two-hundred vision."

I stood up. The bubble of icky feeling in my stomach was still there, prodding at me like I hadn't done enough to help the woman. "I wear contacts."

Gary snorted derisively. I sighed. "I know what I saw."

"Sure." He didn't say anything for another second, looking at the ground. "I know what you didn't see."

"What?"

He pointed, then walked forward a couple of spaces. "Somebody lost a tooth." He bent over and poked at a shining white thing on the concrete, not quite touching it.

I walked over, bending to look at the enameled thing on the ground. It was a tooth, all right, smooth little curves and a bumpy top, complete with bloody roots. "Eww. Somebody got cut, too." I nodded at thin splatters of blood, a few feet farther out than the tooth, that were already dry on the concrete. Gary cast his gaze to the heavens.

"The lady goes 'eww' at a tooth and she's looking for a corpse."

"I'm looking for a person," I corrected.

"And you think she's in the church."

"Yeah."

"So why the hell are we screwing around in the parking lot?"

I looked around. "The light's better over here?" It was one of my favorite jokes, left over from my childhood. I never expected anyone else to get it, but Gary grinned, dug a hand into his pocket, and tossed me a quarter. I caught it, grinning back. "Now that we've got that taken care of."

We walked back to the church together.

I was right. The doors swept open, impressively silent. I felt like I should be leading a congregation in search of the light, not a linebacker-turned-cabby in search of a corpse. I stepped through the doors, half-expecting a floorboard to creak and mar the enormous silence.

Within a few steps I was sure a floorboard wouldn't have dared creak in this place. It wasn't the solemn, weighty quiet of old churches or cathedrals. Those places could absorb the sound of heels clicking and children laughing with dignity and acceptance. This church simply forbade them. I wasn't even wearing heels, and

I found myself leaning forward on my toes a little so that my tennies couldn't possibly make any excessive noise on the hardwood floors. This was a church where "Sinners in the Hands of an Angry God" would be performed and harkened to weekly. I noticed I was holding my breath.

It was stunning, in an austere, heartless way. The A-frame probably carried sound beautifully, but the only natural lighting was from a wall of windows behind the pulpit. I use the term natural loosely: there wasn't much natural about the violent, grim images of Christ's crucifixion, or Joseph and Mary being turned away from the inn, or Judas's betrayal, or any of the other scenes I recognized, more of them jimmied into the stained glass than I would have thought possible. This was a church where you came to be terrified into obedience, not welcomed as a sinner who has found the true way.

The pews were hardwood, without cushions, and the choir books looked as though they'd never been cracked open. I guessed you'd better know your music before you came to church. It was not a friendly place.

It was also completely empty of human life other than my own and Gary's. I looked back at him. He frowned faintly before meeting my eye. I couldn't blame him.

"I don't know where she is," I said before he could ask, and lifted my voice. "Hello? Hello?" My voice bounced up to the rafters and echoed back at me. The acoustics were incredible, and I tilted my head back to look longingly at the ceiling. "Wow. I'd love to sing in here."

"Yeah? You sing?"

I shrugged. "I don't scare the neighbors."

Gary bent over and looked under the pews. "Yeah, well, maybe you can sing yourself up a dame. There ain't nobody here, Jo."

A muscle in my shoulder blade twitched. "Y'know, nobody calls me that except my dad."

"What, did he want a boy?"

"Not exactly." That seemed like enough information to volunteer.

Gary unbent a little, hooking his arm over the top of a pew as he looked at me. Enough time passed to let me know that he was politely not asking about my dad before he asked, "Then what do they call you?"

"Joanie, or Joanne, usually. Sometimes Anne, Annie."

Gary straightened up, hands in the small of his back. "My wife was named Anne. You don't look like an Anne to me."

I smiled. "What'd she look like?"

"'Bout four eleven, blond hair, brown eyes, petite. You gotta be at least a foot taller than she was."

"Yeah." It came out sounding like a laugh, and I smiled again. "So call me Jo, then."

"You sure? I don't think you get along with your old man."

"I don't not get along with him." How had I ended up in a church looking for a body and discussing my home life? "It's okay. I don't mind Jo." I waited for the muscle in my shoulder blade to spasm again. It always did when I was tense. This time it didn't. Maybe I really didn't mind being called Jo. Who knew?

"There's nobody in here, Jo," Gary repeated. I tried to stuff my hands in my pockets, only to discover I didn't have any. The thing I'd learned about traveling was that it was slightly less miserable if I wore stretch pants with an elastic waistband. The ones I was wearing were black and comfy and had nice straight legs, but no pockets. I hooked my thumbs into the strap of my fanny pack, instead. I hated the things, but I never learned to carry a purse, and a fanny pack is at least attached to me. Makes it harder to forget.

"C'mon, let's go. Nobody here."

"No, wait."

Gary sighed, exasperated, and leaned against a pew, arms folded across his chest. Seventy-three or not, he made a pretty impressive wall of a man. "Then do your thing and find the broad."

I looked at him. "My thing?"

"You got some kinda thing going on here, lady. Normal people don't stick their heads out a plane window and see dames that need rescuing. So do your thing and rescue her. My meter's still running."

Oh, God. It probably was, too. "Hope you take credit cards." I walked to the front of the church and around the pulpit.

I really, honest-to-God, expected to see the woman cowering in the back side of the pulpit. That she wasn't came as a shock. "Well, shit."

"What? You find your body after all?" Gary shoved off his pew and came long-legging it up to the front.

"No, you ghoul. There's nobody here. I really thought she would be."

"I'll cut you a break and won't expect a tip, just for the satisfaction of being right." He leaned on the pulpit, grinning whitely at me. I had the sudden urge to pop him in those nice straight clean teeth. It must have shown in my face, because his grin got even wider. "You wanna try it?"

"No," I said sourly. "I think you'd break me in half."

"Only a little bit."

"Gee. Thanks." I backed up a couple steps and leaned on the edge of the...hell if I know what it's called. Looked like an altar to me. All gilded and dour. It had probably never been introduced to a woman's behind in its whole existence. Or maybe it had been. You always heard stories about the priest who's a pillar of the community but turns out to be having affairs with half the congregation. Seemed to me if you're going to sin, you might as well do it right. On the altar would be a nice big sin. "I thought she'd be here."

"Why?"

I shrugged. "I don't know. Churches are supposed to be sanctuary, or something. I thought she'd be safe in here. Consecrated ground."

"What century are you living in, lady?"

"The wrong one, I guess." I thumped on the edge of the altar, annoyed.

The top slipped.

I leaped off it like it had bitten me. Gary's bushy eyebrows went up. We both stared at the inch-wide crack at the edge of the box where the lid had pushed back. "You don't believe in vampires, do you, Gary?"

"God damn it," he said, "I was trying *real* hard not to think that way."

"Kind of fits, though, doesn't it? Scary-looking church, big old crypt in the middle, the living dead ris—"

"It's past dawn," Gary said hastily. "No vampires after dawn. Right?"

"There's no such thing as vampires, Gary."

He stared at me dubiously. I stared at the crypt dubiously. Funny how a second ago it had been an altar and now it was a crypt. "Well?" he demanded. "Are you gonna look in it?"

"Yeah."

"When?"

"As soon as I get up the nerve."

He prodded me in the small of my back, pushing me forward. I admired the resistance in my body. I felt like he was trying to move a me-shaped lead weight. I expected to hear my feet scraping along with the sound of metal ripping up hardwood. Instead, I stumbled half a step forward, then glared over my shoulder at

Gary. "You're a big strong man. Aren't you supposed to be plunging into danger before me?"

"You're forty-seven years younger than me, lady," he pointed out. "And almost as tall as I am. And you're in my weight class. And it's *your* vampire in the coffin."

"I am *not* in your weight class," I said, offended. "You've got to outweigh me by at least forty pounds." I edged a quarter of a step closer to the crypt. "And it's not a vampire."

"How much do you weigh?"

"Isn't it rude to ask a woman how much she weighs?"

"Nah, it's rude to ask how old she is, and I already know."

Oh. Damn. I stepped forward, holding my breath. The crypt didn't do anything. "I weigh one seventy-two."

"No shit?"

"I'm almost six feet tall, Gary, what do you want me to weigh, a hundred and thirty? I'd be dead." I peeked into the little hole the lid made where it had slid over. If there was a vampire in there, it was a very small, very hidden vampire. Or maybe it blended with shadows well. Vampires were supposed to do that, weren't they?

I was scaring myself. "Give me a hand with this."

Gary crept forward. "I outweigh you by sixty pounds."

"That's why you're a linebacker, and I'm not. Push on three. One, two, three!"

I underestimated how much push we could provide. The lid shot off the box, crashing to the floor with a thud that rattled the rafters. I fell forward, shrieking, with visions of being sucked dry by vampires supplied by my too-vivid imagination.

Halfway into the crypt, I was met by another shrieking woman on her way out.

CHAPTER THREE

My head hit the floor with a crack only slightly less impressive than the crypt lid had made. My vision swam to black, and my tailbone decompressed like a series of firecrackers. I wouldn't need to visit the chiropractor after all.

Vision returned in time to see something bright and glittery arching down at me. I flung my hand up, barely deflecting the fall of a knife. My wrist hit the woman's with the solid thunk that meant a week from now, after I'd forgotten this had happened, a bone bruise would color half my arm. The woman's grip loosened and the knife glanced off my cheekbone instead of driving into my throat. I hit her again, and the knife skittered away, bouncing across the hardwood floor.

The woman shrieked again—or maybe she hadn't stopped—and scrambled after the knife. I tackled her, flinging my arms around her. Her white blouse suddenly stained red where my cheek pressed against it.

Gary pulled her out from under me and to her feet, pushing

her elbows in against her waist and holding her still. His hands looked bizarrely large in proportion to her waist. She winced and hissed, her head down as I got up unsteadily and touched my face. Blood skimmed over my fingertips and into my palm, coloring in the lifeline. I watched vacantly as it trailed all the way around the side of my hand and down my wrist. My face didn't hurt. It seemed like it should.

"You got lucky," Gary said. "She was gonna cut your throat right out. What should I do with her?"

I looked up, startled and vacant. "Oh, fer Chrissakes," he said, "You're shocky, or somethin'. Get something to stop the bleeding."

That seemed like a pretty good idea. I looked around, silver catching my eye again. The knife she'd cut me with lay against the foot of a pew, a nice heavy butterfly knife. I picked it up and cut a piece off the altar banner, holding it to my face while Gary asked again what to do with the woman.

"Um," I said, and *then* my face started to hurt. For a minute I was too busy blinking back tears to give a damn what Gary did. I croaked, "Hold her for a minute," and tried increasing the pressure on my cut to see if it helped the pain any. It didn't. I looked up through teary eyes. It had to be the same woman. She had hip-length dark brown hair with just enough curl to make me covet it. "You're the one I saw from the airplane."

She lifted her head to look at me, eyes wide. I dropped my hand from my face and the makeshift bandage fell to the floor as I gawked at her.

She was beautiful. Not your garden-variety pretty girl, not your movie-star kind of beautiful. She was the sort of beautiful that Troy had gone to war over. High, fragile cheekbones, delicate pointed chin, absolutely unblemished pale skin. Long-lashed blue eyes, thin straight eyebrows. A rosebud mouth, for God's sake. There were very fine lines of pain around the corners of her mouth and eyes, and the nostrils of her perfectly straight nose were flared a little, none of which detracted from her beauty.

"Jesus." I suddenly had a very good idea of why she'd been chased.

"What?" Gary demanded. I just kept ogling the woman. She had a perfect throat. She had great collarbones. She had Mae West curves, too, a real hourglass figure. She was at least eight inches shorter and fifty pounds lighter than I was. It said something for her momentum that she'd knocked me flat on my ass. I didn't think I could have knocked Gary over, if I'd been her and he'd been me.

I hated her.

I was so busy staring and hating her it took a while to notice there was drying blood on her shirt, not just the new stuff I'd put there, but sticky, half-dried brown spots. "Shit. Let her go, Gary."

"*What?*"

"Let her go. Her arms are all cut up. You're hurting her."

Gary let go like his hands were on fire. The woman made a small sound and folded her arms under her breasts, shallow gashes leaking blood onto her shirt again. I expected her voice to be musical, dulcet tones, with an exotic accent. Instead she was an alto who sounded like she was from Nowhere In Particular, U.S.A. "You saw me from an airplane?"

People kept saying that. I took a breath to respond and realized I didn't feel like I needed to throw up anymore. The twist of sickness in my belly had disipated. My shoulders dropped and I let the breath go in a sigh. I wasn't a fan of my innards guiding my actions. Now all I had to do was explain myself so I could go get fired and go home to sleep. "At about seven this morning. I was flying in from Dublin." As if that had anything to do with anything. "I saw you running, and something was after you. Dogs, or something. And a guy with a knife." I looked at the knife I was still holding. "This knife? How'd you get past him? How'd you get away from the dogs?"

"I ran away from the dogs," the woman said, "and I kicked the guy with the knife in the head."

Gary and I both stared at her. She smiled a little bit. A little bit of a smile from her was like spending a little bit of time with Marilyn Monroe. It went a long way. "I guess I don't look like a kickboxer," she said.

"That's for damned sure," Gary mumbled. He looked even more awed than I felt. I guessed it was nice to know some things didn't change even when you hit your eighth decade. "So how'd you get all cut up?" he asked.

She shrugged a little. "I had to get close enough to kick him."

"That his tooth out there?"

Her whole face lit up. "I knocked a tooth loose?" She looked like a little kid who'd just gotten her very own Red Ryder BB gun for Christmas. I almost laughed.

"You knew him? Why was he chasing you?" Even as I asked, I knew the question was idiotic. Men have hunted people down for much less attractive prizes. I *liked* being tall. Next to this woman I felt as ungainly as a giraffe.

"Why did you come to save me if you don't know who he is?" she asked at almost the same time. We stared at each other.

"Let's start again," I said after a long moment of silence. Then I had no idea where to start with someone who'd been attacked and who just tried to cut my throat out. Names seemed like a good place. "I'm Joanne Walkingstick."

It's physically impossible to look at your own mouth in astonishment. I gave it a good shot. I hadn't called myself by that name in at least five years. More like ten. Gary raised his bushy eyebrows at me curiously.

"You don't look like an Indian," he said, which really meant,

"How the hell did you end up with a last name like Walkingstick?" I'd heard it for the first twelve years of my life.

"I know." I hadn't known that a practiced tone of controlled patience could lie in wait for the next time it was needed, but there it was. It hadn't been needed for years. It meant I wasn't going to say anything else, and if you wanted to make a big deal of it, you'd end up in a fistfight.

I was good at brawling.

Gary, the linebacker, let the tone blow right over him and stayed there with his arms folded and eyebrows lifted. The woman studied me through drawn-down eyebrows. It made a wrinkle in the middle of her forehead. On me, that wrinkle was scary. On her, it was cute. I hated her some more.

Gary was wrong, anyway. I did look Indian. My coloring was wrong, but in black-and-white photos I looked like I didn't have a drop of Irish blood in me. I'd changed my last name to Walker when I turned eighteen and graduated from high school. Nowhere official. I just filled out every piece of paperwork, even the diploma application, with Walker. My birth certificate was the only piece of paper I owned that had Walkingstick as my official last name.

"My name is Marie D'Ambra," the woman said.

"You don't look Italia—" I nearly bit my tongue off.

"Adopted," she replied, amusement sparkling in her eyes.

Oh. "My mother was black Irish," I said after a moment. "I got her coloring." It seemed like a fair exchange of information. "Why was that guy after you? What was *chasing* you? It didn't look like a dog pack. Exactly."

Marie inclined her head. It looked gracious. How did she do that? "It wasn't. His name is Cernunnos, and he is the leader of the Wild Hunt. It was the Hunt who chased me. Why did you come to help me?"

I looked sideways at Gary, who shrugged almost imperceptibly. I wouldn't think a guy with shoulders that wide could shrug imperceptibly. It should be more like plate tectonics. I hoped I was in that kind of shape when I was seventy-something. Marie waited patiently, and I shrugged more perceptibly. I really didn't want to say, "I felt like I was going to puke if I didn't," but I heard myself saying it anyway. I curled a lip, shook my head, and added, "You looked like you needed help. I felt like I had to try to find you."

One half of her mouth curved up in a smile. I stopped hating her. I couldn't hate a smile like that. Her smile made the world seem like it would all be okay. "A *gwyld* at the crossroads," she murmured, and I frowned at her.

"A what?"

She shook her head and did the wonderful half smile again. "Nothing. I'm sorry for cutting you. I thought you had to be one of Cernunnos's people. I couldn't imagine why anyone else would be looking for me."

"One of his people? Not him himself?" That sounded wrong. "He himself."

Marie shook her head. "Christian earth. Even Cernunnos can only stand on it a few minutes. None of the Hunt can at all."

I looked at Gary. Gary looked at me. We both looked at Marie. She smiled the tight little smile of someone who knows she sounds crazy. It made me feel better. "This isn't the best place to talk about this," she said.

"Why not? You just said the guy who was after you can't come here," Gary said.

"No, but he can send people who can," I said before Marie could. She nodded. "If he couldn't, she wouldn't have thought we might be trouble." I touched my cheek gingerly. It was still bleeding. "An emergency room might be a good place to go. This is going to need stitches, and you should get looked at, too."

Marie extended her arms, palms up. Half a dozen cuts still oozed red as she looked at them. She looked like a clumsy suicide attempt. "They'll heal," she said dismissively. "He knows I was hurt. I'd rather not go somewhere so obvious."

"You'd rather *bleed?*" I demanded. Gary cleared his throat.

"I got a first-aid kit in the car."

I glared at him. He smiled and shrugged. "Sure," I said, "the pretty one whose face isn't cut up gets her way. Fine." I stomped off the dais, picking the butterfly knife up off the pulpit. It made a satisfying series of clicks as the blade and handles slapped against each other when I closed it.

"Hey. That's mine." Marie had to take two steps to every one of mine, even after she ran to catch up with me.

"Not anymore, it isn't. Call it a finder's fee."

"You didn't find it."

"I found you." I shoved the knife into my waistband. Two steps later the elastic shifted and the knife slid down my leg and out of my pants, clattering to the floor. Gary choked back a guffaw and Marie grinned broadly.

I picked up the knife with as much dignity as I could muster and stalked out of the church.

I thought going into a diner all bloody and bandaged was more conspicuous than going to an emergency room, but Marie insisted. Gary butterfly-bandaged my cheek and wrapped up Marie's arms while I sulked. As a gesture of peace he turned the meter off, but my face hurt too much for me to be grateful.

I dragged a coat out of my carry-on and pulled it on over my bloody T-shirt as we went into the diner. Marie walked in like she was daring the world to comment on her bloodstains. No one did. We sat down, silent until the waitress brought us our drinks. I didn't know what it was about food, but it always seemed to make it easier to talk.

Marie folded her hands around an enormous glass of orange juice. I had a coffee. Actually, this being Seattle, I didn't have just a coffee, even at a cheap diner. I had a grande double-shot latte with a shot of amaretto. Just the smell of the stuff got me high.

"Cernunnos leads the Wild Hunt," Marie said to her orange juice. "They ride to collect the souls of the dead." She looked up to see if that cleared things up for us. Gary just waited. He really was having a regular black coffee. I didn't even know they made that anymore. He'd ordered breakfast, too. I was hungry, but between adrenaline and no sleep, I was pretty sure food would just come back up again. Now that I thought about it, the injection of caffeine probably wasn't such a great idea on that combination. Food would have been better.

"You ain't dead," Gary pointed out. Marie winced, producing a pained smile.

"An oversight."

"Fill in us dumb ones," I said. "What's a wild hunt?"

"*The* Wild Hunt," she corrected.

"Okay, *the* wild hunt. What is it?"

She sat back, her hands still wrapped around the orange juice glass. She hadn't drunk any yet. "Cernunnos was an old Celtic god," she said slowly. "When Christianity came to Ireland and Britain, his cult was so powerful that it took a while for it to die out. And it never entirely faded."

"Like any pagan religion," I interrupted. Marie lifted her eyes to look at me. The muscle in my shoulder blade twitched again and I shrugged, trying to loosen it. "The Peop—the Cherokee still practice their old ways, too. Faith is hard to stomp out." The People. Walkingstick. What was wrong with me?

"Like any pagan religion," she agreed. "Cernunnos is the Celtic

Horned God, essentially a fertility figure but with very deep ties to death as well. There are Norse and German counterparts, Woden, Anwyn, rooted in a common ancestry." She waved her hand absently, brushing aside the trivia.

"And he's after you." I infused my voice with as much sarcasm as I could. It was pathetically little. She was too pretty to be sarcastic at, even if she was crazy.

"Yes." Marie nodded and dragged her orange juice to the edge of the table.

"You seriously think you got some kind of god after you?" Gary asked. Marie nodded. Gary turned to me. "I vote we drop her off at a loony bin and run for the hills."

"Are you asking me to run away with you, Gary? After such a short, violent courtship?" It wasn't that I didn't agree. In fact, I pushed my latte away, getting ready to stand up. Gary did the same, looking relieved.

"Sorry, lady," he said, and stood. I put my palms on the table and looked at Marie. She looked bone-tired, more tired than I felt. She looked like she'd been through this a dozen times already, and was just waiting for the time that she screwed up and didn't live through it.

Dammit, I'd jumped off a plane and come tearing through the streets of Seattle to find this woman. I didn't feel like I'd seen it through to the end yet. I settled back into my seat.

"Aw, hell," Gary said, and sat back down. Marie bit her lower lip, holding her breath while she watched me. When I didn't move again, she let her breath out and began talking again, without taking her eyes off me. If she thought she was pinning me in place, she was right. Girls weren't really my thing. Hell, I didn't even like women much, as a species. I had no idea why I wanted to help her so much. Marie took a deep breath.

"I gather neither of you are mystics."

Gary laughed so loudly I nearly spilled my coffee. A tired-looking blonde behind the counter turned around and looked at us. Marie twisted a little smile at her orange juice. I suddenly felt sorry for her, which was new.

"Okay," she said in a very small voice. "Can you handle the idea that there's more to the world than we see?"

"There are more things, Horatio, than are dreamt of in your philoso-phy." It was the obvious line. What wasn't so obvious was that Gary beat me to it, and said it in a rich, sonorous voice. Marie and I both looked at him. "Annie liked 'em big, not stupid," Gary said with a grin. "Sure, lady, there's more than we see."

Marie glanced at me. "Why does he keep calling me lady?"

"I think it's an endearing character trait. When he really gets to know you, he'll start calling you 'dame' and 'broad,' too."

"Yeah?" She looked at Gary, then back at me. "How long've you known him?" I turned my wrist over to look at my watch, which was still wrong.

"About ninety minutes. So what're we missing in our philoso-phies, Marie?"

She smiled. It was radiant. Honest to God. Her whole face lit up, all warm and welcoming and charming. Gary looked pole-axed. I pretended I didn't and allowed myself the superior thought: *Men.*

"I'm an anthropologist," Marie said. "I've been studying simi-larities between cultural mythologies for about ten years now."

All of a sudden she had an aura of credibility. Well, except I thought she looked about twenty-five. I stole a glance at Gary, who didn't look disbelieving. Either he thought she looked older than that, or his so-called useless talent was a load of bunk. "How old is she?" I asked him. He lifted a bushy eyebrow, glancing at me, then looked back at her.

"Thirty-nine," he said, in tandem with Marie. Her eyebrows

went up while my jaw went down. Gary looked smug. After a few seconds she shook her head and went on.

"It's hard," she said carefully, "to immerse yourself in a study, in mythology and belief, without beginning to understand that even if *you* don't believe it, that someone did, and that it has, or had, power. I don't consider myself particularly susceptible to bullshit."

Looking at her, I could believe it. She had to have heard every line in the book, by now. It would take genuine effort to remain gullible, and she didn't seem gullible. She finally lifted her orange juice and drank half of it.

"Certain legends had more power for me than others. They were easier to believe. They tended down Celtic lines—my mom says it's blood showing through. But the Morrigan, the Hunt, banshees, cross-comparisons of those legends to other cultures were more fascinating to me than most other things. A while ago a gloomy friend of mine pointed out that they weren't just Celtic legends. They were all Celtic legends that had to do with death or violence."

She took a deep breath, looking up at us with those very blue eyes. "Right after that I started to be able to sense who was about to die."

Silence held, stretched, and broke as my voice shot up two octaves. "You're a fucking *banshee?*" The tired blonde behind the counter looked our way again, then shifted her shoulders and turned away, uninterested. Marie's thin straight eyebrows lifted a little.

"I thought you didn't know anything about those legends?"

"I just got off the plane from a funeral in Ireland."

Understanding and curiosity came into Marie's eyes. "Whose funeral?" she asked.

"My moth—what does that have to do with anything?"

"I was curious. You don't have the sense of someone close to you having died."

"We weren't close," I said shortly. This was the second time this morning I'd said something about my family. I was breaking all sorts of rules for me. I really needed sleep. The waitress came by and slid Gary's breakfast in front of him. Three eggs, fried, over a slab of steak, three huge pancakes, hash browns, bacon, sausage and a side of toast. I got full just looking at it. Gary didn't pick up his fork, and after a couple seconds I frowned at him.

The big guy was actually pale, gray eyes wide under the bushy eyebrows. He stared at Marie like she'd turned from a golden retriever puppy into a king cobra. I did a double-take from him to her and back again, wondering what was wrong. "Gary?"

"Don't worry," Marie said, very softly. "I don't see anything about you."

Gary focused on his plate abruptly, cutting a huge bite of steak and eggs to stuff into his mouth. His eyebrows charged up his forehead defiantly, like he expected Marie to make an addendum to her comment. Her mouth twitched in a smile, but she didn't say anything else.

"Does being a banshee have anything to do with why what's-his-face wants you?" I reached over and snitched a piece of bacon off Gary's plate. He noticed, but didn't stop me.

"Cernunnos. I don't know. Maybe."

"Because, what, the Hunt isn't scary enough without you?" I heard myself capitalize the word, and wondered why I'd done it.

"I haven't had a conversation with him about it," she said. "I don't really *know* what he wants me for."

"So how do you know he wants you?"

"Having a pack of ghost dogs and rooks and a herd of men on horseback chase you down the street gives a girl a pretty good idea that she's wanted for something," Marie said acerbically.

I had the grace to look embarrassed. "Okay, it was a stupid question."

"Couldn't it have been vampires?" Gary asked wistfully around a mouthful of hash browns. "Vampires are at least kinda sexy. What's sexy about packs of dogs and birds? No such thing as rooks around here anyway."

"They come with Cernunnos." Marie kept saying these things like they were obvious.

"Marie, what *are* you?" I asked. She shrank back, looking surprisingly guilty. "Banshees are fairies," I said. "Please don't tell me you're a fairy."

"Not much of one, anyway," she said to her orange juice, "or I wouldn't be able to hide on holy ground, or use that knife." She nodded at the butterfly knife I'd set on the table at my elbow. I picked it up without opening it and looked at her curiously. "Iron," she said, "steel."

"What about it?"

Have you ever had someone look at you like you were a particularly slow child? That's the look Marie gave me. Come to think of it, Captain Steve had given me that same look earlier. I was beginning to think I should be offended. Marie interrupted before I got up the energy. "You really don't know anything about the mystical, do you?"

"Why should I?"

"I thought Indians knew that kinda stuff," Gary put in. I looked at him incredulously. He shrugged. "Well, you got all them powwows and stuff. What were you doing during the powwows?"

"Reading books on evolution," I said through my teeth. Apparently that tone was scarier than the one I'd employed earlier, because Gary closed his mouth around another forkful of food with an audible smack. "That's like saying all big guys are stupid, or all blondes are dumb, or—"

Gary pushed his food into one cheek, squirrel-like, and nodded. "Yeah, yeah, I gotcha. It was a joke, Jo. Jeez."

"Perpetuating stereotypes through joking isn't funny."

"I'm *sorry*." Gary sounded like he meant it. I frowned at him, then sighed and put my face in my hands.

"Forg—*fuck* that hurts!" I jerked my hand away from my cheek, expecting to see fresh new blood on my palm. I was spared that, at least. This was not my morning.

"The Celtic fair folk aren't supposed to be able to bear the touch of iron," Marie explained, once more interrupting my downward spiral of misery before it began. "Not even their gods. And I don't know what I am, not in the way you're asking the question. I'm an anthropologist with an unusual skill."

"Skill? Like you learned it deliberately?"

Marie shrugged. "Talent, skill. I hesitate to call it a gift." She caught Gary's eye, and flashed a quick smile. "Although I could make a killing in insurance," she said quickly. He snapped his mouth shut around another bite of food, beaten to the punch. I grinned. It made my cheek hurt. "In any other aspect," Marie said, "I'm ordinary."

"You are not," I said, "ordinary." My voice came out about six notes lower than normal. I felt color rush to my cheeks, which made the cut throb furiously. Marie's mouth quirked in a crooked little smile. I bet even a smirk would look good on her.

"Thank you," she said, easily enough to make my blush fade. I could feel Gary looking at me. I very carefully didn't look at him.

"You're welcome." I lifted my hands to my temples and held my head. My shoulders ached. I needed a hot shower, a massage from a tall bronze guy named Rafael and about sixteen weeks of sleep. "All right, look. Let me take you at face value."

Marie pulled a wry little moue, and Gary let out a deep chuckle. I felt a little smile creep over my face and split my cheek open again. I was going to bleed all day long. How fun. "Let me take your *story* at face value," I amended. Marie laughed.

"I'm sorry," she said. "I was about eight when I figured out being taken at face value meant people were going to let me get by on my looks. If I'd had a different family I'd never have learned to think at all. Why would I need to?" The way she said it made me think she'd used her looks just as much as she'd used her brain to get where she was in life. There are beautiful people who know they're beautiful, and use it like a weapon. I got the impression Marie used it as a tool. I couldn't blame her.

"You're being hunted by an ancient Irish god who wants you for his own nefarious purposes. Dead or alive will do. Have I got that right?"

Marie nodded.

"Right," I said. This was completely insane. "How can I help?"

"He's gaining power," she said. "He will until the sixth, and then he'll be banished to the otherworlds until Samhain. It's the cycle he's bound to."

"Until what?"

"Halloween," Gary and Marie both said. I looked at Gary. He shrugged and ate a piece of bacon. I pressed my eyes shut, wished it didn't make my cheek hurt, and opened them again to look at Marie. She kept right on *not* looking as if she were completely insane.

"Just out of morbid curiosity—the sixth?"

"It's the last day of Yule."

I wished she would stop saying things like that as if it explained everything. I waved my hand in a circle, eyebrows lifted as I shook my head. Apparently the connotation of "yeah, so?" got through to her, because she sat back with a quiet sigh.

"Yuletide used to be very important in the Catholic Church. It's the twelve days from Christmas to the sixth of January, and it marks the days of Cernunnos's greatest power as he rides on this earth."

"You're telling me some random church holy days hold sway over an immortal god." That time the sarcasm came through loud and clear, whether she was pretty or not. Her shoulders drooped.

"Those dates are closely tied to the solstice and the half-moon cycle after the solstice," she said very quietly. "There aren't any written records, of course, but I've always suspected the lunar cycle had more to do with when the Hunt rode than our calendar."

"Oh." I stopped being so sarcastic, the wind taken out of my sails. "Okay. I guess I can buy that." Insofar as I was buying any of it. What was I *doing* here? "So what's he want with you?"

Marie shook her head again. "I don't know. I've been trying to stay away from him since Halloween, traveling all over the place. He kept finding me." She shivered, wrapping her arms around herself. "All over the world. So I kept moving. But since Christmas I've been…this morning was the closest. I'd never actually *seen* him before. Never touched him." She dug into her pocket and pulled the tooth out, putting it on a napkin on the table. "I didn't even think something like this could be done to him."

I stared at the tooth. "Eww. I didn't know you'd picked it up."

"While Gary was bandaging your face," she said. "It's a good thing to have. It gives us a physical connection to him. It may help us build shields against him."

"Build what?" Gary asked. He'd cleared two-thirds of his plate. I reached over and stole a piece of bacon. He stabbed at my hand with his fork, but not like he meant it. The bacon was really good, so crunchy it practically melted. I stole another piece. "Cut it out," Gary said. "I gotta watch my figure."

"Shields," Marie said. "Protection."

"How do I protect you from a god?" I demanded. "I could get

you thrown in jail for a few days. The sixth is what, three days? He can't get through steel bars, right?"

"Two. It's the fourth. And no, he can't, but he could send someone who could," Marie pointed out.

I shrugged, hands spread out. "Fourth, okay, whatever, it's morning, you've still got all day to get through. That makes three days. Anyway. So what do I do?"

"Build me a circle of protection."

"Uh-huh," I said. "You want me to get a bunch of people to stand around you with iron crosses and this tooth and only let people you say are okay come in?"

"No, a——" Marie broke off with an ugly little gasp. I was looking right at her. I couldn't mistake the color draining from her eyes. All that gorgeous deep blue spilled away, even eating away the pupil, until there was just blind white, and then she blinked. Color came back to her eyes, but not the right color. Her irises were all black, tinges of gold and blue around where the pupils ought to be. She blinked a second time, and blanched, then spoke in a very thin voice, staring straight at me.

"You're going to die."

CHAPTER FOUR

An announcement of impending death sure could take a girl's appetite away. The knot of weary tension in my stomach contracted around the bites of bacon I'd stolen, cold threads of terror seeping down like a net. The rational part of my mind dismissed it all.

That would have been a comfort, except it appeared a lot more of my mind wasn't rational. I seized on to panic and ran with it. All of a sudden I understood why Gary had been so uncomfortable with Marie's gift. I clenched my teeth together, wondering why my hands were so cold. I wrapped them around my coffee cup and tried to stare at Marie without looking at her eyes. They were still unnervingly black, and I never wanted to see anything like that again.

"Something just changed," she went on, still in a whisper. "You weren't supposed to die, but now you're going to." There was conviction in her voice. She didn't blink. Her eyelashes were as black as her eyes, not brown like her hair.

"So I'm going to die because of you." I meant to sound challeng-ing. Somehow it came out sounding more like a frightened little girl. Marie nodded, dismay vivid even in her altered gaze.

"Well, fuck that." There. That sounded more like me. I stood up. "I'd like to help you, lady, but not enough to die for you." Great. Now I sounded like Gary. He scrambled to his feet beside me, favoring Marie with an unhappy glance. I dug into my fanny pack and came up with a five dollar bill and three Irish punts. I threw the five down and picked up my butterfly knife. "Gary, cover the rest, will you?" I headed for the door ignoring the sudden bubble of sickness that erupted in my stomach again, just as it had when I'd seen Marie through the plane window. Gary, thank God, didn't argue, just pulled out his wallet.

"Wait!" Marie's voice came after me, plaintive. I didn't stop. "Maybe I can help you!"

I turned around in the door. The tired blonde behind the counter looked a little more awake, watching first me, then Marie. "You think you can *help* me?" I demanded. "Weren't you the one just telling me I was going to die?"

Marie stood up. "The possibilities changed very quickly," she said softly. "If I'm with you, maybe I can see them change again. Maybe I'll know what you should do to avoid dying." She tossed a bill onto the table, too, as Gary came around it. The waitress was going to get a major tip.

"What are you, a banshee or a precognitive?" I asked. I was still in the door having the conversation. That wasn't a good sign, as far as I was concerned.

"To see someone's death, you have to be precognitive," Marie said. "I thought you didn't believe in any of that."

"Just because I don't believe doesn't mean I don't know the names." I put both hands on the door's center bar and shoved my way out of the diner, listening to the bells chime as the door swung shut behind me.

A SCUD missile hit me in the chest. I smashed back into the door, glass shattering with the impact. The center bar hit me in the small of the back, and I rotated around it. God did not intend anybody's back to be used in that fashion, except maybe those bendy Cirque du Soleil acrobats.

Unfortunately for me, I wasn't one of those acrobats. I flipped over the bar and slammed the back of my head against the still-intact glass in the lower half of the door, then collapsed on my face onto glass-littered linoleum. My cheek split open again as I hit the floor. More glass fell into my hair and onto the floor around me, sounding like falling stars.

The possibility of passing out crossed my mind, but I just *had* to see who was running around suburban Seattle with a SCUD. Lifting my head told me all sorts of painful things about muscles in my neck that I didn't want to know. I clenched my teeth together on a whimper. Whimpering seemed undignified. No one ever whimpered in the movies after getting smashed through a glass door.

There was no missile launcher in the parking lot. Instead there were very large hooves a few feet outside the destroyed door. While I waited for that to make sense, they disappeared and reappeared again, moving forward.

Have you ever heard the sound of tearing metal? It's a high-pitched scream that sets your teeth on edge and lifts the hairs on your arms. It's the kind of sound a mechanic gets used to, but in the diner, along with the rattle of more breaking glass and some other noises I couldn't place, it was incomprehensible. The hooves disappeared again, and I wondered where my knife had gone. Glass and dust and spikes of wood fell down around me.

The floor wrenched apart with a shriek of sound as one of the enormous hooves smashed down inches from my face. I twisted my head up, whimpering again at the pain in my neck. An extraordinarily broad chest was about four feet above my head. It reared up, which seemed wrong somehow, but I was too busy rolling frantically out of the way to give it more thought. Glass crunched under my arms as I rolled. I felt tiny cuts opening up on my arms.

I ended up sitting with my back against the counter, gasping while the rest of the world caught up with me. The tired blonde behind the counter shrieked with the regularity and volume of a car alarm. Gary had moved maybe two feet from the table, which suggested that despite the slow clarity I was experiencing, the attack had happened very quickly. Marie was shouting in a language I didn't understand. It didn't sound like Italian.

The horse made more sense now, for some nebulous value of the word sense. It had been able to rear up because after it kicked me in the chest it had torn out the entire door structure, and part of the roof had fallen down. The rest of the roof was on fire. I wasn't sure how that had happened, but it didn't seem to bother the horse.

Horse is such a limited word. The beast in the diner had the grace and delicacy of an Arabian and the size of a Clydesdale, multiplied by two. It shimmered a watery gray, bordering on silver, the color so fluid I thought I might be able to dip my hand in it. Despite myself, my gaze jerked up to its forehead. There was no spiral horn sprouting there, but I wouldn't have been surprised if there had been. It was Plato's horse, the ideal upon which all others are based.

It was trying to kill me, and all I could do was admire it.

Then it screamed, shrill and deep all at once. The blonde behind the counter shut up, but I screamed back, a sort of primal response without any thought behind it.

Just for a moment, everything stopped.

There was a rider astride the gray, arrested in motion by my scream. He wore gray himself, so close to the color of the horse I could barely tell where one ended and the other began. The reputed Native American belief that white men on horseback were one exotic creature suddenly seemed very plausible.

The rider turned his head slowly and looked at me. His hair was brown, peppered with starlight, and crackled with life, as if touching it would bring an electric shock. It swept back from a massively sharp widow's peak, and was held in place by a circlet. His face was a pale narrow line, all high cheekbones and deep-set eyes and a long straight nose.

The impression he left was of living silver. I locked eyes with him, expecting to see that liquid silver again. Instead I met wildfire green, a vicious, inhuman color, promising violence.

He smiled and reached out a hand, inviting me toward him. His mouth was beautiful, thin and expressive, the curve of teeth unnervingly sharp, like a predator's. I pushed up the counter, using it to brace myself, and wet my lips. Marie was right. I was going to die. The rider wanted my soul and I was going to give it to him without a fight because of that smile and those inhuman eyes. I took a step toward him.

The second SCUD of the morning hit me in the ribs and everything started to move again. I slammed into the floor under Gary's weight, sliding across linoleum and a zillion sharp pieces of glass. We stopped when my head hit the far wall. I opened my eyes to find the butterfly knife lying against the wall a few inches away from my nose. The horse screamed again and reared back, missing my head by half an inch as he crashed back to the floor.

Gary's breath smelled like syrup and bacon. "Are you outta your *mind?*" He popped up onto his knees and hauled me to mine by a fistful of shirt at the back of my neck. I snatched up the knife as the horse smashed down again, right where my head had been. I looked up at the rider, and the horse kicked me in the ribs with a toe. I felt the bone crack inward, and didn't even manage a scream, just a pathetic little grunt.

From a very long way away, I heard Marie scream a warning, in English this time. Before I could react, Gary hauled me over backward. A tip of silver glittered through the air where my throat had been. The rider looked genuinely startled before his eyes narrowed and he urged the horse farther into the diner. They were huge, taking up all the room, all the air. I gasped and scrambled to my feet, clutching Gary's arm with one hand and my ribs with the other. Breathing hurt.

"Leave them alone." Marie sounded thin and tired and at the end of her bravery, but there she was at my side, looking up at the rider with a set chin. "I'll go with you. Just leave them alone. They were only trying to help."

I let go of Gary's arm and shouldered forward. The rider watched me. Neither Gary nor Marie moved. Behind me I heard the blond waitress fumbling with the phone, and her panicked, "Hello? Police? Hello?"

"He'll kill us anyway," I said, very low. I couldn't get enough breath to do anything else. "Because it's what you do, isn't it? It's nothing personal. You're the Hunt, and when the Hunt is loosed, you kill until someone binds you away again. *Cernunnos.*" Terrifying conviction gave my voice strength. Twenty minutes ago I'd never heard of the thing standing in front of me; now the knowledge of who and what he was felt like the only thing I'd ever been certain of in my whole life. I didn't like that at *all*.

The rider's eyes widened, and then he smiled, inclining his head.

"The Horned God." I lifted my eyes to his circlet again, which wasn't a circlet at all. It was more like Caesar's crown, but it was part of him. It began at his temples and swept back in an elegant bone pattern, horns curved to the sides of his head and meeting at the back, woven together there. Very practical. No catching your head on tree branches that way. I wondered if he shed them yearly and grew them again, or if they were as eternal as he was.

"They grow with my power," he replied. Chills ran through me. It wasn't that he responded to an unasked question. *That* seemed perfectly normal from this being. It was his voice, dark and rich and earthy, deep enough that a roar from him would shake the world. That, and I was quite certain he hadn't spoken English or any other language I knew.

"What'd he say?" Gary whispered. Out of the corner of my eye I saw Marie shake her head fractionally.

"You cannot stop me," Cernunnos said, little more than a murmur.

"What do you want?" I still couldn't breathe enough to get a real voice out. He laughed, and it took everything I had to not run away.

"To ride free and hunt," he answered. "That is what we all want."

"All?"

"My host." He flicked his hand casually at the parking lot. I knew I shouldn't, but I looked anyway.

"Jesus, Mary and Joseph," Gary said.

"Not exactly," Cernunnos said, and that time Gary understood him. He flinched, jerking his eyes from the parking lot back to Cernunnos. I couldn't have looked away from the lot if someone paid me to. Everything I didn't believe in had come to roost there, things that just hadn't *been* there a moment earlier. It was like someone pulled the bandage off in one swift rip, exposing a world I didn't believe existed in full Technicolor glory.

The riders moved too quickly, or maybe not enough in this

world, for me to get an accurate count. There were close to a dozen, though, and one magnificent pale gold horse with no rider. Animals and riders alike faded at the edges, sunlight draining through them. Around their knees crept enormous sleek white dogs, with lowered heads and reddened eartips and violent red eyes. They avoided the few cars in the parking lot, milling around them but never touching them. Settled on the cars were narrow, long-beaked birds I'd never seen before, whose cries sounded like lost children. The dogs growled and snapped, every once in a while one baying at the sunrise. I could hear the horse's hooves against the asphalt, but the bridles made no sound, and neither did the riders as they drifted, waiting for their master.

"That isn't possible," I whispered. Cernunnos laughed again.

"You name me the Horned God and yet say my host is impossible? What are you, little mortal?" He put the silver sword against my chin, and turned my face toward him. I held very still, meeting his eyes.

Apparently I do not learn quickly. Meeting his eyes was a terrible mistake the second time, too. They were phenomenal, promising power and passion and eternity. All I wanted was to be with him, part of his ancient world. His blade caressed my cheek, opposite the cut Marie had made earlier. It felt like a lover's touch, and I wanted all the more to be with him.

"You could be," he murmured to the unspoken desire, "but then you would interfere, little mortal, and I am very tired of being interfered with. A shame, to end all your unrealized power, but more of a shame to be closed into the night again."

They say watch the eyes, when you're about to get into a fight. There are some people who can hide the telegraph of their actions from their eyes. Cernunnos wasn't one of them: he had no need to be. It just took a flicker, before he drew the sword back and punched it forward. It was all I needed.

I jolted forward, *into* the sword, instead of away. I tried to twitch enough to one side so the blade would catch my shoulder, instead of something vital. The horrible cool straightness of metal slid through me, fiery pain filling up the right half of my body. It hurt so badly my knees collapsed, and for an instant the sword through my torso was the only thing holding me up. I was pretty sure the next breath I let out would have blood on it.

But now I had his blade trapped.

And I had steel.

One-two-three. The *clack-clack-clack* of the butterfly knife sounded very loud to me, over the pounding blood in my ears. I coughed, and that made the sword scrape up and down my lung. I spat a mouthful of blood at Cernunnos, pleased that he flinched back. I dragged myself forward along the blade, and took a handful of his shirt, half-expecting it to slip away through my fingers like melting cotton candy. But it held, and as his horse neighed and reared up again, I kept my fist in his shirt and pulled him down. He fell, weighing more than I expected. My knife slid between his ribs, and he screamed.

The windows shattered. My eardrums shattered. I shrieked back, soundless into the overwhelming, unearthly noise that he made. I could see the scream vibrating from his throat even when blood slid from my ears and down my chin. His eyes weren't compelling anymore. They were filled with seething rage, green fire boiling over. I waited for it to spill out onto me, to set me on fire, and after a few seconds I smelled it: flesh burning. It was sick and sweet and horrible.

It took a long time to look down and see that it was the hole I'd put in Cernunnos's ribs that burned, not me. Silk singed around the knife, sticking and reeking. Beneath the fabric, his skin blackened and festered, bubbles beginning to burst. I screamed again, and jerked my hand back. The knife came out, and Cernunnos dropped to the floor. I began a long, slow collapse, Cernunnos's sword still stuck in my lungs. Beyond it, I could see his mouth moving, and even though I couldn't hear anything else, I heard him promise, "You will pay for this, little mortal."

The floor came up in a rush and hit me very hard.

CHAPTER FIVE

For a few moments it was very, very dark, and then it was very, *very* bright. I thought, *So this is what it's like to be dead,* and then, *Shit, man, I didn't want all that crap about a white tunnel to be true.*

I squinted. The brightness wasn't really very much like a white tunnel. It was actually a lot like staring directly into the sun. I closed my eyes, and a giant ball of green danced behind my eyelids. It turned red, then blue with red outlines as I squinted my eyes open again. Outside of the white light there was blue that looked suspiciously like the sky.

Lying there, under the suspiciously ordinary sky, I heard a drumbeat. It faltered, unsteady, like the drummer didn't know what he was doing. I turned my head toward it, scraping my cheek against hot earth. Tears from staring at the sun ran over my nose and wicked away into desert sand.

My cheek didn't hurt. I rubbed it against the ground a little, and it kept on not hurting. In fact, none of my body hurt, and that seemed wrong. I was pretty sure that only a minute ago there'd been all kinds of holes in it.

Overall, not hurting was an improvement. The sun was hot, and the sand, for ground, was comfortable. I closed my eyes again and relaxed. The drumbeat missed a beat.

"I wouldn't advise going to sleep right now."

My eyes popped open and I blinded myself with the sun again. Dammit. I pushed up on one elbow and looked around. No one was there.

Somehow, I wasn't surprised. I flopped onto my back again.

"Do you hear the drumbeat?"

"Of course I do," I snapped. The drumbeat sped up for a few beats, then slowed again.

"You should get up and follow it."

"I'm comfortable." I closed my eyes more firmly. I was *not* having a discussion with an invisible man.

"I'm not invisible. You just can't see me."

There was a lovely piece of logic. I sat up, glaring around.

If this was my subconscious's idea of paradise, I needed my head checked. Sulfur-colored sand dunes swept up against robin's egg-blue sky, both broken periodically by huge outcroppings of rough red stone. Wind hissed across the sand, smelling dry and old. Under my hands, fine particles of earth gritted against each other and melted away, leaving depressions for my fingers. The whole place reminded me of Arizona, only more so.

"This isn't even the kind of Indian I am," I protested. The drumbeat sped up a moment, getting louder. I twisted toward the north, where it was coming from. I wondered if I really should follow it.

"You should," the voice said helpfully.

"Why? I can't even see you. Why should I listen to you?" I looked around through my eyebrows, trying to find the voice's origin. "Why *can* I listen to you? Hear you, I mean. What are you?"

"You sure ask a lot of questions. You can't see me because you don't believe in me. You can hear me because you're dying, and it's letting me slip in." The voice sounded like this was a normal thing to say.

Despite the burning sunshine, shivers ran through me, and the drumbeat faltered. "Am I really dying?"

"Oh, yeah. You're really dying." The voice had a casual bedside manner. "You can choose not to, if you want."

"Why the hell would I *choose* to die?" I climbed to my feet. He had to be around here somewhere.

"Because living means changing your entire worldview. That can be a very difficult thing to do." His voice came from the same direction as the drumbeat.

"Oh, and dying is easy?" I began walking toward the north, glowering at the invisible voice.

"Dying is remarkably easy. Just stop going toward the drum, and in a few minutes, it'll stop."

"And then I'll be dead?" I didn't exactly break into a run, but I picked up the pace a bit. The drumbeat accelerated. "That's my heart, isn't it?"

"Yep," the voice said.

"Are you a spirit guide?"

There was a pause that felt considering. "Yep."

Yeah, that's what I thought. "Are spirit guides supposed to say 'yep'?"

He laughed. "Yep."

"How far is it to my—" I couldn't say, *to my heart.* "To the drum?"

"Not too far. Would you like me to lead you there?"

I took a deep breath. "Please. I don't want to die."

A small coyote bounded in front of me, like he'd always been there. I looked behind us. His tracks were tangled with mine, across the sand. He yipped, and I looked forward again. He smiled a coyote smile, and leaped out across the sand in a long, lean run. "I can't keep up with a running dog!"

"I'm not a dog. Come on." He stretched out and I swore, but I began to run. The drumbeat sped up again, and my strides got longer, until I was running an easy fast lope across the dunes, my feet kicking up sprays of sand. The coyote stayed a few yards in front of me, cresting over a dune.

I followed recklessly, and the earth dropped out from under me. It turned scarred and pitted, like an asteroid crater with deep, sharp sides. I hit the ground where it began to slope again and rolled ass over teakettle, trying to protect my head as I bounced. The drumbeat sounded once, then stopped again, a rare staccato. The coyote ran on, much more gracefully than I, then looped back to snap his teeth at me.

"Hurry. You don't have time for this."

"I *fell!*"

He bared his teeth in a snarl and pranced away, jerking his head to urge me on. I stumbled to my feet and began to run again. The coyote snapped his teeth again, satisfied, and forged ahead.

The crater narrowed into an impact spot, less than a foot across and plummeting into blackness. The coyote dove into it, just barely fitting. I couldn't possibly squeeze into it.

On the other hand, I couldn't possibly be running across an uber-Arizona landscape inside my head, either, and that seemed to be happening without the slightest regard to what was possible. I took a deep breath and dove after the coyote—

—and the impact spot got much bigger, or I got much smaller. It turned into a tunnel, plunging downward. A trickle of water appeared. I loped after it, running on four feet like I'd always done it. My hands *felt* like hands, but as I watched them flash under my nose, they were pawed and clawed, like the coyote's. The water widened, becoming a stream. I ran along the bank after the coyote, feeling a tail swishing behind me. The sand turned into rich dark topsoil, and then into solid granite, the stream cutting a swath through it. Every once in a great while I felt my heartbeat shaking the stone around us.

"Is time slowing down?"

"No," the coyote said, "your heart is."

Damn.

The stream disappeared without warning, sinking into stone, and the tunnel veered up at a steep angle. I dug unaccustomed claws into the hard rock, scrabbling for a purchase, and wriggled my way up the tunnel, shouldering past the coyote. Stone gave way and I burst through the earth into a pool of numbingly cold water. I kicked frantically toward the bright surface, dragging myself onto the bank a few seconds later. My hands were hands again. I wasn't a coyote anymore. It felt strange.

The drumbeat, my heartbeat, ricocheted around me, shockingly loud. The coyote ran out of the pool and shook himself furiously on the bank, then trotted through a sparse, stingily kept garden to an unmoving lump on the ground. I rolled onto my stomach and pushed to my hands and knees, watching him.

He nosed the lump on the ground, then sat down beside it, head cocked at me, expression full of expectation. "Physician, heal thyself."

I crawled over to the lump, still shivering. "Jesus *Christ!*" I reared onto my knees, backing away.

The lump was me. I looked like hell. Blood matted my hair, which hadn't been clean to start with. The bandaged cut on my face was almost lost among dozens of other tiny, glass-infested nicks and scratches. My shining new silver necklace was stained red, the cross settled in a pool of blood at the hollow of my throat. My ribs on the left side looked deflated, bent inward, and the sword was still stuck in my right lung.

I—the one sitting, not the lump—fell onto my butt and began crab-walking backward. "I'm *dying!*"

"I thought we'd established that," the coyote said. He hopped over my body—the one lying there—and grabbed my shirt in his teeth, tugging me forward again. "Heal yourself. It's in you."

"Dammit, Jim, I'm a mechanic, not a doctor." The coyote was strong, pulling me forward even as I resisted. "I don't know *how.*"

He let go of my shirt and lay down with his chin on his front paws. "You know how to fix cars, right? You know where everything goes."

I nodded. He lifted his bony shoulders in a shrug. "Pretend you're a car. It's a nice analogy."

Are spirit guides supposed to know what analogies are? The coyote grinned at me, even though I hadn't spoken aloud, and tipped his head toward my body. "You don't have much time."

"Pretend I'm a car. Right. Okay." I scooted closer to my body, hesitantly, mouth pressed closed. "A car. Right. Start with the obvious." My co-workers tell me I talk to myself when I'm working. I'd never noticed it before. "I'm leaking. What leaks? Oil filters leak. Great. I'm an oil filter." I put a hand on my chest, grabbed the sword's hilt with the other, and tugged. It stuck for a moment, grating against my ribs, and the drumbeat stopped entirely.

"No!" I yanked the sword harder, and it slid out with a liquid sound. I threw it to the side, and hit myself in the chest. I—the one on the ground—coughed, and the drumbeat made a sad little thump. Dark, important-looking blood spurted out, covering my hands.

"Patch it up," the coyote said.

"I don't know how," I whispered, closing my eyes. I could imagine an oil filter, emptying itself onto the ground. I ran through the process of changing it—loosening the drain, oiling the gasket on the new filter, screwing it back onto the filter pipe. Uncertainly, I tried overlaying those images on my body, envisioning my torn lung as the old, burned-out filter, imagining the new one sliding into place.

Something clicked in the center of me, below my breastbone and just above my diaphragm in exactly the same place, the sickness that had impelled me to help Marie had been. It felt like cartilage popping, a thick painful feeling, as if a lock, stiff with age, had reluctantly opened. I felt it in both my bodies, the one I was consciously inhabiting, and the one lying all but lifelessly on the bloody grass. Energy surged through that place with the same cool feeling as drinking water on an empty stomach. It lined the insides of me and reached out, connecting my kneeling self to the dying body under my hands. For a few seconds I thought I could see *through* myself, the ridiculous oil filter analogy at work repairing my lung. The energy I felt was centered there, coiling inside the ruined cavity and patching it. Then the sensation faded and dizziness swept through me. I tilted over sideways, suddenly exhausted. "I don't think it worked."

"Take a look," the coyote murmured. I pried my eyes open and looked down at myself. Ichory black blood still covered my chest and my hands, but when I pushed my shirt out of the way, the hole was gone, the skin unscarred.

"Holy shit."

The coyote chuckled. "Now reinflate your lung."

"What, like a tire?"

"Just like that." He sounded approving.

Flat tire. Filled tire. It doesn't take that long to fill a tire, but I had the horrible idea that I would explode my lung if I filled it too fast. The drumbeat thumped unsteadily, then fell into a more reassuring pattern as I envisioned air being pushed into a tire. I felt the same energy coil behind my breastbone again, shimmering through both bodies. It spilled out as I dragged in a deep breath. Beneath my hands, the other me did the same thing, and the alien pool of energy went dead again. This time it left me with the faintest sensation of still being there, waiting. I swallowed hard. "What is that?"

"It's your destiny," the coyote said.

My heartbeat missed another pulse, but overall it was much better. I let out a high-pitched laugh. "My destiny. I'm a car and I'm fixing me and it's my destiny? Great, that's just great, in a completely fucked-up surreal way."

"The ribs next, I think." The coyote sounded serene. I reached for the unlocked knot of energy more deliberately this time, and laughed again, a little hysterically, when it responded.

"How can I be doing this?" My broken ribs were like a body frame that had been torn apart. I pressed them back into shape, cautiously realigning them, welding the weak points carefully. Pressure I hadn't consciously realized existed slowly eased, and I could breathe more easily. My whole body felt more aligned, stronger, just like a car felt solid with its frame intact. The energy I was using spilled from me like it was part of my bone structure, like it was integral to my being, but I'd never felt anything like it before.

"You're finally beginning to accept a path you abandoned a long time ago," the coyote answered. "You have gifts, Joanne Walker, that your spirit cries out to use. Healing is chief among them."

"I don't understand." I sounded young and frightened, but even as I made the protestation I moved, without being told, on to the next of my injuries. The cuts and scrapes on my arms and face were a paint job. Using the coyote's analogy worked: it gave me a way to focus the cool rushing power inside my belly. It was bewilderingly easy, almost instinctive. The surface damage of the cuts and scrapes called for less of that energy than the lung or the ribs had. I felt myself making choices I barely understood, siphoning just a fraction of the power available to deal with the smaller injuries. The rest settled behind the unlocked place above my belly, waiting. When the "paint job" was complete, the extension of energy faded back into me, joining the rest of the power behind my breastbone. I felt a little like a battery charging up.

I opened my eyes uncertainly, looking down at myself. I couldn't do anything about my clothes. "I think I'm okay now."

"What about that one?" The coyote poked his nose at the long cut on my cheek from Marie's butterfly knife. I put my hand over it; the new paint job hadn't entirely taken care of it. Instead of disappearing, it had scarred over, a thin silver line along my cheek. After a moment I shrugged.

"It wants to stay."

Very smart dogs can look approving. The coyote did, then snapped his teeth at me. "I'm not a dog."

"What *is* it with people reading my mind today?" I looked down at myself, the one lying in the grass. I still looked horrible, my skin a ghastly pallor that made very faint freckles stand out across my nose. My face wasn't one that did sunken flesh well. My nose is what you might politely call regal, and my cheekbones are high, making my cheeks look very hollow and fallen. Lying there like that, I looked two breaths from dead. The drumbeat, my heartbeat, was still thudding with a degree of uncertainty. I put my hand out over my torso and chewed my lower lip. "There's still something wrong. Like..." My car analogy almost fell apart. "Like the windshield is all cracked up and burnt from the sun."

The coyote did the approving look again. "This is the hard part."

I frowned at him nervously. "What do you mean, the hard part?"

He pushed his nose out toward the me that was dying, there on the grass. "You have to change the way you see the world."

"Isn't this place enough proof of that?" I asked, pitch rising. The coyote's ears flicked back and he sat up primly, offended.

"Is it?" he asked. "Do you believe what's happening here?"

I looked down at my body again. My heartbeat was drumming much too slowly. "I don't know. It feels real, but so do dreams."

"This place shares much with dreams." The timbre of his voice changed, deepening from a tenor into a baritone. I jerked my eyes up, to discover a red man sitting there on his butt, arms wrapped around his knees, loose and comfortable. He wore jeans with the knees torn out, no shirt, and he was genuinely red. Brick red, not a color skin comes in, not even sunburned skin. Long straight black hair was parted down the middle, and his teeth were better than Gary's. His eyes were golden, as golden as the coyote's. I blinked, and the coyote was back.

"Is Coyote even a Cherokee legend?" I kept blinking at him, hoping he'd turn back into the red man. He stayed a coyote. Still, if men like that were wandering around here, I'd take it as a good argument that this garden had a lot in common with dreams.

"It's a little more complicated than that," Coyote said. "You don't have a lot of time, Jo. Is this real?"

I scowled down at my body. *If this is a dream,* I decided, *when I look up, he'll be the guy again. I'm aware, so it's a lucid dream, so I can affect it, and he'll be the man because I want him to be.*

I looked up. The coyote was sitting there, head cocked, waiting for me.

"Dammit," I said out loud. A thin line in the spiderweb I felt inside me made a hissing sound like cracking glass, and disappeared. The drum missed a long, scary beat, then fell into a natural, reassuring rhythm.

"Time to go back," Coyote said, and the garden went away.

CHAPTER SIX

Shit, I thought again, *I didn't want all that crap about a white tunnel to be true.* I closed my eyes. The light continued to bore into my eyelids until I opened them again. The paramedic squatting above me clicked the penlight off, announcing, "She's back," to someone out of my line of sight.

"I'm back," I agreed in a croak, and closed my eyes again. Perhaps if I was very lucky I'd go away again.

"Getting the crap beat out of you isn't gonna make Morrison feel bad enough not to fire you, Joanie," the someone said, then lifted his voice. "Forget the ECG, Jimmy. She's back with us. Looks like the other guy got the worst of it. What happened," he said, addressing me again, "his gang dragged him off to die?"

My arm weighed about twenty thousand pounds, but I picked it up and dropped it on my chest, trying to find the hole the sword had poked in me. I found it by proxy. There was a gash in my shirt, a nasty hole stiffening with dried blood. Beneath it, my rib cage seemed to be unpunctured. I rolled my head to the side, somewhat amazed that it stayed on, and croaked, "Gary?"

All I could see were feet. I didn't know what kind of shoes Gary wore, but I was pretty sure they weren't open-toed blue leather heels, absolutely impractical for Seattle in January.

"Who the hell is Gary?"

I rolled my head back to where it had been and tried to focus on the paramedic. "Oh," I said after a while. "Billy. Cabby."

"No, Billy Holliday, sweetheart. You've always been easily confused." He squatted by me again, pushing my eyelid back and inspecting my pupil. "How many fingers do you see?"

"I don't see anything, Billy, somebody's got his damn thumb stuck in my eye. What happened, you get called in early?"

"How'd you know?" He took his thumb out of my eye and elevated his eyebrows at me.

"The shoes."

Billy Holliday was, as far as I knew, Seattle's only cross-dressing detective. I'd met him three days after I was hired: dispatch asked me to rescue an off-duty officer whose car had broken down. Dispatch hadn't mentioned that the cop in question would be wearing a pale yellow floral print dress and had biceps bigger than my head. Billy looked better in a dress than I did.

Not that I could remember the last time I wore a dress.

Billy inspected his feet. "I shoved my feet into the first thing I found next to the door," he admitted. "Do you like them?"

I decided I was feeling better, and began to sit up. Billy pushed me back down. "I think they're great," I offered, and tried to sit up again. The admiration didn't appease him, and we had a good little tussle going when Gary's knees intruded in my line of vision. He crouched while I wondered how I recognized his knees.

"You oughta be dead, lady."

I let Billy win and dropped onto my back. "Yeah?" I asked. "What's Marie got to say about that?"

"You ought to be dead," she said from above my head. I tilted my chin up and looked at her foreshortened form through my eyebrows.

"That's reassuring." I closed my eyes. "What happened?"

I felt Marie and Gary cast uncomfortable glances at Billy. "Billy," I said without opening my eyes, "go change your shoes, would you?"

Mortal offense filled his voice. "What, so you can get your story straight? What kind of detective do you take me for?"

"It's a little more complicated than that." I tried to remember where I'd heard that recently. Oh, yeah. Coyote.

My head began to hurt again.

I pushed up on an elbow, opening my eyes. "I'm asking as a friend, Bill. Or I'll steal your distributor cap."

He grinned reluctantly. "Friends don't threaten friends' distributor caps. Look, you sure you're okay, Joanie? You look like hell."

"I'm sure. I'm fine. I swear I'll explain it later."

"Arright." Billy stood up. So did Gary. They sized each other up while I worked on climbing to my feet. Gary nodded tersely, and Billy walked off. It all smacked of some sort of bizarre male testosterone thing. I tried hard to ignore it.

"What happened?" I asked again. My balance was off. I spread my arms out, trying to find my center. Then it occurred to me that Coyote wanted me to do exactly that, and my head hurt more. I rubbed my temple, then my face, and that didn't hurt at all. Fascinated, I prodded at my cheek. No pain.

"You got a scar," Gary pronounced, staring wide-eyed at my face. "On your cheek. Where she cut you. A real thin scar. It was still bleeding just a minute ago."

I slid my fingertips over my cheek, feeling the thin line, perfectly healed. "What," I asked for the third time, "happened?" The scar felt weird. I'd always had good skin.

"The Hunt took Cernunnos away," Marie said. "I'm not sure anyone's ever hurt him like that before."

"Bully for me." I kept rubbing my cheek. "How'd I get into the parking lot?"

"I carried you," Gary volunteered. "The diner was on fire."

I turned around and looked at it. Sure enough, it was on fire. There were firemen there now, and I realized I'd been hearing the sounds of water and steam and men calling to one another since I woke up. Clouds of steam and smoke rose up, and, as I watched, a section of the roof fell in. All and all, I was glad Gary hadn't left me in there. "Thanks. What happened to the sword?"

Gary jerked a thumb toward his cab. "In the back seat. I thought we oughta leave it in you until the paramedics got here, but Marie kept sayin' we had to get it out. Guess I'm not much good at sayin' no to a dame."

"Yeah," I said, "you look like the henpecked husband type." My fingers drifted back to the hole in my shirt, feeling skin through it. It felt perfectly normal. I pulled the collar of the shirt out and peered down. Gary guffawed. I muttered, "Oh, shut up," and kept looking.

My bra was a bloody mess, and there was a gash in it. "God damn it," I said, "that was a new bra."

Gary laughed again, and I looked up long enough to glare at him. "Sure, laugh. It cost sixty bucks. Goddamned men don't have to buy goddamned expensive underwear...." I peered down my shirt again. There was no indication the bloody mess on the shirt and bra was from my own bleeding. Breasts, bra, blood, no hole in my chest. Lookit that. I felt like an X-File.

"You kept flashing between living and dying," Marie said. "I just had the feeling that you wouldn't live if the sword stayed in you."

"You were right." I stopped peeking down my shirt. It was too weird.

"So she made me pull the sword out," Gary said, his whole face wrinkling up in a grimace. "And then..." He trailed off. Marie drew in a breath.

"And then you began to heal. Just like magic."

"It was magic," I mumbled.

"What?" Gary laughed again.

"It was magic," I repeated, unconvincingly. Marie developed a smug grin. Even smug looked attractive on her. It wasn't fair.

"I thought you didn't believe in magic," she said with a reasonable amount of diplomacy. Unfortunately, her grin ruined the sincerity of the moment.

"A lot's changed since then," I muttered. A cord tightened around my heart, then loosened, like a bowstring snapping. A sudden vision of the cracked windshield blurred my vision, and a spiderweb-thin line in it sealed up, healing. I shivered a little and wrapped my arms around my ribs. "C'mon. Let's go talk to Billy."

"Wait." Marie caught my arm. "We have a problem."

Those were not the words I wanted to hear. It took a long time to convince myself to say, "What kind of problem?"

"Cernunnos wasn't the one I fought at the church."

I frowned at her without comprehension. "He couldn't have been," I said after a minute. "You took that knife from him." I felt terribly clever for figuring that out, especially when surprise, followed by embarrassment, washed across Marie's face.

"You're right. I didn't even think—but who was he, then? The Hunt *was* after me," she insisted. I unfolded one hand from around my ribs to head off her protestations.

"I know. I saw. Maybe it was somebody human who's working for him." I admired how I said that, all casual-like. I could handle my world being turned upside down and shaken like a snow globe. No problem. I was cool. I was good. Yeah.

"Then why didn't he follow me into the church?"

I stared down at her, at a loss. So much for being cool. "I don't know. Look." I shook my head. "Let's go talk to Billy and get that part of this over with before we try to figure the rest of it out, okay?" I glanced at Gary. He nodded. So, after a reluctant moment, did Marie.

We went to talk to Billy.

Once upon a time, a nice young half-Cherokee half-Irish girl went to college and got the ultimate would-you-like-fries-with-that degree: English. I had no illusions that I'd get a job in my field when I graduated from college, but I'd never planned to. I already had a day job. I'd started learning how to fix cars when I was barely old enough to walk, and I never really wanted to do anything else.

When I graduated from the University of Washington, my part-time college gig at a local mechanic's shop couldn't upgrade me to full-time, so I hired on with the North Precinct police department. The best part about it was I didn't have to move out of the apartment I'd been renting since my sophomore year of college.

There was just one itty-bitty catch: my then-supervisor, Captain Nichols, wanted me to go to the police academy. It was the black-and-white photos they took for station ID that did me in: my Native American blood showed through like a waving red flag, and Nichols couldn't resist a bonafide Indian woman on the roster. It made the department look good. I went to the academy, managed to survive it and gratefully slunk back to the garage, there to stay.

A year later, Nichols retired and Captain Michael Morrison replaced him.

Odds are that Morrison and I never would have so much as spoken, if I hadn't brought my car to the precinct car wash fundraiser. I was not prone to doing that sort of thing: my car, Petite, is my baby, and I prefer to wash her myself, but Billy's oldest kid begged and pleaded with me, and I was weak in the face of big-eyed nine-year-old boys. So I brought her to the car wash.

How any red-blooded American male could mistake a 1969 Mustang for a Corvette, even an admittedly sexy '63 Stingray, I will never understand. But Morrison did, and I laughed in his face. If I were to be totally honest, I might go so far as to say I mocked him mightily, before, during and after laughing in his face.

I didn't *know* at the time that he was my new top-level supervisor.

I say that like knowing would have made a difference.

I generally went to some lengths to avoid admitting to myself that I'd behaved like a complete, unmitigated jerk. It was like a horrible, embarrassing reversion to elementary school, where you indicate you think a boy is cute by throwing rocks at him. Once I'd lobbed the first rock, so to speak, I didn't know how to stop, and the relationship hadn't exactly improved with time. As far as I could tell, neither Morrison nor I had much life at all outside of the station, so we ran into each other often enough to develop a long-term, standing animosity. We were like Felix and Oscar without the good moments.

So when I'd asked for some personal time off to go meet my dying mother, Morrison'd been in a hurry to tell me that the department could only afford me six weeks of leave, and then they'd have to replace me. I told him I'd be back in a month.

That month stretched to two, then three. When I called to say it was going to be another month, Bruce at the front desk sounded downright grim, and told me that Morrison wanted my ass in his chair the minute I got off the plane.

Which was why I was now on Morrison's side of Morrison's desk, in Morrison's remarkably comfortable chair, with my feet propped up on Morrison's scarred gray desk. I just had to push my luck.

The office was large enough to not be claustrophobic. The door opened against a half wall of windows that let in the mild winter light. Two chairs that fit under the category of "comfy" were on the opposite side of Morrison's desk, the side I was supposed to be on. Another three folding chairs were tucked around a long brown table shoved under the windows and into the back corner. The table, like Morrison's desk, was buried beneath chaotically distributed paperwork.

Morrison's desk looked out onto the offices through another set of windows, floor-to-ceiling, Venetian blinds hanging at the tops. He usually left them open. When they were closed, somebody was in huge trouble. I couldn't decide if I was relieved they were open now.

Three calendars, with the past, present and next months turned up, were tacked on a bulletin board above a quietly percolating coffeemaker on the other side of the office. Around the calendars were clippings from cases, past and present, overlying one another until the board below them was virtually invisible. Next to the coffeemaker was a Frank Lloyd Wright clock. I wondered if it had been a Christmas gift, and who had given it to Morrison. There were no photos of family on his desk. I doubted he had any.

I eyed the clock. He'd kept me waiting seventeen minutes. It only seemed fair, since I'd kept him waiting four and a half months.

A moment later the door banged shut and I flinched upright, startled out of the first sleep I'd had in days. Morrison glowered at me from the doorway. I cast another glance at the clock. I'd been asleep less than three minutes. Just enough time to make the worst possible impression. I hoped I hadn't drooled on myself.

"Get," Morrison growled, "the hell. Out. Of my. Chair."

I beamed. "Bruce was very specific," I said in my best innocent voice. "'Morrison wants your ass in his chair the minute you get off the plane.'"

Morrison took a threatening step toward me. I cackled and waved a hand, climbing to my feet. "I'm getting. Don't get your panties in a bunch." I walked around the desk to the chair I was supposed to be in, and sat.

Or that's what I meant to do, anyway. What I actually did was take two steps, tread on my shoelace and collapse in a sprawl at Morrison's feet. I lay there wondering why I couldn't breathe. I could feel Morrison staring at the back of my head.

The floor was pretty comfortable, all things considered. Maybe if I stayed there, Morrison would just have me thrown in a nice quiet cell where I could sleep for two or three days. Except there were no quiet cells at the station, and I knew it. I groaned, pushed myself to my hands and knees, then sat back on my heels.

"Don't do it, Joanie!" someone bellowed, loud enough to be heard through the window. "The job ain't worth it!"

It took several seconds for my position, relative to Morrison's, to sink in. Then I turned a dull crimson, too tired to even get up a really brilliant shade of red. Morrison glared over his shoulder and stomped around the desk to take his seat, all without ceasing to scowl at me. I climbed to my feet in a series of small movements, using the desk to push myself up incrementally. Eventually I got turned around and met Morrison's frown.

"You look like hell," he said, which wasn't what I expected, so I blinked at him. He waved at the chair. "Siddown."

I sat. Not, thankfully, right where I was standing: I had the presence of mind to stagger the couple of steps to the chair. Morrison watched me. He was in his late thirties and looked just like a police captain ought to: a big guy, a little bit fleshy, with cool investigating eyes and strong hands that had blunt, well-shaped fingernails. He was good-looking in a superhero-going-to-seed kind of way, which is probably one of those things you're not supposed to notice about your boss. I sank into the chair and closed my eyes.

Morrison leaned back in his chair. It creaked, a high shriek that made hairs stand up on my arms. "You overextended your personal leave by three months, Walker."

"I know."

"I hired your replacement ten weeks ago."

"I know." Damn, but I was a stunning conversationalist. My eyes were glued shut. I rubbed at them, and the sticky contacts suddenly made tears flood through my lashes.

"Jesus," Morrison said in mystified horror, "don't tell me you're crying."

"It's my contacts," I snarled.

"Thank God. You never struck me as the weepy sort." Morrison was quiet a moment. I didn't have the energy to look up at him. "It seems like half the department's been by to make googly eyes on your behalf."

I snorted into my palms, undignified laughter. "Googly eyes?"

"Googly eyes," Morrison said firmly. "For some reason they like you."

"I fix their cars." It was true. On particularly bad days—of which this was one—I thought it was because I had no way to relate to other people except through cars. On better days, I acknowledged that I just loved the job, and the fact that I'd made friends because of it was a bonus. "Come on, Morrison, give me the ritual 'I divorce thee' three times, and let me go home and get some sleep." I pushed a hand back through my hair. Morrison winced. "God, do I look that bad?" I hadn't checked a mirror. Maybe I should have.

"You look like you got hit by a truck. What happened?" Morrison actually sounded curious.

"I got into a fight." I dredged up a little smile. "But you should see the other guy."

Morrison snorted and stood up, coming around his desk to lean on the edge of it, arms folded as he looked down at me. I checked the impulse to get to my feet. Morrison and I were exactly the same height. I'd been known to wear heels sheerly for the pleasure of looking down on him. He was looming on purpose. "I'm moving you to the street beat." He sounded alarmingly pleasant.

I stared at him for a long time. "What?"

"I'm moving you to the street beat," he repeated. "Corner cop duty."

"You're supposed to fire me," I blurted. I'd never done time as a cop. I didn't really want to. Morrison grinned, and pushed away from his desk to get himself a cup of coffee.

"The chief wouldn't let me. You're a woman, you're an Indian, you're a cop, all you've done wrong is not show up to work for a few months, and that was because of a personal family emergency. It's not enough to fire you for. Not in this quota-happy age." He opened a fridge under the coffeemaker table and poured milk into his coffee.

My eyebrows shot up. No one had ever actually mentioned quotas out loud. It was just one of those silent givens that nobody talked about. Morrison turned back, lifting his mug of coffee. "Want some?"

"Sure," I said dazedly.

Morrison poured a second cup of coffee and handed it to me. I took a sip, burned my tongue, and clutched the cup with both hands, watching Morrison nervously.

"So I'm putting you on the street."

"Why?" My voice rose and broke. Morrison beamed at me. I'd never seen him smile so broadly before. It was unnerving.

"Because I figure you'll quit. You're a mechanic, not a cop. You haven't got the stuff. Want to save us both time and do it now?" Morrison didn't burn his tongue when he sipped his coffee. The bastard.

I ground my teeth together so hard it hurt. I couldn't do it. I just couldn't do it. Not in the face of that grin. I couldn't prove him right, especially by quitting before I'd even tried.

"No," I said through my teeth, standing up and putting the coffee cup aside. "No, I don't think I do. Sir."

It took every ounce of will I had available to close the door gently on my way out.

CHAPTER SEVEN

No fewer than eight cops—all of whose cars I tinkered with regularly—lingered outside Morrison's office, ostentatiously reading files or exchanging stories over their desks. Every one of them fell silent as I carefully closed Morrison's door and stepped away from the office. Bruce, a thin blonde who had no business being away from the front desk, put on a mournful smile. "Well?"

"The son of a bitch fired you," Billy guessed before I had time to draw breath. An uproar met his speculation, a wall of outrage entirely on my behalf. Rex, short and stout as his name, flung his hat on someone's desk and stalked toward me. I backed up into Morrison's door, alarmed. The doorknob hit me in the butt.

"Get out of the way, Joanie." Rex sounded like a bulldog, low-voiced and growly. "I'm gonna give that bastard a piece of my mind. He can't do this to you! You were on *family leave,* for Christ's sake!"

I edged to the side. "Um, actually..."

Rex stormed past me and flung Morrison's door open, banging it closed behind him again. Around me, furious cops swore and waved their hands and lined up, God help me, actually lined up to be the next one to take on Morrison.

"Actually," I mumbled, "he didn't fire me."

Nobody listened. I rubbed my hand over my eyes, setting my contacts to tearing again, and sighed. Bruce appeared at my elbow and guided me to a desk to sit down. "It'll be okay, Joanie," he promised. "You're a fantastic mechanic. You'll get a job in no time. Heck, you could probably keep yourself busy just fixing our cars, huh guys?"

"I fix your cars anyway," I pointed out. "Nobody pays me for it." Bruce had exactly one hobby: running. His wife's car, a 1987 Eagle station wagon with a manual transmission, broke down more often than soap opera stars. I wasn't sure he knew how to drive it, much less fix it. "Look, Bruce, I'm—"

Bruce patted my shoulder reassuringly. "Elise wants you to come over for dinner Friday. She's going to raise holy living hell about you getting fired."

Elise made the best tamales I'd ever had, and was convinced I was killing myself eating macaroni and cheese for every meal. "Elise is an angel," I said, "but—"

Rex burst out of Morrison's office, cheeks bright red with exertion. Billy marched through the still-open door. Even over the general noise I could hear Morrison's, "Oh, for *Christ's* sake!" A moment later Billy backed out of the office, herded by Morrison, who stopped at the door, broad-shouldered and impressive.

"Joanne Walker has not been fired!" he bellowed. "All of you get the hell back to work!" He stepped back into his office, slamming the door behind him.

Eight officers of the law turned as one and stared at me accusingly.

"That's what I was trying to tell you," I said weakly. "He didn't fire me. He busted me back to foot patrol." For a moment I wondered if a mechanic could technically be busted back to anything.

Everyone was silent for about as long as it took me to wonder that, and then the cacophony began again. I tried, briefly, to explain, then gave up and let Billy defend my dubious honor as an honest-to-God cop with a badge and everything. I wasn't sure where that badge was. I remembered they'd given me one when I graduated from the police academy, but my best guess was that it was in my sock drawer. Or possibly in the glove compartment of my car. Or maybe in the junk drawer in the kitchen. I slunk out while the debate about whether I was *really* a cop heated up.

Gary and Marie were waiting impatiently in the lobby. "You're a cop?" Gary demanded as I came through the turnstile.

"No. Yes. No. Shit! Why?" I flung myself onto a bench and scrubbed my eyes.

"Jeez, lady, I didn't mean to ask a tough question. What happened in there? Why didn't you *say* you were a cop back at the church? Or the airport? I thought you were nuts, goin' after some broad you saw from a plane." Gary towered over me, hands on his hips. Marie hovered in the background, looking just as curious as Gary.

"I'm not a cop. I mean." I sighed, pinching the bridge of my nose. "I am a cop. I guess I'm a cop. I'm a *mechanic*. That's what I do. Except now I don't. Now I write jaywalking tickets, or something. I wonder when I'm supposed to be back at work. Shit."

Gary and Marie stared at me. After several seconds, I mumbled, "I make more sense when I've had some sleep." I pried my eyes open. Tears welled up again. Gary became sympathetic all of a sudden.

"All right, all right. I'll take you home. Tonight we'll get together and figure this out." He actually patted my shoulder, just like Bruce had done.

"We?" Marie and I spoke together. She sounded surprised. I sounded small and pitiful.

"What, you think I'm gonna miss out on what happens next? Crazy dames." Gary shook his head and pushed his way out of the station, muttering to himself.

Gary dropped me off at my apartment complex. I stood on the concrete stairs and waved as he drove off, then staggered up to my apartment, navigating to the bedroom without turning the lights on. No one lived there but me; it was a safe bet that there wouldn't be anything unexpected on the floor except four months worth of dust. I was right: falling face-first into the bedcovers dislodged dust and made me sneeze, but nothing worse awaited me. My last conscious thought was that I'd forgotten to take my contacts out.

The apartment was empty of unexpected things. My dreams were not. Coyote was waiting for me. He looked warily approving while I frowned at him groggily. "How d'you do that?" I demanded. "Dogs don't have that much expression."

"You've never owned a dog, have you?" Coyote asked. "Besides, I'm not a dog."

I put my face in my hands, eyes closed. "Whatever. Where are we? What do you want?" I peeked at him through my fingers. "Are you always going to be bothering my dreams?"

"This isn't a dream." Coyote cocked his head to the side, looking around. After a moment I did too, wearily. I had to admit I'd never had a dream that looked like this one. Even falling dreams, which weren't big on detail, usually had a gray sky and a very long drop. This one didn't even have that much, just dark storm clouds pushing at each other with no particular pattern or intent. I thought I preferred falling dreams.

I dropped suddenly, a sickening distance in no time at all. Coyote yipped, a short sound of annoyance and alarm. I flinched upright, back where I'd started. "Pay attention," he said sharply.

"I am," I protested. "What was that? Where *are* we?" There was nowhere for me to have fallen. Coyote and I drifted, in the middle of it, sitting on nothing.

"You called a dream up," Coyote said patiently. "We're in a place between dreams."

"Why? I'm so *tired.*" I was whining. I made a small sad sound and straightened up, trying to behave like an adult. Coyote licked his nose.

"You did a good job this morning," he said. I blinked at him slowly.

"Is that why I came here? So you could tell me that?" I didn't mean to sound like a snappy, ungrateful bitch. I was just so damned tired. Coyote let the tone blow over him.

"Partly," he agreed. "Ask the banshee to help you with your shields. You're going to need them."

"My shields?" I wasn't used to feeling this thick.

Coyote smiled. I didn't know dogs could smile. "I'm not a dog," he said, and, "she'll know what you mean. Now get some sleep." He dropped a golden-eyed wink and disappeared.

Or at least, I ceased to be aware of him. Instead I became aware of someone pounding on my door with the patience and rhythm of a metronome. I stayed very still for what felt like a very long time, hoping the pounding would go away. It didn't. After six or seven years I rolled out of bed and crawled toward the front door.

I made it to my feet somewhere in the living room and was rewarded for my monumental effort by barking my shin on the coffee table. I reached for the doorknob and the injured shin at the same time, pulled the door open, and slammed myself in the forehead with the edge of the door. Collapsing onto the floor in a sniveling lump seemed the only thing to do, so I did it. It was only when tears started to unstick my eyelashes that I realized that I not only hadn't, but couldn't, open my eyes. I took turns rubbing at my shin and my forehead and my stuck-together lashes. Somewhere up above me, Gary said, "Jesus Christ, Jo. You look like someone ran you over and backed up to see what he hit."

"Nice to see you, too, Gary." Not that I could see him. I put a hand over my throat. I sounded like a bulldozer had dumped a load of gravel into my chest. "What time is it?"

"Seven-thirty." He crouched; I could tell by the location of his voice.

I pried one of my eyes open. "No way. I just went to sleep." I turned my wrist over and tried to focus on my watch. I couldn't, but that was okay, since it was wrong anyway. "No way."

"Yep. Seven-thirty. We're supposed to meet Marie in half an hour at her place." Gary straightened up again. I got my other eye open, and blinked tearfully at him.

"Okay. I guess, uh. Let's go." I swallowed, trying to loosen my voice up some, and worked on getting my body moving in a direction that felt like 'up'.

"Uh," Gary said.

I could only do one thing at a time. I stopped trying to stand and squinted at him. "What?"

"You might wanna think about taking a shower and changing clothes."

I looked at him without comprehension for a while, then looked down at myself. And, in growing horror, looked some more. After a while, I said, "Oh yuck."

I wouldn't have thought sleeping in bloody gory clothes could be beaten for general yuckiness, but adding in a layer of dust over all that made me a fine imitation of a desiccated corpse. "Come in," I grated. "I'll shower." I crawled away from the door without waiting to see if he came in.

* * *

The reflection in the mirror was marginally kinder fifteen minutes later. My hair was clean and slightly gelled into spikes. I was still pale, but only from lack of sleep, rather than from blood, dust *and* lack of sleep. I'd managed to unstick the contacts from my eyes and was wearing an old pair of glasses, thin gold wire frames with long narrow oval lenses. The gold did cool things to my eyes, or at least it did when I wasn't still suffering from bloodshot-from-hell eyeballs.

I stared at my reflection, fingering the thin white scar on my cheek. It began just behind the glasses lens, next to the corner of my eye, and ended in the faint smile line above my mouth. It wasn't exactly detracting, but it sure as hell wasn't something I was used to. Bumping my fingers over it didn't make it go away. I finally looked away from the mirror and wove my way into my bedroom to find clothes.

The first T-shirt I found was black, probably the worst possible color to wear when I was one step paler than death, but it was clean, and the V-neck didn't mess up my hair as I yanked it over my head. Sometimes that's all a girl can ask for. It would've shown off my new necklace well, except I'd had to abandon that until it spent some quality time with silver polish and goo remover. Blood did not go well with silver.

For a girl who didn't wear jewelry, I felt weirdly naked without the necklace. I dug up the only other piece of jewelry I owned, a copper cuff bracelet my father'd given me for Christmas while I was still in high school. It went on my left wrist, having left the dysfunctional watch on the bathroom counter. The etchings around the outer edges of the bracelet were Celtic knots, which I'd never realized before. For the first time, I wondered if Dad had done that on purpose. I stood there staring mindlessly at the bracelet for far too long, tracing a fingertip over the line etches of various Cherokee-favored animals between the two bands of knots, then shook myself. I was supposed to be getting dressed. I could handle a task like that. Really.

I clawed through my sock drawer and came up with socks, a G-string and the police badge. I threw the badge back in the drawer and pulled the G-string on. Not my favorite kind of underwear, but slightly better than going without. I tugged a pair of jeans on and went out to the living room with my socks in one hand.

Gary was on the couch with one of my secret weaknesses: an entertainment magazine, now four months old. I sat down on the love seat and pulled a sock on. "Are we going to be late for Marie's?"

"Nah." Gary looked over the edge of the magazine. "She doesn't live too far from here. Hey, you don't clean up so bad."

It took a minute to work my way through that. "Thanks. I think."

"Sure," he said, and went back to the magazine. I got my socks on straight and went looking for shoes. All my favorite pairs were in my luggage, at the airport. I snagged a pair of boots that weren't too reprehensible, went back into the bedroom, got a pair of skinnier socks that would fit better under the boots, and left the ones I'd had on in the middle of the floor. Such are the joys of living alone. No one can yell at you for doing things like that. "Okay, I'm ready when you are."

"Just a sec." Gary didn't look up from the magazine.

"You can borrow it." I grinned and went into the kitchen for a drink of water. When I came back Gary was on his feet, waiting.

"Damn," he said, and looked at my feet. So did I. The boots had heels, nice thick sturdy ones. Cludgy, in fact, but I like cludgy boots. I have big feet and can't wear sexy skinny little shoes, so I always went for the opposite extreme. In those shoes I was every bit as tall as Gary was, maybe a little taller. I grinned at him.

"Lady, you scare me," he said, and opened the door for me. I went out feeling pretty good about myself.

* * *

Marie lived barely ten minutes from me. My all-day nap had evidently made a dent, or at least I'd caught another wind, because I took the stairs up to her condo two at a time, leaving Gary behind. "She said it'd be open," he called as I looked both ways down the hall. "Number one twenty-one." I took an arbitrary left as Gary caught up, found Marie's door and did a staccato rap before pushing it open.

"Hey, Marie, it's us." The entryway was a short hall with a longer hall to my right and a kitchen to my left. At the end of the entryway, in front of us, was a Néné Thomas print, a woman surrounded by ravens. "I like the print," I called, and went past the kitchen, past the print and around a corner into the living room, still smiling.

Marie's very dead body lay sprawled across her living room floor.

CHAPTER EIGHT

I backed up and crashed into Gary, elbowing him in the gut. He grunted, offended. "What the hell was that for?"

"She's dead," I whispered.

"What?" Gary crowded me forward again. "Are you sure?"

"Pretty sure." I swallowed. Gary did the same, right behind my ear.

Marie lay on her back on the floor, one arm flung above her head, a classic faint. Except it wasn't a faint. A hole had been torn through her midriff, starting just to the left of her breastbone. It rose up at an angle, and it didn't take much imagination to envision the heart muscle cut neatly in half beneath the crimson blood. There were no superficial wounds that I could see. It looked like someone had walked in, jerked a knife up through her chest without warning, and walked out again. I rubbed my chest where Cernunnos had stabbed me, nervously. "Where's that sword?"

"In the trunk of my cab," Gary whispered back.

"Are you sure?"

"Yeah."

"I wonder if that's good or bad."

We stood there staring at Marie's body. "Maybe we should call the cops," Gary suggested.

I pulled my glasses off and rubbed my eyes, then put them back on. Marie was still lying there, dead. "Shit," I said after a while. "I *am* the cops." I backed up again and went looking for a phone. I found one in the kitchen, lying beside the tooth Marie'd collected from the church parking lot. She'd cleaned the blood off it and it looked innocuous, like it was waiting for the tooth fairy. I picked it up and stared at it, then folded it into my pocket as I got the phone and went back into the living room, dialing 9-1-1.

We were still standing there twenty-five minutes later when the real cops showed up. They bustled us down to the station in separate cars. I thought if we were really criminals, we'd have either abandoned the place or worked out our story while we were waiting for the cops, but no one wanted to listen to my point of view.

Gary had an all-day alibi; he'd been at work until two, then at a senior's poker game until he came to wake me up. I had no alibi at all. A cop I didn't know questioned me for over an hour. He kept getting hung up on the fact that I'd seen Marie from a plane in the first place. Everybody was having trouble with that idea. I made a mental note not to play Rescue Chick from the air again.

He let me go after verifying I really was a cop. Gary was waiting on the station stairs for me. We stood there watching splats of rain hit the sidewalk.

"You think it was Cernunnos?" Gary asked after a while.

"I don't think his horse would fit in that apartment." I sat down hard on the steps. Gary looked down at me in surprise. I smiled up at him weakly. "I haven't eaten this week." I didn't think I was even exaggerating.

"You could eat?" he asked in horror.

"Either that or I could pass out." I gave him my hand to pull me up. He did, and put a steadying hand at my waist when I wobbled. I smiled dizzily at him. "You know, Gary, if you were forty years younger I could get to like you."

"Yeah," he said. "That's what all the girls say. Where we going? My cab's at Marie's."

"There's a Denny's right around the corner."

"No doughnut shop?"

I grinned a little. "Down the street. But I need real food."

"You could eat," he said again, sort of admiringly. I nodded and teetered down the street.

A plate of mozza sticks, a grilled chicken-with-cheese-and-bacon sandwich, a copious number of fries and a chocolate milkshake later I could think again. Gary watched me eat with silent fascination and didn't so much as steal a fry. When I ordered a hot-fudge brownie sundae and sat back to wait for it, Gary judged it safe to speak again. "So *do* you think it was Cernunnos?"

I pulled my glasses off and chewed on the earpiece. "I don't know. Do ancient Celtic gods go around murdering people in their apartments?"

"Dunno. Never met any before. Don't know why they wouldn't."

I looked up and squinted, trying to resolve his fuzzy edges into something more solid. My vision wasn't that bad—I could drive without my contacts, if I had to—but I'm nearsighted and things more than about three feet away took on the Christmas tree-light effect. "I think maybe we should start with something a little less esoteric."

"Sure," Gary said, "like a jealous rival in the anthropology department." He stared at me until I wrinkled my nose and put my glasses back on.

"It could happen," I mumbled.

"Could," Gary agreed. "You think it did?"

"No," I said reluctantly. "I think Marie was into something weirder than that."

Gary nodded, satisfied. The waitress came back with my sundae and I poked at it with a fork, no longer hungry enough to eat it. "It was too clean to be Cernunnos."

"Whaddaya mean, too clean? Didn't you *look* at her?"

"Yeah, but." I waved the fork around. "Think about his host. Dogs and birds and guys on horses. Do you think he goes around killing people all by himself? What if it was that other guy?"

"What other guy?"

"The one with the knife. She said it wasn't Cernunnos, but she'd thought it was up until the diner this morning." I frowned at my brownie, and took a bite. It was pretty good. I took another bite.

"The human guy?"

"I donno. I wonder if there are any humans associated with Cernunnos. Maybe we should find out."

"I don't think the library's open this late, Jo."

My eyebrows went up. "Doesn't matter. I've got a computer at home." The brownie really was pretty good. I ate some more.

"Never touch the things," Gary said disdainfully.

I grinned. "Try it. You'll like it." I finished my dessert, paid the bill and we went home.

I have a little sign on my computer that says: On The Internet, Nobody Knows You're A Dog. I dusted it off while the computer booted up. Gary stood back about four feet, looking wary. "It isn't going to bite you, Gary."

"That don't look like the ones on TV," Gary announced.

I shook my head. "I'm running Linux."

Gary squinted at me. I inhaled to explain, and gave it up as a bad job before I even started. "It means I'm a computer geek."

"Right." Gary edged closer. I opened up a Web browser while he watched curiously. "And you know what you're doing?"

I grinned over my shoulder at him. "Welcome to the twenty-first century, Gary. Anything you want, you can find it on the Net. It takes hardly any effort to find one hundred percent right answers, and one hundred percent wrong answers."

He leaned over and planted a hand against the corner of my desk, peering at the screen. "How do you tell which is which?"

"Personal prejudice, sometimes. But for this kind of stuff—" I waggled my fingers at the screen "—you can check through half a dozen sites or so and pick up the information that's common to all of them. That's pretty close to being true. I mean, we're talking about Celtic gods here, Gary. I don't think there's a real unquestionable expert on the topic, you know?" I clicked through to one of the sites. Gary dragged a chair over and we both read the screen.

There were a lot of origin stories for the Hunt. Some of it was what Marie had told us already, though some of them mentioned someone called Herne the Hunter. Those ones said the Hunt was made up of mortal hunters who had worked for Richard II of England. The rest suggested it was either of "faerie," which looked like an obnoxious way to spell "fairy" to me, or made up of great warriors from the past. Even King Arthur was listed among the riders.

"His punishment for killing the children," Gary said when we got to that bit.

"What?" I pushed my glasses up, peering at him.

"Arthur had hundreds of kids killed."

I stared at him. "I never heard anything like that."

Gary shrugged. "It's one of the stories. Sort of like the Pharaoh killing all the kids trying to get to Moses. Except Arthur was trying to destroy Mordred. Maybe he's riding with Cernunnos as his punishment for killing them."

"Where'd you learn all that?"

Gary cocked an eyebrow at me. "I'm an old dog, lady. You pick up a few tricks along the way."

Great. Apparently I was the only nonbeliever in Seattle. Well, me and Morrison. Somehow that didn't make me feel any better. Gary reached out and clicked back to the search engine, and through to another site. I half smiled.

"I thought you never touched these things."

"Don't tell anybody. You'll ruin my rep." He leaned forward, jutting his jaw at the screen while we waited for a slow-loading page to resolve. "So the only mortal mentioned with Cernunnos is this guy Herne. Is he our guy?"

I slid down in my chair, sighing. "I don't know. Some of the descriptions sound like they might just be the same person. Which doesn't do us any good. Dammit."

"What's that?" Gary leaned forward, examining the screen. Badly rhyming nonsense filled the page in a painstaking handwritten font.

I call on the East Gate to close and bind thee
I call on the gods who would listen to me
I call on the wind and the earth and the sea
I call on fire to help bind thee
In this god's name I set my geas
That this binding cannot be broken
By my will and by these words
By these powers and by my skill
I bind thee for eternity.

"In Cernunnos's name I set this geas?" Gary asked, grinning. I reached out and clapped a hand over his mouth, startling even myself. Above my fingers, his eyes widened. *"Wwwf wng?"*

I looked back at the chant. It still looked like nonsense, but I shivered anyway, discomfited. "I don't think we should read that out loud."

Gary's eyebrows went up a little and he glanced at the computer before shrugging. "Okay."

What, that was it? Just "okay"? My surprise must have shown on my face, because he shook his head, smiling. "Jeez, lady, don't you ever go on gut feelings?"

I spread my hands. "No."

"Well, that's what you been goin' on since I met you. Better get used to it."

"God, I have been, haven't I?" I looked around for my glasses and put them back on. "Tomorrow," I said firmly, "I will wake up normal and rational again."

"And have answers to all your problems, right?"

I smiled halfheartedly. "Right."

"Sounds like a good plan to me." Gary sighed and ran a hand back through his hair. He didn't have a lot of it, and what there was, was white. It was the only thing that made him look somewhere around his age. Even his wrinkles were sort of Ernest Hemingway wrinkles, like they were from too much squinting into the sun rather than age. They made him look dependable, not old. "Well, lady, I'm an old man and I've been up since early, so I'm heading home. I gotta go to work in the morning."

"Yeah, okay. Me, I'm going to..." I trailed off and frowned at the computer.

"Gonna what?" Gary prompted. I shrugged.

"I'm going to find out who murdered Marie."

"No fair having all the fun without me. My shift ends at two. I'll see you then, maybe."

"All right. In the meantime, don't pick up any guys with swords. Oh, hey. Your car. You want a ride to Marie's, um, to where Marie lived, um, to your car?" I stood up, digging in my pocket for my car keys as an attempt to keep my mouth from running off and making me sound even more idiotic.

"You don't have to do that," Gary dissembled, but I'd just spent weeks in Ireland. There's a certain protocol I'd learned there.

In Ireland, you go to someone's house, and she asks you if you want a cup of tea. You say no, thank you, you're really just fine. She asks if you're *sure*. You say of course you're sure, really, you don't need a thing. Except they pronounce it *ting*. You don't need a *ting*. Well, she says then, I was going to get myself some anyway, so it would be no trouble. Ah, you say, well, if you were going to get yourself some, I wouldn't mind a spot of tea, at that, so long as it's no trouble and I can give you a hand in the kitchen. Then you go through the whole thing all over again until you both end up in the kitchen drinking tea and chatting.

In America, someone asks you if you want a cup of tea, you say no, and then you don't get any damned tea.

I liked the Irish way better.

"No, really," I said. "It's the middle of the night and there's a crazy man with a knife between here and there, and besides, I need to stop at the store and get something to eat for breakfast tomorrow. There's no food here at all."

"Well, if you're sure," Gary said, and I fought back a grin as we headed for the door.

I sat in the parking lot after Gary pulled out, both my hands on the steering wheel. I was tired, but it was the kind of twilight tired where I felt a little lighter than air and not quite like I could sleep. I knew I could, but as long as the false high was with me, I thought I should run with it. Somewhere not very far above me was a dead woman who'd needed my help, and somewhere inside my head things had happened that I didn't understand. I leaned forward, folding my hands on top of each other on the steering wheel, and rested my forehead against them. I could smell the old leather on the wheel, and a faint lingering scent of a perfume I rarely wore.

Cars are my refuge, my comfort food. My first real memory is looking out the window of my father's great big old Oldsmobile. I was about three, too little to know I'd be making a trip like that every few months until I left home. Dad tells me that when I was too little to see the cars, I'd hear them and go, "Oom!" because that's what I thought they sounded like. He got into the habit of saying, "Zoom!" and "Vroom!" to make me happy. I still do it myself, from time to time.

Marie's murder was a little too surreal for me. People you've just met aren't supposed to end up dead twelve hours later. I shook my head and let my mind slide off that for a moment.

Of course, that left Cernunnos and Coyote to think about. You want to talk about surreal. I groaned quietly and thumped my head against the wheel. I should be going home. I should be *at* home, looking up Native American legends on the Net. Native American legends, and dream interpretation, and the name of a good psychologist, since it was pretty clear I was losing my mind. I rubbed the heel of my hand over my breastbone. It kept right on not having a hole in it. I kept right on not being dead. This was beyond mortal ken.

And dammit, I didn't believe in beyond mortal ken. What did an atheist do if God shows up on the doorstep? I'd invited him in for breakfast.

A sharp rap on the window startled me into bolting upright. I drove the heel of my hand into the horn. A broad face under a blue hat leaned over the windshield, wincing quizzically. I puffed my cheeks out and took my hand off the horn, opening the door to hang out of it.

"Was I speeding, Officer?"

"Didn't know it was you, Joey. Just wanted to check and make sure everything was okay."

"Hi, Ray. Define okay." I smiled wanly. Raymond was a short wide guy whom I was pretty sure could bench press a Buick. Not the fastest on his feet, but between him and a nuclear bunker, I'd take him every time. He stuck his hand out, and I stood up, leaning over the door to shake it.

"Heard you got your balls busted," he said sympathetically. Ball-busting was Ray's favorite term and he applied it with blithe disregard to gender-based improbability. "Guess I never thought about you going to the academy. But you're a real cop, huh? What're you doing out here?"

"I'm a real cop," I agreed. "Sort of." The other question was easier to answer: I pointed a finger up toward Marie's apartment. "I found the body a few hours ago."

"Coming back to the scene of the crime? Common criminal mistake, you know. You know this is the fifth murder like this in the past couple weeks?" Ray shook his head.

My eyebrows went up. "I didn't. Just got back from Europe." God, that sounded pretentious. "What do they have in common?"

Ray shook his head again. "Not much. Different age ranges, different races, different day jobs, different genders, no phone calls to or from the same numbers, not even pizza joints. Different parts of the city, different everything."

"No, there's something linking them," I said absently. I tugged my glasses off and pinched the bridge of my nose, glasses dangling from my fingertips. A piece of wire contracted around my heart and I took a deep breath, trying to shake the feeling off. A brief image of the spiderwebbed windshield flashed behind my eyelids. I frowned, trying to shake that off, too.

"Yeah? Don't suppose you can tell me what it is." Ray reached up and twisted his hat on his head. His hair was visibly thinner right where his hat sat on his head, from doing that for years. It occurred to me that I knew the guys at the department inside and out, but I couldn't remember the last time I'd had a date. My heart was still tight, the spiderweb image still bothering me. I put my shoulders back, trying to breathe.

"No, but there's something. Can I look at the files?" The web inside me loosened a bit and I was able to catch my breath.

Ray twisted his mouth in much the same way he habitually twisted his hat. It dug deep lines around his mouth. Being a cop left its mark. "I don't know. You're not a detective."

"Christ, Ray, the woman was murdered practically under my nose. Gimme a break."

Ray frowned at me, then waved his hand. "Arright. I've got copies in the car. I thought this might be another by the same guy, so I brought 'em to compare pictures to the placement of the body."

"And?"

He shrugged. "And there's nothing to compare. There's no ritual in how the bodies have been laid out. They've all been punched through the chest with a sharp weapon, but that's the only common element. Looks like they've all just been left to lie as they fell."

"Is that good or bad?"

"Neither. The repeat use of the weapon is good, the lack of any other ritual is bad. Nothing to pick up, nothing to deviate from. I don't like it." Ray twisted his cap around on his head again.

"Do you *usually* like horrible murders?"

Ray eyed me. I held up my hands in supplication. "Can I borrow those files?"

"You said look," he objected.

"Look, borrow, whatever. I'll be careful with them. Promise."

I made my eyes all big and wide and hopeful before remembering they were bloodshot. Eww.

Ray frowned at me for a while, then turned around and went and got the files. "Don't let Morrison find out or he'll be busting *my* balls," he said as he handed them over.

I flipped one open, not really listening to him. "I won't. Thanks, Ray."

"Yeah, well, my car needs work."

I looked up with a crooked grin. "As soon as I find out my new work schedule."

"It's a date." He nodded at the files again. "Don't mention where you got 'em."

"I won't." I watched him walk back to his car, wondering if it really *was* a date. Not that I particularly wanted to date Ray. It was just that fixing guys' cars seemed to be my idea of a pretty good date, which probably explained why I didn't get out more. Maybe I could start my own escort service. Oil change and dinner. I'd have to come up with a catchy name for the place. The only things that came to mind involved lube jobs, and that was just bad.

I got back in my car and went home before I started taking myself seriously.

CHAPTER NINE

Wednesday, January 5th, 12:30 a.m.

Ten minutes later I spread out the files on my kitchen table, standing over them. There was no file on Marie yet, but I'd seen that in living—or not—color. Raymond was right. The victims didn't appear to have anything in common. Nothing obvious, but there had to be something. I could feel it practically vibrating in my eardrums.

What did I know about Marie? She was an anthropologist who started believing in what she studied. She had a talent that let her see more than the average person saw, things that could be politely labeled esoteric. I yawned, and the wire around my heart went *spang,* releasing so fast it hurt. I swallowed a whimper and rubbed my chest again. I could almost feel spiderweb cracks sealing up.

All right. What if that was what they had in common? They were all banshees. The spiderweb fissured again, and I sighed. "Okay, that's not it," I muttered. "How about they're all, uh…aware of another plane of existence. Not the kind of thing you're going to talk about, right?" The wire-web relaxed and let me breathe again. I scowled hugely at the photographs. It was Oh God Thirty and I was standing in my kitchen talking to heartburn. Talking out loud, no less. I needed sleep. Or a dog.

"Sleep," I said out loud. "If any of you want to tell me what your gig was, stop by dreamland. Otherwise I'll figure you out tomorrow." I turned the lights off, went to bed and lay there a long time in the dark, looking at the ceiling, faintly white in the dimness. I used to do this when I was a kid, zone out until I could feel myself floating about three inches above my body. I always fell back down into myself as soon as I noticed. I felt like that now, very slightly detached from my flesh.

It was not a comforting feeling after a day like today. I tried closing my eyes and found out they were already closed, but the ceiling still glowed faintly white up above me. I blinked. Darkness came and went, but I didn't feel my eyelids move. A shock ran through me, radiating out from my heart like the sudden release of a metal-on-metal lock, sharp and high-pitched and tingling through my whole body.

And then I was free, looking down at my shape under the covers. I looked very comfortable. I looked down at my feet, the ones I was standing on. I could see the carpet through my toes.

Something tugged at me, pulling me up. I turned my face up, and disconnected with the floor entirely, floating upward.

Next time I go for a flight, I'll go out through the window. Even a glimpse of what the upstairs neighbors were doing—well, I honestly hadn't known human beings could get into that position.

The world outside glowed. I was sure there'd been no moon when I came home, but a brilliant crescent lit the sky with more wattage than usual, silver-blue light weighting down tree branches as if it were snow. Leaves glittered with color, reds and golds and greens that had more to do with neon than nature. Pathways and streets were dark blue streaks undershadowed with something else, like an artist had slapped paint on and let it slide down the canvas to expose other shards of colors beneath it. I stood in the sky, looking down over the streets as the dark blue slowly blurred away.

One exposed path led under an arch of trees that reminded me of Anne Shirley's "White Way of Delight." It twisted, sliding underground, and somewhere down it I could feel a heavy presence waiting for me. It felt like it could drink down the light and me with it, like the rabbit hole pulling Alice in. I reached up to tug a leaf off one of the trees, watching it glow a soft silver in my palm. It brightened into a beacon as I scrambled down the pathway.

It met the mouth of the cave, sliding underground. I hesitated at the dark entrance, lifting my leaf up to try to light the way. I saw a reflection, a glimpse of something bright, in the instant before a wall roared up, damming the cave's mouth. I put my hand against it, the leaf gleaming, but nothing changed except the sensation of the thing waiting for me. It was somewhere beneath the earth, and amused, and patient. I stayed where I was a few moments longer, then slowly turned back up the White Way. The one who waited suddenly felt much more distant, and then I couldn't feel it at all.

The world changed around me again, then again, and again, until they came so fast I could barely distinguish one from another. Some of the permutations I recognized: glimpses of Paris and New York, places that looked as solid as reality, overlooking the vibrant glow that had nothing to do with city lights and a great deal to do with things I didn't want to think about. Others were harder to grasp, African plains with seas of violently purple grass, Australian Outback with a sky as bloody red as the stone beneath it. Every one got farther away from civilization, until I exploded into a place of absolute stillness with the hard white light of the stars pricking my skin.

"Well, she's no good," a tart little voice said. "Look at her. A baby, spilling out all over the place. You want a cosmic bed wetter to take care of this? She can't even see us."

"That's no way to speak to our guest," another voice said very firmly. This one was rich and dark and full of very round vowels, chocolaty, like James Earl Jones. "She's come a long way on nothing but faith."

"She's come a long way on *our* faith," the tart voice said. It sounded like Granny Smith apples. "She hasn't got any of her own."

"She's a newborn," a third voice broke in. He sounded like mellow cheese. "She didn't mean to invite us, but she's willing to help." Two more voices chimed in, everyone bickering and sniping at one another until they sounded like a flock of geese. I turned around in a full circle twice, trying to see the people the voices belonged to. The starlight jabbed at my eyes unrelentingly, no shadows or shapes to go with the voices clouding them. It suddenly felt weirdly familiar.

I hadn't seen Coyote until I believed in him. I had a sinking feeling in my gut that I'd better believe in the voices, because I was pretty sure I *had* invited them to do...whatever they'd done. Hauled me out of my body to somewhere that horribly murdered people hang out.

My brain just shut down around that thought.

"Look," I finally said. It got very quiet in the star field. I turned around one more time to find a handful of people behind me, all staring at me with wide, curious eyes. "You're wrong. I can see you." I wasn't sure which one was the Granny Smith, so I fixed them all with a gimlet eye. "And I'm not all that inclined to help somebody who called me a cosmic bed wetter, when you get right down to it." A tall woman's long nose twitched. I guessed her to be Granny Smith and removed the gimlet eye from the others to give it just to her. Her nose twitched again.

"Sorry," she said after being elbowed in the ribs by a short man whom I guessed to be the James Earl Jones voice. He didn't look anything at all like Jones. I was hideously disappointed.

"You'll have to forgive Hester," he said. "She's not taking well to having been interrupted."

"Interrupted." My eyebrows flew up. "You mean murdered?" I was sure these five were the files I had lying on my kitchen table. They were all the right general sizes and shapes, even if I'd only seen photos of their corpses.

He made a moue. "I suppose so. It's really just an inconvenience, but Hester is young."

I peered at Hester. She looked like she was well into her fifties, at least. Her mouth pursed up like she'd bitten into one of the apples she sounded like. "Not as young as *this* one," she sniffed. I scowled, and suddenly there was an enormous distance between myself and the five, the star field endlessly expanded. I could see, with sharp-edged clarity, the alarm on all five faces.

"Dammit, Hester," one of the others said, "you're going to put her off us entirely before she'll agree to help us at all." Her voice was absolutely clear despite the distance between us, like she was standing on a sound stage. It echoed faintly. Hester flared her nostrils, then lifted her chin.

"I'm sorry." It was much less grudging this time. "Roger is right. I was in the middle of something important, and I'm not sure I'd done enough to make it last. But that's no reason to be rude. You've been extraordinarily generous with your invitation already, even if you didn't know it." Her voice was still tart, but it was more like the tart of apple pie. I began to wonder if I was hungry. "Will you stay long enough to let us tell you what we know?"

"Well, I'm here," I said. Distance contracted again, so that the five and I were only a few feet apart, stars glittering around us. "I might as well listen. Maybe you can tell me what the hell is going on." There was a note of miserable confusion in my voice. I straightened my shoulders and pretended I hadn't really sounded that pathetic.

"You almost died this morning," a petite blond woman said. She had dumpling cheeks that went with Earth Mother curves. I remembered from the file that her name was Samantha.

"Yeah, I was there for that part." I rubbed my breastbone uncomfortably and screwed up my face.

"Do you know that near-death experiences often open people's eyes to another world?"

"I know that's what they *say*," I replied. Samantha smiled a tolerant little smile. It occurred to me that my current position was a fragile one for argument. "All right." I gritted my teeth and pushed the words out. "So maybe there's more than meets the eye." I rubbed the heel of my hand over my breastbone again and took a deep breath. "All right, there *is* more than meets the eye," I said defensively. "Normal people don't start burning and smoking when you stick a knife in them. The guy who stabbed me this morning was definitely not normal."

Hester snorted faintly. Roger elbowed her again. "Be quiet. That's quite an admission for her."

"Must it be an admission to come around to stating the obvious?" Hester asked. Apparently sour was just her nature. The moment of grace earlier must have come hard-won. It had worked to make me stay, but she wasn't earning any brownie points.

"Give me a break, Hes," I said. She looked up sharply. I bet nobody had called her that since third grade. "Yesterday the world made sense and today I'm standing in a star pit talking to ghosts." I looked back at Samantha. "So what happened to me?"

"You got to make a choice. Most people don't get to."

I spread my hands. "Why me?"

"You must have a lot to offer," she said. "Many times, those who need the most healing are the ones who can in turn heal the most."

I took a step backward, a scowl falling down my face like pitch, until I was glaring at her through my eyebrows. "What do you mean, need the most healing," I said. She was clever enough to withhold an answer. Instead, she spread her hands, a polite mimicry of my earlier gesture.

"I did not mean to intrude," she said so deferentially that the anger drained out of me again. "What do you know about shamans, Siobhán Walkingstick?"

My eyebrows went up and my jaw went down until my face was as long as a donkey's. My father had taken one look at the unpronounceable Gaelic first name my mother had bestowed on me and had given me another one. I'd looked up the pronunciation when I was a teenager, but I actually hadn't been sure that the bizarre combination of letters was pronounced *She-vaun,* not *See-oh-bawn,* until my mother used the name when she called to ask to meet me. Aside from that one conversation, not even she'd called me Siobhán. It was even less a part of me than the Walkingstick name I'd abandoned a decade ago. "How did you know that name?"

Samantha drew an outline around me with her fingertip, a loose general shape. "It's a part of you that you've been denying your whole life, and now it's spilling over. Think of it like a floodlight shining on you, illuminating all the information you've been keeping filed away. It's very clear to anyone who knows how to read it. It's eager to be acknowledged. You have a remarkable heritage, Siobhán. You ought to explore it, not turn your back on it."

I stood there and stared at her. After a while I tried to crank my jaw back up. Part of me wondered why I was reacting physically when my body, as far as I could tell, was tucked safely in bed, back at home. Wherever back at home was, from here. "Right," I said eventually. "This is getting a little too thick for me." It came out exactly right, casual bullshit. I was very pleased. The thing was, right down in my gut, I believed her.

"You're not a very good liar, are you?" The fifth person finally spoke up. He was taller than me and had a wonderful Grecian nose and broad cheekbones. He hadn't looked so good in the murder photos. It was too bad he was dead, or I'd have asked him on a date. His mouth curved in half a smile, and I had the sinking feeling he'd somehow heard that. Coyote and Cernunnos had certainly heard things I hadn't said out loud.

"Don't worry," he said. "I won't tell anybody. But thanks." He winked, and the half smile turned into a grin. I told myself I couldn't possibly blush, without a body handy. I think it even worked.

"I always thought I was a pretty good liar," I finally mumbled.

He shook his head. "There's nothing wrong with your delivery. But the truth flares up around you like a spotlight. We probably don't have much time, Joanne. Let's save the pretenses for later."

"Subtle, Jackson." Samantha smiled. He grinned and shrugged.

I opened my mouth to argue, and let all my air out in a rush. "Okay. Okay. So maybe I'm kind of on-purpose dense about American Indian—" I waved my hand around "—stuff. I just hate playing into stereotypes, you know?"

"Actually, you're afraid of it," Jackson murmured. I straightened my shoulders, offended.

"What's there to be afraid of?"

"Power," every single one of them said. I took a step back.

"Responsibility," Samantha said, and Hester said, "Change."

Roger smiled and shrugged a little, as if to say, what can you do?, and added, "Love," to the list. "Death," said the woman who'd been quiet except for swearing at Hester, and Jackson breathed, "Life."

"I'm not afraid of any of that," I threw back. "Not that I'm eager to die, but—"

"You've been very closed off since you were about fifteen," Samantha said, sympathetic again. I felt my stomach knot up, and took another step back. "The world was a lot more wonderful before then, wasn't it?"

One of those cracks I'd seen inside me tore open, surgery with a battle-ax. For a moment there was nothing but pain and rage and a terrible sense of loss, memories that I'd kept safely locked away in a small black box in my mind. "How do you kn—"

I clenched my jaw on the words. I was not having this conversation with dead people in a star field somewhere outside of my own body. I felt a little tug around my heart and ignored it. "What is it that you five have in common," I said flatly. "There has to be some kind of pattern."

All five of them exchanged glances, and Jackson spoke up. "Sam asked earlier. What do you know about shamans?"

I shrugged, stiff. "I don't know. They're medicine men. They do magic. What do they have to do with me?"

"The world has a lot of people and a lot of problems these days," Hester murmured. "It needs more shamans than ever."

"A shaman's job is to heal," Roger said. "Whatever needs healing. That's what we did, in life. Most of us have been doing it for many lifetimes."

I stared at him for a while, waiting for the punch line. When it didn't come, I rubbed my eyes, noticing that here, I could see perfectly clearly without glasses or contacts. "So why would someone go around murdering cosmic caretakers?"

"Power," the quiet one said wryly. She sounded English. Hester frowned at her.

"It doesn't work that way."

"Not our power," the quiet one said patiently. "His own power. We're all people who could have fought or helped him, and so we threatened his power."

"Fought? You just said you were healers."

There was a little silence while they all looked at each other again. "There are different paths," Jackson finally said. "Some of us are warriors. Others are less confrontational. The end purpose is the same, to take away pain, physical and emotional, to heal."

Very, very slowly, a light came on at the back of my head. "That's not what I've gotten myself into." I figured this was the moral equivalent of asking for a no. It was like asking, "You wouldn't want to help me paint the fence, would you?" Put it that way, and you were setting up for denial.

I really, *really* wanted to be denied.

"We rarely understand the consequences of our decisions at the time they're made," Samantha murmured, which didn't sound much like the answer I was hoping for.

"I didn't have a lot of time," I snapped. Another tug pulled at my insides, a little stronger than last time. I rubbed my breastbone absently and took a deep breath. I wondered if my body back in bed did the same thing.

"The important decisions usually come when there's not much time to debate," Roger agreed. I frowned at him. He seemed so nice and down to earth, and I was unconsciously counting on him to back me up. My hopes and dreams were obviously being lined up to be crushed.

"Well, Christ, there's got to be a way out of this, doesn't there?"

"Of course there is." Hester'd become even more disdainful, which I wouldn't have thought possible. "Ignore it."

"Will it go away?" I asked hopefully.

"No. You'll keep struggling with the urge to help people, and every time you turn your back, a little part of you will die. Eventually you turn into a prune."

I stared at her. I could have nightmares about turning into someone like her. To my surprise, she threw her head back and laughed. "Oh, I might rub *you* the wrong way, Walkingstick, but there are people who respond to me fine. Listen to this—a shaman is a trickster. To heal someone, you need to change their way of thinking, if only for a moment. Your armor is fractured. One good hit—" She flicked her middle finger against her thumb, like she was thumping me in the chest. The tug returned, painful this time. "—And you'll come apart into a thousand pieces. Keep your promises, and you might not shatter."

I hated suspecting people were telling me God's own truth. I gulped against another painful tug, and the five of them suddenly seemed distant. "Oh, hell," said the quiet one. "We've wasted too much time. She's too tired to stay."

"She's very young," Roger reminded her.

"I know, and she's come a long way, but—" The quiet one broke off and stared at me intensely. "Listen to me—"

"Wait," I said. "Marie wasn't a shaman, was she? What did she have in common with you?"

"I don't know Marie," the quiet one said impatiently. "Find him, Siobhán Walkingstick. His power and his pain will bleed off him. Find the scent of it and follow him back."

"But who is he?" My voice sounded very thin and distant, even to myself. The tug was a steady pull now, and the stars were streaking by me, disappearing as I faded away.

"I don't know. But he controls the—"

I took a sharp breath, woke up and rolled over. Something crunched in my palm. I opened my hand and blinked through the dimness at the shimmering leaf there. After a few moments I sighed quietly and went back to sleep, cradling the leaf carefully.

It was seven-thirty and I'd woken up to a still-dark sky before I remembered that it was January and there were no leaves on anything but the evergreens.

Wednesday, January 5th, 8:30 a.m.

I don't go to confession. For one, I'm not Catholic. For two, the whole idea of being absolved of your sins by telling a priest about them has always struck me as a little strange, probably because I'm not Catholic.

On the other hand, a priest isn't allowed to call up the loony bin and have you committed after you tell him all your crazy little stories, and he's a whole lot less expensive than a shrink.

St. James Cathedral in downtown Seattle was the only Catholic church I knew of for certain. I parked in one of the lots at the corner of 9th and Columbia, having made it from the University District in thirty-seven minutes. On a weekday morning, that was a record-breaker. Finding a parking spot put it off the charts.

St. James didn't exactly look like it was imported wholesale from Europe, but it had all the impressive dignity a cathedral ought to. Buff-colored brick and two very tall bell towers defined the place; that, and a sixty-foot arched entryway. I felt properly awed as I went inside, cradling my shimmering leaf in my palm. I kept expecting it to disappear and leave lines of fairy dust on my hand.

I edged around the pews and up to a confessional booth, sliding inside. The leaf gleamed slightly.

There was a thump in the other half of the confessional, and a gusty sigh.

"Ever had one of those days?" the priest asked. "Where you're doubting everything?"

I'd never done this before, but I was pretty sure that wasn't supposed to be his line. I'd been sort of looking forward to the bit where I said, "Forgive-me-father-for-I-have-sinned," and he'd ruined the pattern already.

"Don't get me wrong," he said, "I like my job. But don't you ever get up and wonder if you've made the right decisions? Wonder if you've really got a calling, or if it's just all some sort of infinitesimally large joke? Catholics don't mind the ancient-earth theories so much. I can see that God might call a billion years a day. Life is complicated like that. It's just that every once in a while something happens that really shakes the hell, excuse my French, out of my faith."

I blurted, "What happened?" He flashed me a sad little smile through the lattice.

"You haven't seen the news yet, have you? There was a massacre this morning at one of the high schools. Four children were killed. The really sick thing is that it was some lunatic with a knife. Not a gun. He went and tore every single one of their hearts out, all those innocent souls. How could God let that happen?"

"They didn't catch him?"

The priest let out a bitter laugh. "How do you *not* catch someone who's sticking knives into kids? But no, they didn't. Their teacher was knifed, too. And nobody saw anything."

"No one saw anything?" Had I done this? Was it vengeance for knifing Cernunnos yesterday? I closed my eyes. How long did it take for a god to heal? What possible purpose was there in the deaths of four kids? Did it give him strength? Hester said power didn't work that way.

"No." I spoke aloud, my eyes popping open. *Shamanic* power didn't work that way. Cernunnos was a god, not a shaman. Maybe his power was some kind of death power. The Web pages hadn't said.

"No," the priest agreed angrily. "No one saw. So what's the point?" I saw the shadow of him move, leaning forward to put his face in his hands. "If God can let this happen, how can I have faith in Him?"

I stood up slowly. The priest turned his head and watched me rise. His eyes were brown and his face unlined, in the unobtrusive confessional light. He couldn't have been much older than I was. "Don't worry, Father." I took a deep breath. "If God can let this happen, then he can put people on Earth who can stop it, too."

"But where are they?" he asked softly. I lifted my hand and pressed my palm against the lattice. The leaf crunched quietly and shattered in a tiny splash of light.

"I'm right here."

He reached up and pressed his hand opposite mine, separated by a few centimeters of wood. He was quiet so long I thought he might laugh at my arrogance. But then he smiled, the kind of smile a priest ought to have, gentle and compassionate and full of serene confidence that there's a better place than this world. "Go with God."

He left me standing alone in the confessional, a fading imprint of leaf dust glittering on my palm.

* * *

"They were shamans." Out of everyone I knew, Billy Holliday was the only person I would dare say that to. Billy was as enthusiastic as Mulder, a true believer in the things that went bump in the night. New people on staff always gave him shit about it— God knows I had—but it invariably faded into being one of those accepted quirks that make people interesting. Billy had more than his fair share of those quirks, but for the moment I was more or less grateful there was somebody I could talk to without Morrison throwing me in a nuthouse.

I plunked the files Ray lent me on Billy's desk, doing my best to look triumphant and in control. Billy blinked up at me, eyebrows climbing up his forehead like caterpillars.

"Where'd you get those?" he asked first, to his credit for keeping the security of the department, and, "Who were?" second.

"I found them in a garbage can."

He eyed the stack of paperwork. "You're an officer, you know? Not a detective."

"I've been with the department more than three years. I'm up for detective." I widened my eyes. Billy snorted.

"Yeah, right. Who were shamans? Are you supposed to be here?"

"I dunno," I admitted, glancing in the general direction of Morrison's office. "He didn't tell me what shift I was on. I think he expected me to quit."

"Have you ever quit anything in your whole life?"

"Not much. Shift change is at eleven, right? It's ten-thirty. I can be all perky and on time. Listen to me, Billy. These five murders in the past couple weeks, they were all shamans." I pushed my fingertip against the files. My knuckle turned white.

"How do you know that, Joanne?"

I straightened up, squared my shoulders and said, firmly, "I met them dream-walking."

Well. It was supposed to be firm. It was really more of an embarrassed whisper. Billy held my gaze for longer than the priest had, until I twisted my shoulders uncomfortably and glanced away. "Look," I said very quietly.

"No," he said, "I believe you."

Despite his rep, I was taken aback. "You do?"

He stood up. "Let's get some coffee. Down the street."

That was the usual cue for the good cop to leave the room while the bad cop terrorized the witness. I didn't usually think of Billy as the bad cop sort, but I sucked my lower lip into my mouth nervously and stuffed my hands in my pockets as I followed him out the door. On the street, he said, "You're about the most rational person I know."

I drew on what little dignity I had left. "Thank you."

"I like you and respect you even though you've been laughing up your sleeve at me for years."

I winced. "I gave up laughing ages ago, Billy. I just…"

"Think I'm nuts."

I winced again. "In a good way. Look, I mean…" I sighed. "I mean, why *do* you believe in that stuff, Billy?" I'd never thought, or maybe dared, to ask before.

He glanced at me, mouth drawn in a thin line. "I had an older sister."

"Had?" I tried to remember if I knew anything about Billy's childhood, other than the unfortunate name his parents had given him. Nothing surfaced.

"She died when I was eight. She drowned." Billy's shoulders were tight, his voice quiet.

"God. I'm sorry."

"Me too." He glanced at me again, stopping outside the coffee shop door. "When I was eleven, I woke up from a dream that I was suffocating. Caroline was sitting at the edge of my bed with her fists knotted in her lap. She told me that my best friend, Derek, had fallen into the slurry a neighbor was pouring for the concrete foundation to their house. I woke up the whole household and we all went running over there in our pajamas."

My own hands were knotted at my sides. "And?"

"My dad pulled Derek out of the slurry. It was half-set and crushing his ribs. My dead sister saved his life."

I hauled in a deep breath of air and rubbed my breastbone. "Jesus." I smiled lopsidedly. "So you're telling me you see dead people?"

Billy shot me a look, seeing if I was teasing him. I was, but it was the only way I could get through the conversation. I didn't mean to hurt him, and after a moment he realized that. His shoulders relaxed and he smiled back, crookedly. "Yeah. Not like the kid in that movie. Not nearly that often. But yeah, I do. You remember the Franklin murder a couple years ago?"

I shuddered. "Yeah."

Mrs. Franklin had killed her fourteen-year-old daughter, Emily, after the girl claimed she could see her new stepfather's past, and that he was a rapist. Mother and daughter had a screaming fight, ending in the girl's death. Mr. Franklin's police record proved Emily correct, too late. It was the sort of case the cops hated to have on the news; the tabloids made a huge fuss over it, while the coroner's office held its tongue about whether Emily had been sexually abused. The news crews took the coroner's silence as an implicit yes. The police department didn't like to talk about the fact that she hadn't been. It led to unanswerable questions about the little girl's apparent psychic abilities.

"Yeah, I remember. The whole thing was insane." I wasn't supposed to have been there. I'd been out with Billy, trying to hear the hitch he claimed was in his engine, when he was called to the murder scene.

"Emily Franklin was in the corner watching you the whole time you were there, like you were the sun and had just come out." Billy turned and pulled the door to the café open for me.

"Emily Franklin was dead, Billy."

"I know."

Hairs stood up all over my body, like someone'd dropped an icicle down my back. "You're telling me there was a ghost watching me?"

"The ghost of a clairvoyant little girl. She said you didn't have any past at all. She'd never seen anyone like you. She wanted to see what was going to happen to you. After a few days she let go, but I've been waiting ever since to see what happens to you. With you." He ordered a large decaffeinated espresso and waved his hand at me to order while I stared at him unhappily. "Go ahead and get something." He dug in his pocket for cash.

"Hot chocolate with mint and whipped cream," I mumbled. Forget cars. I needed real comfort food. "A grande. Why didn't you ever tell me that, Billy?"

"Would you have believed me?" He pulled the top off his drink and blew on it before taking a sip. I frowned at the counter.

"No," I admitted.

He shrugged. It was answer enough. "So something finally happened." He took a bigger sip of his drink and cursed, sticking his tongue out in an effort to reduce the burn's pain. "I've been waiting two years. You do this kind of about-face, I'm prepared to believe it. You wouldn't be here if you didn't believe it yourself. So tell me about the shamans. Was your friend one, too?"

I got my hot chocolate and found a couple dollars to give him for it. "I don't think so. She had something else going on. Look, where do I start, Billy? I've got a feeling I've got a lot of catch-up work to do. Starting right now, and starting with some old Celtic gods." I said it with a hard C, the way Marie had, and Billy looked both surprised and impressed.

"I woulda thought you'd say 'Seltic,'" he said. I wrinkled my nose at him.

"I just got back from Ireland," I pointed out, let a beat pass, and admitted, "Marie said Celtic. I didn't know better before then."

"There's no soft C in the Gaelic language." Billy took another sip of his coffee, then set it down. "Okay, tell me about this...god? God, Joanie. You start believing and you go whole haul, huh? I've just got dead people."

"Lucky me." I shook my head. "The guy I fought with yesterday wasn't a gang member. He was...Marie thought it was Cernunnos. An ancient Celtic god."

Billy sat back, pressing his lips together. "What do you think?"

"He wasn't human." It was strange to hear myself say that. I felt like an alien had taken over my body. Billy nodded slowly.

"You think he's the one who killed Marie? Who did the other five murders?"

"I don't know. I hurt him pretty badly yesterday, and I don't know if he could heal from it that fast. And then there's the high school this morning."

Billy nodded again. "Same M.O. Is it your guy?"

I wrapped both my hands around the paper cup. "Marie thought there might be someone else involved. It doesn't feel right to me, pinning this on Cernunnos." I barked laughter. "Doesn't feel right. God, listen to me."

"I am," Billy said seriously.

Hot chocolate splashed as I set the cup down. "And that freaks me out even more."

Billy studied me as he took a long drink of his coffee. "What's it like?" he finally asked. I dropped my head and looked into my hot chocolate.

"The good news is it's keeping my mind off having to walk the streets." I scowled at my drink. "That came out wrong." I pushed the chocolate away and lowered my head to the table, resting it on my forearms. "You remember the first time someone you loved died, Billy? It's like that. I can't believe it, but I can't not believe it, either. At the very least I should be in a hospital bed breathing through a tube. I should probably be dead." I sat up, fingers drifted to my sternum again. "It's like the whole world is a badly tuned engine. I'm starting to feel when it misses or lurches. And I've got this stupid idea that I can fix it."

"The world," Billy said. I smiled thinly.

"Let me just start with Seattle."

I turned up at Morrison's door, still carrying my hot chocolate, at five minutes to eleven. He stared at me like he'd never seen me before. "You didn't tell me when my shift started," I said with all the aplomb I could manage.

Morrison continued to stare at me. "I don't have a patrol uniform, either. I do have my badge!" I dug it out of my jacket pocket and waved it at him.

He stared at it.

"So now you pair me with an old curmudgeon, right? Somebody to show me the ropes? Somebody who hates paperwork and foists it all off on me? That's what happens now, right?" That's what happened in the movies, anyway. I frowned at Morrison. "You okay?"

"What the hell are you doing here, Walker?"

I straightened up, startled. "What'd you think I was gonna do, not show up so you'd have an excuse to fire me? Y'know, I might have loads of stupid, Morrison, but I'm not quite *that* bad."

"Walker." Morrison walked around to my side of his desk, pausing to close the door. My heart lurched. "You are a suspect,"

Morrison said, the words measured, "in a murder case. Walker. Do you really think I'm going to put you on the street?"

I swallowed hot chocolate wrong, and coughed until my eyes teared. Morrison stared at me impassively. When I could breathe again, I croaked, "Suspect? But they let me go."

"It looks bad. You chased that woman all over hell and breakfast, and twelve hours later she's dead? The papers will have a field day. Murdering cop put on foot patrol. The department can't afford that kind of publicity, Walker. The only place I want to see you in the next week is nowhere near here."

"If I'm nowhere near here how can you see—" Morrison's eyebrows shot upward. I shut up.

"Since you're here, go get a uniform and the rest of the equipment. Then stay outta my sight until this thing is cleared up."

"But—"

"Get!"

I got, stopping by Billy's desk on the way out. "Swing shift?" he asked. I snorted.

"No shift. I'm on temporary leave of duty until this murder's been taken care of. Morrison thinks I'm the prime suspect."

"Isn't it nice to have co-workers who have faith in you?" Billy shoved the paperwork I'd gotten from Ray at me, grinning. "So go clear yourself."

I retreated to the coffee shop to study the files, reading about the murders and trying to figure out what they had to do with Marie. None of it made any sense to me. The last of the shamans, the quiet woman whose name I hadn't been able to remember, had died on New Year's Eve. Her next of kin was listed as Kevin Sadler, and there was a contact phone number. Maybe I hadn't missed the funeral.

I'd never called up a stranger to ask about a dead person before. Kevin Sadler had a quiet voice and told me I'd missed the funeral but he would appreciate a visit; the house was very quiet and empty now. Nervous, uncomfortable and glad I wasn't in uniform, I drove to the address he gave me.

The man who met me at the door was as unprepossessing as his voice, with thinning ashy brown hair and weary hazel eyes. He was at least my height, but his shoulders stooped and he gave the impression of being much smaller. Despite the shadows under his eyes, he smiled at me and offered his hand. "I'm Kevin. I don't think Adina ever mentioned you, Joanne."

I shook his hand and came in as he ushered me. "We only met once, very briefly," I said awkwardly. "The circumstances were unusual."

A genuine smile flickered over his face. "Things with Adina often were. Can I get you some tea? I have the kettle on."

Despite my discomfort I smiled back. "If you're sure it'd be no trouble, I'd love some tea." I followed him into the kitchen, looking around.

The Sadler home was tiny, small enough to be called a cottage. The kitchen was country-style, with innumerable calico cat figurines, besieged with flouncy bows, on wall racks and littering the counters. The walls were butter-yellow where they could be seen behind pine cupboards, and the counters a cheerful orange that somehow avoided being overwhelming. Only one small window, with pretty gingham curtains, gave the room natural light, but it seemed bright and pleasant anyway. A calico-printed kettle puffed madly, a promise that any moment now it would whistle and the water would be ready.

"I think the first thing I heard Adina say was swearing at someone," I commented, still looking around. "I don't think this is the kitchen I would have expected from her."

Kevin smiled as he took down teacups from a cupboard. They

looked like real china, with cats on the sides. "Adina liked to shake up people's preconceptions. When did you meet her?"

"I was looking for help." I couldn't find a tactful way to say "last night" to this quietly mourning gentleman. "I think she may have had some answers, but I didn't have time to ask her." The whistle blasted. Kevin took the kettle off and poured boiling water over tea bags.

"What did you need help with?" He reached out to pat one of the calico cats on the counter. It opened its eyes and purred. I leaned back, startled.

"I'm trying to find someone," I temporized, then suddenly went on a gut feeling and corrected, "I'm trying to find the man who killed her."

All the smile went out of Kevin's face. "He's a very dangerous man. A lunatic."

"I know. But a friend of mine was murdered last night and the police think it's the same man. Four kids were massacred this morning, and I think it's the same man. I don't—" I took a breath and gulped down air. "I don't have much to go on. He seems to be attracted to different kinds of power."

Kevin glanced over at me. "What kinds of power?"

Damn. I was going to have to say it out loud. "Shamanic power. And—and death power."

Kevin nodded slowly. "Adina believed in those kinds of things. Do you?"

I let my breath out, relieved he hadn't laughed and shown me the door. "I didn't used to," I admitted, "but some pretty convincing things have happened to me lately. Adina said she was a shaman and that...I was too." I didn't like saying it out loud. "But I don't know much about it. I'm running blind."

"But you think you can stop this man."

"I promised a priest." I smiled a little. "Seems like the kind of promise you shouldn't renege on."

Kevin smiled back without it touching his eyes, and turned away to take the tea bags out of the tea. He offered me a cup. I sipped and watched him struggle for words. "Adina went back east for Christmas," he finally said. "To visit her family. She came home early to surprise me, and—" He took a shaking breath.

"Hell of a Christmas present," I mumbled, and clapped a hand over my mouth when I realized I'd said it out loud. Kevin lifted his teacup in a mock salute, a ghost of an unhappy smile on his face.

"And a Happy New Year."

CHAPTER ELEVEN

I left Adina and Kevin's home with a list of books to check out and no more information at all about Cernunnos or anyone who might be working with him. I stopped off at the University Bookstore on the Ave., found all but one of the recommended books, and went home to check my e-mail. There were two messages promising I could lose fifty pounds in thirty days, and another telling me I could make twenty thousand dollars in the same amount of time. My spam filter was getting sloppy. I manfully resisted these temptations and sat down with one of the books. I was still reading when Gary pounded on the door.

"You look better," he announced when I let him in. "I was half afraid you'd be dead, too."

"Gee, thanks. I didn't think you'd come by." I let the door swing shut and went into the kitchen to start some coffee. Gary followed me.

"Lady, you're the most interesting thing that's happened to me since Annie died. You think I'm gonna miss out on all of this? So what'd you find out?" He leaned against the counter and folded his arms across his chest, looking for all the world like he belonged there. I wasn't sure I'd ever seen a man who looked as comfortable in my kitchen as Gary did. He filled up the room in the same way I imagined Sean Connery might, so easy with himself it was like the air around him vibrated.

I put the distracting but otherwise appealing thought of Sean Connery out of my mind and lifted a hand to tick off my accomplishments for the day. "Priests are losing faith, the police don't want my help and shamanism is kind of interesting."

"Shamanism." Gary's bushy eyebrows climbed up toward his receded hairline, making deep solid wrinkles in his forehead. "I leave you alone a few hours and I miss all kindsa things."

"You have no idea." I frowned at the countertop, trying to find a place to start. There was a crack that ran along the edge of the counter. It had been there since I'd moved in. It had never bothered me before, but it looked dark and uncared for after Adina's kitchen. I bumped my fingertips over it, shaking my head. "Funny thing is, a lot of this stuff makes sense to me. I mean, drug-induced spirit journeys, I'm not sure if I think that's real. It could just be the drugs. But trance-induced, that's easier to take. It's not being brought on by mind-altering drugs, you know? It's something your psyche is doing all on its own. But on the other hand, how much of it is influenced by what you've read or been told or have held in your subconscious somewhere? Does it *matter?* Is it any more or less real because it's been influenced by something?"

"Jo," Gary said politely, "what in hell are you talking about?"

I looked up and laughed. "Can you play a drum, Gary?"

He leaned back, eyebrows quirked. "I can keep a beat, sure."

"I want to try an experiment. I went somewhere yesterday when Cernunnos stabbed me. I want to see if I can go there again."

"Spirit journey," Gary guessed. I nodded. "Thought you Injun types knew all about that." He grinned as I rolled my eyes. "Got a drum?"

"Nope. I thought you could use one of my stainless steel pots."

Gary blinked at me. I laughed out loud, and his blinking faded into mild chagrin. "Makin' fun of an old man," he grumbled, but his gray eyes held a spark of humor.

"I don't see any old men here," I said as I went back through the living room into my bedroom. I heard his snort of pleasure and the creak of the floorboard as he followed me out of the kitchen. I came out with a drum and handed it to him, trying not to look proud. It must not have worked, because he took it with a great deal of grace and care.

"Where'd you get this, Injun?"

Trying not to sound proud didn't work, either. "It was a birthday present. One of the elders made it for me."

I didn't own much that qualified as art. In fact, the drum was probably the sum total. It was about eighteen inches across, thin stretched hide evenly tanned and evenly pulled over the wooden frame. A raven whose wings sheltered a wolf and a rattlesnake was dyed into the leather, bright colors that hadn't faded in the fourteen years I'd owned it. Bone and leather strips decorated the frame, hand-carved polished beads dangling down from the ends of stays that crossed under the head to make a handle. The drumstick that went with it had a knotted leather end and a cranberry-red rabbit fur end. I brushed my fingers over the soft drumhead, smiling. "He said I'd need it some day. I thought he was crazy, but it was the most beautiful thing anyone'd ever given me. No one ever made anything just for me before."

Gary grinned. "Not even a valentine?"

"I wasn't ever at any schools long enough to get valentines." Half-truths were a lot easier than whole truths, sometimes.

Gary brought the drum and drumstick together with a deep ringing boom. "Looks to me like that was their loss."

"You're too old to flirt with me, Gary." I grinned, though. I'd been complimented more in the day I'd known Gary than in the past year put together.

"Listen to her. A minute ago she's sayin' she didn't see any old men. 'Sides, the day I'm too old to flirt is the day they nail the coffin shut, lady. Keeps you young." He reached out and poked me in the chest with the drumstick. "You oughta remember that. This gonna wake up the neighbors?" He knocked the drumstick against the drum again.

"I don't care if it does. I have to listen to them having kinky sex at two in the morning. They can listen to my drum at two in the afternoon."

Gary sat down on the couch. "How do you know it's kinky?"

"You don't want to know," I said fervently. "Can you keep a heartbeat rhythm?"

The answer was a pair of beats, the sound of a heartbeat. I snagged a pillow off the couch and stretched out on my back on the floor, eyes half-closed. The drum had a deep warm sound, and Gary's rhythm was close enough to my own heartbeat to send a wash of chills over me.

"How long we playing for?" Gary asked over the drumbeat.

"Half an hour after my breathing changes." I admired how confident I sounded, just like I knew what I was talking about. "I'll wake up when the drum stops." Well, that's how the book said it ought to work, anyway.

"Gotcha," he said, and I drifted.

I knew where I was going this time. I wasn't sure if I could get there, but I knew what I was looking for. The drum bumped along steadily. I wondered, briefly, about the sanity of inviting someone I barely knew to sit in my living room and watch me zone out, but the idea set off no alarm bells and I performed a mental shrug.

The room wasn't quite warm enough for this kind of behavior. I could feel a cool draft from somewhere, and while I'd always appreciated the breeze in the summer, discovering it while lying on the floor in January wasn't as pleasant.

On the other hand, the floor was remarkably comfortable. I'd slept on it for two months after I'd moved into the apartment, too broke to afford a bed. The carpet was soft enough to sort of sink down into, like I might fall through the floor.

I *did* fall through the floor, and into the coyote-sized hole I'd traveled before. It got smaller and smaller, and so did I, until I was mouse sized. A stream appeared alongside me and I jumped onto a palmero leaf that bobbled along the water's surface. A moment or two later it dropped over the edge of a newly appeared waterfall, and I spread hawk wings to glide to the edge of the pool before landing on my own two perfectly human feet. I felt dizzy and exhilarated by the shifts, even if I didn't know how I'd performed them. I stretched my arms, feeling like I might be able to sprout wings again, then relaxed.

"You're back soon," Coyote said. He hadn't been there an instant earlier, but somehow it didn't surprise me as he trotted up beside me and sat down. I scratched his ears and his tongue lolled out blissfully while I looked around.

The garden was healthier than it had been yesterday. There had been a lot of function, no form, precise trees and neatly cut grass, like an English maze. The trees had been browning, as if they needed watering, and nothing had bloomed, like the flowering season was long over. I was surprised at how much I remembered. I didn't think I'd looked around that much.

"It's your garden," Coyote said lazily. "You should know what it looks like." He stuck his nose in my hand and flipped my hand back on top of his head. I skritched his ears again, obediently, and looked around some more.

It still favored function, with austere stone benches and narrow pathways leading from bench to bench, to the pool, and to flowerbeds that had been empty of life yesterday. Today they were greening, and wind dusted up fallen leaves, shuffling them away in favor of growing grass. There were, I could see clearly, twigs sticking out from the carefully clipped trees, so they were no longer perfectly symmetrical.

It was very quiet, though. "Is everyone's garden this quiet? I don't hear any birds or squirrels or anything."

"Some people like it quiet." Coyote snapped his teeth together and wagged his tail, eyeing my hand hopefully. "I didn't think you'd come back so soon. What happened?"

I sat down cross-legged and scruffled his ears again. "Is it undignified to scratch a spirit guide's ears?"

He thumped his tail against the grass. "Not if the spirit guide likes it." He lay down and put his nose against my leg, looking hopeful. I grinned and rubbed the top of his head.

"I went and visited a bunch of dead people."

Coyote's ears pricked up in alarm. "That's dangerous."

"Now you tell me. Did you know you were making me a…shaman?"

He sat up, paws placed mathematically in front of him. "I didn't make you anything. You almost died. You chose to live, and that woke possibilities in you."

"But you knew it was going to happen."

He lay down again, chin on his paws. "There are so many people." He sounded sad. "There are lots of new shamans, and they make a difference, but the Old Man thinks he needs someone with a little extra power."

My eyebrows went up. "Old Man?"

Coyote licked his nose. "Grandfather Sky. The Maker. He has a hundred names. Brand-new souls are hard to make," he said. "He worked hard on you. I knew if you chose to live everything you keep inside would start to spill out."

"Damn," I murmured. "I like my intestines where they are." Coyote snapped his teeth at me again, like I was an aggravating fly. "I know," I said. "That's not what you meant. You meant..." I trailed off again. "What *did* you mean? Somebody *made* me? On purpose? Come on, Coyote. There've got to be jillions of new souls every day. There's lots more people than there ever were before. Besides, who would make *me?*"

"The Old Man would. There are many more people than there used to be, but there are far more souls than there have ever been people. They recycle."

"You don't look like a Buddhist."

"Is there anything you believe in?" Coyote sounded impatient.

I thought about that. "I suppose this is an inappropriate time to say, 'I believe I'll have another cookie.'"

The coyote gave a very human-sounding sigh. "There's no talking to you."

I sighed back at him. "What's this good for, Coyote? What do I do with it? Why *am* I the shiny new soul?"

He shifted his eyebrows, peering up at me until he was certain I was listening. "The Old Man wanted to bring together two very old cultures to make a child who would bridge both of them. There've been lots of Celtic-Cherokee crossbreeds before, but he wanted someone who could grow to her full potential. You can't be tied down with a lot of back story, to do that."

"Back story?"

"We carry the scars of our past lives with us. He thought starting fresh would be best."

I pulled my knees up to my chest, wrapping my arms around them. "I've got plenty of scars."

"I know." Coyote's voice gentled. "I'm not sure the Old Man remembered that we carry the wisdom of our past lives with us, too."

I didn't like where this conversation was going. I hunched my shoulders and scowled. "So what do I do with it?"

One of his ears pricked up, like a human lifting an eyebrow. "It's a lever," he said after a while.

"You don't look much like Archimedes, Coyote. I bet he was taller than you, for one."

How long does it take for the human eye and brain to register something it sees? For exactly that amount of time, Coyote was the golden-eyed Indian man again, stretched out on his belly with his chin in his hands, grinning at me. "Not really," he said, and it was the coyote who said it. I blinked at him.

"*Stop* that." He grinned, a toothy coyote grin, and I rubbed my eyes. "Shouldn't it take more than a blink of an eye to shape-change?" I demanded waspishly. He laughed, a mixture of human laughter and a coyote's cheerful yip.

"Not when you've got as much practice as I do." He sat up, lining his paws up together again. "It's a lever, Joanne Walker. Siobhán Walkingstick. You *can* move the world. It won't be easy, but I told you that before. You have the power to heal." He leaned forward and butted his head against my shoulder. It was like having a block of furry concrete smack me. I rubbed my shoulder, frowning at him.

"But what am I, a physician's assistant or a surgeon? I don't understand this, Coyote."

"You're both." He stuck his nose under my palm and asked for more scritches while he spoke. "Heal the patient, Jo. The patient—"

The drumbeat stopped and I opened my eyes on a sigh. "—is the world."

"Eh?" Gary set the drum aside and leaned forward, looking down at me.

"The patient is the world," I repeated, then slowly grinned at him. The euphoria of the drumbeat surged through me even though it had ended. The colors were brighter, noises sharper. Gary looked different. There was an air of contentment around him, knowledge of a life well-lived. "God *damn,* Gary, I feel good."

He chuckled, like a nice big V-8 engine purring. I bet his Annie had been a V-4, higher pitch to complement his deeper sound. Divisible numbers, too: one went into the other. It fit. I wished I'd been able to meet her. Gary stood up and put the drum carefully on top of my computer desk. "Glad to hear it. You get anywhere?"

"Yeah," I said. "Yeah, I did." I got up from the floor, whistling "I'm A Believer." Gary pursed his lips like he was trying to fight off a smile. "You hush," I told him happily. Another crack fused shut, a feeling of heat and sizzling deep inside me. I rubbed the heel of my hand over my breastbone and grinned at Gary. "You hush," I repeated. "You just let me be giddy and weird here for a minute. I'm jumping between worlds here. This is too wild. You just hush."

Gary laughed and I stuck my nose in the air and went into the kitchen to put some water on for coffee. Gary followed me, leaning in the door. "Tell me something."

"What?"

"How come you don't know anything about your heritage?"

I was in a good enough mood that the question didn't even piss me off. I turned around and leaned on the counter while the coffeepot started up and looked for a place to start. Some of the good humor fell away, but not enough to make me clam up. "I was about twelve when I told my dad we were going to choose one place to live and stay there until I was out of high school. My whole life we'd been picking up every three or four months and going somewhere new and I was sick of it. He looked at me like he'd never seen me before and the next time we got in the car we drove to North Carolina, where he'd grown up. Eastern Cherokee Nation."

I shoved my hands in my pockets, looking at the floor while I spoke. "I knew he was Cherokee, but he hadn't ever talked about growing up. He taught me pretty much my whole primary school education, math and science and English. I mean, I went to school, but we were always moving, so I was never anywhere really long enough to get the curriculum. Anyway, he didn't tell me anything about the People. So I got to North Carolina and I was already years behind in what a lot of other kids had just grown up with. And I'm all horrible and pale like my mother was. Not that there aren't other Native kids who're pale, but I was really sensitive about it." I spread my hands, looked at them, and shrugged. "So I worked really hard on not learning anything. Not caring."

"Were you born contrary or did you have to work at it?"

I looked up. "Born that way."

"So where was your mom?"

I snorted and looked over my shoulder to check the coffee. "Ireland. I was the unexpected product of a one-night stand during an American holiday." God. Apparently I was the deliberate product of a one-night stand. It was just that the deliberation wasn't on the part of my parents. I fell silent, trying to adjust to that thought.

"And?"

"Um. And she brought me back to the States when I was three months old, handed me over to Dad and went back to Ireland for good."

"I thought your dad was on the move all the time. How'd she find him?"

"That," I said, "was the last time he spent more than five months in one place." Gary winced.

"But you said you'd gone to her funeral. So she turned back up?"

"Why are we playing Twenty Questions About Joanne's Life?" Everything was still a little too clear, the smell of coffee brewing sharper than normal. My question didn't come out as acerbically as I'd meant it to. I felt too good to be really bitchy, and I was still trying to absorb what Coyote had said.

"I guess she'd been corresponding with my dad for pretty much my whole life. Once every couple years. She sent letters to his parents in North Carolina and they'd forward them on to wherever we were."

"And your dad didn't mention this?"

"No." I didn't feel like adding anything else to that. "Anyway, so Mother just called up one day and said she was dying and she'd like to meet me before she keeled over. I was furious. I mean, who was she to ignore me my whole life and then turn around and pull something like that?"

"Your mother?" Gary offered. I sighed and nodded.

"That was basically what I came up with, too. I mean, I spent a really long time..." I went quiet, choosing my word carefully. "Resenting her. Maybe even hating her. She abandoned me and I was like any other kid who figured her life would've been way better, way different, if she hadn't. But in the end I thought, you know, if I don't go meet her, I'll never know. Maybe I'll find out it was best that way."

"Was it?"

"I still don't know." I leaned on the counter, dropping my head. "Her name was Sheila MacNamarra. She looked a lot like me. Black Irish. She liked Altoids. Um." I pressed my lips together. "We spent four months together and I feel like all I really know about her was she liked Altoids. I didn't really like her. I didn't really dislike her, either." I touched my throat, where the necklace she'd given me wasn't. "She gave me—I don't know if you noticed it. A necklace. I was wearing it yesterday."

"The cross thing, yeah. I saw it."

"Yeah. It was literally the last thing she did, giving me that. I don't know why she did it, really. It didn't seem very much like something she'd do. It was this weird personal touch after months of hanging out with a stranger. She didn't ask me very many questions and she didn't talk about herself, the whole time. She was a lot like my father. He doesn't like talking about himself either."

Gary's eyebrows rose. "The apple don't fall far from the tree."

"What?" I poured two cups of coffee, frowning at him.

"I mean, you don't open up so easy, either. I'm askin' you questions all over the place and you're real careful about choosing your answers. Maybe she couldn't figure out how to say anything to you." Gary took his coffee and watched while I ladled sugar and milk into my own.

"She was my mother," I said, frowning.

"So what? That means she was s'posed to be able to just know how to talk to you? You're an adult. I bet it's pretty hard trying to talk to a kid you left behind almost thirty years ago." Gary waved his coffee cup as I frowned more deeply.

"So you're saying it's my fault I don't know anything about her?"

Gary shrugged and waved his coffee cup again. "I ain't sayin' anything. What'd she die of?"

I exhaled. "Boredom, I think."

Gary lifted his eyebrows skeptically. I shook my head. "No, really. I think she was done. She'd seen what she wanted to see and she'd met me and she was done. So that's the kind of person she was. I don't know. Tidy. Focused. Capable of dying of boredom, or at least dying when she was done with her checklist of things to do."

Gary pursed his lips. "'Scuze me for sayin' so, but I think you're still resentful. That's a big thing to get stuck with. A mom who didn't think you were interesting enough to stick around and get to know?"

"Thanks, Gary, that makes me feel a whole lot better. Can we change the subject now, please? What about you? You've got kids, right?"

He crinkled his eyebrows at me. "Kids? Me? No."

I took a sip of coffee and eyed him over the top of the cup. "You said you had to get married when you knocked your old lady up."

"Oh, that. I was tellin' stories." Gary grinned disarmingly and sat down at the kitchen table. I stared at him, morally offended. "C'mon, siddown," he said, still grinning. "Stop looking so put out. An old man's gotta keep himself entertained somehow."

I shook my head, muttering semiserious dismay at him, and came to sit down. "Entertain yourself with figuring out what's going on with Cernunnos. I still think Marie doesn't fit." I planted my elbows on the table, supporting my head with fingertips pressed into my temples. It gave me a headache. Instead of stopping I rubbed little circles against my temples and frowned at the table.

"You said that." Gary drained his coffee cup and got up for a second. "If the guy's a death god, why doesn't it fit?"

I frowned more. "Because why kill a bunch of shamans and then start taking out banshees and school kids? Where's the connection?"

"I thought you were a cop. Aren't you supposed to be good at this kind of thing?"

I lifted my head to glare at him. "I'm a *mechanic,* Gary. Mechanics *fix cars*. For some reason solving murders just didn't end up on my résumé."

"My garage needs somebody," Gary said. I let my head fall to thump against the table.

"I can't quit now. Morrison expects me to," I said into the varnish. "If I can't hack it I'll come talk to your garage. But this week I'd like to learn how to be a shaman and try to solve a murder, if that's okay."

"Well," Gary said slowly, "if that's all you think you can handle...."

I looked up incredulously to see a broad grin showing off those perfect white teeth. "You," I said, "are a sonnovabitch." Gary put a hand over his heart, looking wounded.

"Good thing my mammy's in her grave to not hear that."

"Your mammy, my ass." I got up to get another cup of coffee. Gary handed me his to refill. "Do you have the world's largest bladder, or what?"

"Lotsa practice drinking beer," Gary said sagely. I grinned and poured him another cup of coffee. "So Marie's murder and the school kids don't fit, and you're out of coffee. Now what?"

"I don't usually have to make it for more than one person." I frowned at the sludge in the cup. I was getting a lot of practice frowning lately. "I think now I go to the school."

"School's gonna be empty. They're not gonna keep the kids there after what happened."

"I know. I probably should have thought of it this morning. But Adina said the guy who was doing this would have a sense of power about him. Maybe I can get a scent of it."

"You're a bloodhound now?"

"I'm playing by ear, Gary. Besides!" For once I felt certain of something. "I bet I can tell if it's Cernunnos, if I go over there. I know what he feels like." That much I was sure of. I didn't think anybody could forget what the horned god's raw power felt like once they'd met it head-on.

"You didn't get that off Marie."

"I didn't know I should even be trying. Now I do. If I can get even an idea about what's going on, I shouldn't pass it up, right?" I drank some of the coffee, shuddered, and added more milk.

"Guess not. Who's Adina?"

"One of the dead ladies I talked to last night." I stared at Gary over the edge of my cup, just daring him to comment. He shut his jaw with an audible click. I grinned into the coffee cup and went to get my shoes.

CHAPTER TWELVE

Wednesday, January 5th, 3:35 p.m.

When I was about nine, my father told me that forgiveness was easier to obtain than permission. I wondered, even at the time, about the wisdom of telling a kid that. In retrospect, it was smart: I tested the premise occasionally, discovered he was right and probably got in less trouble than I would have otherwise. The end result, seventeen years later, was me walking into Blanchet High School like I belonged there. Forget permission. Just act like you belong. I felt very smooth.

Until it turned out it didn't matter. One hall, cordoned off with yellow police tape, was still packed with reporters, paramedics, cops and traumatized teachers. No one was paying attention to anything else. I watched the throng for a few minutes, then turned down another hall and began pacing through the school, looking for nothing in particular.

I hadn't been inside a high school since I'd graduated ten years earlier. Blanchet High had a lot more money than the school I'd gone to did. The wide halls were carpeted, and walls above tan lockers gleamed white, like they'd been repainted over Christmas break. Florescent lights hummed, altering the color of posters cajoling students to turn out for the weekend's basketball and wrestling tournaments. Water fountains seemed to be about two inches lower than I remembered them being. Either I'd grown since high school, or Blanchet was full of short kids.

I pushed open a heavy door of solid wood with no window in it, and stepped inside a small theater. It was dark except for one white light in the sound booth, and smelled a little of makeup and sweat. I let the door close behind me and walked in quietly, taking the steps down to the stage in near-darkness.

"Long cold note on a tenor saxophone," a girl's voice said very clearly. I stopped where I was, halfway to the stage. She came out on it, nothing more than a pale shadow in the darkness. She had terribly blond hair, long and thin and straight, just like she was. She wore a pale sweatshirt that added bulk to her narrow form, and her legs faded into darkness, not even a shadow. Dim tennies were on her feet.

"Life's brief candle, a moment in the dark / laid down beneath the blade of sound." She knotted her arms around her ribs, like she was holding herself in. Her voice was as thin as she was, a clear soprano that rose and fell as she delivered the poem. When she quavered in speaking, she didn't try bullying through it, just let her voice shake, words falling to a whisper.

"Let me fold a thousand paper cranes / longing for a wish that cannot be." Hairs stood up on my arms, and I shivered. I had no right to listen to the girl's private grief, but I was afraid to move and warn her I was there. *"Loss is pure in its first hour, jaded by time."* She sank down onto the stage, wrapping her arms around her legs and burying her face in her knees. Blond hair fell over her arms as a choked sob broke the silence.

I turned and left the theater as quietly as I could.

* * *

Out in the hall, under the florescent lights again, the air was thick, like I was breathing in sadness. I leaned against a wall and kept my eyes closed until the tears stopped leaking and my heartbeat slowed down a little. I could feel something inside me, a knot of appalling rage, fueled by the girl's sorrow and the rough poem. It lit up all my own scars, all the cracks in my windshield, and threw them into sharp relief until they throbbed with the need to be answered. I slid down the wall, lowering my head and lacing my hands behind my neck. I felt like a beacon, flared up with terrible, unfocused fury that burned through the walls of everything else. I couldn't remember the last time I had been so angry, horror mixed with sorrow and disbelief, and the rage pulling in every other emotion after it, drowning them.

This has to be stopped. The thought, unnervingly clear through the anger, made me lift my head, staring sightlessly across the hall. *This has to be stopped,* and, *I can stop it.* I grasped the idea with sudden understanding, much deeper than the promise I'd given the priest. For one instant it was painfully obvious. Anger was a tool, and there was a choice in how to use it.

The Gordian knot of rage inside began unraveling, bright orange and yellow lengths of rope springing out to run through me instead of tying me up. Around the rage wound pale blue, thick ropy strands of compassion, feeding off fury. It all happened inside of an instant, and then I could breathe again. The unlocked center of me gobbled it up, storing all the burning energy for later use.

I could still feel the anger pulsing through me, self-righteous and forthright fury that someone could do what had been done. Compassion tempered it, though, delivering me the one step of distance that changed what I needed to do from vengeance to healing. Whomever had done this, whether it was Cernunnos or someone else, was terribly sick, and sickness could be healed.

"Joanie?" Billy's voice interrupted me, deep and worried. I startled and looked up. He was crouched right in front of me, big hands dangling over his knees, eyebrows beetled down in concern. "You all right? I said your name about three times."

"Sure." I blinked at him, then shook my head and nodded. "Yeah. Yeah, I'm fine, thanks."

"What are you doing here?"

"What are *you* doing down here? The party's at the other end." If I hoped it would sidetrack him, I was wrong.

"Taking a look around. It's my job." Subtle emphasis on the last word. I closed my eyes. "It's not," he pointed out, "your job. You," he added helpfully, "are suspended."

"Thanks for the reminder, Billy. I heard it all yesterday." Had it been yesterday? *They* said hitting the ground running was the best way to deal with jet lag. I bet *They'd* never had two days like I'd had.

"That was this morning." He stood up, offering me a hand.

"I was afraid of that." I took his hand and stood up.

"Haven't caught up on sleep yet, huh?"

I smiled thinly. "There hasn't really been time."

He nodded. "What're you doing down here?"

Damn. I hadn't distracted him enough. "Sniffing around."

"For what?"

I shrugged stiffly. "Some sense of who's doing this. Trying to see if it's Cernunnos. Trying to get a feeling for his..." I swallowed, uncomfortable with what I was saying. "His power. His...whatever's driving him."

Billy folded his arms across his chest and frowned at me. "You think you can do that?" He sounded skeptical. I couldn't blame him.

"Figured I could try. I've got to start somewhere."

"You're not supposed to start anywhere, Joanie." He jerked his head down the hall and started walking. "C'mon."

I followed sullenly. "What, I warrant a police escort from the building?" Billy looked over his shoulder at me and kept walking. It took me a minute to realize we were heading for the crime scene, not the front door. I blinked and jogged a few steps to catch up, not questioning the decision.

"Still got your ID?" he asked, lifting the yellow tape for me to duck under.

"Morrison took my badge away," I muttered. It figured. One minute I didn't want to be a cop and the next I was sulking because I wasn't. "But I've got my station ID." I dug my wallet out of my pocket and flipped it open to the ID photo. A cop I didn't know gave it a cursory glance and waved us by. It seemed like half the North Precinct was there. It occurred to me this would be a good time to perpetrate other crimes, if I were the sort of person who did that.

Working for the police in any capacity had clearly been bad for me. I never would have thought that, back in the day. A couple guys I knew looked surprised but greeted me, and Billy went to talk to a hulk of a man who stood outside the classroom door. I stood around watching the reporters, who practiced looking good for one another, and waited for Billy to come back.

He did, looking grim. "Morrison's gonna have my eyeteeth if he hears about this," he muttered, "but come on. I told them you're on the serial killer case and you're coming in to see if there's any connection with these kids."

"You sound like you've done this before, Billy."

He threw a tight grin over his shoulder and led me into the classroom.

Afternoon sunlight streamed in the windows, glaring off whiteboards. Red and green and blue marker printed out class assignments more neatly than I remembered chalk doing. The teacher's desk was in front of the boards, and rows of one-piece chair-and-desk units were settled in uneven rows.

For a second, it all looked perfectly normal.

And then the smell hit me. Sweet and tangy and sharp all at once, the air conditioning filtered some, but not enough, of it away. I blinked one time and the haphazard rows of seats resolved themselves into a mishmash that pushed out from the center of the room. Three of the units were overturned, half blocked from sight by the desks around them. From where I stood, still in the doorway, I could see the beige carpet's discoloration as blood dried.

I didn't want to see more.

"Joanie?" Billy took a step back toward me, a hand extended and his eyebrows lifted. I shivered.

"I'm okay," I lied, and walked forward. There were footprints of blood on the floor, dried tennis-shoe shapes, from where the other children had run from the room. I could almost hear them screaming.

Three steps farther into the room any illusion of normality that was left dissolved. Four bodies lay sprawled on the floor, three boys and a girl. Three of them lay touching, arms slumped over ankles. All of them had died with expressions of mixed disbelief and terror. The girl had long brown hair, blood stiffening it to black. Every one of them had died the way Marie did, with one vicious knife thrust from the rib cage up through the heart. I stopped again, trying to control my breathing. I didn't want to vomit all over the crime scene. It smelled enough as it was.

"Joanie?" Billy asked again.

"I'm all right," I said, more sharply than I intended. "Just give me a second here."

He nodded and fell back a couple of steps, letting me walk forward alone, which was about the last thing I wanted to do.

I did it anyway. A second round of police tape circled the bodies, at about knee-height, wrapped around the desks. I stopped and stared into the circle of tape. I really, really didn't want to do what I heard my voice asking if I could do. "Can I cross this line, Billy?"

"Do you need to?"

I nodded mechanically. I could *feel* it, malevolence so close if I put my hand out it would be like touching a wall. "What kind of shoes are you wearing?" he asked. I looked at my feet.

Thick-soled boots, no heels this time. "All my clothes are still at the airport," I realized out loud. "They're made by somebody called Endura. Wide shoes for women. Size ten and a half."

"Got it," somebody else said. "Go on in."

I stepped across the police tape and into the blood.

Nothing happened. I was shocked enough to take a staggering half step backward. Billy, for the third time, now alarmed, said, "Joanie?"

"It's okay," I said distantly. I could hear Coyote's voice, faintly: *Ask Marie to help you with your shields. You'll need them.*

I was pretty sure I'd figured out shields all on my own. I still felt the malevolence, all around me, not quite able to touch me. And I knew I was the one keeping it away.

Great. I'd figured out how to shield. How did I take the blocks down?

Imagine you're a car. Coyote's advice, again. I almost looked over my shoulder for him. Instead I closed my eyes. A car with something blocked that I had to get to. Had to be in the dashboard, those were the worst bitch to open up and put back together. I envisioned searching out screws, and all the damned fine wiring. I dragged the dashboard open, the moral equivalent of unhinging the top of my skull and flipping it back.

All sorts of hell broke loose in my brain.

* * *

For what felt like about five hundred hours, pain and rage and chaos swam together inside my head, trying to tear my mind apart. They screamed together, telling me the horror of death and the glory of murder and the sheer unadulterated joy of power. Somewhere along the line my car analogy broke down, because now I was drowning. There was blackness, streaked with silver and gray, the not-colors rushing up beyond me as I fell down and down and down. The weight of despair pushed me farther and faster until it seemed I would pop out the other side of the earth. I tried to catch the streaks of light. Where I touched them, they turned crimson and bled, color sticking under my fingernails, but I kept falling, and they kept screaming.

I had to stop falling. In the Coyote dream, all I had to do was concentrate and I stopped falling. Here, I could hardly hear myself think, much less concentrate, and there wasn't much point anyway, because I was clearly going to die, just like the kids had. I felt them around me, cold fragile wraiths, nothing like the shamans I met dream-walking. *Those* dead men and women grasped the cycle of life. *These* kids still thought they were immortal, and the shock of death turned them into shadows. Not even so much as shadows, all their essence drawn away by the murderer—

—*by the son of a bitch who had killed* children—

All the colors of darkness stopped with a shock so hard I bounced. For one blessed moment, there was silence.

"Oh, no," I said into the quiet. "You don't get to take me that easily."

And the howling started again, but I wasn't alone anymore. Four children, less than insubstantial, stood around me, watching with pleading in what was left of their souls.

"I'll find him." My voice cut through the howling so sharply I knew they'd heard me. One by one they gave me thin, ghostly smiles, and one by one they flew up like the silver and gray had flown.

This time I followed them.

I took one staggering step and opened my eyes, expecting the sunlight to be gone, expecting the police guard to have changed, expecting the world to be completely different.

It was exactly the same. Billy didn't say my name this time, but I felt him standing less than an arm's length away, just on the other side of the yellow tape. Goose bumps stood up on my arms and I shivered, looking down at the four bodies. I felt him, the murderer, could feel what he'd done.

"They were lucky," I heard myself say very quietly. "Something stopped the circle from being completed." I crouched and touched the hair of the last boy, whose outflung arm and sprawled legs were inches away from the legs of the two closest him.

"Lucky?" Billy asked, not as incredulously as I would have under the same circumstances.

"It was supposed to be a power circle of some kind," I whispered. "I can feel his exultation at the last death. And then rage. Something stopped him from aligning them properly. North, east, south, were all closed. West wasn't closed. He took their life essence." My voice shook and I couldn't stop it. "Drained them. But he meant to take their souls. Bind them to..." I shook my head and stood up unsteadily. "I don't know." I was crying. "But the circle wasn't closed, and their souls escaped."

Someone let out a very gentle breath. It changed the current in the room for just a moment, displacing air-conditioned air, adding moisture and warmth. I felt it as potential, like the butterfly who makes a storm in China. I could feel everything living in the room, an awareness a little bigger than my skin.

"Can you recognize this guy's power again?" Billy's question was quiet, but intense, spoken just behind me.

I took a deep breath, tasting copper on the air, tasting death and power and the last burning emotions of the murderer, his glee and his fury. "Yeah. I'll know him when I feel it again. I'll know the fucker."

CHAPTER THIRTEEN

I should have expected the wall of flash-photography that hit when Billy led me out of the classroom. Should have: that I didn't was a flag that I was a complete novice, just in case I hadn't figured it out on my own. Someone actually shoved a gray padded microphone under my nose, which I thought only happened in movies. I squinted into the flashbulbs and recognized one of the local TV anchors, Laura something. Corvalis. Laura Corvalis. She was some kind of exotic blend of ethnic backgrounds, Filipino and black and something else, probably white. Her eyes, just a little tilted, were blue in a café latte face.

And she was yelling at me.

In fact, a lot of people were.

Officer Walker, can you tell us—local police officer Joanne Walker—who did this, Officer?—are you ready to make a statement, Offi—three-year veteran of the SPD—the wave of murders that has Seattle talking about the Christmas Killer—arrival on the scene—

I retreated one bewildered step. Billy's voice broke over them all like a tidal wave. "The police department has made all the statements it's able to at this time, ladies and gentlemen of the press," he all but bellowed. I admired how he didn't even sneer at the last six words. The hubbub died down suddenly.

Laura Corvalis stepped forward into the silence, the mike back at her own mouth. "Detective Holliday, can you at least tell us some details about the serial murders Seattle's been besieged with the past two weeks? Do the deaths today match the pattern? Are you any closer to finding the killer? How about you, Detective Walker?"

"I can't," Billy said at the same time that I said, "I'm not." Everyone looked a little shocked, including me. Billy's shock turned to alarm and he shook his head minutely at me. Laura Corvalis's shock turned to delight and she moved in for the kill.

"You're not what, Detective Walker?" She shoved the microphone under my nose long enough for me to inhale, then pulled it back to demand, "What do you have to say about that, Detective Holliday?" and to push it at Billy.

"Ms. Corvalis," Billy said with the patience of a man who'd been through the exact same routine dozens of times, "I've given you all the information I can—"

"I'm not a detective," I said under him. He kept his expression schooled, but exasperation flashed in his eyes. I should have kept my mouth shut. Laura thrust the microphone back in my face.

"Don't tell me you're a civilian, Ms. Walker. Detective Holliday, has the Seattle Police Department fallen so far that you're allowing civilians on the scene? In which case—" she produced a delightful, flirtatious smile. "How about letting me in?" Laughter sounded from the press corps, and Ms. Corvalis looked pleased with herself.

"I'm a police officer," I said, still quietly. "Just not a detective.

I just wanted to be sure you got your story right." Billy's big hand closed around my biceps.

"I'm afraid this is the end of this interview, Ms. Corvalis," he said very firmly. He propelled me in front of him, using me to shoulder our way through the photographers and cameramen.

"Wait! Can you tell us why you're here, Officer Walker? Can you give us any information about today's killings? Damn," Laura Corvalis said as we made our escape. "Cut the tape. Maybe we can get something out of this."

Billy threw me in his car before he started yelling. "Would you care to tell me what the hell that was?"

I rubbed my forehead where I'd cracked it against the door frame and looked at him sullenly. "I'm *not* a detective. I can just see Morrison coming down on me like a load of bricks for giving myself an on-screen promotion. Anyway, I didn't say anything damning." I didn't think I'd said anything damning. Please God, let me not have said anything damning. "It probably won't even be on the news."

"You shouldn't have said anything. You've been suspended, for God's sake, Joanne. You've been suspended and you just showed up at a murder scene and don't think for a *minute* that Laura Corvalis isn't going to do her homework on you. It'll be on the news. 'Suspended officer, suspected of murder, visits crime scene'. God, why didn't you keep your mouth shut?"

I shrank down in my seat. "I'm sorry."

Billy glared more, then sighed. "I didn't tell you not to say anything. It's as much my fault as yours." He went silent, then sighed again, more explosively. "Did you get anything in there?"

I sighed too, shrinking farther down into the seat. "Yeah. Kind of a good news/bad news scenario."

"Give me the good news first."

"It's not Cernunnos."

Billy hit the steering wheel with the heel of his hand. "What's the *bad* news?"

"It's not Cernunnos."

"Shit." Billy didn't say anything for a couple of blocks. "All right, well, it's something. We're not dealing with a Celtic god here. Good. Great. Fantastic." The sarcasm dripped. "You know, Joanie, I'm glad you don't think I'm crazy anymore, but—"

"But now you think *I'm* crazy."

He glanced at me. "You could've picked a smaller way to break into the wonderful weird world of the paranormal, yeah."

"I guess I didn't get the memo on that one." I slid my fingers over the thin scar on my cheek. "Do we have a physical description of this guy?"

"About six-one, mid-thirties, Caucasian, long light brown hair, green eyes, big shoulders but overall a slender build, carries a very sharp knife."

"A teenager told you he was in his mid-thirties?" I remembered distinctly when twenty-six was old. I was pretty sure I wouldn't have recognized mid-thirties as such, when I was fifteen.

"No, the teacher, Mrs. Potter, did. She gave us most of the description."

"Where is she?"

"Hospital. You said they got lucky, the circle wasn't closed? That's probably thanks to her. She tackled the guy. Got cut up pretty good herself, two stab wounds to the abdomen and a lot of minor cuts."

"Brave lady." I sucked my lower lip into my mouth, staring out the windshield. "I think I need to go see her."

"They won't let you in without a police escort."

I looked at him. "Well, you're in trouble anyway."

* * *

Hospital antiseptic is chemically balanced to cut through the smells of blood and vomit and urine and death. It also makes me sneeze so hard I cry.

Gary arrived in time to stand next to Billy and watch the end of the sneezing fit. They were both grinning and not trying to hide it when I unfolded from a fetal position and looked up with watery eyes. "Oh, shuddup," I said thickly. Gary offered me an enormous red handkerchief that looked like it hadn't been used. I wiped my nose and stuffed it in my own pocket, on the assumption that he didn't want my snot in his pocket. He didn't object, so I figured I was right. "Thanks," I said as politely as I could. "What're you doing here, anyway?"

"He called me up while you were on your way over." Gary tipped his head at Billy. "Said you were gonna need a ride back to your car and he had to go down to the station to get his ass chewed."

"Oh." The minute Billy had agreed to take me to the hospital I'd fallen asleep. He could have run a brass band over my head and I wouldn't have noticed, not with the comforting thrum of wheels against concrete soothing me.

Mrs. Potter was in a private wing down a rat's maze of gated hallways. Billy stopped and talked to the guard, who opened the gates and ushered us through into a corridor that looked like its sole purpose was keeping important people safe. There were no windows, the walls were prison gray and the lights did nothing to cheer it. My boots echoed on the linoleum. "What do they do, bring people down here to encourage them to die?"

"It's a little morbid, isn't it? Supposed to discourage people from exploring down this way." Billy waved a hand at the nearly empty hall.

"Like they can get past the guards," Gary muttered. "What's the point?"

"Used to be a psychiatric wing."

"Sure," I said. "Like crazy people need *another* reason to be depressed."

Billy scowled at me. "They converted it about ten years ago, and the primer color paint got donated. These days it's used for celebrities, criminals and emergencies. The isolation helps keep sightseers and ambulance chasers away."

"And visitors," I opined. "I'd have gotten discouraged three corridors back. What happens if sainted Aunt Sally wants to visit her precious movie star nephew who got hurt filming on location?"

"First sainted Aunt Sally gets a background check, then she gets brought down here with a police escort. Just like you did." Two more guards stood at attention as we came around a corner and up the hall. I wondered if they'd been like that the whole time, or if there was a poker game hidden around the next corner.

"Does that mean you did a background check on me?" Gary asked. Billy ignored the question, walking up to the guards. Gary grinned. "Bet that means no." Billy gave him a dirty look and pushed the door open, gesturing me in.

I had an image of Mrs. Potter built up in my mind. She was young, in her early thirties at the most, with heavy blond hair she usually wore up. It would be down now, and she would be pale under her light tan. She'd be tall, although not as tall as me, and muscular like a swimmer. She'd have blue eyes and not need much makeup.

A woman who was at least in her mid-sixties lay on the bed, the oxygen mask they'd given her set askew on her face. An orderly tried steadily and without the slightest success to get her to put it back on.

She had gobs of white hair that stood out in random directions, a state that seemed natural rather than caused by a traumatizing day. She was, in fact, both tall and muscular, and she had an amazingly solid feeling to her, like Mrs. Claus on steroids. "My lungs, young man, are perfectly functional," she was saying as I walked in. "I do not need this ridiculous contraption and I will not wear it. The doctor has verified that my brain is operating quite within normal parameters. If you insist, I will sign paperwork absolving the hospital of all responsibility should my lungs suddenly collapse, leading to my demise through suffocation, but I have had quite enough of that silly mask."

"You like *Star Trek?*" I asked, surprised. Mrs. Potter removed her gaze from the orderly, who sagged in either relief or resignation, and fixed it on me.

"I do," she said crisply. "How ever did you deduce that?"

I grinned and walked forward. "I don't think anybody who wasn't a *Trek* fan would say 'operating within normal parameters.' Hi, I'm Joanne Walker." I stepped up to the side of her bed and offered my hand. She had a strong grip.

"Good evening, Joanne Walker. My name is Henrietta Potter. To what do I owe the pleasure of your acquaintance? And who are these two ruffians?" Sharp blue eyes glanced over Billy and Gary, and she waved a hand. "Who is the one ruffian," she corrected herself. "I see our detective with the unfortunate name has returned. You are a very polite interrogator, young man."

Billy grinned and half bowed, all charming modesty. "I try, ma'am. This is Gary Muldoon." Gary hung back in the door, trying to look small. It didn't work.

"Well, Gary Muldoon. I normally prefer to be a little more attractively attired before entertaining gentlemen callers, but you may as well come in." Henrietta returned her gaze to me. "You were about to launch into a detailed explanation of why you were here," she reminded me. "As I have never seen you before, I can only gather that either you are involved in the police investigation of this morning's events, or you are a shyster hoping to trick the last few pennies out of a dying old lady." The precision of her tone never failed, but I saw tremendous pain flicker in her eyes as she referred to the morning.

"I don't think you're dying," I said slowly. I could all but feel determination pouring off her, a refusal to be beaten by the injuries she'd sustained. I wondered how much of the strength she was showing was a facade, and how much she was buying into it herself. *I* was buying it, anyway. "You may be agéd, but I'm not sure old is exactly a word that applies to you, Mrs. Potter. If I'm a shyster, I'm in trouble."

She graced me with a small smile. "It is the morning's tragic business that brings you here, then. Sit down, child, and tell me who you are. Go fetch us some coffee," she added imperiously. Billy, the orderly and Gary all flinched and started for the door. The orderly recovered first.

"Ma'am, you're not to have any caffeine for at least forty-eight hou—"

"Then make it decaffeinated," she suggested, and this time all three of them bolted for the door. There was a moment's struggle while they stuck there, before the orderly squirmed out and Gary and Billy had room to follow. After a few seconds, the door swung shut.

"Wow," I said, impressed. "How did you do that?"

"Years of practice," she said modestly. "I had six suitors, at one time. I had to find some way to deal with them. Now, what can I do for you, Joanne Walker?"

I studied her curiously for a moment, trying to see the young woman who had had so many suitors. It wasn't hard: she still had magnificent cheekbones and a firm chin, and I realized suddenly that she bore a striking resemblance to—

"——Katharine Hepburn, yes, I know," she said patiently. "And no," she continued as my jaw fell open, "I don't read minds. I've heard that from nearly everyone I've met since I was fifteen, and everyone gets the same expression just before they say it. I never," she added, for emphasis, "met Spencer Tracey. Now," she said again, and pushed herself up carefully, a faint wince crossing her features, "tell me why you're here."

I didn't know where to start. "A friend of mine was murdered yesterday evening," I finally said. Had it really only been last night? "I think by the same man who came into your classroom this morning."

Henrietta's expression tightened. "I'm very sorry."

"Me too." I stared at my hands. "I'm..." I trailed off. Henrietta waited patiently.

"Young lady," she said eventually, when I didn't speak, "the creature that killed my students walked into my classroom without anyone seeing him. Mark was dead before we saw his killer. Whatever you are trying to work yourself up to telling me, I don't believe it can possibly make my day any more unpleasant."

"Sorry." I looked up. "I need to find him. I have to try to help him."

Her eyebrows, white as her hair, shot up. "Help him?"

"He's very sick." I remembered the bleak fall through blackness and found myself standing up, taking a few steps as if I could get away from the memory. "Help him. Stop him. I think they're almost the same thing. Can you tell me everything you remember about him?"

"The police have already taken my statement." She pushed herself up a little farther, wincing again. "I presume you've received the physical description. As tall as you, brown hair, green eyes?"

I nodded. "Very well," she said. "The classroom door was closed. I never heard it open. I have no idea how he entered. I was writing on the chalkboard—whiteboard," she corrected herself, "and for a moment I thought the sound I'd heard was the marker against the board. It was that kind of sound, a high-pitched squeak, enough to raise hairs on the neck without causing real alarm. But then the children started screaming." Her voice shook.

I could feel the unlocked energy inside me bubbling with the impulse to help her somehow, to ease her pain. I came back to the bed and sat down, taking her hand.

The touch opened a link, unexpectedly vivid. Memory bludgeoned into me, relegating Henrietta's words to the distance: "I turned around."

I/Henrietta turned around to unfolding horror. Mark, a sandy-haired basketball player who got poor grades because he was lazy, lay sprawled on the floor, dark blood spilling from a gash that opened his chest. Jennifer, voice choked off by a hand around her throat, was dangling in the air, struggling against the man who held her up. Her killer cast her aside and her body caught on one of the chairs. Blood drained down her shirt as she slowly tilted over. Other children screamed, knocking desks over and pushing them out of the way as they tried to get away. The memory resonated peculiarly before I realized what was wrong with it: high school kids weren't children, to me. They were, well, kids. Henrietta's thoughts defined them differently. I felt a wave of dizziness that had nothing to do with what was going on in front of me and a lot to do with breaking down the walls of my own perceptions. I shivered, wondering if it was Henrietta or me doing it, and brought my attention back to what was going on.

The man in the children's midst was not large; he merely seemed that way, wide shoulders and gore-covered hands adding a terrifying depth to him. Long light brown hair splashed over his shoulders, drops of blood coloring it. He reached out with inhuman speed to close a massive hand around another boy's arm. "Anthony," Mrs. Potter said, very faintly. "Oh, no. Not Anthony." I wasn't sure if the words were spoken out loud, or if I was hearing her thoughts at the time the memories came from.

With one savage jerk the killer shoved a knife into Anthony's chest and yanked it up. The boy fell to the floor. Jennifer's body collapsed over his, her hair spilling over his legs and onto the floor. Perhaps five seconds had passed since the first bewildered, terrified squeak.

I could see more, now, through Henrietta's memory. The blond girl I'd seen in the theater stood pressed up against a far wall, screaming. Other children scrambled by her. A boy grabbed her arm and pulled her down to the floor. She disappeared in a flash of pale hair as the killer swelled. Blood and ichor seemed to fill him, making him appear too large to fit into the room. What Adina said about power spilling over from the inside suddenly made sense.

Oh, God, I was so far out of my league.

Paralysis left my—Henrietta's—muscles, and I leaped forward, crashing into the killer's back an instant too late, another child already dead in his hands. He stumbled forward, dropping the boy. A tiny sound cut through the killer's roars of frustration and my own incoherent screams: the clink of dog tags. The last dead boy was his mother's only child, Adrian, and he wore the tags from a father who'd died in a war fifteen years earlier.

I looked up into the killer's eyes. His voice, thick and distorted with rage, filled my mind. *Fool!* he screamed. *The circle is broken!* His eyes were green, brilliantly green, inhuman, like Cernunnos. The snarl he gave me showed eyeteeth that curved into unnaturally vicious points.

Then there was pain, white fire plunging into my belly. I screamed, my memories separating from Henrietta's and leaving me with a final conscious thought: *Oh no. Not again.*

CHAPTER FOURTEEN

Oak trees surrounded me, so large and neatly spaced I began counting them. I reached thirty-five before realizing I wasn't seeing the forest for the trees. I shook myself and took a better look around.

The oaks weren't the only foliage; they just dominated it. Slighter trees grew between them, stretching up toward slate-gray light. It was drizzling, most of the rain filtered out by the enormous trees. The forest floor was very green, soft moss rolling up over gentle hills. Everything was muted, clouds and moss combining to quiet the sounds of the forest. I took a deep breath of damp cool air. Only then did it occur to me to wonder where the hell I was. I was getting jaded.

I looked around again. In my limited experience, wondering where the hell I was made somebody show up and tell me.

No one showed up. I stood there for a minute. "I'd like to go home now," I announced hopefully. Wind ruffled my hair, but I didn't think it was responding to me. I shrugged and stuck my hands in my pockets and went for a walk. I hadn't been in a forest since I left North Carolina. I was surprised at how much I'd missed the sound of wind and rain on the leaves. In ten years I hadn't even thought about it.

There was a lot I hadn't thought about. I was pretty sure it was all going to come home very soon now. I pushed the idea away and kept walking.

A stag walked out of the forest in front of me, so calm I expected him to say something to me. He didn't. We gazed at each other across several yards of empty space, and then he tossed his head and bounded off into the woods as silently as he'd arrived. I grinned after him. I wasn't just getting jaded. I was turning into a world-class freak. Talking stags. What next?

As if in answer, a branch snapped behind me. I turned curiously.

A monster, more than half my height and twice as wide, charged out of the trees on four short, thick legs. Beady, vicious eyes sighted me and it swerved toward me, bristly head lowered in a charge that would end with me impaled on yellowing ivory tusks.

I shrieked and flung myself to the side, suddenly comprehending why wild boar hunting had been considered such a dangerous sport. The boar swerved again, barely missed trampling me and made a passing nod at goring me. Then, just like the stag, it disappeared into perfect silence.

I lay propped on my elbows, gasping after the animal. "Note to self," I whispered when it appeared it wasn't coming back, "do not ask 'what next?' in realms unknown."

A horse leaped over my head and I shrieked again, curling up in a little ball. With my head pressed against the ground I could feel the vibrations of what seemed like a herd of horses pounding the earth. Then rough-voiced men shouted cheerfully over the rattle of tack, and I lifted my head cautiously. Six grinning men on horseback made a half circle in the woods, all of them facing me, right in the center of their circle. I froze. They jostled back and forth, changing position into some preferred layout that I couldn't appreciate.

What I could appreciate was that none of them seemed to be paying attention to me. I let out a sigh of relief and uncurled.

"Stand ready, my liege," someone said. "The boar comes."

That was *not* what I wanted to hear. I jumped up and sprinted for the safety of a tree just as the boar burst out of the woods again, this time with half a dozen men in full and glorious pursuit. In the boar's position, I would have been terrified. He just looked furious, like he knew he was going to die and he was going to take as many of the green-clad bastards with him as he could. The green-clad bastards in question all let forth howls of delight, and charged forth to meet the angry boar. Spears flew, horses leaped, and somehow all the weaponry missed the giant pig. It ducked beneath a horse, twisting its squat neck up and around. Its ivory tusks ripped the horse's belly out. Rider and beast fell together.

Another rider flung himself off his horse, landing on top of the fallen man, and beneath the boar's hooves. The boar squealed and slammed its head forward, tearing a bloody line across the second man's stomach.

The forest faded away around me, thinning to younger trees. The second man, with a calm and bitter smile, sat atop a horse, a knotted rope around his neck. "Is this how you repay me for your life, my liege?" he asked, the last words he ever spoke. A man slapped the horse's hindquarters and it bolted.

At my elbow, the second man watched himself hang, and said to me, "Do you enjoy a good hanging, my lady?"

I'd like to say I didn't so much as flinch, but I almost jumped out of my skin. "No." I watched the dangling man with sick fascination. "What is this? When did this happen? Who are you?"

"Six hundred years ago," the man beside me said. He was green-eyed and broad-shouldered, light brown hair worn loose over his shoulders. Malevolence flowed off him in such force that I shivered, just standing by him. "I was called Herne, then. Herne the Hunter. The man I saved, who had me hanged, was Richard, my lord king and liege. Would you care to walk?" He offered me his elbow, a fluid elegant gesture.

I took it against my own volition, then flinched again, trying to pull away. Herne smiled, keeping his lips closed. "This," he hissed, "is *my* garden, and you are here of *my* will, not yours. You will walk with me."

And I did. We walked away from his twitching body and into open fields, following a footpath worn into the grass. My skin felt soiled and grimy where it brushed against his, but I couldn't break away. "What am I doing here? What do you want with me?"

Herne smirked. "You're interfering. I intend to deal with you now, once and for all. Here, where I have absolute power."

"Here." I shivered again. "This is your garden, and it must be England, but where...?"

"These were my lands."

"He hanged you on your own lands?" I blurted. Herne looked down at me.

"Oh, yes, my lady. Such is the kindness of a king."

"How did you end up in Seattle?" It was a stupid question, but I had an idea at the back of my mind and I wanted to keep him talking until it germinated.

"On a boat, hand-built of wood, and then with many years of traveling west on foot."

"When did you leave England?"

"Two centuries?" He shrugged. "I haven't counted the years. I go back." His eyes flashed deeper green. "I will not leave my lands unprotected."

"But how?" The footpath we followed ended abruptly and began again a few feet later, a flaw in Herne's garden. It reordered itself as we walked over it. I frowned, pushing my will forward, at another section of path. The unlocked energy beneath my breastbone tingled through my blood, like it approved of what I was trying to do. "How can you still be alive?"

Herne looked positively disappointed. "Can't you guess? Ah, but you see only the ordinary man I was. Would it help..." He released my hand, took two steps forward and stopped in front of me with a little flourish. The path under his feet disappeared briefly. I frowned again, partly to hide a grin at the path's reaction to my push and partly because I didn't understand what I was supposed to see.

Then the subtleties of how he had changed hit me. His cheekbones had sharpened, chin lengthened a little, and the vividly green eyes tilted more noticeably. A pattern of bone distorted his temples just slightly. He looked ever so slightly more fey, no more slender through the shoulder, but with a degree of translucence to his skin, a hint of finer bones in his hands and face. He smiled, and I took a step forward, compelled.

"Oh, my God," I whispered. "You're his son. Cernunnos is your father."

"Not your god," Herne disagreed, "but a god, at least. Now you understand, of course, that you have to die."

I didn't understand that at all. "Wait! Shouldn't you be speaking French?" Even as I said it, I wondered what kind of stupid question *that* was. Even as a gambit for time, it had to be one of the dumber things I could have said. But it worked: Herne stared at me while I frantically searched for the flaw in his garden that had let me reshape the path. He'd said something, something important, if I could just understand what to do with it.

"I was born a landowner, not nobility. English is my native

tongue. And do you not imagine, *gwyld,* that in six hundred years I might learn another language if I needed?"

"Oh." I was genuinely embarrassed. "That was a dumb question."

"Yes," Herne agreed, "it was." Then his will rolled over me like thunder, transmuting, forcing me to the shape he chose for me. I thickened, arms and legs shortening as I dropped to all fours and tossed my head in panic. My head was too heavy, attached to my neck wrong, and my vision was dismal. On nothing but instinct, I charged forward. Herne laughed and stepped to the side, and I found myself bolting through forest with a handful of horsemen on my curling tail. I squealed in rage and fear and let the weight of my body drive me forward as I ran.

I burst into a clearing, toward a line of men seated on horseback. One moved forward, and I recognized the scene with a jolt of fear. Richard's hunt, the one that ultimately cost Herne his life.

Only this time I was the boar.

My clarity of vision returned abruptly, enough to let me see Herne's thin smile. Even as I charged forward, desperate, a plan crystallized in my mind. It was easy to gore Richard's horse, to bring the animal down and the king with him. Herne flung himself off his horse to protect the king. I brought my head up, ripping a glancing blow across Herne's belly; it had looked much more impressive when I was hidden behind the tree, watching. Herne flung a fist upward, catching me behind the ribs with a knife. I squealed in pain and staggered a step. Triumph lit Herne's eyes and he rolled out from under me, rolled off Richard, and drew his sword as he came to his feet.

I stumbled again, my breath coming in ugly little wheezes. The ground gave under my foot, and I collapsed to my knees, on top of Richard. He grunted and I felt the absurd desire to apologize. But Herne was driving his sword down, and there wasn't any more time.

I crushed my eyes shut and *chose*.

I *chose* to be there, in Herne's garden. That was the thing he'd said, the wiggle room I needed. With my choice, the shape his will held me in shattered. I snapped back to my own form, rolling to the side with a gasp. The knife wound Herne had put in my belly was still there, throbbing with agony.

Herne slammed his blade down into the place I'd been an instant before. Into Richard's abdomen. Richard's eyes went very wide and bright. I whispered, "Sorry," while my blood spilled through my fingers to mix with his. We stared at each other for another instant, before Herne's scream rendered the air and I staggered once more, forcing my head up to meet his eyes.

"It is not possible," he rasped. "My place—my power—"

I clutched the hole in my belly where he'd stabbed me and straightened up as far as I could. It wasn't very far: to breathe through the pain I had to stay a little hunched, but at least I could meet his eyes. "Your will," I whispered back. "I'm not here. Of your will. Anymore." I couldn't breathe. It hurt so badly I could hardly think, flares of pain steady with my heartbeat. "Chose. To be here." I hadn't been sure it would work. "Choosing. To leave now. Too."

I collapsed over the silent, broken form of Richard, king of England. Herne's scream of fury echoed in my memory for a long time.

When I opened my eyes again I was on my knees in my garden, doubled over with one forearm against the ground and the other wrapped around my belly.

"This one's a little more complicated," Coyote said. "Can you feel them?"

I lifted my head up, beads of sweat draining into my eyes. I couldn't feel a goddamned thing except the spiking pain in my gut, and the blood slipping through my fingers.

"Try harder," Coyote said. He lay on his belly with his head on his paws, gold eyes intense on mine. I whimpered without any dignity and tried to feel something beyond myself. Just on the other side of pain was a source of amusement, smugness and concern.

"Not me." Coyote sounded patient. "Past me." I grunted and tried to reach past him, my fingers creeping forward in the grass like the physical motion would help the mental. For a moment there was a scattering of sensation, the feeling of someone waiting. I recognized it from my dream-walk and reached for it. Coyote snapped at my crawling fingers. "Farther out."

I drew a deep breath to try again, then couldn't do *anything* for a few seconds. Blood drained through my fingers with more enthusiasm. "Fuck." Nausea made a stab at settling into my system, but I was too hurt to hold on to even that.

I stretched one more time, past Coyote, past the one who waited for me, and finally found what Coyote was after. Two thin silver lines ran through me, attached to one another, using me as a conduit. They flickered, unevenly, unsynchronized and as weakly as my own pulse. One disappeared into darkness, its far end so distant I wasn't sure where it led. The other had no visible end, either, but it *felt* closer, like I could reach out a hand and grasp the arm of the body whose life it sustained.

"They're tied together through you," Coyote said softly, as if he was afraid a full voice would shatter my fragile grasp on the cords. "Don't you see?"

"Mem'ry," I whispered. Blood drooled to the grass. "Henrietta's. Mem'ry. Herne's. Will. Tied me to. Richard's life." I understood. The energy coil inside me bubbled eagerly, sending out pulses of power along with my blood. "More engine work," I mumbled, and fell through six hundred years of time, healing the schoolteacher and the king.

* * *

I opened my eyes and sat down hard in the chair. "You saved them," I said.

Henrietta Potter stared at me. "Anthony and Mark," I said. "Jennifer and Adrian. You broke Herne's circle. He took almost everything but you broke the circle that would bind their souls. They'll get another chance." My whole body hurt, and I was exhausted beyond belief. My thoughts were too thick and slow to be chaotic, but they felt that way anyway. I needed to go sit somewhere, quietly, and figure out what had happened. What it *meant*. I pushed to my feet and wove my way to the door.

I bounced off Gary as he and Billy returned with coffee. Gary dropped both the cups he carried, swore, and grabbed my shoulders as my knees gave out and I tried to follow the coffee to the floor. "What in hell happened to you? You look like you saw a ghost."

"Bad day at the office." I giggled. Billy and Gary exchanged glances. Billy pushed the door to Henrietta's room open and went in. "C'mon," I said to Gary. "I wanna go home. Tired."

"You were fine two minutes ago, lady."

I smiled up at him and patted his cheek. "Aw. Gary. Didn't know you cared." My knees went out from under me again and this time I did drop, flopping to the floor like a rag doll.

Into the spilled coffee. I stuck a fingertip in it. "Aw, man. Now my panties are gonna smell like coffee." I put both my hands into the air and let Gary pull me to my feet as Billy came back out of the hospital room, looking pale.

"What in hell did you do?" he demanded. I stared at him without comprehension.

"Aw, shit. She's not dead or anything, is she?"

"Not quite," Henrietta Potter said from behind Billy's shoulder. He moved out of the way and she stepped out, looking surprisingly dignified in just a hospital gown and bare feet.

"You oughta be lying down," Gary said sternly. He kept a firm hand around my waist, which I thought was sweet of him.

"I believe, actually, that I'll be checking out as soon as someone is kind enough to fetch me some clothes."

"You could borrow mine," I said too loudly, "but they all smell like coffee now." I was very tired. If Gary didn't keep his arm around my waist, I thought I might just collapse again and not wake up for a week or two. No, I couldn't do that. I had to think. I nodded several times to myself, big motions that took on a life of their own as I forgot why I was nodding.

Mrs. Potter looked up at me, amused. "I'm tall for my generation, Joanne Walker, but I would trip on your sleeves."

I stopped nodding, astonished. "But they're short," I protested. Henrietta quirked a smile.

"So they are," she agreed.

"What did you *do?*" Billy asked again. I waved a hand at him.

"Just a lil' fixer-upper. Noooo big deal. Do it anytime. No problem. Lil' hole in the tummy to kill a king? Sure. Hey. To kill a king." I snickered against Gary's arm. "That's funny."

"Detective," Gary said, "Jo needs to go home and sleep."

"Oooh, *good* idea." I tilted over, then frowned and started shaking my head. Big swinging shakes of my head. "Nooo. Can't sleep. Have to *think.*" Now I was nodding again. It was all very confusing, and I was losing my balance. Gary tightened his arm around me. I giggled and patted his shoulder. "Nice Gary."

This was starting to get embarrassing. I peeled out of Gary's grasp and carefully began maneuvering my way down the wide, empty hallway. After several steps, with a gentle thump, I maneuvered my shoulder right into the wall opposite Henrietta's room. That wasn't at all what I'd been aiming for, but it struck me that the wall would help me walk in a straight line. I leaned on it and concentrated on putting one foot in front of another. Left. Right.

Left. It wasn't all that hard, as long as I kept my head down and watched my feet. Feeling rather proud of myself through the haze of exhaustion, I picked up a little speed.

"Joanie..." Billy's voice bounced off the gray walls, a warning. Another pair of shoes intruded themselves on my line of vision. I didn't exactly have momentum in my favor, but I still didn't manage to stop until the top of my head ran into the chest belonging to the intrusive shoes.

I didn't even bounce, just lifted my head and found myself toe to toe and nose to nose with Captain Michael Morrison.

CHAPTER FIFTEEN

Morrison was close enough to kiss. He had tired shadows under his eyes, and his hair had silver threads in it, neither of which I'd ever noticed before. We stared at each other, almost cross-eyed, our noses nearly touching. He drew in a magnificently deep breath through his nostrils in preparation to launch a tirade. I lifted my hand and put my fingertips over his mouth, clumsily. His eyebrows shot up, as much surprise as I'd ever seen on Morrison's face.

"Shh," I whispered. "There's lots of sick people here. Yelling makes bad juju. You don't want to make anybody die, do you? Shh."

In a very modulated tone that did nothing to hide his anger, Morrison demanded, "Are you out of your fucking mind?"

It seemed increasingly likely that I was. I rocked back on my heels, lost my balance and staggered half a step backward, which took me well out of kissing distance, if not out of Morrison's personal space. One of his hands flashed out and clamped around my biceps, steadying me. I was too startled to answer him.

He didn't really want me to answer anyway. "What the hell are you doing here? I have this dream," he charged on as I tried to formulate an answer. "I have this dream that I'll get up one day and the whole damned world will make sense. Being a practical man, I know that's not going to happen." Morrison's volume was building. "But it seems like I should at least be able to stop by for a visit with a key witness without finding the mechanic I suspended yesterday hanging around a police-protected wing of the hospital!"

I found the wall with one hand and leaned on it, letting Morrison's crescendo break and wash over me. It took a great deal of careful thought to manage, "I thought I could help." My voice sounded thick and fuzzy, like I'd been snacking on polar fleece.

"Help? What the hell do you know about helping in a murder investigation? You want to be a mechanic. And even if you *wanted* to be a police officer—"

I leaned against the wall a little harder, closing my eyes. If he'd only choose one pitch and stay at it, I could probably go to sleep standing here, but the fluctuations in volume forced me to listen to him.

"—I don't want *anyone* I've suspended to 'help' with criminal cases they're involved in. If you have information that will help, give it to the police and we'll take it from there. You *know* that's how it works, Walker. There's nothing you can do that we can't."

"On the contrary."

I peeled my eyes open to discover Mrs. Potter had come up the hallway and was standing at Morrison's elbow, waiting for him to acknowledge her interruption. He glared at her.

"Thank you, ma'am, but I don't need your opinion right now. You—" The last word was directed at me, and then Morrison's head snapped back around as he recognized the schoolteacher. "You shouldn't be on your feet."

"As I was saying," Henrietta said equitably, "I believe Miss Walker may be able to do a number of things you can't."

The next few hours got very blurry while people asked me the same questions over and over, sometimes several at once and frequently in a staccato series. I kept looking up to see if there was a single hard white light bulb dangling over my head. All I wanted to do was leave. There was something important I had to go think about, but I couldn't think with all the noise and the yelling and the questions. I needed sleep. The world would make more sense once I'd had some sleep.

What I got instead was Morrison's scowl and doctors who wanted desperately to know how I'd done what I'd done. I remembered shouting, "I'm not a goddamned faith healer! I don't talk to God! I'm a mechanic and her goddamned engine was broken!"

They left me alone for quite a while after that.

I waited for the nice young men in their clean white coats to arrive. When they didn't, the bed Henrietta had abandoned was too tempting to ignore. The nice young men could wake me up.

Gary woke me up instead, gently shaking my shoulder. "Wake up, lady. Jo?"

"Lady Jo," I mumbled into the pillow. "Kinda like that. Sounds like a romance heroine."

Gary paused, distracted. "You read romances?"

"S'my deep dark secret. Go 'way."

"Can't. The ten o'clock news just came on. You might want to get out of here before Morrison gets back."

I tried to peel one eye open, but my contacts were glued to my eyes again. "Whu?"

"You're all over it. C'mon, let's go."

"Oh, God." I turned my face and buried it in the pillow. "I don't care. Let him kill me. As long as I get some rest."

"You've had five hours of sleep," Gary said without sympathy. "You've only got another day to solve this case, y'know."

I pulled one eye open long enough to look at him. It teared up and shut again of its own volition. "What're you talking about?"

"Most murders go unsolved if the murderer isn't caught in forty-eight hours." Gary spoke with an air of great authority.

"Serial murders are different. Go aw—" An alarming thought drained through my sleep-heavy brain. "What's the date?"

"Fifth of January."

I rolled onto my back, blinking tears away as I frowned at the ceiling. "Tomorrow's the sixth?"

"There's a bright girl," Gary said approvingly.

"His power peaks tomorrow night."

"Whose does?"

"Cernunnos. Yuletide. That's what Marie said. His power peaks and then begins to fade until the summer solstice, and then he's banished back to…"

"Wherever Celtic gods are banished to," Gary supplied.

"Until Sa— Halloween."

"Samhain," Gary said. *Sow-ehn,* he pronounced it. I shook my head.

"I saw that word on the computer. When I look at it I see 'Sam-hane.' How do you remember how to say it?"

Gary shrugged. "Old dog. So what's the big deal? After tomorrow, you get the upper hand. Sounds like a good way to play the game to me."

"If I live through it." The words made a little pit of sickness in my stomach. There was a very real possibility that I was going to end up dead tomorrow. I'd certainly come close enough in the past couple days. Gary frowned and jerked his chin at the door.

"Come on. You won't live through tonight if your friend the police captain gets his hands on you."

I groaned and rolled off the bed. "There's a reassuring thought."

"I do my best," Gary said modestly. I chuckled through exhaustion. An alarming number of things were striking me as funny. I wondered if I'd ever get enough sleep to get over that.

"All right. All right. I didn't even *say* anything to that stupid reporter. How can he kill me?" I opted against looking in the mirror, dragged the door open and walked into Morrison for the second time that evening. This time I bounced back a step while he stood there like a wall. "We've got to stop meeting like this."

"I oughta have you arrested." Morrison was nose to nose with me again. I looked down at his shoes, tilting my head to the side a little. The soles of his shoes were the same thickness as mine. If I thought he could have, I would have guessed he'd done that on purpose.

"For what?" I looked back up at him. I could feel Gary looming behind me. It obviously didn't bother Morrison at all, but it made me feel a little better.

"Interfering with a police investigation."

"Have I interfered?"

"You've wasted my time and that of one of my officers for the past seven hours by keeping us here at this hospital."

My eyebrows crawled up my forehead. "I've been asleep for the last five hours. How'd I keep you here? Hell, Morrison, you didn't even know I *was* here when you showed up. You can't blame me for you still being here."

"You affected a principal witness in the case, Walker."

"'Affected.'" I stared at him. "How's she doing, anyway?"

"The doctors can't even find any scar tissue. What the hell did you do?"

"I healed her and Richard the Second of England through a psychic link with a Celtic demigod drawn out of her memory of the murders this morning," I said flippantly, knowing Morrison wouldn't believe it, even if it was God's own truth. Or possibly *because* it was God's own truth. His hand bunched into a fist and loosened again. I almost wished he'd hit me. A good old-fashioned hands-on ass-kicking might do me some good right now. I didn't even much care whose ass got kicked.

"I always liked you, Walker," Morrison said out of the blue. My jaw dropped.

"You did not."

Morrison snorted, a sort of laugh, and admitted, "No. But you always seemed to have a head on your shoulders. No tact, but a head on your shoulders. But now you're talking like Holliday. What the hell happened to you?"

I felt old and tired suddenly. "I'd love to sit down over coffee and tell you, but you wouldn't believe me. It's been a rough couple days, Morrison. I think something bad is going to happen tomorrow night and I have to find out what and stop it."

"*I* have to, dammit! It's not your—"

"My job," I agreed wearily. "I know. It's your job. I just don't think you can find what's doing this, Morrison. I'm not sure *I* can, and they're talking to me."

"Who are?"

"The old gods." I half laughed. "Dead people. This is not what I signed up for, dammit!"

"What did you sign up for?"

"Living another day, I guess. I didn't know it was going to get so complicated." I pinched the bridge of my nose, squinching my eyes closed. The contacts finally loosened up a bit and I could feel moisture in my eyes again. "Morrison, are you gonna charge me with anything, or can I go home now?"

"Are you going to *go* home?" He sounded like a belligerent bull.

"Yes," I promised.

"Are you going to stay there?"

"What are you, my mother? Tell you what. I'll stay home for the rest of my life if every two weeks you'll cut me a paycheck I can live on." I stepped forward to see if it would make Morrison move out of the doorway. It did. I was very impressed with myself. "I'm going home, Morrison. Good night." Gary followed right on my heels, like an oversized protective shadow. I was halfway down the hall when Morrison's voice followed me.

"Walker."

I turned around reluctantly. Morrison frowned down the hall at me. "Stay home. This guy's dangerous."

"You're making me all sentimental, Morrison. Knock it off before I get weepy." I got all the way to the gate and out it this time.

"I think he likes you," Gary said as the gate clanged shut. I laughed, a sharp bark of sound.

"Morrison wouldn't like me if I were kind enough to never darken his doorstep again. He'd find me easier to tolerate, that's all."

"He likes you," Gary said again, with an air of certainty. "He's just afraid of you." He slowed and let me go through the open half of a double door in front of him, while I glared over my shoulder at him.

"Afraid of me? Why would he be afraid of me? I'm not scary. You're not scared of me."

Gary pursed his lips. I stopped and looked at him, arms folded, waiting.

"You've done some scary things since I met you," he volunteered after a moment. I snorted.

"Yeah, well, I didn't start rising from the dead until *after* I met you. Maybe you have that effect on people. There's no reason for you or anybody, especially Morrison, to be scared of me. He's hated me for ages, anyway. He's not afraid of me." Scowling, I started back down the hallway. "Where are you parked, anyway?"

"Visitor parking. Gotta leave through the main lobby. You don't gotta get so huffy, Jo. There's lots of work for scary people. Body-guarding, for example."

"Bodyguards look like professional wrestlers." I eyed Gary. "Don't you dare say I do."

Gary held up his hands and wisely didn't say a thing. I waited, then nodded, satisfied. "Okay. Can I go home now?"

Gary not only brought me back to my car, but followed me home afterward. I couldn't decide if he was overprotective by nature, or if he was one of those strays that moves in and takes over your life. I made coffee and logged on to the computer. There were three more spams, something from one of the online political organizations I belonged to, and a note from Kevin Sadler saying, *It was nice to meet you. Adina would want me to help you learn anything you can. If I can even be a sounding board for you, let me know.*

"He likes you," Gary said cheerfully.

"Please. His wife was just murdered. I don't think he's hitting on me. And I don't need you setting me up with every guy I come across, jeez."

"You sure?"

"Yes, Gary, I'm sure." I frowned at him, then at the screen and hit Reply. *Thanks, Kevin. I appreciate the offer. Some bizarre stuff happened today. Want to get together for lunch and hear about it? I can probably spare an hour tomorrow. —Joanne.*

"What am I?" Gary demanded. "Chopped liver?"

I grunted and sent the message, then fidgeted impatiently for several minutes, hoping for a reply. "It's eleven at night," Gary finally said. "He's probably in bed."

"Yeah, yeah." I yawned myself, eyes tearing, which reminded me to go take my contacts out. I came back into the living room wearing my glasses and still yawning. "I hate not being able to see."

"Least you've had time to get used to it," Gary said. "I hit about fifty-five and all of a sudden my arms were too short to read."

"Maybe you should stop writing on your arms." I grinned at his expression. "You did okay with my magazines and the computer screen."

"Takes a while for a headache to set in," Gary said. "How long've you worn glasses?"

"Since I was nine. You want to know the horrible thing? I felt like it was a big secret, that I couldn't see, and I figured everybody'd point and stare when I came to school with glasses. Nobody even noticed. I'd spent all that time psyching myself up for the trauma of being teased. The trauma of not being noticed was worse."

"Kids are self-centered."

"Humans are self-centered," I corrected. "Don't let kids have all the credit."

"How'd you get to be so cynical so young?"

I snorted. "I'll introduce you to my dad sometime."

"That would be interesting," Gary said so neutrally I thought I should be offended. I frowned at him for a minute while he maintained the careful neutrality. I finally looked away.

"Don't you have to be at work in five hours?"

Gary looked at his watch. "Six and a half. I'll be fine."

I grinned. "What makes you think I'm worried about you? I'm worried about your passengers. You're terrifying to ride with even when you're awake."

"Hey, you're alive, aren't you?"

"No thanks to you," I said happily, and Gary laughed.

"I didn't get you stabbed," he pointed out.

"Details, details. Where's that sword, anyway?"

"At my apartment. Couldn't keep it in the back of the cab while I was working. You want it?"

I thought about that for a minute. "Yeah, I think so. Can you bring it by tomorrow?"

"Before or after work?"

"Um." I sucked on my teeth. "Before."

"Okay." Gary stood up. "I'll be by around five-fifteen."

"Gah. I'll try to be awake."

"You're young. You can survive on a few nights of not much sleep."

"Easy for you to say. You haven't been fatally wounded twice in two days."

Gary's bushy gray eyebrows shot up. "Twice?"

"Um." I rubbed my hand over my stomach. "The second time was at the hospital. It didn't exactly happen on this plane of reality." I winced as I said it. Gary's eyebrows remained elevated, but he didn't say any of the sarcastic things Morrison would have said.

"I got myself knotted into a couple of other people's lives," I mumbled. "If I hadn't been able to fix them, I think I'd have been dead when you came back with the coffee."

"Richard the Second," Gary said, in that carefully neutral voice again.

"Yeah." I scowled defensively. "He put Herne the Hunter to death."

"Herne the Hunter."

"*Yes.*"

"The one we read about on the computer."

I nodded. Gary spread his big hands and shook his head. "What's he got to do with anything?"

"It was Herne at the school today," I said impatiently. "I borrowed Mrs. Potter's memories and Herne dragged me into his playing field." I was sure I'd told him about this already. From his expression, my mind was playing tricks on me.

"Borrowed?"

I sat down. "She was telling me about what happened at the school and I wanted to help her get through the bad memories. Something happened. I shared her memories, like we had some kind of hive mind thing going. And then Herne dragged me out of her memories into his own. And I got all caught up in something that happened hundreds of years ago. It was like I was really there."

"How?"

"I don't know."

Gary was very quiet. I looked up to find him frowning at me. "Why didn't you tell your captain any of that?"

"I—" I broke off, my forehead wrinkling. "Didn't I?"

"No," Gary said. "You didn't."

"Oh." I considered the question for a minute. "Because he's a sanctimonious asshole?"

"I get it," Gary said sagely. "You like him, too."

"For God's sake. Go home, Gary, you're getting delusional from lack of sleep." I remembered thinking Morrison was close enough to kiss, and groaned. "Go home," I said again. Gary finished his coffee and put the cup in the sink, looking at me with what I was beginning to recognize as his expression of concern. It looked a bit like a polar bear with indigestion.

"You gonna be all right here, Jo?"

"I'll be fine," I promised, absurdly touched by his worry. "I'm just going to read for a while and then go to bed. No crazy antics. I promised Morrison." I made a face.

"No, you didn't."

Damn. "I don't think he noticed that."

"Don't count on it. I'll be by around a quarter after five," he reminded me. "Lock the door." I nodded and followed him to the door to lock it behind him, then stood there for a full minute, waiting for another shoe to drop.

CHAPTER SIXTEEN

Nothing happened.

Nothing kept right on happening while I fell asleep leaning on the door. My knees buckled, jolting me awake, and I staggered to the computer chair. There had to be something I could find about Herne, something that would tell me what was going on. If it wasn't on the Internet, it didn't exist, right? So it had to be, some kind of information about Cernunnos's sullen son. I clicked through to a new site, slumped in my chair and wondered how many shoes had already dropped.

"Shoes," I said out loud, and looked at my feet. My luggage. I hadn't actually promised Morrison I'd stay home, and I was out of underwear. I glanced at the computer screen, where the page loaded with excruciating slowness. Stifling a yawn, I went into the bedroom and kicked over my carry-on, digging through it until I found my baggage ticket. The page still hadn't loaded when I came back out, so I switched the screen off and left it to load, grabbing my keys on my way out the door. Airports seemed nice and safe. They had all those metal detectors that would keep peo-ple with swords from coming after me, and lots of security with no sense of humor to discourage someone if he evaded the metal detectors.

Not that it seemed even slightly plausible that airport security could handle Cernunnos. Or Herne, for that matter, since he seemed to be the one going around actually killing Seattleites. I switched lanes and listened to the uneven pattern of changing as-phalt textures under the wheels of the car. Headlights flashed by, going the other direction, rhythmic whisks of light and sound in the dark. When this was over, I promised myself, I was going to go take a nice long drive to somewhere very quiet and try to get a grip on my shiny, weird new life.

Which task I would obviously accomplish with the copious spare cash hanging around in my savings account, during the long periods of free time I'd have between writing parking tickets.

An old Cadillac, big as a boat, flashed by. I remembered the church and reached across the car to open the glove box, letting the butterfly knife tumble forward with the various papers stuffed into the box. It made a solid thud, cushioned by paper, and I glanced at it while I drove.

Marie swore it hadn't been Cernunnos waiting for her outside the church. I believed her: Cernunnos was not someone I would ever mistake for somebody else. That suggested it was Herne; cer-tainly he appeared to be the one who'd murdered her. I closed my eyes, trying to remember the shape of the man I'd seen from the air, wondering if he fit Herne's shape. Then I remembered I was driving. Maybe I should stop thinking until I wasn't on a freeway.

I left the knife in the car when I got to the airport. Security might not be able to stop Herne, but they could certainly stop me. There was a Back in Fifteen Minutes sign on the baggage claim desk, so I wandered upstairs to one of the cafés to find some food, half-expecting to see someone I knew. I always expected to, at airports.

I got an overpriced but surprisingly good hamburger, and a cup of too-hot coffee. I took my bounty and found a table by a window, where I could watch the midnight international flights take off in the distance while I gnoshed on my burger.

"Waiting for someone?"

I focused on the reflection in the window, a broad-shouldered man in a sweatshirt, wearing his long brown hair tied in a ponytail. "Yeah," I mumbled. "My boyfriend."

He grinned. "Your large, bad-tempered, jealous boyfriend?"

"Yeah," I repeated. "Big. Bigger than you. Samoan," I added in a fit of inspiration.

"Mind if I join you?"

I looked over at him. "I'm not a prostitute or out looking for a good time, and I've had a bad day," I warned him. "If you make one pass at me, I'll kick your ass right back to the Carolinas."

"It's good to see you, too, Joanne."

"What the hell are you doing here, Casey?" I stood up and hugged him, letting out an *oof* as his hug popped my spine.

"Looking for lost souls," he said by my ear, and put me back down. "Did I find one?"

"Funny you should say that. You look good. You bulked up."

"It's been a couple years. People change."

"It's been three and a half. And you always looked good." Round-faced and quiet, Casey O'Brien didn't come anywhere near what I considered my type, but he had graceful hands that I'd lusted after in college. He never stood up straight, which drove me crazy, because he was three inches taller than me but came across as shorter.

"You're lying." Casey sat down across from me, wrapping his hands around mine. I discovered I hadn't stopped lusting. "What *are* you doing here?"

"What?" I looked up from his hands. "Um. Trying to locate my luggage. It got left here a couple days ago. What're you doing here?"

"On my way back up to Alaska. New job up there."

"Congratulations. Hey," I said suddenly. "Do you know a Doctor Marie D'Ambra?"

"Not personally. I've heard of her. She's kind of a kook. Claims to know when people are going to die. I think she's been reading too many fairy tales." Casey turned my hand over and traced his thumb over my lifeline. "Why, did you meet her?"

"Yeah," I said. "She's dead."

Casey looked up, pale blue eyes shocked. "You're kidding."

"No. I met her yesterday morning. She was murdered last night."

"Jeez, Joanne, I know you go on first impressions, but you really think you should start killing people you don't like?"

Despite myself, I laughed. "Is that my mistake? I'll work on that." I shook my head, sobering. "She thought someone was after her. Look, you're an anthropologist. Do you think..." I trailed off, uncertain of what to say. "Do you think studying old civilizations can make you susceptible to their beliefs?"

"You're asking the wrong person. I'm an archaeologist, not a cultural anthropologist." Casey pressed his lips together. "I don't think an anthropologist should dismiss the reality of what she studies. But claiming you can tell when someone's going to die? If she could do that, how come she's dead? Shouldn't she have known to run away?"

"She thought she was going to die," I admitted. "She thought..." I really didn't want to tell Casey that Marie had thought an old Celtic god was after her. Not even if it was true. The only reason I believed was because I'd come face-to-face and blade to blade with something that pretty definitely wasn't human. "She thought I was going to die," I said instead.

"You're looking pretty perky for a dead girl." Casey studied me, then reached out and turned my face, frowning. "How'd you get that scar? I just noticed it."

I rubbed it. "Guess it's not wildly disfiguring, then. Marie D'Ambra cut me with a knife."

Casey's eyebrows crinkled. "What'd she do that for? I thought you said you met her yesterday."

"Yeah."

"But it's all healed up."

"I know. Have you ever had a week so strange it was inexplicable?"

"Um." Casey studied me again. "I don't think so."

I picked up my coffee cup. "I'm having one. If I live through it and manage to get some perspective, I'll tell you about it." The coffee was cool enough to drink, and I took a grateful slurp. "Tell me something. Do you think the world needs saving?"

"Needs? Sure. Deserves? Dunno about that." Casey reached across the table and stole one of my fries. They were cold, so I didn't stop him. "People basically suck. Maybe we should kill 'em all and let God sort 'em out. Let the planet start over."

"Do you really think that?" I pushed the plate toward Casey as he took another fry. He chewed slowly, thinking about his answer.

"Sometimes," he said after a minute. "What do you think?"

I took another sip of coffee and stared at the dwindling pile of fries while I thought about it. A few days ago I would have laughed and agreed. Kill 'em all, let God sort 'em out.

But I'd told Billy I felt like I could save the world—or Seattle, anyway. I'd promised the priest I'd stop the nutcase who was murdering children. I'd told Kevin I'd find the guy who'd killed his wife. "I guess I don't think people basically suck. I think...I don't know what I think." I put the coffee cup down and my head in my hands, trying to work my way through a thought. "I think we lost our sense of direction," I finally said. "I think we need to..." I looked up. Casey's eyes flashed emerald-green at me, like a reflected light was somewhere behind my head.

A thin trickle of cold followed the warmth of the coffee down the inside of my throat, spreading out through my stomach. "I think we need to heal the people who are hurt." I picked up my coffee again and twisted around to look behind me. There was nothing green, not even as much as an exit sign. "Heal the ones who can do the most harm, first, and then work our way down through the ranks." I turned back to him. "I think we should start with you."

Casey's eyes shifted. "Me? Since when did I become one of the bad guys?"

"I think you always were," I whispered. "Herne, son of Cernunnos." Names had power, I'd read that. Casey began to stand up and I reached across the table to knot my fist in his shirt, locking eyes with him.

"Give me my friend back. Now."

Color bled out of Casey's eyes, pale blue giving way to virulent green. A small numb part of me watched it and knew I should be scared, but after watching all the color drain from Marie's eyes, after reliving the memory of the teenagers' deaths, all that I could feel was rage replacing the fear that had chilled my belly. I saw surprise deepen the color of his eyes: he expected me to be afraid. I hauled him forward a few inches, and snarled, "Give me back my friend."

"What if he was never here?" Casey's voice tinged with a nasal, arrogant accent. Herne's voice in his garden had been richer, fuller and far more heavily accented, but the intonations were the same.

"All the better," I growled. "Then you're the only casualty I'll have to worry about."

"You can't," he murmured with absolute confidence. "Healer." The word was an epithet. I tightened my fingers in his shirt and moved around the table, until I was face-to-face with him. I could feel power again, the way I'd felt it earlier, roiling through me. It was free now, unlocked and ready to be used. There were other patrons in the restaurant, some of them watching us openly, a few of them pretending very hard not to see us. I didn't *want* them to see us.

All I'd used the power inside me for was healing, so far, but my skin felt abused by the pressure of light on it. Invisibility was just a matter of bending light waves around something. I pushed the bubble of energy inside me out, expanding its surface so that it swallowed Herne and me whole. It felt silver-clear to me, ticklish, as if the rules of the universe had changed in the space I was standing in. I guessed they had: I could see, from the corners of my eyes, that the watchers were frowning faintly, then dismissing what they'd seen—or not seen—as impossible. In a few seconds no one was looking our way at all. My fingers tingled with the outpouring of energy.

Beyond the restaurant, the airport hummed with power, the energy of people leaving and returning home. I only had to redirect all that energy, and I could fry Herne right here where he stood, without any witnesses. I began pulling it in, as natural as breathing, even as the idea made me shudder.

Herne smiled, thin-lipped. "Healer," he spat again. He looked nothing like Casey any longer, canines dangerously curved and build resuming its natural narrow-hipped shape. "You can do nothing here. What will happen to these people if you draw on the energy output here? How many planes will come down when the airport falls off the radar? How many children will you frighten with blackouts? Let me go, little healer. I know how to choose my battlegrounds."

Like a heartbeat, the truth of his words pounded into me. Cause and effect. I could destroy him here, on the physical plane, and it would cost hundreds of lives. I would be as bad, worse, than he. I loosened my hold on the invisibility that wrapped around us, unsure if maintaining it might cause damage, too.

"Why didn't I recognize you?" I didn't release my grip on his shirt. "I was sure I would. After today. After the school. You don't feel like Cernunnos. I thought I'd know you."

He put his hands over mine, surprisingly cool and very large. His nails were thick and heavy, hinting of claws. "Because I can mask myself deeper than you know how to go, little healer. And you have no time to learn."

"But I did better than you expected." I hadn't taken my eyes off his, depthless and green. His gaze had none of the drowning power that Cernunnos's did, but like Cernunnos, it betrayed him. Under his confidence was a layer of concern. I worried him. Once I tasted that fear, the totality of his power swept over me, thundering, meant to drown me. I tightened my fingers in his shirt a little and lifted my chin, letting it wash all around me like Moses and the Red Sea.

Herne's memories weighed heavily, a man caught in a position of something less than a god, but granted hundreds of years beyond a man's lifespan. His mortal life had at least had purpose: he guarded his lands, and faint recollection told me the land had once responded to him. He'd been the Green Man, not a god, no, but at least a protective spirit. But he was too much between two worlds: a taint ran deep in him, all the way back to the half-shared moment where he'd lifted his sword and driven it into his king's body instead of mine.

Real! It slammed through me like a shock. That moment had been *real*. His power had dragged me back through time, displacing me. If I had died there, I would have died here, too. Henrietta would have died.

And Richard the Second would never have hanged the Hunter. From the very beginning of his immortal life, Herne had been something less than he could have been. That knowledge poisoned him as much as—

He wrenched back from me, breaking eye contact and tearing loose from my grip on his shirt. The memories I'd delved in to shattered, losing me any further insight to the half god standing before me. "I'm stronger than you think I am," I said.

"Not strong enough." Herne's eyes were glassy, with no more openings to his power or his soul. "Not strong enough," he repeated. "You don't have enough time."

"I have a day," I said calmly, and smiled as shock rose in his eyes. "See? I know more than you think I do, too." It occurred to me that I'd just played my trump card by telling him that. I didn't know half as much as I needed to. Shock faded from his gaze, replaced by wariness. Hell. If he thought I knew what he was doing, he'd be all the more cautious, and all the harder to track. Oh, yeah. I'd blown it. Good form, Joanne. I needed a neon pink shirt that read NOVICE in big fat letters. Just in case anybody had any doubts on the matter. Herne and I stared at each other another long moment. Then a rangy security guard materialized at my elbow.

"Everything all right here, folks?" he asked casually. As if by mutual agreement, Herne and I broke off from looking at one another to fix the guard with equally grim expressions.

"Fine," I said shortly, then muttered, "was I speeding, officer?" The guard frowned at me. "Nevermind," I said out loud. "We're fine."

"Maybe it's time for you to go on and catch your plane, or head home, ma'am, sir. It's late, and nobody wants any trouble." The guard actually looked as if a little trouble might be welcome.

Herne and I looked at one another again. "Twenty-three hours,

Siobhán Walkingstick," Herne said, and I flinched. I didn't like this thing where people were reading my birth name out of my mind. He hadn't used it before. Had I given away as much in that memory link as he had? I was going to have to do something about this, about all of it. Assuming I survived the next day. Funny how making it through an hour or a day at a time had never been an issue before.

"Twenty-three hours, Hunter. Sorry for the fuss, officer." I stepped past them both and went to pick up my luggage.

CHAPTER SEVENTEEN

The desk attendant handed over my luggage with a perfunctory glance at my tickets and I was out of the airport and on the way home within ten minutes. It felt like a bad omen, that actually getting the luggage had gone so smoothly. It wasn't good when things going easily seemed like a sure sign of doom. I was going to need some extensive therapy when this was all over.

Halfway home I passed a bad wreck, two cars and the freeway wall. Paramedics loaded a body bag into the back of an ambulance as I went by, and Herne's pointer about the effects of using my new power stood out vividly in my mind. I slowed as I rounded a corner, then pulled over, shivering as I unpeeled my death grip from the steering wheel and shook my hands until blood started flowing again.

When my fingers started tingling from returning blood, I wrapped my arms around myself and folded over, my forehead against the wheel as I tried to take deep breaths without hyperventilating. I'd been so sure I would recognize Herne, and the only reason I had at all was a sheer chance of light. It had taken him, a killer, to warn me of the consequences of my actions. I was so far out of my league it wasn't funny, and it was going to get me killed.

I didn't *want* to die.

Light colored in my eyelids, red and blue. I sat up to squint at the cop car that was pulling over in front of me. I didn't recognize the cop who got out, but I hardly knew every cop in the greater Seattle area. I rolled down the window and leaned my head against the steering wheel, waiting for the ritual.

"Everything okay, ma'am?"

I sighed, straightened up, and looked at her. She was pretty. Blue eyes, and blond hair tucked neatly under her hat.

"Everything's fine." I couldn't think of a good explanation as to what I was doing pulled off on the side of the freeway, so I didn't say anything else.

"Car troubles?"

"No, ma'am."

"Been drinking?"

Would I be dumb enough to answer that in the affirmative if I had? "No, ma'am," I repeated. "Just coming back from the airport."

"Late flight, huh? Tired?" She smiled. It was a nice smile that didn't have anything to do with Celtic gods or shamans. I smiled back.

"Yeah. I just needed a breather. I'll be on my way in a second here."

The cop nodded. "Drive carefully, okay? And have a good night, all right?"

"I will. Thanks." I watched her walk back to her car, then smiled and stuck my head out the window. "Hey, officer?"

She turned back, eyebrows lifted under her cap. "Yes?"

"You'd be good at playing Questions, you know that?"

She laughed, a sound as pleasant as her smile. "What makes you say that?" She climbed in her car and drove away, leaving me feeling like the world was a better place. I sighed and slumped back in my seat with a yawn, eyes closed for a moment before I reached for the gear stick.

Light filled my eyelids again. Shimmering, pearly silver light that was about as much like headlights as peacock feathers were. For a long moment I refused to open my eyes again, under the dubious logic that if I couldn't see whatever was making the light, it couldn't see me.

"It doesn't work that way," a sibilant voice murmured. I wasn't at all sure if I'd heard it in my ears or my head. It didn't matter. I knew the voice. Since it didn't work that way, I gritted my teeth and opened my eyes.

Cernunnos's host swarmed around my car, flickering with quite literally unearthly light, as if they were no more than figures on an old silent movie screen. The horses skittered, not quite touching the car. Red-eared hellhounds slunk under the horses' bellies, baring gleaming white fangs at me through the window. One rider glared down through the windshield at me, craggy face bearded and stern. If he weren't undead, I might have considered him handsome.

"Not undead," Cernunnos corrected. A few of the host melted away as he approached on his enormous stallion. "The undead do not *bleed*." Hatred seeped into his voice with the last word. He straightened in the saddle and I saw that he held an arm wrapped around his ribs. He sat tight as a bowstring, the elegant line of his jaw clenched. He was pale, even in comparison to the others, even bearing in mind the color-leaching lights along the freeway.

"I thought you'd have healed." One of the hounds made a lunge at the open window, his teeth snapping shut centimeters from my arm. I flinched back, and the hound dropped a few inches, smacking his chin on the window frame. He let out a high-pitched yelp of pain and backed off, snarling at the car.

"We do not heal well from iron," Cernunnos said, warm liquid voice still distorted with fury. The dog slunk toward his master and lay down between the stallion's forelegs, lips pulled back from his teeth as he looked at me.

"So I really hurt you," I whispered, watching the hound. Cernunnos let out a bark of laughter. My eyes snapped up to his. His distance and the stallion's restless shuffling kept his eyes from having the drowning power I remembered from the diner, but even through the amber lights, they were compelling, violent green, filled with rage.

"Oh, yes." He edged his stallion closer. The hound jumped up and slunk around to the horse's back heels, his head lowered, crimson eyes as dangerous-looking as the ivory canines. I watched them, and shrank back a little farther into my car.

"Am I safe in here?" I wondered out loud. "The steel?" I was suddenly very glad I didn't like show cars like Corvettes, all fiberglass and no substance. Petite was solid steel through and through. She felt safe.

At least, she felt safe until Cernunnos laughed, a sound that could scratch glass. "Safer than you would be outside of it. Not safe enough. Glass holds no power to hurt, and your window is open." He lifted a hand, graceful, though his nostrils flared as he pulled at the injured tissue in his side. One of his host raised a bow as tall as I was, and sighted me down the long narrow shaft of an arrow.

I saw a special on PBS once, with a Welshman demonstrating the power of a longbow. Standing much farther away from his target than Cernunnos's man was from me, he put an arrow through platemail armor, through the dummy body, and out again through the back of the platemail.

All of a sudden Petite didn't seem nearly so safe. Cernunnos edged his stallion to the side, to give his man a clear shot. The archer was tall and slender and very blond, his expression almost sympathetic and clearly bored. Shooting at mortals in tin cans apparently wasn't much sport. I certainly didn't think it was very sporting.

I flung Petite into Drive. She roared and leaped forward. Fire burned over the back of my shoulders as the arrow sliced through shirt and skin without hitting anything vital. It embedded in the passenger door with a shriek and I winced, the injury to my car more offensive than the injury to myself.

Two of the ghostly hellhounds disappeared beneath Petite's wheels, making horribly solid thunks as the Mustang hit them. For one moment, one of the host stood in my way, the bearded man on a washed-out roan. We met eyes, and I braced myself for the impact, knowing none of us, not horse and rider nor car and driver, were going to survive.

The roan gathered himself, catlike, and sprang forward, in so little time I barely saw it happen. Hooves flashed over Petite's windshield, silvery shoes glittering. I wondered what kind of metal fairy horses were shod with, and in the rearview mirror saw the roan come down lightly, back feet tucked up to miss Petite's tail end as she careened forward. The rider put a hand solidly against the roan's neck, and turned to watch me go without the slightest expression on his face.

I caught one glimpse of myself, wide-eyed with shock, in the rearview, then snapped my eyes back to the road, twitching the steering wheel as I tried to avoid a hellhound stupid enough to fling himself at the Mustang. I heard Petite dent, but the dog bounced off with a painful yelp. It rolled away and didn't get up again.

Another sharp *chink* sounded as Petite's wheels squealed and we tore off down the freeway, zero to sixty in about seven seconds. I pushed her up to ninety for maybe two minutes, then remembered the cop who'd stopped to talk to me, and slowed down to somewhere around the speed limit. There was no possible way a herd of riders were going to catch me.

Petite coughed, a sick little sound, and lost power for a second.

"Oh, no." I breathed the words over the steering wheel. "Be good, girl." The gas gauge was lower than I remembered it being, but it had been a long drive out to the airport. Petite coughed once more, then rumbled contentedly. I sank down in my seat. "Good girl," I whispered again. "That's my baby." Don't *tell* me talking to your car doesn't help.

She coughed again, lurching as her power drained. "What? What'd I do? I'm sorry I left you in a garage for four months. This is fun, though, right? Out on the freeway, driving fast? This is fun. Come on, baby. What's wrong?"

We drifted to the side of the road, where she gave one more pathetic little cough and settled into a heap with an apologetic sigh. I leaned my forehead against the steering wheel for a moment, eyes closed. "Okay, nice cop lady," I mumbled. "Come check on me again." I opened my eyes and peered under the top curve of the wheel at the dashboard. The oil was fine, but the gas registered below empty. "You got thirsty awfully fast, baby." I flipped the hazards on and climbed out of the car.

The smell of gas was so strong I wondered why I hadn't noticed it before. *Oh, adrenaline, maybe?* a sarcastic little voice in my head said. I hoped I'd always talked to myself that way, and it wasn't another shiny new improvement that came along with being a shaman. There was a neat round hole through Petite's purple rear end, punched through steel like it was plastic wrap. I popped the trunk, my teeth set together, and sure enough, there was another neat round hole jammed at an angle down through the bottom of my trunk. The gas tank was directly below the trunk. I hardly needed to get the flashlight out of the glove compartment to go look, but indeed, there was a neat round hole

through the gas tank, too. An arrow was caught in it, scant centimeters from the asphalt. If the arrow'd been another two inches
longer, sparks from the metal rubbing the freeway as we sped
along would've blown me and Petite to Kingdom Come.

I lay on my back, methodically going through all the swear
words I knew. When I ran out, I yanked the arrow out through
the hole it'd made and climbed to my feet, staring at it.

Then I broke it into as many pieces as I could with my hands,
dropped them, jumped up and down on them and swore some
more. A few cars whisked by. One slowed way down so the guy
in the passenger seat could take a photo. The flash made a sharp
shadow on the freeway wall, and I started laughing with furious
hysteria as I kicked the arrow bits around and crunched them
under my boots. It took about a minute for the novelty to wear
off. When it did, I kicked the rest of the wood shards out of my
way, got my jack and emergency duct tape out of the trunk, and
jacked the car up so I could reach the gas tank.

Duct tape may not be the ultimate answer to everything, but it's
the best temporary ultimate answer I know. I slapped two strips
together and taped them over the hole with four more strips, then
crawled out from under the car to watch Cernunnos's host, led by
the god and a riderless horse, gallop down from the sky toward me.

For a moment I just stood there, disbelieving. This couldn't be
happening.

The riders forged on. Apparently it was happening. I kicked the
jack out from under Petite, who crashed down with a reproach-
ful smash. "Sorry, baby." I flung the jack back into the trunk and
yanked the four-month-old five-gallon emergency gas container
out all in the same movement. I untwisted the top and poured a
good-sized splash of gasoline out onto the concrete, and because
I was moving too fast to be careful, also all over my shoes and shins.
"Shit! Dammit, dammit, dammit, shit!" At least I was pretty sure

I'd gotten rid of any water that might have built up. I poured the rest into the tank, threw the open container into Petite's trunk with another apology, slammed the trunk closed and ran around to the driver's side just in time to almost impale myself on Cernunnos's sword.

"Oh, look," I said. "You got a new one. And me without my knife." I flung myself sideways into the open door, across Petite's front seats, as the stallion lunged forward, bashing into the door.

I scrambled for the gas pedal and the ignition all at once. Unfortunately, my head was in the passenger footwell, and the pedal and ignition weren't. I twisted around and sat up as a battle-ax smashed into Petite's windshield. The glass shattered and caved inward, breaking the ax's momentum only enough that it didn't follow through to split open my breastbone. For a couple of seconds I stared at the gleaming metal edge that had broken through the windshield, then cranked the ignition. Petite, God bless her little steel soul, started with a roar.

The ax tore along the windshield in an agonized squeal of glass and metal as I gunned her and shot forward. The thick-shouldered rider on the roan reflected in the side-view mirror for a moment, startled and shaking his hand where Petite's sudden acceleration had yanked the ax away. Then he caught up his reins and whirled the roan around as Cernunnos's host began to give chase.

A little belatedly, it occurred to me that running from a hunt was probably the very last thing I wanted to do.

Somehow, I didn't find any comfort in the thought that it was probably *going* to be the very last thing I did, either.

I knew foxes went to ground when they were hunted. I couldn't think of a single damned place that I could go to ground. I didn't know how, but Cernunnos had found me toodling down the freeway. That didn't bode well for losing myself in a crowd, and besides, it was already clear the Hunt didn't mind a little property damage. I hardly wanted to give them the opportunity to start killing people. Other people, at least. They already seemed pretty fixed on the idea of making me dead.

Petite's speedometer climbed past ninety before the Hunt showed any sign of losing ground. Cernunnos fell back, distantly reflected expression furious, and all the host but one slowed with him.

The riderless horse came on, eating great lengths of distance with each stride. It was impossibly fast, and so clear in its motions that even watching in the mirror I could see the play of muscle under pale golden fur, bunching and releasing as it closed the distance between us. I glanced at the speedometer; I was still adding speed, heading toward a hundred now.

And the riderless horse was gaining on me.

A knot of certainty tied itself in my stomach. If Cernunnos were uninjured, all the Hunt would be gaining on me now. I pressed on the gas pedal and Petite responded with an urgent hum of power as she accelerated. I wasn't surprised that the riderless horse still gained on me. I topped out at one-fifteen, more out of respect for my poor abused car than being unable to push her faster, and watched the pale horse put on a surge of speed that brought it to my side.

It—she—was huge, as tall as Cernunnos's stallion, and there was nothing wasted in her. Admiration and envy stung through me. Sparks flew where the mare's feet made solid connection with the ground she ran on, though I'd seen the Hunt ride and I knew she wasn't constrained by having to run on the unwieldy concrete. She ran effortlessly, stretched out long and lean, so low that her head was nearly on a level with mine.

She turned her head to look at me, the almost-full-on gaze that horses do, and the weight of her body followed the lead of her head. For the second time in under an hour I braced for the impact, and for the second time the horse avoided it, this time with a tiny burst of speed. She leaped ahead of me, one hoof denting Petite's hood as she sprang into the sky and wheeled, galloping back to the Hunt, leaving me careening down the freeway alone.

CHAPTER EIGHTEEN

Thursday, January 6th, 5:13 a.m.

I woke up on my feet, my heart pounding wildly in response to a mysterious sound that I couldn't hear anymore. The lights were very bright and my glasses were smashed against my face in a tell-tale fashion that suggested I'd gone to sleep on my face while wearing them. It took a few seconds to recognize my own living room and the indentation in the couch pillows as where I'd been sleeping. The details of getting home were sketchy, but since I was here, apparently I'd made it. The distressing noise sounded again. After another several seconds I recognized it as the doorbell. I staggered to the door, adjusting my glasses as I pulled it open. Gary stood there, looking unfairly awake. He laughed at me.

"Morning, sweetheart. Thought you said you'd be awake."

"Did I say that?" My voice was hoarse. I waved him in and staggered to the kitchen to get a glass of water. Gary followed, brandishing Cernunnos's sword, and dropped into what looked to me like a pretty good en guarde position. Of course, what I didn't know about fencing would fill a library.

"You did." He made a little feint at me. I batted at the sword before I remembered it was sharp, and was glad I hadn't made contact with it. Gary straightened up. Old guys weren't supposed to look that solid. I examined that idea while I drank my water. It wasn't like I knew that many old people, but the ones I saw usually seemed to look fragile.

"I want to look like you when I grow up," I told Gary blearily. He laughed again.

"When you're old, you mean. I tell you what, lady, if you don't quit doing whatever it is you did to your car, you're not gonna get old. What happened?"

"Cernunnos and I had a race down the freeway. I got away, but they chopped up Petite. I think it was a draw. D'you want some water?" I admired how matter-of-fact I sounded. I was trying hard not to let myself think about the damage to my beautiful car. If I started crying, I didn't think I was ever going to stop.

Gary wrinkled his eyebrows and looked at me for a while. When I didn't find anything else to say, he asked, "You gonna be all right here alone, Jo?"

"Oh, sure. I was right. Today's the day. So I just gotta live through it." My words were slurred. I turned around and poured the rest of my water into the coffeemaker and dug around for fresh grounds and a filter. My coffee cup was already sitting under the drip. I didn't remember putting it there.

"You're sure today's it?"

"Herne said so. No." I shook my head, frowning as I tried to form enough coherent thoughts to elaborate. Gary scowled at me expectantly. "Verified it. Marie told me. Us. She was right. Herne was all upset I knew, so she had to have been right." Gary didn't look like I was clearing matters up any. I groaned.

"I'll tell you on…" I looked at my fingers vacantly, like I had the date written on them. "It's Wednesday? I'll tell you Saturday." That sounded like enough time for me to catch up on my sleep.

"It's Thursday," Gary said.

"Saturday," I said firmly. Gary grinned.

"No, Thursday."

I glared wearily at him. He laughed and held up his hands, Cernunnos's sword dangling from his fingertips. "All right, I'll stop giving you grief. Kids these days. No sense of humor." He waggled the sword at me. "What should I do with this?"

I discarded the first two suggestions that leaped to mind as being unnecessarily rude. Gary grinned like he knew what I was thinking, and put the sword on the kitchen table. "I'll just leave it there," he suggested.

I nodded. "Good idea." Gary stood by the table a moment, still looking expectant, and I dredged up a sleepy scowl. "I hate morning people," I told him. He laughed and held up his hands again.

"Okay, okay, I know a hint when I hear one. Stay alive, why doncha?"

"I'm trying," I promised, and let him find his own way to the door. It was only ten feet. I figured he could make it. The water turned slowly into coffee, dripping steadily into the coffee cup. It was a pink cup. I didn't consider myself a very pink person, but it had my name on it, so I'd bought it. When it was three quarters full I stuck the usual pot under the drip, filled what was left of the cup with milk and sugar, and went to turn on the computer screen.

The Wild Hunt rode out of the screen at me, in such fine detail my first thought was that I wouldn't put artwork that good up on the Net without degrading it some, to make it harder to copy. Then my hands began to shake and I had to put the coffee cup down as I stared at the painting.

It was good, maybe of professional caliber, but it was also terrifyingly accurate. Cernunnos's eyes were filled with the unholy green light that would haunt my nightmares if I ever again got enough sleep to dream. The elegant bone horns swept back along his skull and he smiled as he urged his stallion onward. The silver animal's broad chest so well rendered I half expected it to pull in its next deep breath as I watched.

Beside Cernunnos, almost in front of him, ran the pale gold mare who'd kept pace with me only an hour or two earlier. She wasn't riderless, though: a feral-eyed child with hair as wheat-pale as Cernunnos's rode high in the saddle, mouth open in a shout of joy at the speed his horse ran at.

Others of the Hunt poured down out of the fog, riding down from the sky, the dark shadows of rooks around their heads and the sleek white bodies of the hellhounds running at their heels. Even rendered indistinct by fog, I could pick out the shape of the thick-shouldered man, and the archer. I leaned back and picked up my coffee cup just to give my shaking hands something to do, and took a sip. Not enough sugar. I took another sip, staring at the painting. It was titled *And A Child Shall Lead Them*. Whoever had painted it had seen the Hunt.

In fact, he'd seen more than I had. There wasn't any child riding with Cernunnos now. I found the artist's e-mail address and scribbled out a note. Is it scribbling if it's typing on a keyboard? It seemed like scribbling.

Hey. I just came across your painting of the Wild Hunt, and it's incredible. Scared the hell out of me, in fact. It's so real I'm gonna guess you're not going to think I'm crazy when I tell you I've had a run-in with Cernunnos myself, that he almost killed me. But there was no kid riding with him. Can you fill me in on who the child is? It's important. Please write back.—Joanne.

I sent it and immediately regretted it. For a couple of fruitless

that kid. Herne and the Hunt were both in Seattle. It stood to reason that the missing child was, too. All I had to do was find him.

All.

I got dressed, printed out a copy of the painting, and went to the police station.

CHAPTER NINETEEN

I stopped by The Missing O on the way and got not only an apple fritter, but also a four-man police escort, headed up by Bruce, to the station. "It hasn't been that long," I pointed out. "I'm pretty sure I can still find my own way in."

Bruce grinned and put his hand on top of my head, pushing me into a slump. I was ushered past Morrison's office in a little herd of grinning cops.

"You're going to get in trouble." The other three peeled off, leaving me walking down the hall toward Missing Persons with Bruce.

"My car really needs a tune-up." Bruce shrugged. I laughed. "You could set up your own cottage industry, Joanie. Become the department's personal mechanic. It'd beat foot patrol."

"In exchange for meals?" I asked, amused. "I still need to pay rent, Bruce."

"Well, you don't have to take it out in trade. You could, y'know. Charge."

"Right, except for you, 'cuz Elise makes awesome tamales, and except for Billy, because he and Melinda bring me clothes shopping, and except for——"

"All right, all right." Bruce laughed, waving a hand. "I get your point."

"And then the guys who aren't taking it out in trade get jealous," I went on, feeling ridiculously cheerful, "and next thing I know the Better Business Bureau busts me——"

"Very alliterate," Bruce interrupted approvingly.

"Thanks. And then I'm on the wrong side of your bars here and not only do your cars break down horribly, but I get all gray and long in the tooth and none of you will sneak me doughnuts in the morning. It'd be a terrible tragedy, Bruce, I'm telling you."

He laughed. "You forgot fat. If we're sneaking you all those doughnuts, you'd not only get long in the tooth and gray, but fat. We don't exactly have exercise equipment in the cells."

"I said you *wouldn't* bring me doughnuts, but so what, now you're bringing doughnuts but not letting me out for my morning constitutional? Man, you think you've got friends, and look what happens."

Bruce pulled the Missing Persons' office door open and leaned heavily on the knob, looking at me. "You're in a good mood this morning."

"What you mean is, I'm remarkably chipper for someone who got switched to a job she never wanted and then suspended, and who's been running all over hell and breakfast getting herself involved in murder cases, right?" I leaned in the door frame and lifted my eyebrows at him.

He pursed his lips. "Obviously that's not how I would have put it, but yeah, that's about what I mean. Morrison was already in when I got here this morning. Came out to tell me not to let you in, then went back into his office. He's wearing the same clothes he was yesterday."

I clucked my tongue to mask a sudden seizure of guilt. "I told him he should still be letting his mother dress him. Why'd you sneak me by him if he said not to let me in?"

Bruce held up three fingers in a Scout's oath. "I never saw her, Captain. She must've come by while I was in the bathroom." He blinked, wide-eyed and innocent.

I laughed. "The other guys gonna say the same thing?"

"What other guys?"

"You're a doll, Bruce. If Elise weren't scary, I'd give you a kiss for being such a good guy."

Bruce held up a hand at a fraction over five feet and raised his eyebrows. "Elise? This Elise? Little Elise?"

"Little is hardly synonymous with sweet-tempered. She'd beat me up."

"Nah. You could just put a hand on her forehead and lean away. She wouldn't be able to touch you." Bruce fell silent for a moment, then cleared his throat. "You don't, ah. Have to repeat that."

I giggled. "If I ever need to blackmail you, I'll use that."

"You would, too." Bruce smiled, then sobered. "Really, Joanie. You doing okay?"

"Aside from the murder, mayhem, inexplicable activities and new job description, I'm perfectly fine." I saw the worry in his eyes and smiled. "I'm all right," I said a little more gently. "A little giddy on caffeine and too little sleep this morning, and I've got an awful lot to do today."

Bruce nodded. "Still coming over for dinner tomorrow?"

Oh, God. I'd forgotten. "Yeah, but call me before you leave work, or I'll probably sleep through it. It's gonna be a late night." I just couldn't fathom being lucky enough to wrap this whole mess up by noon. It was a nice thought, though.

"All right." Bruce tilted his head at the main office. "You might want to pull a fire alarm instead of risking Morrison on your way back out. He really doesn't want you to be here."

"I know. But there's stuff I need to do." I ducked into the Missing Persons' office.

Even Morrison's desk wasn't quite the picture of efficient chaos that the MPO was. Every spare inch was covered in photographs and drawings, sometimes years' worth. Active cases were out on desks, and heavy dark gray steel cabinets lined most of the walls, so overstuffed they looked like caricatures.

For some reason, I found the MPO to be the most depressing branch of the department. It had a desperation to it, especially in the walls of missing children, that none of the other departments had, not even homicide. It wasn't that homicide was lacking the desperation, but it was filled with other things, too. Anger, betrayal, passion. Missing Persons was bleak.

I stood in the doorway and realized that I could feel that desolation far more deeply than I ever had before. This was a good place for the new me to go if I ever decided I needed just a little push over the edge toward suicide.

"You coming or going, Joanne? Either way, make up your mind. You're letting a draft in." The woman who appeared from around the corner was dark-haired and attractive in a no-nonsense way.

"Hi, Jen. I was looking for you."

"You're not supposed to be here." She came forward to shake my hand. Jennifer Gonzalez always shook hands when someone came into a room. For the first time I wondered if it gave her a sense about the person she couldn't get from just looking at him.

"You psychic, Jen?" I asked. Her eyebrows rose.

"Don't have to be psychic to know you got suspended. It's all anybody's been talking about since yesterday morning."

"Well, it's good to know I don't even have to be here to destroy productivity. Morrison must be so pleased."

"Morrison's pretty shook up, especially with the high school yesterday. Give him a break, maybe." Jen hitched one hip up onto a desk. "Whatcha got for me?"

"A semi-missing person." I hesitated. "My life's gotten a little weird this week, Jen…"

She pointed two fingers at my right cheek. "So I've heard. They're taking bets on whether you've been assigned to visit the shrink yet."

"Heh. Not yet."

"Good, that's where I put my money. All right, so who's missing? I'll trust it's not you, missing your mind." Jen's eyes sparkled, just a hint of laughter. I smiled lopsidedly.

"I'm pretty sure I am, but I'm not looking for it right now." I unfolded the enlargement I'd made of the missing Rider and handed it to her.

"This is a painting, Joanne."

"That stunning grasp of the obvious is why they pay you the big bucks, right?" I leaned against another desk. "The kid on the gold horse is the one who's missing." I held my breath for a few seconds. "The problem is, I'm not sure if he's real."

"Well, he's a she. Not that it'll help if she isn't real, but at least you'll be looking in the right half of the population." Jen handed the printout back to me, her eyebrows lifted in amused challenge.

I stared at her, then took the paper to stare at it. "How can you tell it's a she?"

"Why do you think it's a he? Look." Jen leaned over the page and traced the line of the kid's shoulders, then a fold in the fabric of his shirt. "It's a teenager. The collarbone and shoulder are awfully delicate, even for a skinny boy. And her biceps are pressed in to make the line of the chest smooth on the outside, but the fabric's filled out and wrinkles here like there's flesh there. A boy skinny enough for that shoulder breadth almost certainly wouldn't have anything like enough muscle mass to fill out the shirt that way, even if there wasn't enough shadow below to indicate breasts. It's an androgynous kid, but it's a girl. When was this painted?"

I gaped at her and the painting, back and forth. Now that she'd pointed out the error of my ways, I could see the feminine traits, but left to my own devices, I'd have been looking for a boy until doomsday. "Uh." I lifted my eyebrows, trying to remember. "I think it had a copyright date of last year."

"All right. Assuming this is based on a real person, which, frankly, is a hell of an assumption, Joanne—"

"I know," I interrupted. "But it's all I've got to go on."

Jen nodded. "Taking that assumption as writ, you're looking for a girl somewhere between twelve and fifteen, maybe slightly older, probably not much younger. Now, also assuming she has a real life from which she is missing, when would she have gone missing?"

I shook my head. "I'm guessing any time from around the solstice up till...today. I don't know."

Jen studied me. "You're not making this easy, Joanne. Can you tell me why you're not sure this girl is even real?"

I wrinkled up my face, then dropped my chin to my chest. It took more than a minute to nerve myself up to talking again. "The other visible riders in the painting are real. Based on real people, I mean. But they're not..." The only person I'd said this to so far, at least in a straight-forward fashion, was Billy. I'd snapped at Morrison, but I never expected *him* to believe me. I discovered that I desperately wanted Jen to believe me, but I knew in her position I never would have. "They're not human," I said very quietly.

Jen was silent. I stuck my jaw out, setting my teeth together, then forced myself to look up at her. She had an expression of sympathy that was worse than outright mockery. "Look, I'm really *not* crazy—"

She held up a hand, then took the paper back. "I'll put out a bulletin to see if anyone matching the description has gone missing in the past two weeks. Are the eye and hair color accurate?"

I took a breath. "The coloring for other people in the painting is dead on, so I think hers is, too. So yeah."

"Okay." Jen glanced at the clock. "It'll probably be ten or so before I get anything back, maybe even later. Want to meet me for coffee around then?"

I managed a weak smile. "Thus getting me out of here before Morrison sees me? Yeah. Around the corner?"

Jen nodded. "Yeah. Make it ten-thirty. Do you have a cell phone?"

I shook my head. "I'll call around ten-fifteen to make sure we're still on."

"Okay. See you in a couple of hours." Jen picked up a sketch-pad from a desk and went back around the corner. I stood where I was for a minute, pressing my lips together. I wanted to ask why she believed me, but I was afraid she'd say she didn't. I decided I'd rather not know I was being humored, and edged to the door, cautiously tugging it open. Would skulking around draw attention, or should I brazen it out and try to slip past Morrison that way?

Having worked myself up into a fine dither, I opened the door farther and peeked out.

"You're causing a draft!" Jen shouted a few seconds later. Guilty, I slipped into the hall and closed the door behind me.

Rather anticlimactically, I made it all the way to the garage entrance—the back way in—without encountering the Dread Morrison, whom I'd worked up as being nearly as bad as Cernunnos, by now. Nearly. Despite not knowing anything about cars, Morrison had never stuffed a sword into my ribs, and that had to count for something.

"Here, hey, can I help you?" A blond guy a couple years older than I was stood up from behind a car, a tire iron held behind his shoulders like Bo's baseball bat. I froze, then scowled.

"Did they hire you about three months ago?"

"Sure did. If you're here about the computer loan, I swear the check's in the mail."

I looked down at myself. I never thought I looked like a bill collector before. Did bill collectors wear jeans and sweaters on the job? Maybe they did. "Actually," I said to my feet, and looked up again, "I'm a mechanic."

There was a phone in the garage I worked at in college that whoever was closest was supposed to answer. Whenever I did, the person on the other end would always ask to speak to a mechanic. Whenever I said I was one, there was always a long deadly silence, no matter if the caller was male or female. The blond guy produced the same kind of long deadly silence. I seriously considered kicking him. "No," I said, "really. They gave you my job."

His eyes widened. "You're Joanie?"

Wasn't that nice? They talked about me enough for him to know my name. "I'm Joanie," I agreed. "You're...?"

"Incompetent, compared to you, I guess. Do me a favor, won't you, and walk on water. The guys've been swearing you can do it."

Somehow, I didn't think I had a new friend here. "Only at Easter. Sorry if they've been giving you a rough time."

He gave me an unfriendly look. "It got worse a couple days ago. When you got back."

"Sorry," I repeated. "I think they thought I was like their mascot or something. The Girl Mechanic." He was good-looking, in a tall, blond, broad-shouldered, Thor-like way. If you like that type. Which I did. And we obviously already knew we had cars in common. It was too bad he'd set out to dislike me. "Is anybody else around?"

"They went for coffee."

"You don't like coffee?"

"I don't like crowds."

He was a real charmer. Kind of like a pit viper. "Right," I said. "And two's a crowd. I'll just get out of your hair." His long, thick, blond, wavy hair. I needed another cold shower. I glanced at the car he was working on as I went by, and cleared my throat. "That's Mark Rodriguez's car. Check the axle alignment. I never saw anybody yank more wheels out of whack than Rodriguez." What the hell, Thor was determined to dislike me anyway. He and Morrison could have a nice bitchfest about me someday. "Brakes probably need work, too. He's got a lead foot for braking."

Thor gave me a look over the top of the car. "He brought it down for brake work," he admitted. I felt just a little smug. "Hang on," he said. I looked back over my shoulder. He took a hand off his tire iron and spread his fingers at the car. "Aren't you gonna show me your stuff?"

"Never on the first date, mister." Pleased with myself, I stuffed my hands in my pockets and went out whistling.

It was probably inevitable that Morrison was at the street corner. He opened his mouth and I held up a hand. "Go talk to your boy Thor in the garage," I said. "He doesn't like me either." I stepped around him and got far enough down the street that I thought I was actually going to get away with it before he caught up with me.

"I'm addicted to the doughnuts, Morrison," I interjected into his next indrawn breath. "Can't help myself, there's just nowhere else in the city that makes them quite like The Missing O. Swear to God, that's all I'm here for. A nice apple fritter." Maybe I could keep this up and just not let him get a word in edgewise. It sounded like a good plan to me.

"I'll buy you one," he offered with a tight smile. I crinkled up my face. Not only had my nefarious plan not worked, but apple fritters were filling and I'd already eaten one.

On the other hand, I couldn't pass up the opportunity for Morrison to spend money on me, even if it was only a dollar twenty-nine. "You talked me into it. Be careful, though. People will talk." Bruce was right. I was in a good mood. If I closed my eyes and concentrated a little, I could feel the city's people, millions of lives wrapped up in their own quick paces. I could affect them if I chose to.

I could also walk right out into traffic. Morrison's big hand closed on my shoulder and hauled me back from the curb. My eyes snapped open and I stared up at him. "What the hell do you think you're doing?" we both barked, and then neither of us would give in to the little surge of laughter the doubly demanded question deserved.

"I've known geniuses who couldn't be trusted to keep their heads from the clouds long enough to cross a street, Walker. Are you gonna turn into one of those?"

"Why, Morrison." I grinned after all. "Are you saying you think I'm a genius?"

"Oh, for God's sake." He let go of my shoulder and crossed the street. I followed, trying not to give in to the urge to do a little jig. Even if I did get killed, I'd gotten the better of Morrison three or four times inside of a day. It seemed like a pretty good legacy, just then.

The Missing O was incredibly busy, the whole neighborhood stopping by for their morning cuppa joe. The garage crew was there, so I made Morrison stand in line while I said hello and collected hugs. They departed en masse when Morrison returned with not only an apple fritter, but a hot chocolate for me, too. "Why are you being nice to me?" I asked suspiciously. I took a bite of the fritter, though. It seemed unlikely that he'd gotten the barrista to poison it.

"I didn't want to deal with the paperwork I'd have had to fill out if you'd walked into traffic." He sat down. "Sit."

I sat. He'd just bought me breakfast, after all. "Glad to know you're only being self-serving. For a second there I thought you might be concerned. What do you want, Morrison?"

"People walking out into traffic does concern me. What do *you* want?"

I lifted my eyebrows. "Love, justice and world peace. But I'll settle for solving a murder."

"You're sus—"

"Suspended. Yes. We've been over that. What's your point?"

"I could fire you for insubordination."

"Fine. Fire me. I'll go get Henrietta Potter to hire me as a private investigator." That wasn't a bad idea, now that I thought of it.

Morrison set his coffee cup down and held up a thick finger. "One," he said, "you don't have a P.I. license. Two." He held up another finger. "You don't know much about investigating anyway. Three, this is personal for you. Personal gets in the way of impartiality. And four, you irritate me."

I held up four of my own fingers, then folded them down and closed my thumb over them, jabbing at my own jaw. "And five, on general principles?" I asked. Morrison picked up his coffee again, almost smiling.

"Don't tempt me. What were you doing at the station?"

"Why do I bug you so much?" This was probably not the time

to get into it, but I was suddenly incredibly curious. Morrison arched his eyebrows. "No, really," I said. "I mean, I know we got off to a bad start, although I still can't believe you didn't know a Mustang from a Corvette—"

"I was never into cars."

"Obviously. What *were* you in to?"

Morrison stared at me over the edge of his coffee cup, then put it back down. "Being a cop."

"What, when you were like nine? Fifteen? You wanted to be a cop, not to drive fast cars and pick up girls?" I took an incredulous bite of the apple fritter.

"Yeah. I never wanted to be anything but a cop. And that, Walker, is why you irritate me." Morrison looked like he was at war with his own body language, trying to force himself to relax back into his seat while the intense low pitch of his voice drove him to lean forward, speaking to me sharply.

"You fell into a job I spent my whole life working for. You irritate me because I think being a police officer is a calling and a solemn occupation and you're carrying a badge without it meaning a damned thing to you. You hang out with my officers in your off time, being just that damned cool, an attractive woman who talks cars and drinks beer and arm wrestles. None of them give a damn that you were in the top third of your class at the academy and that you're wasting your skills in Motor Pool playing with engines. But it bugs the hell out of me. *That* is why you irritate me."

I gawped at him. Morrison exhaled loudly and looked away. "What were you doing at the station?"

Thank God he'd said something else. I might've gawked at him the rest of the day, unable to speak. Attractive? Morrison thought I was attractive? Morrison knew where I'd graduated in my class? Christ, I usually played that down. He had to have looked it up.

Morrison thought I wasn't, for God's sake, living up to my potential?

I swallowed the impulse to apologize for disappointing him. "How do you know I was at the station?" It was a stupid question, but it was marginally better than apologizing.

Morrison just looked at me. I shrugged, took a sip of my hot chocolate, and nearly choked. It was mint-flavored and topped with whipped cream, the way I like it. It didn't go at all well with apple fritters, but to the best of my recollection, I'd never once ordered hot chocolate with mint while Morrison was around. I stared at the cup, then stared at Morrison, while he looked almost perfectly bland. I bit down on rabid curiosity and refused to ask, taking another sip of chocolate instead, just like he hadn't completely outmaneuvered me. Twice.

"I was seeing if anyone had filed a missing persons report," I said when I put the cup down. I couldn't think of anything to tell him but the truth. Besides, Jackson had told me I wasn't a very good liar. If a dead man could see through my lies, there was no way I could fool Morrison. "I don't think anything's going to come of it, but it's worth a shot."

"Who's missing?"

"A kid. A girl. Maybe. I mean." I closed my eyes. Here I went again. "She might be missing, if she's...real."

When I opened my eyes Morrison was looking at me like I'd lost my mind. "You think someone who might not be real is missing," he said in disbelief. I cringed.

"I know she's real. I don't know if she's got a day-to-day ordinary life to be missing from." One like I'd had until the beginning of the week. I ran my fingers over the scar on my cheek, then rubbed the heel of my hand against my breastbone. I wondered if the nervous hollow feeling there would ever go away. Morrison watched me.

"That diner had security cameras, did you know that?"

I looked up and shook my head, suddenly grateful for the hot chocolate. I took a sip before getting up the courage to ask, "And?" I had the hideous feeling the tapes had all been wiped blank, or had recorded static. It would just figure.

"I watched the tape this morning. Right from you and your friends walking in to you coming back from the dead. I didn't believe you until then."

"You believe me now?" My voice sounded very small and hopeful to my own ears.

Morrison took another sip of his coffee. "You should have a hole in you."

"You want I should flash you and show you that I don't?"

To my surprise, Morrison grinned. "Maybe another time." I gaped again. I didn't know Morrison knew how to flirt. Particularly with me. "I didn't believe your friend Mrs. Potter, either."

"Despite being faced with direct evidence? You're a contrary bastard, Morrison."

"Indirect evidence. I didn't see it happen, and the hospital security tapes show you flopping over her and then getting up. And then Mrs. Potter getting up a few minutes later."

"C'mon, Morrison, how direct do you want?" I was arguing for something I considered impossible three days earlier. Oh, what a tangled web we weave.

"It's piling up in your favor." Morrison took another sip of coffee, then put the cup down. "Which is why I'm considering the possibility that you might be of some use after all."

That, somehow, didn't sound like something I really wanted to hear. A cold little ball of dread formed in my stomach and started sending tendrils out through my guts. "What happened?"

Morrison took a deep breath and leaned back in his chair. "Henrietta Potter was murdered this morning."

CHAPTER TWENTY

Black fog rolled into my vision, narrowing it down until all I could see was Morrison, and even he looked distant and unreal. The memory of Mrs. Potter's bright eyes and crisp speech blotted him out for a few moments. Then my sight expanded again, the edges brightening to white until I could see the entire café. It disappeared in a flash of brilliance. I stood alone in the star field again, shouting for help, and no one came.

There was a distant hunger, though, a mawing blackness between the stars. It drew closer as I shouted, like a great cat studying its prey before it pounced. I hadn't noticed it before, but I suddenly remembered Coyote's warning that speaking with the dead could be dangerous. I was very sure the darkness was home to the danger. I shouted for help one more time, into silence too immense to even echo. The stars blurred away into images that raced by, too quickly to comprehend, until the doughnut shop resolved itself around me and Morrison was crouched beside me, shaking me.

"...nne? Joanie?" he said distantly, and then, sharply, "Jesus, Walker. What the hell was that?"

My vision pounded back into focus and I whimpered, lifting my hands to my temples. I felt like I had a three-day hangover. "She was fine last night."

Morrison straightened, looking down at me. "Yeah, well, apparently getting to know you is bad for people these days." He moved back to his side of the table, frowning as he sat down again. "If you hadn't pulled that stunt at the hospital last night—"

"—she'd still be there under guard and alive," I finished in a miserable whisper. Morrison glanced up.

"No. She *was* there under guard. If you hadn't pulled that stunt, they probably would have thought she died from complications, but half the staff saw she'd been healed up. Still, the wound that killed her was nearly identical to the original." Morrison was silent for a long moment. "How the hell did you do that?"

I closed my eyes, remembering the absurd car analogy. "Do you really want to know?"

"Yeah. I really want to know."

I took a fortifying sip of my chocolate, then spoke to it. "I had a near-death experience Monday morning. It's apparently not uncommon for people with shamanic potential to be jolted into an awareness of that potential in near-death experiences. In fact, there are whole rituals...nevermind. Shamans are healers." That much, at least, I'd grasped. "Healing requires belief." I looked up. "I've never been big on belief." He let out a snort of amusement. "But you'd be surprised at how far getting a sword punched through you and waking up unscarred will go for a girl's belief."

"I might be," he said noncommittally, and waved his doughnut, an unfilled maple bar, at me. "Keep talking."

"The shaman has to believe, but so does the one being healed." I picked at my apple fritter, eating little bites. "She was unconscious. I guess it's harder to have an opinion when you're unconscious. She's really dead?" My voice was hollow. Morrison nodded.

"She's really dead."

"I liked her," I whispered. I wasn't going to cry in front of Morrison, dammit. Especially when I didn't have my contacts in as a cover-up.

"Shit happens," Morrison said. I looked up, angry, and caught the flash of frustration in his eyes. Maybe it wasn't as easy for him as he pretended it was. I'd give him his white lies if he'd allow me mine. We were both silent for a few seconds, composing ourselves without looking away from one another.

"So why did you tell me this?" I finally asked. Morrison finished his doughnut and his coffee, then compulsively straightened the silverware on the table before answering. I watched, fascinated. Captain Michael Morrison was not a particularly fastidious man. "You're fidgeting." What a wonderful place the world was, that Morrison could be made to fidget. "Am I one of the suspects again?"

He glared at me, which seemed to restore his equilibrium. "Do you have an alibi for five o'clock this morning?"

I blinked at him. "Astonishingly, yes. Gary dropped by at about ten after."

"Then you're not. Who's Gary?"

"My secret lover, Morrison, who else? He's the guy who was with me when I met Marie. When we found her body. The cab driver. He was at the hospital last night. Big guy. What's it to you, anyway?"

"Oh, Mr. Muldoon. Didn't know you were on a first-name basis with him."

"Just because I've known *you* for three years and I'm not on a first-name basis wi—" It occurred to me that he'd used my first name, when I'd blacked out a few minutes earlier. I wouldn't have sworn Morrison even *knew* my first name. "My life has gotten very peculiar all of a sudden," I said a little randomly. "Maybe I should go now." I stood up.

"Siddown."

I sat down.

"What was Mr. Muldoon doing at your house at five in the morning?"

"Do you want to know professionally or personally, Morrison?" Sarcasm seemed like a good way out of bewilderment.

"Professionally," he said icily.

"Well, then, I probably shouldn't answer that question without my lawyer present, should I? For Christ's sake, Morrison. He was dropping something off before he went to work."

"What?"

"Work. You know. That thing that I don't have to go to right now, 'cuz some bastard suspended me?"

Morrison turned purple. I felt better about the world. "What," he said precisely, "was Mr. Muldoon dropping off at your house?"

"That," I said just as precisely, "is none of your fucking business. What's going on, Morrison? Five seconds ago I wasn't a murder suspect and now you're treating me like one." Gary'd said Morrison liked me. It was absurd, but it was a nice cheap shot and I wasn't feeling big enough to pass it up. "If it weren't completely insane, I'd say you were jealous."

"Oh, damn," Morrison said, all wide eyes, "I've been found out. What was he dropping off?"

"A rapier," I said in disgust. "The one Cernunnos stabbed me with. I thought it would make a nice souvenir. If Mrs. Potter died of a wound like the one she had earlier, the rapier is shaped all wrong to make it. I hate to disappoint you. Now what the hell do you want from me, Captain?"

"I want you to find this guy," Morrison snapped. I thought it was probably a lot easier on both of us, being angry. We could deal with each other as adversaries that way, like we were used to. Moments of connection only made things screwy. I spread my hands, lacing my voice with sarcasm.

"Yes, sir, Captain, sir. Why the change of heart?"

"Because he walked past two of my guards and murdered a woman this morning, and nobody saw a thing." Morrison set his empty cup down on the table, hard. "You tell me something, Walker. If I bring you in on this case as a specialist, are you good enough to solve it?"

"No," I said flatly. Morrison leaned back, shocked. Shocked, and maybe a little admiring. Silence drew out a moment before he dropped his chin, half a nod.

"Why not?"

"Because I don't know what the hell I'm doing, Morrison. I'm in way the hell over my head in a game I don't know the rules to. I'm learning awfully fast, because as near as I can tell, anything else and I'll end up dead." I took a sip of chocolate and put the cup down with a little less emphasis than Morrison had. "I'm not good enough," I repeated, "but I don't know what other choice you've got."

Morrison swung his hand around in a little circle that meant "keep talking." I pushed my cup away. "Cernunnos and Herne. They're at the heart of this. Know anything about them?" Morrison snorted. I half smiled. "Neither did I. Cernunnos is a god, Morrison. An ancient Celtic god. He's not evil. He's more…" I closed my eyes, envisioning the hard narrow face and the slender fey lines of the god's body. "Primal. The other one, Herne, is his son. And he *is* evil. He's twisted. He's the one killing people. And I don't know why. What I *do* know is that Cernunnos tried to kill me so I couldn't bind him again, and Herne seems to have developed a personal vendetta against me. So no matter what else, I'm the one you need because they're both gunning for me."

"Can you stay alive?"

Electricity ran through me, a warm shock of life that made my fingers tingle. For a few seconds I forgot about the world, feeling the blood coursing through my veins, feeling the beat of my heart and the fill and fall of my lungs. My vision blurred again, and, looking at my fingers, I could see each layer of skin, the tendons and the bones, as clearly as I could see the coffee cup my hands were wrapped around. One more blink, and I would see the cells skimming against one another, bouncing off the surface tension that was skin. Instead I shivered and met Morrison's eyes. "I decided this morning that I wasn't going to die."

Morrison's shoulders were lifted, expression tense. "Your eyes are the wrong color."

I blinked. "What?"

His shoulders went even tighter. "They're—they were—gold."

"Must've been the light," I said in a very low voice. Morrison thrust his jaw out. Yeah, I didn't believe me either. Great. Marie's eye condition was catching. I hoped I didn't start doing the pupilless eye thing. "I decided I wasn't going to die," I repeated, hoping Morrison would let it go. I carefully looked at the table, rather than at my hands. I wasn't that keen on seeing my own bones.

He was silent a few seconds before I heard him shift into a more relaxed position. "Nobody gets up in the morning planning to die, Walker. Well," the cop in him amended, "hardly anybody."

I swallowed. "No, I don't think you understand."

He spread his hands. "Enlighten me."

"I can see my bones," I said softly, and dared look at my hands again. They looked perfectly normal. "I don't think anything short of brain death can kill me right now."

"Are you telling me you're immortal?"

"No," I said irritably, "I'm telling you I can stay alive."

"Why the hell didn't you just say so?"

The wall was too far away to hit my head on. "Does that mean I'm no longer suspended?"

Morrison puckered up like he'd bitten into a lime. "Yeah."

"Do I get my badge back?"

"Yeah."

"Cool," I said. "How about a raise?"

Morrison's expression went tight.

"Hey," I said, "I'll be detecting. Detectives make more than mechanics, don't they?"

Morrison stared at me. "I really don't like you."

I smiled brightly. "It's good to be back. Boss."

It took half an hour to get my badge back, and another forty minutes on the range blowing holes in distant targets to assure Morrison I wasn't going to shoot myself or anyone else unless I intended to.

"That's it?" I asked when Morrison pulled off his earmuffs.

"That's it," Morrison said, still scowling. "You shoot well."

"Thank you. My dad taught me. I like rifles better, but I guess one wouldn't fit in a shoulder holster." I tucked the gun awkwardly into that self-same holster. Morrison looked like he felt better when I didn't do it well, which made no sense. I would rather someone very competent was tucking and untucking guns from shoulder holsters, but Morrison was having a bad enough morning as it was. For once I let it go, asking, "That's it?" again. "Now I get to go out and defend the innocent and protect the weak with my trusty sidearm and shiny star?"

"I can't tell you how much I already regret this," Morrison growled. I sighed happily.

"No, but you'll probably try."

"This isn't a game, Walker." Morrison was grim.

"No shit."

"Walker." There was a dangerous note in Morrison's voice. I looked up from trying to arrange my pistol comfortably and rubbed the heel of my hand over my breastbone. It was getting to be a nervous habit, but I couldn't get over the uncomfortable feeling of having a sword through my lung.

"I know, Morrison. Okay? I never planned to be a card-carrying member of any law enforcement agency. I really just wanted to be a mechanic. I'm not taking this lightly."

"Coulda fooled me."

I shrugged my jacket on over the shoulder holster to see how it fit. Not bad. Felt a little strange, but I'd adapt. "Did it ever occur to you that might be the point?"

He was quiet and I looked up again to see a faintly satisfied expression in his eyes. I wished he wouldn't do that. Discomfited, I adjusted my jacket again and shifted my shoulders. "There anything else?" I asked my shoes. They were regular waterproof winter boots today. Morrison was wearing similar shoes. We were the same height. I smiled a little.

"Just try not to talk to the press, Walker."

I dropped my voice half an octave. "This is Special Investigator Joanne Walker, reporting for *Tabloid TV.* I've learned that at the heart of a series of bloody murders is an ancient Celtic god and his estranged son. Tune in at eleven tonight for more."

Morrison tried not to grin, producing a wicked sparkling smirk instead. It wasn't James Dean, but it wasn't half-bad. "None of that."

"Who would believe me?"

"The kind of people who watch tabloid TV. Just spare the department the embarrassment. Spare *me* the embarrassment."

"Why, Morrison, are you asking me a favor?"

He glared at me. Funny how most of the time, Morrison's glares made me feel better about the world. They were a kind of reliable continuity, and I could use all the continuity I could get right now. I held up a hand. "All right. Look, this will be over tonight, Captain. Anything else can be dealt with to—Monday."

"To Monday," Morrison echoed, eyebrows elevated.

"I promised myself I could sleep until Friday afternoon if I lived through this," I explained, "and I've got a dinner date Friday night, so I'm not doing anything else until Monday at least. And right now I'm going up to see if Jen's got anything on the missing persons report I filed."

"Who's the date with?"

I smiled brightly. "Wouldn't you like to know?" As I brushed by him, I had the distinct impression that he would. I took the stairs up into the station two at a time, grinning. Morrison followed me up and broke off at his office, muttering under his breath. I went back to the Missing Persons department and Jen lifted her voice as I came in the door.

"Got nothing."

I puffed my cheeks out, closing the door behind me, mindful of the draft, as I went around the corner to her desk. "Too early?"

She nodded, waving a handful of papers at me. "Too early, or your girl isn't missing. I did a sketch from the painting and sent it out around the city. Nobody's reported back. You're early, by the way."

I glanced at a clock; it was five after ten. "Yeah, well, the world just came to an end."

"Really?" Jen looked around. "I always thought all the paperwork would go up in flames when the world ended. One big poof of spontaneous combustion. I'm disappointed." She sounded like she really was.

"Maybe it was just one of the seven signs of the Apocalypse, then." I took out my badge and tossed it on her desk. I was going to have to get a flip-open wallet. All of a sudden, I understood their appeal: not only did they not require digging through pockets, they were terribly theatrical.

Jen put her papers down and picked up the badge. "You've gotta be shitting me."

I cackled. "Nope."

"This didn't come out of a Cracker Jack box, did it." The statement verged on a question, full of disbelief. I cackled again, unable to help myself.

"Nope. Straight from Morrison's own delicate little hands, it is."

Jen stuck a pen in her mouth and looked up at me. She quit smoking two years ago and still put things in her mouth. Around the pen, she asked, "What'd you do, blo—"

"He's not my type," I said hastily, and grinned. Jen grinned back.

"Nobody's your type, Joanne. How'd you swing this?"

"His idea. Look, if nothing turned up yet, how about I swing by in a few hours just to see if I've gotten lucky? Maybe around two."

"Sure. Hope I've got something for you." She took the pen out of her mouth and grinned again, intoning, "Officer Walker."

I was going to cackle for the rest of the day. Possibly for the rest of my life. I flicked her a jaunty little salute and took the main route through the station as I headed for the front door. Morrison gave me a dour look as I went by his office and waved. I left feeling like I could conquer the world.

CHAPTER TWENTY-ONE

Walking out of the police station in a mood that good probably meant somebody was preparing to kick me in the metaphorical balls. I stopped at the base of the steps, looking up and down the street. That line of thinking, I realized, along with my newfound phenomenal cosmic powers, would probably get me kicked less metaphorically and more physically. They say the world is what you expect it to be. Right now I was expecting to get kicked. Not a good attitude.

On the other hand, I was expecting to live through it, which was a lot more than I'd thought when I got up. Does it count as getting up if you only slept in the shower?

"My name is Walker," I said to no one in particular, grinning like a fool. "I carry a badge." My badge and I went down the street, the latter of us whistling cheerfully. About half a block past The Missing O, I remembered I'd tried to set up a lunch date with Kevin Sadler, and swung back to the café to check my e-mail. The barrista, grinning, offered up another apple fritter, and I realized I wasn't anywhere near hungry enough for lunch.

Of course, it wasn't anywhere near lunchtime, either. There was a note from Kevin suggesting we meet at a restaurant near where he lived. I got directions and fired off a note agreeing, then headed out onto the big bad street again.

The problem with being cocksure and full of attitude was that it frequently hides the fact you don't know what the hell you're doing. I strode along briskly for about two blocks, then wondered where I'd parked my car and what exactly I thought I *was* doing.

The car, I could find. I backtracked another half block and climbed up on the hood. It wasn't Petite; she was in no shape to be driven. It was a rental, a recent-model Ford with about as much personality as a shoelace. I really hoped I wasn't going to have another run-in with Cernunnos while I was driving it. My paycheck was going to stretch thin covering Petite's repairs, nevermind the rental agency's fees if I got one of their vehicles hacked up. I was practically certain my insurance policy didn't cover acts of gods.

I studied the wall on the opposite side of the parking lot, not really seeing it. I'd been running on adrenaline and impulse for days now. There were fourteen hours until midnight, so no matter what, this thing was almost over. The idea of uninterrupted sleep was nice, but I'd already spent way too much time reacting instead of proacting. I needed to think. The concrete wall across from me, however, seemed to be inspiring very little other than a pleasant pale haze in my mind.

I didn't know why I was assuming whatever was going to happen would happen at midnight rather than, oh, noon, or an even more civilized four in the afternoon. Midnight was just very dramatic.

It was also the final quarter of the day, as winter was the final quarter of the year. It was good enough for me.

I'd read that some shamans could get a sense of the future by opening themselves up to the world and accepting all the possibilities. The most likely possibilities would be brighter, more obvious senses of potential. It was a matter of disregarding time and trusting the universe. I already knew what sliding through time felt like, although that had been going backward, and controlled by Herne. Undaunted, I closed my eyes and tried to stretch myself forward in time.

It was like a cat trying to push its way out of a canvas bag. I prodded around inside my head, feeling muffled, with absolutely no sense of direction. The only information I was able to gather was that Manny, a big guy working on a building at the back of the lot, thought that he was underpaid, overworked and ready for lunch, and I got that from his rarely pausing soliloquy, not through any more esoteric means. Finally I sighed and opened my eyes. Herne had guided the last jaunt through time. Left to my own devices I didn't know which buttons to push.

That left logic, a commodity I had precious little of just now. Logic and a police badge. "Okay." I frowned at my feet. Overlooking the fact that Herne and Cernunnos both wanted to kill me, there was something else they had in common: Marie.

What the hell did Marie have to do with any of it? I took the tooth she'd stolen from Herne out of my jeans pocket and examined it. I'd like to say I studied it thoughtfully, but I'm afraid it was more of a vacant gaze. You take what you can get, I guess. The tooth didn't do anything, just gleamed in the mild way that ivory gleams. I curled my fingers around it and went back to staring across the parking lot at the wall while I thought.

"She saw dead people," I said after a while, out loud. Thank goodness there was no one around to hear me talking to myself. Well, there was Manny, but Manny was talking to himself, too, so I figured he didn't have any room to point fingers. "No, no, *Billy* sees dead people, Marie saw when people were going to die. Okay. So…what?"

The wall across from me was not forthcoming with answers. I pinched the bridge of my nose and puffed my cheeks out and lay back on the hood of the car and made faces at the sky. Then my stomach muscles contracted involuntarily, pulling me halfway upright again. "Oh shit!"

Manny looked over his shoulder at me, quizzical and concerned. I waved him off and my hand kept up the motion, flapping with excitement. "She saw when people were going to die!"

Cernunnos is primal, not evil. That's what I'd told Morrison. Cernunnos had told *me* he wanted his freedom. To ride as he chose. Without the girl, he could do that. Why replace her, then? Why add another Rider?

Unless without a full complement of Riders, the Hunt couldn't fulfill its—sacred?—duty. Unless without someone who knew which souls to harvest, someone who knew who was going to die, they couldn't Hunt at all.

Without the child, there's nothing to stop them from riding forever. The e-mail had told me that, although God knows if it was safe to be trusting random e-mail sources. On the other hand, the guy'd been able to paint the Hunt, so I was willing to run with it. It wasn't like I had a lot of other really good options.

I closed my eyes and pressed my fingers against my temples, working my way through the idea methodically. My mind felt thick and puddinglike. "Okay. The girl led them to souls, and led the Hunt back to the Otherworld. No, wait." I thumped the heel of my hand against my forehead. For somebody who'd been hit on the head and knocked around as much as I'd been the past few days, I certainly seemed willing to keep doing myself injury. And the thumping wasn't helping me think. I stopped.

"She *bound* them to the Otherworld." I opened my eyes and

stared at the wall. "How can she bind them anywhere if she's a girl here?"

The wall continued to not provide answers. "She's not here," I said to it in despair. "I don't know why she's not with Cernunnos, but it's not because she's here. Dammit." I'd sent Jen on a wild-goose chase. I put my hands over my eyelids and thunked the back of my head against the windshield. "So where is she? How do you lose a Rider of the Wild Hunt?"

You don't. You *steal* a Rider. I let out a half-voiced yell and sat up again. "That's what he's done!"

Manny turned around and eyed me. I shrank down into myself and gave him a cheesy, apologetic smile, but as he turned away again I smacked my fist into my palm triumphantly. "He controls, that's what Adina said." God, I hoped I'd always talked to myself. I really couldn't remember. I was almost excited enough not to worry about it. Almost. "He controls the *child*. Which means he controls—oh, shit."

The Hunt. By controlling the missing Rider, the youthful one, Herne could control the Hunt. Cernunnos had to know that. That's why he'd needed Marie: to replace the child and to lead the Hunt. She could find the people whose souls needed to be taken, but she had no ties to whatever Otherworld Cernunnos and the Hunt were born to. With Marie to guide them, the Hunt could have ridden forever.

I pressed my eyes harder closed as I tried to think. "But Herne controls the real Rider," I mumbled. "Somehow. Shit. So he couldn't let Cernunnos replace that Rider with Marie, because he'd lose whatever advantage he's trying for. But what's he—"

I remembered his expression as I'd twisted out of his illusion, the glee wiped out by shock and horror as he drove his blade into his king. The same disbelief had been there when Richard had seen him hanged, not just on the face of the long-remembered man on the rope, but in the eyes of the one who'd stood behind me as he watched his own memory play out again.

The same expression had been there when Henrietta Potter had broken the circle of bodies, too. Betrayal, every time, that something could have gone so terribly wrong. I rather imagined my own expression had been similar when Cernunnos stuffed his sword into me up to the hilt, and hell, I'd meant for that to happen. Still, I hadn't thought it would hurt quite that badly. I'd be very happy to never hurt that much again.

Well, shit, Joanne. I opened my palm, exposing the tooth I held to the air. *He doesn't want to hurt anymore. He thinks if he controls— if he leads—the Hunt, he'll be invulnerable.*

The thought resonated, like a violin string, shivering through my body and out into the city. With my eyes closed I could see it stretch, vibrations shaking the air like it was water. It dove and twisted through the gray Seattle morning until I saw a startled pair of unearthly green eyes lift, then flinch away.

My eyes popped open. *Start with one true thing.* I forgot who'd said it, but it was how he always began his writing, with one true thing. I'd hit on one true thing about Herne. I closed my eyes and reached for that resonance again, confident. It lay there, just below the surface of my mind, stretched taut across the city toward Herne. All I needed was to follow it to him.

Unlike trying to stretch through time, thought and action were one. I leaped forward psychically, careening through Seattle as I followed the thread back to Herne. Pure delight and pride splashed through me, making me feel bright as a beacon. I had finally figured out how to do something right!

And then I ran up against a wall of pure granite. I bounced off so hard I recoiled back into my body and slumped into the windshield. Something dripped onto my mouth. I wiped the back of my hand across my nose and it came away smeared with blood.

My ears rang like I'd been at a concert for three hours, and my head pounded.

"Jesus, lady, you okay?" Manny the construction worker stood a few yards away from his building, a sledgehammer in one hand and a look of consternation on his face.

"Yeah," I croaked. My bottom lip was cut, too. I touched it gingerly with the back of my hand and winced.

"Looked like somebody hit you in the face with one of these, man, only I didn't see nobody." Manny hefted the hammer. I coughed and touched my lip again.

"Yeah, feels like it too." I licked at the blood and slid off the hood to see if my rental car had any tissues. It didn't. I swore, before remembering my new little trick. What did a bloody nose count as? Touchup on the paint? I closed my eyes and fell inside myself for a few seconds, deliberately reaching for the bubble of energy beneath my sternum. It responded, sending a thrill of glee through me. I laid my paint job analogy over the power, guiding it through the steps of "repainting." Primer, then the expensive glossy paint applied with an airbrush.

I sneezed explosively, my body reacting to the idea a little more thoroughly than I wanted: I wasn't wearing a protective mask, and I felt like I'd just breathed in fine paint particles. Sneezing through a banged-up nose is not to be recommended. After a few seconds the throbbing went away and I prodded gingerly at my nose and lip, testing to see if the paint job had taken. The energy coil inside me settled down, as if satisfied. All but a thread of it, at least: I could still feel the faint link to Herne, stretching right from the center of me.

My face didn't hurt anymore. I sighed in relief and let my shoulders slump.

"You some kinda *bruja,* lady?" Manny stared at me, slapping the hammer nervously into one hand.

I touched my bottom lip again and found half a grin for him. "Yeah. Yeah, Manny, I'm some kinda *bruja*. A, um, *bruja de la luz,* if there is a such thing. Don't worry. I won't put a curse on you."

"That's good. I never did no *bruja* no harm. You be careful, *bruja*. There's nasty things out there." He nodded, eyes dark and serious, then turned and went back to his work. My smile got a little bigger.

"Thanks." I slid off the hood and climbed into the driver's seat, sitting sideways with my feet on the ground. It crossed my mind again that I was way out of my league, but by now the thought was almost reassuring. At least some things weren't changing.

I'd found Herne, that much was clear. The pulsing line of truth was still pulled tight between us, disappearing into his granite defenses. If I was going to follow the line back to him, I'd have to be a little more subtle. I touched my mouth one more time and chuckled. Morrison would attest to me never having learned subtle. It appeared I was going to have to cope with a whole series of disconcerting changes to my lifestyle.

Much more cautiously, I closed my eyes and grasped onto the shimmering line that ran toward Herne. The world dimmed, like low thunderclouds had just rolled in. I opened my eyes to discover the same effect. For a moment I was tangled up in uncertainty about whether I'd opened my real eyes or my astral eyes, and that all led to wondering if I was a man dreaming he was a butterfly. The world brightened again, as if irritated with me.

"Sorry," I mumbled. The clouds rolled back in with a decided aura of "hmph."

My body stayed put, but my sense of self left it to stand in front of the rented Ford. Off to the left, Manny kept up his interminable bitching, but he glowed with contentment as he swung his hammer into the brick. For a few seconds I could see his family as clearly as if they stood around him, four-year-old twin girls and a chubby little boy barely old enough to walk, and a slender woman with a fond smile. He was planning to go home and tell them about the *bruja* he saw, who didn't curse him, and that was almost as good as a blessing.

It didn't seem very likely I was ever going to be the sort of person to go around bestowing blessings, but I made a note to send one Manny's way if I ever felt like the time was appropriate for me to do it. At the least, I could think good thoughts for him, though it seemed to me that he had the good thoughts department covered.

I looked away from Manny and toward the city. Seattle spread out before me like a computer simulation, buildings reduced to their infrastructures, thin lines against the sky that let me see through one into the next, on out to the water. The people were blurs of color, shaming the rainbow, with disproportionately high incidences of reds and oranges. I wondered what the colors meant, but they weren't what I was looking for. I was looking for a part of the city that I couldn't see.

And to the southeast, there was an area that was blocked. Not by the granite wall that I expected, but by the solidity of buildings. Bricks were as opaque as mist, and colors drained away from people until they were dull facsimiles of the rest of the city. No matter which direction I approached it from, the half-solid mist remained, too thick to be seen through, but not quite as solid as reality. I could feel Herne's presence behind the mist, his will drawing a line that he wouldn't let me cross or look through.

I let myself fade back into my body and sat blinking thoughtfully at the asphalt. I was heading to that part of the city for lunch anyway. Maybe I could narrow down Herne's location by getting inside the parameters he'd delineated. To continue to protect himself, he'd have to blur smaller and smaller regions, until I could pinpoint him. Pleased with myself, I dragged my legs inside the car and left early for my lunch date.

CHAPTER TWENTY-TWO

Of course, it wasn't that easy. I was early enough and late enough, an hour in either direction, to miss both commute and lunch traffic, but the lack of cars on the road didn't help pierce the veil of obscurity that Herne had flung up around himself. Instead of the field narrowing down, everything that I looked at with my second sight was hazy and thick, just as it had been from a distance. It was like being in San Francisco on a really foggy morning.

It took twenty minutes to find a parking place, so I ended up at the restaurant only half an hour early. I left my gun in the car and went in. By the time Kevin arrived, I was asleep at the table.

"The maître d' is complaining that you're drooling on the table," he murmured as he sat down.

"'Zno maidder-dee." I lifted my head slowly. It seemed to have gained twenty or thirty pounds in the half hour I'd been napping.

"All right," he said agreeably, "the waitress is complaining that you're drooling on the table." He smiled, and I chuckled tiredly.

"Sorry." I drank most of the glass of water that had been left for me, and rubbed my eyes. "Really long night. Keep falling asleep in the weirdest places."

"Your e-mail was from eleven or so last night. You were up after that?" He was wearing a neat, unobtrusive plaid shirt, ironed. I wondered if Adina had ironed it before she died, or if he did it himself. He looked tired, too, almost as tired as I felt, his hazel eyes sad and weary.

"Yeah, until three or four. Then I got up at ten after five, or something. It's been a rough few days." I cringed a little. I had nothing to complain about, comparatively.

He gave me his sad smile. "It has been," he agreed. "What happened yesterday?"

I made a sound of amusement as the waitress arrived, and ordered a grilled cheese sandwich. She gave me a funny look, but wrote it down along with Kevin's order and went away again. "Not exactly an upscale meal," Kevin said.

I shrugged. "I like grilled cheese sandwiches. Comfort food, you know? And I need it. The night got a whole lot weirder after I left that e-mail." I recounted, briefly, my night's adventures. Kevin blanched and looked away.

"What drives a man like that?" he asked, a low dangerous timbre in his voice. "To slaughter?"

"Statistically? Serial killers are in need of control. Our boy Herne doesn't really fit the statistics, though. They weren't meant to quantify six hundred-year-old demigods."

Kevin looked up through his eyelashes. "Is that really what you think you're dealing with?"

"Yeah." I drank what was left of my water. "He's older than I am, stronger than I am, more experienced than I am..."

"Smarter than you are?" Kevin asked with a smile. I swirled the remaining ice in the glass around, and considered the question.

"I don't think so."

Kevin's eyes darkened. "Then why haven't you caught him yet?"

"Older, stronger and more experienced don't count for anything?" I asked plaintively, and he smiled again.

"They might count for too much." The waitress delivered our drinks. Kevin nodded politely to make her go away. "Tell me again what stopped you at the airport."

I shook my head and stuck a straw in my lemonade. "I could feel it," I said softly. "The power in me to just shut him down. But it's all connected." I laced my fingers together and tugged them to the left without pulling them apart. My body tilted slightly with the motion. "I can't move part of me without affecting all of me." I tugged my hands to the other side, tilting again. "See? I move. And the city's like that, too. Probably the whole world. I think you can't move part of it without making everything shift a little.

"It wasn't that *I* was all that powerful, really. I could just *draw* on all that life, all that energy." I let my hands fall, frustrated. "But drawing on it would cost. Not me, so much, as the whole infrastructure. Taking him down then would have caused a power failure, that's how much it would take. People would have died."

"The good of the many?" Kevin asked.

"Outweighs the good of the one, yeah. In this case, the one are..." I trailed off and sighed. "Are people like Adina and Mrs. Potter. I'm sorry. I didn't see any other choice."

Kevin nodded, but murmured, "There's always a choice."

"Yeah. In this case, letting him go seemed like the better one."

"Can you live with that?"

I inhaled. "I have to, don't I? Yeah, I can. I regret it, but I can't say I'd do it differently, faced with the same choice again."

Kevin nodded again. "That's good. Living with the consequences of your actions isn't always easy. Rationality often fails."

"Yeah, well." The waitress delivered our food and I took a grateful bite of grilled cheese, surprised at how hungry I was.

"Up until a few days ago I was the most rational person you'd ever care to meet."

"You've converted?" Kevin had a vegetarian burger. I thought that was one of the weirdest ideas in the world. Those, and the fruit drinks that advertised themselves as flavors never intended by Nature. Nature, I figured, knew what she was doing. Leave well enough alone. Except cran-apple juice. That'd been a good idea on somebody's part.

Grilled cheese and lemonade, incidentally, didn't go together well. I shuddered and screwed my face up, then took another drink of lemonade. Kevin watched, amused. "You enjoy doing that?"

"Yeah." My voice was as raspy as if I'd just had a shot of whiskey. I shuddered again, happily, and took another bite of grilled cheese. "No," I added, "I haven't converted. I think I'm still rational. It's just the world's gone nuts around me. I've gotten a crash course in the esoteric. I don't have to *like* it. I just have to cope with it."

Kevin nodded again and ate in silence for a while. "So why did you want to see me?" he asked eventually. I stabbed a fry into ketchup and bit it viciously before answering.

"Where would you go if you were a demigod on the verge of making a grab for power? Oh," I waved another fry at Kevin's expression of alarm. "Not that *you'd* know, but do you know anyone who could tell me where places of power in Seattle are?"

"Is that what you think he's doing?" Kevin asked cautiously. I shrugged and shook my head.

"I don't know what the hell he's doing, except trying to kill me." That wasn't exactly true, but I'd piled enough on Kevin already. He didn't need to hear my theories about Herne's emotional problems. "I don't know how he plans to do it, but tonight is the night the Hunt is supposed to return to the Otherworld, and I think Herne's going to try to affect that somehow. I don't know what he's going to do, though," I admitted. Kevin let out a worried little sigh.

"I don't know," he admitted. "I tried to stay out of that side of Adina's life. She was very spiritual and I'm...not. I could look in her address book, if you want, and call you if there are any names."

"Names of who?" I asked. "I don't even know what I'd start looking for."

"Anyone associated with power centers. Probably not the kind of thing you find advertised in the phone book."

I made a face, drank more lemonade, and made a worse face. "Probably not. If you would look, though, it can't hurt. I'm chasing wild geese as it is. I thought I would find him here."

Kevin's expression turned furtive, and he straightened up a little. "Here?"

"In this part of the city. I linked to him, but he's blocked me. He could be in the diner and I don't think I'd know." I looked around, displeased by the thought, and caught the gaze of a green-eyed man at the counter. It took distressingly long to shake off the paranoia that settled over me like a cloak and glance back at Kevin, who looked unwell.

"I'm sorry," I said. "Maybe this wasn't a good idea. I'm not exactly the world's most reassuring conversationalist right now, am I?"

He pasted on his thin smile. "It's all right. Neither am I."

I nodded. "If you can, check her address book." I scribbled down my number on a napkin. "Thanks, Kevin. I'll get the check."

He picked up the napkin, nodding, and quietly made his way out the door. I got the check and the receipt, for the pure joy of writing it off as a business expense and annoying Morrison. Pleased with myself, I went back out into the winter afternoon.

* * *

Driving back to the U District was an adventure in burgeoning road rage. I'd caught the end of lunch-hour traffic dead-on, with bumpers to bumpers and impatient drivers leaning on their horns. Seattle'd had a reputation for having the politest drivers in America, back when. Since then, something had gone terribly wrong, kind of like…a thing that had gone very wrong. Yep, there went my grasp of metaphor. I was going to be in real trouble if I needed to do any more shamanic stuff, with that kind of visualization skill at my beck and call.

It was beginning to rain. I rolled my window down while I waited on an on-ramp, sticking my palm up to catch raindrops. Another degree or two colder, and it might snow. That would make for an exciting drive. There's nothing quite like Seattle drivers in snow.

Like the weather was responding to my train of thought, a snowflake fell into my palm, and melted. I leaned my head out the window, looking up, and got a snowflake in my eye for the effort. "Crap." I leaned back into the car. Traffic pulled forward a few meters at a time, creeping ever more cautiously as the snow began to come down like it meant it.

I hoped Kevin would come through for me. If not, I could think of two places in Seattle that seemed like obvious power nodes. One was the Space Needle, just because it *was* so obvious. The other was the Troll Bridge. It was just so bizarre I had to wonder—if I was going to acknowledge this whole other world—if it had been inspired by something more than just the sculptor's imagination.

But I was pretty sure there were more power places in Seattle than two modern constructions that might or might not have anything to do with ancient nodes. Wow, I was getting good at this esoteric speech stuff. See what a few hours of reading and some time on the Internet will get you?

The on-ramp let me access the freeway and for a while all I could think about was the other guy, and making sure he didn't run into me or anyone else. Then I began wondering if I was really affecting whether or not people were driving well, and consequently took a turn too fast and fishtailed all over the slippery road.

After that I just concentrated on driving.

It still took until almost two to get back to the station. I parked in a reserved-for-police parking spot because I could, and took the steps up through the wet snow two at a time. It felt good, not sneaking through the station trying to avoid Morrison. I even nodded at him as I passed his office, and for once he didn't scowl.

Jen was lying in wait for me, or it seemed like it. I walked into Missing Persons and she handed over a small stack of papers like she'd expected me. "Here's your girl. Assuming, which I am, that she looks a little less fey than that painting you showed me. I redrew her to send out. No responses, though—she's not missing."

I glanced down at the papers without really seeing them, then shook my head as I looked back at Jen. "I'm afraid I wasted your time. I'm so sorry, Jen." I rubbed the back of my hand against my forehead, letting the papers fan over my face for a moment. "I don't think she could've been real after all. She had to have been like the others. Not really from this world." I said that like it wasn't a completely insane thing to say. I was starting to understand the tired expression Marie had worn more than once, the one that said, *I know you think I'm nuts, and there's nothing I can do about it, but I can't change what I am, either.* I wished I could apologize to her. "I'm sorry," I said to Jen again, instead. One of the copies slid out of my fistful and I sighed, crouching to pick it up. "I really appreciate you trying to he—holy shit." My fingers, suddenly cold, lost their grip on the rest of the sheets, and a few dozen copies of the drawing spiraled down and spread across the floor.

Jen jerked to attention, looking around the room like she thought I'd seen—I hesitate to say a ghost. "What?"

"I know her." I stayed in my crouch, staring at the drawing, then swallowed and met Jen's eyes. She looked like she thought I'd taken leave of my senses. "I know her," I repeated. "I mean. I saw this kid yesterday. At the high school."

Jen had applied the coloration from the painting to the sketch. Wheat-pale hair fell around a delicate face, not precisely fey, but with high cheekbones and a small, pointed chin. Her mouth was just slightly too wide, no longer stretched in the rider's laugh, and the eyes were disconcertingly green. It was the girl from the theater, the one who'd recited the poem.

Jennifer glanced at her watch. "If that school even held classes today, they'll be over in about forty-five minutes. If you want to find her, you better haul ass."

I stared at her speechlessly, then vaulted out of my crouch and bolted for the door.

CHAPTER TWENTY-THREE

I hit the front steps at a run. My shoes, which had no traction for snow, slid, leaving three feet of skid marks before I reached the edge and went flying at a horizontal angle, feet leading. For one very brief moment in the midst of panic I enjoyed the sensation of being unanswerable to gravity.

Then gravity called me home with a vengeance.

By dint of my head being nearer to the top step than my hips were to the lower ones, I hit it first. I can only surmise that my shoulders, small of my back and tailbone subsequently and sequentially hit the top edges of the next several steps down. I was out cold.

I was getting used to states of unconsciousness bringing about states of altered reality. Bright, exploding balls of pain like silver and red fireworks were a new twist, though. I couldn't say I cared for it at all. I was pretty sure I hadn't killed myself, so I didn't know why it seemed to hurt more than having been stabbed did, but it did. It hurt a *lot*.

"Because you hit your head," Coyote said, distracted. "It's where you perceive your self as being held."

I tried opening my eyes. Stabbing daggers of green light jabbed into my brain. I didn't like it. I closed my eyes again. "Hnnng."

"Kind of an impressive wipeout," he added. "Did you actually need me for something?"

"Hnnng," I said again, and tried to shake my head. Someone drove an icepick into my skull behind my left ear.

"Good." He left me alone with the explosions of pain. Spirit guides, I decided, around shards of shrapnel slicing through my skull, were a pain in the ass.

I'd been through all this before. A little visualization, and I'd heal right up. Just a little concentration.

Too bad I couldn't concentrate with Paul Bunyan hammering my head in. Brilliant spots of light burst into being and faded out again in random patterns, whether I had my eyes opened or closed. They slid by like a starscape, while I wondered if I was going somewhere or if I'd damaged my occipital lobe somehow. I'd hit the back of my head, so it didn't seem likely, but stranger things have happened. A lot of stranger things had happened recently, in fact, so who was I to dismiss the theory out of hand?

One of the spots faded in and slid closer, growing progressively larger and resolving slowly into a more solid image. "And behold Death, who comes on a pale horse," I mumbled. The rider drew to a stop before me, smiling his wicked, devastating smile.

"I have always liked that," he admitted. Stars kept flooding by, but a dais of blackness formed under us, supporting us in the journey through the cosmos.

"You look better." I closed my eyes. Interestingly, Cernunnos's image didn't disappear. Thwarted, I opened my eyes again. It was less disconcerting that way.

"You're not so easily rid of me as all of that," he chided. I didn't want to, but I smiled.

"I should be so lucky. Where are we?"

"Your world." Cernunnos lifted one hand to make a loose fist of it. "And mine." He made a fist of his other hand, and placed one above the other so they brushed occasionally with the small motion of his breathing. He expanded that distance a little, so I could see it was there, and said, "We are here."

"Just a hunch," I said, and pointed at the fist he'd called my world, "but don't I want to be there?"

"We both do," the ancient god replied. He swung down off the liquid silver stallion and walked to the edge of the ebony dais.

"Why? I mean, I know why I want to be there. Why do you?" I watched him crouch and trail his fingers off the side of the dais. Ripples spilled back, sending wavers through the rushing stars. "Am I dead?" I asked, suddenly curious. "This looks kind of like where I met the shamans."

"You are not dead yet." Cernunnos hit the surface of space with the palm of his hand. Another shock of waves splattered the dais with a few drops of midnight. "Nor do I think that you are at the moment dying, though certainly your mortal body is injured."

"You know, I wasn't a reckless kid," I said. "This really isn't like me. Getting hurt all the time."

"Hurt is not something only the physical body feels, little shaman. There is a darkness within you. You hide it well, but it was torn open in our first encounter. Even now I see its mark on you." The god flickered his fingers, a casual gesture.

The spiderweb I'd imposed on myself as a shattered windshield flared into physical lines, a hole that ran all the way through my belly. It felt like a gunshot wound with a concussion of broken glass around it. It was worst around the hole, fogged lines held together by false plasticity. They spread out, down through my groin and into my thighs and shins, to the bottoms of my feet, and up through my breasts and shoulders and out my fingertips. I was glad I couldn't see the dark striations on my face.

It was the only thing at all that I was glad for. Pain lanced through me, memories creeping through the outlets he'd colored into my body.

I was only fifteen, and very, very naive. Fifteen and convinced it couldn't happen to me. Just like every other girl thinks. Just like every girl who was ever wrong.

First Boy. That's how I thought of him, with capital letters. The First Boy who'd noticed me. The First Boy I ever fell in love with. The First Boy, who split for his mother's people in Canada when I got pregnant.

The babies came four weeks early. The little girl, who was so very tiny, was born second. She held on to her brother's hand with all her dying strength for the few minutes that she lived.

First death.

I called her Ayita, which meant "first to dance" in Cherokee, and named the boy Aidan even though I knew his adoptive parents would probably change his name. He was almost twelve years old now and I had never seen him beyond those first few minutes. It was better that way, but it didn't stop me from wondering, sometimes, somewhere deep and private in myself where I didn't let other people get close.

I was never, ever going to make a mistake like that again.

Cernunnos tipped his head to the side, like a bird studying a worm. "I can take that pain away, little shaman." He smiled and stepped closer, until I could see nothing but his deep eyes and the wealth of power he could drown me in. He promised peace, and escape from the aching emptiness that boiled cold through my blood.

I took it.

* * *

They say drowning is an easy death. Not the panic, but the last moments, as your lungs fill with water and you stop struggling in face of the inevitable. That it's not so bad, then. That it's warm and comforting, as from water we are born, and so in drowning we return to water in death.

I'd like to know how the hell they know that.

Still, the warmth of Cernunnos's power was as great a refuge as I'd ever known. Green god, horned god, my god. I rode beside him, neither queen nor consort, but Rider of the Wild Hunt. The purpose of chaos sang in my blood, a raw sound that heeded no boundaries. I was wrapped in it, and gave myself up to it.

"Little shaman," Cernunnos said. I smiled at the name he'd always called me by, endless years of memory coloring the words with affection. "Whither wilt thou lead us?"

"To Babylon and back again, by candlelight." The nursery rhyme popped to my lips unexpectedly.

One elegant pale eyebrow arched. "Then lead us to this land of Babyl, little shaman, and together we shall see if this curse that holds us might be undone."

Curse? a very faint part of my mind asked, but the mare leaped under me, and ran with a purpose unlike anything I'd ever known. I crouched low over her neck, shouting out the glee of speed into the whipping wind. I barely guided her, my hands buried in her mane and my touch on the reins incidental. The slightest movement of my body, leaning to the left or right, sent her into long graceful curves. Behind us the Hunt ran, with Cernunnos himself at my left flank.

Is this not as it is meant to be? he demanded, silent, the question echoing in the bones of my skull. *Tell me of your pain now, little shaman.*

My pain. I remembered it, distantly. I reached for it, and found the warm green of Cernunnos's power instead. It reacted to my touch like it was the caress of a lover, filling me, pure and raw and hungry. I forgot old pain in pursuit of new pleasure. Cernunnos chuckled, low and approving, a sound that somehow carried through the chilly blackness of the star field. I threw a brilliant smile back over my shoulder, and urged the mare on, leading the Hunt.

Something was important about where I rode. The thought was fleeting, and Cernunnos curled around it. *Of course it is important, little shaman,* he murmured reassuringly. *You guide us in our eternal duty.*

"Is that it?" I asked. The task seemed ever so slightly alien, but I couldn't understand why. My thoughts felt thick and slow: it was the inability to speak to Cernunnos's mind. Had I known the trick of mind-speech? Had I forgotten it?

Only will it, and it will be so, Cernunnos said. His power flowed around me, a safety net. I glanced over my shoulder. The rest of the host leaned into their horses, keeping pace. To a man they watched me, dusky eyes drinking me down.

Only will it, one or many of them whispered. Once more something struck me as odd in the multitoned encouragement. I grasped for the something, and it darted just out of reach, a bright flicker like candlelight racing beyond the mare.

Only will it, I agreed. I wondered how I'd forgotten the ease and intimacy of speaking mind to mind.

Yours is a hard road to travel. The touch of Cernunnos's mind was comforting. *For time unending it has been, little shaman. Very soon, though, that will change, and your task will be no more than the rest of us bear.* The pleasure in his sending was a flare of warmth, and I responded without meaning to.

I'll be glad to carry a lighter load, my lord master of the Hunt, I replied. For an instant, I felt a tug through my belly, like a claw hooking my spine and dragging it forward. Images of a misty world ran through the claw and directly into my senses: a gray sky and trees of muted greens, glimpsed through swirling fog. It smelled rich and peaty, like good earth just tilled, and the wind that shook the leaves was cool and crisp with the scent of salt water. There was laughter, crystalline musical sound that cut through the fog. Everything inside me screamed *home!*

The mare's breakneck pace slowed a little.

Not yet. All the vast power of the god came to bear upon me, inside a breath. The misty, shadowy image that cried *home* shattered under his will. New pain, as deep as the old, erupted inside me.

Give it back! I screamed, but Cernunnos's power locked me away from it, solid as iron chains.

Bring us to your Babylon, he ordered, and I flung myself straight in the saddle, throwing my hands high.

"We are here!"

The stars stopped around me with earth-shaking suddenness. I closed my hands, drawing down the starscape like it was a curtain. From behind it emerged a city, growing up around me as if it had always been there.

Structured of stone, it sprawled out with a decadent elegance, broad streets spreading in all directions from where we stood in the center of a square. Towering, twisting spires rose high into the sky, like Joshua Trees reaching a thousand feet tall, gnarled and intricate and as old as time. They stood out, bright white against a blue-gray sky, with branches knotted together to form looping walkways in the air.

Hanging jungles grew from those walkways, thick vines and wild flowers so potent I could smell their rich scent from hundreds of feet below. They writhed with more than the wind, as if they rather bordered on sentience. Leaves and branches wove in and out of one another, creating hammocks and nests as if the trees themselves enjoyed the intimacy of touch. I watched a child fling himself off the walkway with a piercing shriek of joy. The gardens caught him and built a ladder so he could climb back to the pathway above.

Men and women of all ethnicities and colors walked the pathways with no hurry at all, stopping to speak with one another. Their voices rose in a babble, over the sound of wind. If I listened with my ears I heard every tongue imaginable, but when I listened with my mind, I understood every word that was spoken.

Not one of them took notice of the Hunt's arrival like it was anything untoward, though a number of passersby nodded and smiled or called their greetings. I watched curiously as a man and woman met and walked together to the base of one of the Joshua Tree spires, where the man lowered his head to kiss the woman's throat.

Nor was theirs the only such display. Littered here and there, sometimes half-hidden in shadows, but as often not, couples tangled together without the slightest regard for who might be watching.

"What is this place?" Cernunnos asked, fascinated. "What is this Babylon of yours, little shaman?" He dismounted, and with a flick of his fingers sent the host down a dozen different streetways, then offered me a hand as I dismounted as well.

"A land of excess," I said slowly. Remembering was hard; there was a fog in my mind, and it wanted me to remember the passion of the Hunt, not ancient legends from the world I'd once called home. "Where all men could speak to one another, where gluttony and lust held sway over intellect and reason. They say God was angered by the excess and destroyed the city, so that men could no longer speak to each other and instead were made to fight over misunderstandings. They say that to return to Babylon is to embrace corruption." I looked around, listening to the rise and fall of voices and laughter. "It feels to me like...peace."

Cernunnos placed two fingers over my breastbone, where his sword had punched through me a few days earlier. The sudden memory made me blink and shiver before it faded again. "And tell me, little shaman," he said, "are you at peace now?"

A warning note twinged inside me. There was something I was forgetting, a reason not to be at peace. But Cernunnos smiled, shockingly green eyes inviting, and I forgot it again. "I am, my lord master of the Hunt."

"I am so very glad." He curled his fingers under my chin. His hands were cool, even through the leather gloves he wore. I shivered a little. "Don't be afraid," he murmured, and kissed me.

Fleetingly, the thought went through my mind: *This is not right,* and was followed hard by, *when was the last time someone kissed me?* Cernunnos's power closed around me then, no longer a safe blanket of comfort, but tendrils of penetration, enticing passion from deep within me. I made an uncertain sound, closing my eyes against the pleasure in Cernunnos's gaze. Green fire filtered through me, swirling up through my groin and into my breasts, sweet and hungry. His kiss was a taste of freedom, unlike anything I remembered since childhood. It was sanctuary.

"What a child we will make together, little shaman," Cernunnos whispered. "What power, what passion he shall have."

My eyes flew open, reality crashing back into my bones with a gut-wrenching jolt. "No!" I shoved him away as hard as I could. The god stumbled back, his green eyes alight with outraged astonishment. "No," I panted again. "No, and no, and *no,* Cernunnos, I am not yours, and *I will not make that mistake again.*"

Passion ignited into rage in his eyes. "Think on your choices, shaman," he snarled. "Choose me and I'll grant you eternity, riding at my side. You will guide me as I guide the Hunt. Choose otherwise, and you and this place end now." He threw his head back and let out a bellow like a wounded hind, a deep throbbing sound that sent tremors through the Joshua Tree spires. Around us the host faded back into being, unconstrained by observing niceties like traveling through physical space or linear time.

I stared at Cernunnos, far too aware of the heat still in my blood and the taste of his power, almost visible as he stood before me. At least the fog in my brain seemed to have burned away. "You need a thirteenth." I'd figured that much out. Damn, I'd been right. Go team go. But I'd thought he needed Marie specifically. "You need someone to ride in the child's place so you can ride. It can be anybody? You're offering that to *me?*"

"Not anyone," Cernunnos said through gritted teeth. "Someone with power. Someone who can bear the weight of my touch without shuddering. Someone who can bear a child to replace the one that is lost."

Tears burned hot in my eyes, an unexpected pang of shared loss lighting the air between the ancient god and myself. For a few seconds I could hardly breathe, my throat tight with memory and loss. The fire in Cernunnos's eyes burned dark with frustrated rage and sorrow. I shivered and wrapped my arms around myself, holding myself still to prevent myself from going to him and trying to ease his pain.

"Choose," Cernunnos demanded. He closed his fist around the stallion's reins and mounted the animal in a single graceful motion. He looked terribly tall, fury stretching the elegant features gaunt, his power lending breadth to the slender form. He didn't move, but I thought that if he turned his head I would see faint mists of green fire drift away, trails left by the anger in his eyes.

I remembered the sudden longing the silver misty world had

woken in me, and took a startled breath. "She's your daughter. The last Rider, the one who's missing. And she's strong enough to call you home. But me, I'm not from that world. I can resist that call. But I'm not—" I shivered again, staring up at him. "I'm not like Marie, my magic doesn't work like hers. That's why you need me to make a—" I couldn't say the last word, not out loud, not to the primal god on his horse before me. "My magic would overrule the power of that world, the one the Rider calls home. You could use our—" I still couldn't say it. "You could stay in my world. Led by a child with shamanic magic."

"A child would be best," Cernunnos whispered. "Blood of my blood is bound to me whether we like it or not. Blood of your blood would bear much stronger ties to your world than any child I've sired before. Blood of our blood would be *rich* with power." He lifted his stallion's reins in a clenched fist. "But you, little shaman, you will do. Choose!"

"Just as long as you keep me drugged." I touched my temple, remembering the green fog of his power. "No. No!"

A feral grin slipped over Cernunnos's mouth. "Do you know what this place is, *gwyld,* that you have brought me to? Neither your world nor mine. There is no binding here."

A sick feeling knotted my stomach. Cernunnos grinned again, sharp canines curving over his lower lip a moment. "A land of peace, shaman. They are traveling souls, without defenses, and we are beyond worlds." He threw his head back again, ash-colored hair flinging back over his shoulders, and let out another spire-shaking bellow, this one more like a hunter's horn than the wounded stag. When he lifted his head again, his brilliant eyes were narrow slits, full of smug anger. The crown of horn lost its subtlety, sweeping back from his skull in elegant, heavy whorls. His neck and shoulders thickened as I watched, body changing to support the greater weight of the full crown. "You have chosen," he snarled. His smile was wicked, so sharp it made me cold. "We ride."

Morrison waved smelling salts under my nose and I came awake with a shock.

CHAPTER TWENTY-FOUR

"No!" I sat up with a shriek, knocking Morrison's hand away with all the strength I had. The vial of smelling salts flew out of his hand and bounced over the steps, skidding to a halt in the slushy snow. "No, no, oh, shit, no, I've got to go back, I've got to get *back!*"

Morrison stared at me, dumbfounded. I wanted to hit him for not understanding, even though I knew I sounded like a lunatic. "I've got to get back!"

"Funny," Morrison said through clenched teeth, "I thought you just came back."

"No, no! There, out there, I just let Cernunnos loose on, oh, fuck, I've got to get back!"

"Should I sedate her, Captain?" someone behind my back asked. Morrison looked up, disgusted.

"Sedate a head injury. Bright idea there."

All I needed was the reminder. Pain exploded through the back of my skull like it had been lying in wait. It grew progressively worse as I continued to shout at Morrison, frustration and fear rendering me more incoherent by the moment. Finally he picked up a handful of gritty slush and threw it in my face, which shut me up, as much to his surprise as mine.

"Once more," he growled, "from the top, this time with complete sentences."

I took a deep breath and wiped my face clean. Both actions sent ripples of pain down my back, muscle seizing up where I'd hit the stairs. I was sitting on the second one from the bottom, now. Apparently I'd not only wiped out, I'd then slid. And the police station had security cameras running twenty-four/seven. I'd end up in their Greatest Hits collection as soon as they were sure I was all right. I reached back and touched the back of my head. My fingers came away bloody and slushy. Muscles in my back spasmed again.

I explained in as few sentences as I could. Morrison's expression went from disbelieving to disappointed to dismayed as it became clear I, at least, didn't think I was hallucinating.

"You used to be so straight." He stood up, looking frustrated and disgusted. I decided not to follow suit just yet, trying to concentrate enough to heal myself through the rhythmic throbbing of my head. I couldn't, gave it up as a bad job, and concentrated on climbing to my feet instead.

"I've got to find a way back." I clutched at Morrison's sleeve to keep myself upright. It wasn't dignified, but it was almost worth the startled expression it garnered. Maybe I needed to work on the damsel in distress routine.

"You've got a job here to do," Morrison said dismissively. I stared at him, not quite believing I'd heard him right. "Come on, Walker." He handed me off to Bruce, who made quiet fussing sounds while I looked slack-jawed at Morrison. "You want to save a world, save this one. We've got plenty of lost souls right here."

"You don't get it." I let go of Bruce's arm and immediately wished I hadn't. The deed done, though, I took a step forward, trying to tower over Morrison. My shoes weren't tall enough. "For one thing, that place was full of souls and a lot of them were *from* this world. The Hunt's harvest there is going to leave a lot of catatonic dying bodies *here*. But that's not really the point." My voice was rising again. For some reason it did that around Morrison. "The fucking *point,* Morrison, is that I screwed up, and there is *nobody else* to clean up my mess. I've got to get Cernunnos back into *this* world so he and Herne can be dealt with *here*. Ca-fucking-piche?" I'd somehow ended up nose to nose with the police captain again, shouting at him from so close I could have kissed him.

I wished I would stop thinking that.

Morrison held his mouth tight, meeting my eyes without giving an inch. "I understand," he said, low and harsh, "that you are an officer working in my department and you will God-damned well do as your superior officer tells you to do."

"Fine," I said, "I fucking quit." From behind me, the collected officers let out a collective gasp. I yanked the badge out of my jacket pocket and threw it into the slush at Morrison's feet. Snow and water sprayed up over our shoes. His gaze flickered to the badge in the snow and back up to mine.

"You don't want to do this," he said very quietly.

The real bitch of the thing was, he was right. But there I was with the badge in the snow and my dignity all tangled around it, and hell if I could think of a way to back down. The rage poured out of me, though, leaving me tired and remembering that I was injured. My head throbbed along with my heartbeat.

"Then let me do this my way." I didn't have any fight left in me, suddenly. Standing up took almost everything I had, and my voice was quiet. "I have a responsibility, Morrison. You're the one who wanted me to live up to my potential." I spread my hands. "I'm trying."

Morrison looked down at the badge in the slush again, and back at me again. "Somebody get her a paramedic." He stepped around me, leaving me on the second step of the station. I crouched very cautiously and picked up the badge. I guessed I'd won that round, but it didn't feel like much of a victory.

Bruce offered me a steadying arm as I straightened, ushering me into the station. I leaned over his desk and punched out numbers on his phone while Linda, one of the paramedics, tried to doctor the back of my head. It hurt and I kept flinching. She kept swearing.

"Tripoli Cabs," a rapid-fire, unfriendly male voice said into the phone almost before it rang. "This is Keith. Where do you need a pickup?"

"I don't. Can you get a message to one of your—ow!" I glared at Linda, who glared back. "One of your cabbys," I said resentfully.

Keith's voice became a few notes more unfriendly. "This isn't a public service line, ma'am."

"This is an emergency. Please?"

Deep, put-upon sigh. "It's always an emergency. Yeah, what do you need."

"Can you tell Gary Muldoon that Joanne called, and she needs him to go by her apartment, get her drum and come to the police station as soon as he's off work?"

"A drum is an emergency?" Keith mumbled, but I could hear the tap of a keyboard as he took the message down. "Joanne, get drum, police station. He gets off work at two."

I looked for a clock. It was three minutes to two. "I hope you can catch him, then. Thank you. I really appreciate it."

"Yeah, yeah. That's what they all say, but does anybody ever send chocolate? I got work to do, lady."

I grinned at the phone and hung up instead of asking if employees of Tripoli Cabs were contractually obliged to call women "lady."

"Bruce?"

"Yeah?" He sounded relieved that I remembered his name. Linda put something that boiled on the back of my head and I shrieked. Bruce jumped, then glared resentfully at Linda, saving me the trouble of doing it again.

"Where do you order flowers and chocolates from when you're in the doghouse with Elise?"

He pointed at the phone. "Speed-dial number nine," he said in a voice that dared me to laugh.

I laughed. It made my head hurt more, but it was worth it. Linda swore again and reached over my shoulder to grasp my jaw in her hand. "Hold still," she said impatiently, and swabbed the boiling painful stuff onto the back of my head again.

"Ow! What is that, battery acid?"

"Hydrochloric," she corrected as I dialed Bruce's flower shop. "There's all kinds of gook in there. Stop whining."

"Gook," I said. "Is that a technical term?"

"Thanks for calling Forgiven Again Flowers. Hi, Bruce," the woman on the other end of the line said. I laughed again, flinching away from Linda.

"Not Bruce," I said. "Just borrowing his phone."

Three minutes later a vase of wildflowers and a box of chocolates were set to be delivered to Keith at Tripoli Cabs, the ibuprofen was starting to kick in, and I was feeling slightly better about the world.

"I faxed that sketch over to Blanchet High," Jen said from behind me. I turned around. Linda swore yet again and stalked off, muttering disclaimers of responsibility for me. I watched her go, nonplussed, then blinked at Jen.

"And?"

"And there are a thousand students there. The office didn't recognize her off the bat, but they offered to send the picture over to the yearbook staff to see if anybody knew her. I'm waiting for an answer back from them." She shrugged and wandered back down the hallway.

"Thank you," I said, not very loudly, but she threw a smile over her shoulder at me. I sat on the edge of Bruce's desk and rubbed my eyes. Little stabs of pain winked back through my head, but comparatively it was like a soothing massage, so I kept rubbing.

"When was the last time you slept?" Bruce asked. I smiled lopsidedly.

"I donno. I slept in the shower. I'm fine."

"You look like the walking dead."

"Thank you." I laughed. It didn't make my head hurt as much, for which I was grateful.

"Why don't you go take a nap until your drum gets here?" he suggested. I had to admire the perfectly calm collected way he said that, like it was completely normal for people to hang around police stations waiting for drums.

"With a head injury?" I asked, bemusedly echoing Morrison.

"I don't think it'll kill you."

"Mmmph," I said, and looked around the station. Truth was, I couldn't think of a damned thing I was good for until Gary and my drum got here. My head hurt less, but still too much to concentrate through, and I was waiting on the yearbook staff at the school. "Yeah," I said, nodding a little. "If Jen gets anything from the yearbook staff before Gary gets here, send her to wake me up, okay?"

"Sure. Now go on. You'll only get a few minutes anyway."

"Yeah," I said again, and wove my way through desks toward the drop-spot neé broom closet. Much too small for an office, it was ventilated and kept fastidiously clean. Cops whose desks couldn't be seen under the crap they had piled up were known to change sheets on the drop-spot cot, and it got swept out twice a day whether it needed it or not. It was the only really clean area in the whole station, and it stayed that way because everybody knew that sooner or later they'd be collapsing into the cot. Nobody wanted to sleep in someone else's grunge.

I was asleep before my head hit the pillow, which was nice. I didn't need another impact, no matter how soft, to make my head ache more than it already did.

I woke up to the scent of coffee under my nose. Gary sat on the floor beside the cot, Indian-style and grinning, holding a cup from The Missing O a few inches away from my face. I blinked at him slowly, then seized the cup and took a grateful slurp. Not just coffee. Mint-flavored mocha, heavy on the chocolate but with twice the caffeine.

"You are a god," I announced as the first slug trickled down my throat and spread out to coat the lining of my stomach. "How'd you know about the mint?"

Gary chuckled. "Blond guy at the front desk said it was the best way to wake you up. I was polite and didn't ask how he knew."

I snorted. "I think Bruce knows the best way to wake everybody who works in the North Precinct, including Morrison."

"Yeah? Whaddaya do, grab a bullhorn and bellow from far enough away that he can't shoot you?"

I grinned sleepily. "Probably. I've never had to try. What time is it?"

"'Bout two-forty. I got here fifteen minutes ago but they sent me for coffee. Said you needed the sleep and the caffeine. Some little Spanish lady has some papers for you."

I sat all the way up, holding the coffee cup out. "Jen. She's Hispanic, actually. She must've found the girl. Kick ass. Hold this, I gotta change the sheets."

"You've got to what?" Gary watched in bemusement as I stripped the sheets off the bed and put new ones on. "You ever been in the army, lady?"

"Nope. Why do you keep calling me that?"

"You do corners like you were," he said approvingly, then lifted his bushy eyebrows. "Calling you what?"

"'Lady.' I know it's been over nine hours since you saw me and you're old, but I did tell you my name." I took my coffee cup back and grinned at Gary's faint look of offense.

"Part of my charm," he said with immense dignity.

"That's what I told Marie," I reminded him. "I was kidding."

He spread his hands. "Turns out you weren't. Who knew?"

"Are you decent in there?" Jen banged on the door and pushed it open, thrusting a handful of papers at me. I took another sip of my mocha and held the cup in my front teeth while I shuffled through the papers.

"You look like a rabbit," Gary said. I spared a hand to flip him off.

The yearbook staff at Blanchet High had faxed over half a dozen pages of photos of the slender blond girl, most of them with her alone, often reading or drawing. She consistently wore her hair loose, tucked behind an ear when she was bent over a drawing pad.

"Fmmbmmy onna y'buk sfaff—"

Jen took the cup out of my mouth.

"Somebody on the yearbook staff has a crush on her, huh?" I repeated. Jen grinned and Gary looked startled.

"My guess is him," Jen said, and pushed one of the faxed pages over to reveal a gawky kid with a camera leaning over one of the girl's drawings. He had hair that fell over his eyes and good skin, for a teenager, and he would probably grow up cute. The girl was smiling up at him.

"Looks like true love." I smiled and shuffled the picture away. At the bottom of the pile was a two line biography.

Suzanne Quinley, sophomore. Interests: art, drama, volleyball. Birthday: January 6. Goals: being Picasso.

"At least she doesn't want to be John Malkovich," I mumbled.

"She probably doesn't know who John Malkovich is," Jen said dryly. "He's too old for her."

"Picasso's older," I pointed out. "Is this all there is? No phone number, nothing on where she lives?" I shuffled back to one of the photos and compared it to the drawing Jen had done. There were probably about a hundred thousand blond teenage girls in Seattle, but this one felt right. I looked up at Jen, hopeful.

She held out a thin manila folder. "I expect you to worship at my toes."

I flipped it open. It held three pieces of paper and a black-and-white photograph, taken a year or two earlier. One paper was a copy of a birth certificate; the second, an adoption record. The third was a brief biography. I stared at the papers for a moment, then lifted my eyes to Jen's in admiration. "How'd you do this?"

"Magic, *chica*." She waggled her fingers and smiled. "Got a friend in the State Department. Everybody's got an FBI file. Public record."

My eyebrows shot up. "Public?"

She didn't even look uncomfortable. "For some definition of public."

"You're a bad woman, aren't you, Jen?"

"Got what you needed, didn't I? Right down to her home address. Which you're going to need, since school let out twenty minutes ago. You should get going."

"Last time you said that I went and broke my head open on the front steps. I'll go as soon as I can. I've got something else to take care of first." I pushed a hand through my hair, wondering if it looked as bad as it felt. "Gary, did you bring my drum?"

The big cabby nodded. "It's in the cab. I'll grab it."

I took a deep breath. "Okay. Let's get this show on the road, then."

CHAPTER TWENTY-FIVE

We ended up down in the garage break room, the place I was most comfortable in the station. A surprising number of people followed us down, evidently all struck with the need to take a break at exactly the same time. Morrison was conspicuous by his absence, for which I was both grateful and resentful. He, after all, had seen the diner's security tapes and had come around far enough to reinstate me to work on the case. It seemed like he should come keep an eye on me while I did the weird stuff that he'd reinstated me to do.

Maybe I didn't need to work on that damsel in distress routine after all. The idea of Morrison keeping his eye on me implied I might need him to rescue me, which seemed both unlikely and annoying. Fortunately, my replacement, Thor the Thunder God, came in from the garage with the rest of the mechanics. His arrival knocked me out of sulking over the captain.

"This really isn't going to be that exciting," I said to Gary. He had a duffel bag over his shoulder and was carrying it carefully. I assumed my drum was in there, protected against the weather.

"Want me to get 'em out of here?" He looked more hulking than usual, like a rooster with his feathers fluffed out. I almost laughed.

"No, I think it's okay. I just, ah." I stopped arranging an empty space on the floor and looked around at the two dozen men and women crowding the break room. "No. No, in fact, I think I have an idea. All right, look, everybody." I lifted my voice and straightened, arms akimbo. Nearly everyone came to attention, like I was their worst drill sergeant returned to haunt them. I fought off laughter again.

"This isn't," I repeated, "going to be very exciting. I'm going to sit here in a trance while Gary bangs a drum. I take it pretty much everybody's gotten the lowdown by now."

Nobody would quite look at me, or at each other. Especially at me. I couldn't help wondering if they were here to see if my freaky new life was real, or if I'd just lost my mind. Either way, I couldn't help laughing. Nothing traveled faster than gossip, and getting the lowdown had brought most of them here. "Right," I said. Bruce, at least, met my eye with an unapologetic little shrug. "Since you're all here anyway, I'm gonna ask a favor of you."

Maybe a dozen people were left when I was done explaining what I wanted to try. To my surprise, Thor stayed. He glowered and folded his arms over his chest when I arched an eyebrow at him, but he didn't move. I wondered what his real name was as I waited another moment before beginning. No one else left, so I sat down Indian-style in the middle of the crowd. Gary sat down across from me and took my drum out from the duffel bag.

"I brought this, too." He withdrew Cernunnos's rapier, sheathed in leather, from the bag. My eyes widened.

"Don't tell me you had a scabbard just lying around."

Gary shrugged a bit. "Okay, I won't tell you. Take it." He offered the sheathed blade to me, and I placed it across my lap. Curious murmurs rose and fell, but no one asked outright. That would come later, I imagined. A lot of questions were going to come later. Either that or a lot of people were going to start finding excuses not to talk to me ever again. I wondered which route I'd have taken, if someone else had been trying to pull this off.

"Not gonna lie down this time?" Gary asked.

"I think I'll be okay. If I fall over, somebody can prop me up." I inhaled, a long slow breath through my nostrils, and let my eyes drift closed. The first beat of the drum was deep and certain and sent chills over my arms. I straightened my spine involuntarily.

I knew I could do what I wanted to do. I didn't know if I could do it on purpose. I remembered the electric awareness of the airport, the charge in the air that was the life force of hundreds of people coming and going about their business. It had been so available, the urge to tap it obvious and nearly irresistible.

There, on the scale I'd reached for power on, it would have been deadly. Here I wanted only a fraction of that power, and I was asking for it to be volunteered. The drum settled into a rhythm that matched my heartbeat. I exhaled, and with the exhalation stood, leaving my body sitting empty on the floor, motor functions operating while my consciousness stepped out for a breather.

The room's inhabitants glowed with the same peculiar neon life force I'd seen outside my apartment when I'd gone for the inadvertent visit to the dead shamans. It was the same force that had unlocked inside me, although less potent; the same astonishing skinlessness I'd experienced in the coffee shop while talking with Morrison. They were full of life, breathing and pulsing with it. Curiosity caught me for a moment and I looked past them, through the walls of the garage, to study the look of living earth from below instead of above.

I shouldn't have; it was depressing. Bisected and intersected with concrete, there wasn't much living at all. The sunken building walls had their own sense of purpose, their own energy, but it wasn't what I was looking for and I didn't have the time to examine it more carefully.

I withdrew back into the break room, concentrating instead on the brilliant auras of my co-workers and friends. And Thor. Billy had shown up, a stolid wall of fuchsias and oranges. Unlike almost everyone else, he held his hands in front of him, a coiling ball of color writhing between his palms. Jen, nearby, held the same kind of ball, in boiling yellow and brown. I didn't even know brown came in neon.

A few of the others stood that way as well. The others simply stood where they were, casting curious, silent glances at the body I'd temporarily abandoned—not that it was apparent I'd done so—and at the people around them. Their energy rolled off them in waves, flickering away like flame. Some were clearly concentrating on extending goodwill toward me, visible in sheets that dissipated without focus. The rest had less ability to focus, offering not much more than their simple essence.

I reached for the sheets of goodwill first, wondering how to temper the power. Was a wish of good thoughts an infinite gift, or did it exhaust the giver? If it did, I had to make this very fast, or find a way to slow down the output. There was too much I didn't *know*.

On the other hand, there wasn't a lot of time to sit around agonizing over that fact, either. I cupped my hands, siphoning the unfocused power into a ball between my own palms, watching the startling colors spin and dance around one another without quite melding. Where they touched, flashes of gray and black and white blurred them together, making them cohesive without taking away any of the individuality. Mesmerizing patterns formed within the ball, all of them unique and yet still sounding a common theme. I watched a moment, then shook myself. If I was lucky, there'd be time later to study the universal similarities in man. If I wasn't, I'd be dead and it wouldn't be much of a worry for me anyway.

Calling the already-focused power that Billy and Jen offered was easier. Their energy flowed to me when I called them, dancing around the ball I held like electrons around an atom, almost too fast to see. All of the power I held traced thin lines back to its creators, bright snaps of color that wound around each other in intricate braids without ever tangling together.

I wasn't taking anything at all from at least a quarter of the people in the room, the ones who weren't able to offer it up as easily as the others. I could take it outright, borrow some of their life force, just as I'd intended to in the airport, but for now I left them.

Babylon. How did I get back? *By candlelight, and back again.* I closed my eyes and fell inward on myself, reaching backward and within for the starry void. My hands and feet and head sucked inward, collapsing into my belly button. My entire self shriveled and shrunk until with an audible pop I imploded entirely and exploded back out of my belly button again, exactly as I'd been, only facing the opposite direction and looking into the racing starscape instead of the garage break room.

"Hey," I said out loud. "That was cool." The energy I'd borrowed was no longer visible in a ball between my palms. Instead I could feel it settled in my abdomen, a life force there that was, and was not, part of myself. I shuddered and tried to shut myself away from recognizing the feeling. With a jarring shock, spiderweb cracks shot through me, deeper and sharper than anything before.

"Give me a break," I whispered. "This isn't the time." I superimposed clarity over the cracks, and they faded out reluctantly. It occurred to me that all three times I'd found my way to the starscape, the past I'd tried so hard to leave behind had resurfaced. I wondered, very briefly, what exactly this place between the worlds was. Then the candle appeared and I wrapped my hands around it and whispered, "Babylon."

A noise like the end of the world hit me, sending me staggering back a few steps. A huge knobby root caught me in the back of the knees. I sat down hard at the foot of a Joshua Spire, trying to make sense of the chaos that had become Babylon.

The sky had lost its blue-gray color, tinged now with deep, sickening red. The silver Joshua Spires twisted up into the bloody sky, hanging gardens torn and falling down the sides of the trees. They shifted restlessly, not pushed by the wind, but like dying creatures making a last desperate snatch at life before giving away to the inevitable end.

The restless, cheerful babble that had filled the air was gone, too, leaving lonely wind and cries of fear and pain in its place. For one crystalline moment, I saw a long view of human history, reaching far back to the first days of mankind. I saw a small woman with thick curves and dark eyes, recognizable as human, yet alien all the same. She met my eyes and performed a shrug, small, wry, fully understandable.

We came here once, she said, *when we were few.*

This was Babel, I said back. *This is where we came to all speak together. To share and understand each other. When we bred too many...Babel was lost?*

She nodded and smiled, warm and approving.

You're Eve, I said. She threw her head back and laughed, a very human sound.

They called me Mother, when I was there. I was not the first in the way you think of Eve as being. It was not so easy as that. But——yes. Eve might do as a name. But go, she said, *or all my children will lose the place we once had, forever.*

Goodbye, Mother, I whispered. The roar of angry wind filled my ears. I had never left Babel, but I could see it again. The street cobbles were torn, chunks of stone flung at wild angles that suggested an earthquake of devastating magnitude. Where they'd been the warm color of rust before, they were splattered with red, the dangerous crimsons and dark shades that meant vital blood had been spilled. I rubbed my breastbone, feeling sick. There was too much to think about, too much to assimilate and far too little time.

People hid behind every cockeyed piece of street, some dead, some dying, others mourning and still others screaming out their defiance against the Hunt that rode through them. As I watched, a line of soldiers, arm in arm, stood up together and walked forward. Before them, the street shivered and reformed, cobbles lying back down under the force of their will. Behind them, it lay smooth, a gauntlet thrown in the face of the chaos that was the Wild Hunt.

And down the newly relaid road they came, a dozen too-solid riders and the lonely pale mare. Cernunnos rode at their lead, his elegant antlers sweeping back to tangle with his ashy hair. He carried the new double-edged sword. Beneath the blood, it gleamed as bright a silver as the rapier I'd taken from him. As I watched, his stallion leaped a still-broken section of road, and Cernunnos smiled brilliantly at a young woman scrambling to get out of the way. Her lips parted and she went still, fear replaced by the compulsion of the god's green eyes. He laughed, like the music of breaking glass. His deadly bright blade swept down in a gleaming arch, and the girl stiffened, waiting for the blow.

I whispered, "No."

The god's sword smashed into my spoken word like it was a shield, and rebounded. Cernunnos jolted back, and for a moment the entire Hunt hesitated. The girl, freed from Cernunnos's eyes, turned and ran. With precise slowness, Cernunnos transferred his sword from his left hand to his right. He curved the fingers of his left hand down, rubbing them against his palm, and stretched them wide again. Then he lifted his hand, palm up, and looked slowly around with the intent of a deadly, confident predator.

It was suddenly important that I face him before he called me out. I pushed away from my tree root and walked forward, coming into the street ahead of the line of soldiers, who stood still now, remaining arm in arm, waiting and watching. Their healing power still rolled off them, spreading out through the ruined city of Babylon. A wave of fierce protection wrapped around my heart. *I* would die before I let anyone else here die. Let him see nothing but me, I willed. Let him forget them.

Cernunnos watched me silently, fascination visible even in features only half-human. Behind him, the archer and the thick-shouldered rider exchanged glances. The thick-shouldered man smiled before returning his attention to me; the archer nocked an arrow, but didn't draw. I thought it was rather unsporting of him anyway. I'd seen how fast he could nock an arrow, earlier. It wasn't like he needed the extra time afforded by doing it now.

"Little shaman," Cernunnos said. The beautiful voice was harsher now, distorted by the thickened neck and changed vocal cords.

"My lord master of the Hunt," I replied. The thick-shouldered man did smile at that. Cernunnos did too, a twist of a mouth that had the fullness of the man's lips pulled into a stunted muzzle, neither human nor animal. He bowed from the waist, a small gesture as impossibly elegant as anything I'd ever seen him do. It wasn't enough, though, to wipe the blood from the blade he carried. The power I'd borrowed boiled in my belly, asking to be used.

"I hardly expected to see you again, little shaman."

"I hardly intended to leave you here. This isn't your place, Cernunnos."

"Oh, but it is," he murmured, and lifted his hands, bloody sword in one, to encompass the bleak red sky and the death in the streets. "Look what I have wrought."

"You marked it. That doesn't make it yours. Come on, my lord master of the Hunt." The words sounded like they would if I'd said them to Morrison, full of sarcasm. "Mano a mano, eh? You and me. If you win, I take the child's place in the Hunt and you ride unbound. If I win, you leave this place now and forever and return to Earth with me."

"Now and forever?" the god asked, a gleam in his brilliant eyes.

"That remains to be seen," I said steadily. He lowered his head, ivory horns catching the bloody light, and considered me.

"How did you say it? Mano a mano. So it shall be. I swear it by my name and by my power and once more by my immortal life. Should I lose here to you, nevermore shall the Hunt return to Babylon, and with you we will go, to the place you call Earth."

I wondered, briefly, what that name he swore by was. It was not, I was sure, Cernunnos. There was something deeper, more private, that he answered to in the most secret part of his soul, and no one else would ever know that name. *Except maybe the camel,* I thought in a fit of pure irreverence. I hoped he hadn't heard that, and spoke out loud to cover the thought. "I have no immortal life to swear by. Should I swear by yours?"

Scathing disdain filled Cernunnos's vivid eyes. My mouth twisted in a smirk. "Don't have much sense of humor, do you?" I straightened my shoulders. Being a smart-ass might help keep my courage up, but this was important. My heartbeat, steady as the drum, sounded loud in my ears as I spoke. "As you swear it, so shall I, by my name and my power and my all-too mortal life. If I lose to you here, I'll ride in your missing child's place, and try no more to bind you." A constriction came over me as I spoke, a very real compulsion, and it occurred to me once more that I'd gotten in way over my head. There was a proverb about that. Looking and leaping. Maybe someday I'd remember it before I leaped.

God knows what I was expecting. It wasn't the force of Cernunnos's will smashing down on me like a hammer, though. My words were still lingering in the air when he hit me, green strength like a mountain coming down. I dropped to my knees, the air crushed from my body, and held onto the contents of my stomach through clenched teeth.

Cernunnos dismounted with predatory grace, stalking toward me across the new cobblestones. I swayed, watching him and distantly remembering the helpless fear in the woman's face a few minutes ago. I had been here before, weighed down under his power. Unfortunately, Gary wasn't here this time to haul my ass out of the fire. I was going to have to do it myself. I reached for the internalized strength I'd borrowed from my friends, and hesitated.

Not yet. Cernunnos stopped a few feet away from me, easily within the reach of his sword. "Thou art bold, little shaman," he murmured. "Foolish, but bold." He drew the blade back, preparing for a deeply disabling strike. I didn't think he was going to kill me. Not unless he knew a way to capture a newly released soul, which, now that I thought about it, I wouldn't put past him. That didn't make me feel any better.

He lunged forward, and I fell over.

It certainly didn't have any of the grace the god persisted in showing, but it did get me out of his path without me having to fight off the weight of his power to get up. He stumbled, taken off guard, and I rolled forward, into his legs. Gratifyingly, he lost his balance for a moment. I twisted on my back and drove a booted foot up into his groin.

For one horrible moment Cernunnos stared down at me and I was afraid I might as well have kicked one of the Joshua Spires.

Then he screamed, so deep and angry it twisted my bones. The gray veil that I had willed Babylon behind shivered and faded. Cernunnos flung both hands up, his sword knotted in his fists, and drove it down toward me.

The weight of his power was gone, though, shattered by pain as thoroughly as crystal was by sound. I came to my feet as the sword slammed down into cobblestone. As he began to draw it back out I kicked him in the jaw. He spun around, torso moving faster than his legs, one full turn and an aborted half, just like Charlie Chaplin.

Against all the rules of good sportsmanship, I kicked him while he was down. I caught him one solid blow in the ribs, moving his whole body a few inches, but the second time he caught my foot and twisted it hard to the side. Something that shouldn't have popped in my knee and I screamed, collapsing almost on top of the god. For a few seconds we lay there, panting at each other. I saw a flash of anger in his eyes.

It was just enough warning to throw up a shield as his power slammed down on me again. This time I could see it, the deep snarling green of his strength pushing at the silver-gray barrier I'd flung up, testing it for weaknesses.

And finding them. Uncertainty, lack of knowledge, simple fear, they were holes I didn't know how to plug up. Like the Lilliputians with Gulliver, Cernunnos pinned me down through those holes, threading green power into the stone around me. He grinned, feral and strange on the half-animal face, and rolled to his feet, dragging his sword out of the stone.

An incongruous thought made me look away from him, to the thick-shouldered rider in the host. He lifted his bearded chin, a trace of amusement in his face, and then he nodded, a single drop of his chin. Something familiar glittered in his eyes as Cernunnos's sword came free of the stone with a scrape. Then there was no more time to contemplate the riders while I looked for a way to get free of Cernunnos's bonds.

The god rose up and drove his sword into my belly, and I stopped thinking at all.

CHAPTER TWENTY-SIX

One thing I'd learned in the last few days was that a body gets used to different degrees of pain. For example, my head still throbbed, but I'd more or less forgotten about it while concentrating on the return to Babylon. The very bad popping in my knee was excruciating, but letting it distract me from the matter at hand was suicidal, so I didn't.

Getting a sword in the gut for the second or third time in a week was not something you could get used to. I was too surprised to scream; instead I opened my mouth and a pathetic little bloody cough came out. Above me, smiling brilliantly, Cernunnos asked, "Do you yield?"

Interesting question to ask a shish-kabob. He leaned on the sword a little more, turning it slightly. I opened my mouth to scream again and didn't even manage the pathetic cough that time. "Do you yield?" Cernunnos asked again. Pleasantly, even.

My vision faded out, into blood, and back in again with the peripheries stained red. The rest of the Hunt was gathered around us when I could see again. I felt like a particularly novel and newly discovered bug, skewered on an examining table.

"I…" I croaked. Cernunnos, still smiling brilliantly, leaned closer to hear me.

"I'll see you in hell first," I whispered, and did the most amazingly stupid thing I could think of. I released the coil of energy inside me.

It blasted out in every direction, most of its force screaming in a multicolored ball up the sword to smash into Cernunnos. There was one delightful moment of complete surprise on his face before he flew back, ass over teakettle. I heard a dull thud as he crashed into one of the Joshua Spires, and another one as he hit the earth a moment later. His sword made a dull tink against the stones as it landed somewhere between us.

Unexpectedly, all my pain went away. I stood up slowly, my vision turning to swirls of red and blue: infrared and ultraviolet. Detail faded to impressions, splotches of heat and cool. Energy still boiled out of me. It felt exhilarating, utter freedom from constraint, self-imposed or otherwise. I felt as if nothing could possibly stop me. A tiny part of me knew it was a false high, but for the moment I hung on and looked around.

Babylon, behind the mist of obscurity I'd put up around it, was healing. I could see within the Joshua Spires, like I'd been able to see through the city buildings. Men and women formed circles around and inside the spires. I could see power rising from them, flowing out over the mythical city. Where their power touched damage, it healed. Only the bodies the Hunt had left behind remained still and unliving as the shamans worked together to heal their gathering place.

They dared focus on the healing because they trusted me to deal with the Hunt. I could feel that, too. Not supreme confidence, but quiet expectation, the belief that it was safe to pay attention to other tasks. Only the line of soldiers whom I'd seen first still stood linked across the street, watching me. I lifted a hand toward them, meaning to smile, but the sight of my own hand drove all other thought from my mind.

There was no hand, nor wrist or elbow or, as I looked down at myself, any of the other usual flesh and blood extremities that came with being human. I was human-*shaped,* with fingers and breasts and hips and feet, but it was like someone had taken all the coverings off and left me with nothing more than the spirit that filled those parts. No wonder I'd stopped hurting. There wasn't anything physical left to hurt.

Color swam over what wasn't my skin, like oil held in by surface tension. Rainbows gleamed and swirled and mixed and were reborn. It was ridiculously beautiful. For a second or two I just stared down at myself, lost in the random patterns of spirit unbound by flesh.

A small sound roused me, and I looked up, toward Cernunnos. Other than the groan, he hadn't moved since I threw him into the spire. I discovered I was holding him down, just as he'd held me earlier, with the force of my power. The green of his strength met the silver rainbow of mine, pushing against it enough to prevent him from being crushed, but not enough to let him escape. I cocked my head and walked forward.

The host moved back from me, not precisely a retreat, but certainly a respectful and cautious distance. Their features were lost in the reddish haze as they looked away from me to their captured leader. I crouched beside Cernunnos, watching his power push against mine. It wasn't, maybe, fair. I still felt the good will of my friends reaching out to me, pouring in to me, and he had only his own power.

Then again, he was a god. "Do you yield?" I asked, nearly as politely as he had. It seemed like a good protocol, although I knew he'd say no, just like I had.

The problem was, neither of us would ever yield. We could keep fighting until together we destroyed Babylon. At some distant point one of us would destroy the other. The only thing I had on my side was that if Cernunnos actually killed me, he'd have no one to take the Rider's place. Suzanne Quinley's place. Of course, it would leave him free to terrorize Babylon. I had fewer constraints, except I didn't know if the Hunt could be led back into my world, or their own, if Cernunnos himself was dead. I preferred not to find out.

Cernunnos growled, feral eyes full of rage. "I do not yield," he snarled.

"No," I said, "I didn't think you would."

I tested the depth of the power I was tapped in to, not taking my eyes off the god. The power ran deep, but not deep enough: I could feel the bottom of it, like I was reaching through a streambed when I needed a river. I mumbled a prayer and reached for the rest of the people surrounding my physical body, the ones who didn't know how to offer, but who hadn't left the room when I'd explained what I needed.

And my hold on Cernunnos slipped. He roared and sprang forward, knocking me down. My damaged and too-solid flesh came back as I crashed into the cobblestones, the god's taloned nails at my throat. My head hit the stones, and for another moment the gray veil around us wavered again, Babylon visible during that breath. Pain did bad things to my vision, narrowing it down to pinpricks. Cernunnos lifted one hand from my throat, extending it beyond where I could see. Then silver glittered, as he drew the broadsword into my line of vision. For one exciting moment I comprehended just how very long I was going to be dead. I brought my hands up to stop the sword, a futile gesture.

Then I remembered what else Gary had brought to the station.

The surprise on Cernunnos's face was almost worth the near-death experience, as his broadsword bore down and clanged into the flat of my rapier. I held it extended at an awkward angle that barely prevented him from slicing my throat open, but it was all I needed. I gathered my strength with a shout and shoved him off me, rolling to my feet.

That's when I found out, for the second time in two days, how much it hurt to stand up with a two inch hole sliced through your insides. I nearly fell over again right there, content to have done with it, but Cernunnos smiled, a bright flash of triumph. The idea of letting him win pissed me off enough to keep me on my feet. Bleeding and swaying, with an arm wrapped around my abdomen, but on my feet. It's the small victories, I tell you.

It didn't seem fair that he wasn't actually hurt, while I was bleeding and staggering all over the place. He came at me carelessly, an easy overhead stroke that expected nothing in response. Without any particular conscious intent on my own part, the rapier came up, catching the broadsword a second time. Metal rang out again, pure clean tone of a bell, and the god once more looked surprised. Hell, I was surprised, too. I wouldn't have bet on being able to parry a toothpick, much less the heavy blade Cernunnos carried. I could feel the rapier, though, as if it came from the same source the coil of energy within me did. The slender sword's strength was from more than just the metal it was forged with. It was filled with my will and the power lent to me by my friends, and its very presence was a response to my need.

Since I didn't have any world-class fencing skills, I kicked Cernunnos in the nuts again. I didn't have to know how to use a sword to do that, and he was standing there like he was asking for it, so it seemed justified. Shock and rage filled his green eyes all over again as he doubled. I guess there must be rules that people fighting gods usually followed. Next time, maybe somebody would give me a primer. Since nobody had this time, though, I kicked him in the head while he was doubled, and knocked his sword away as he fell gracelessly to the ground. It was the perfect moment to bear down upon my enemy and smite him in a gladiator-inspired hour of triumph. Too bad I was digging the rapier into the ground for support and afraid that if I moved I'd collapse on top of him.

Instead, I did what I'd been trying to do before.

I took all my own power, and the offered strength from my friends, and reached just a little farther and took what the others who had stayed didn't know how to offer. Fear surged through a few of the new links, and those I let go as quickly as I could. The last thing I wanted to do was leave scars in my friends' minds.

The remaining power I wove into a net, visualizing all the colors spinning together, shoring up weaknesses and sharing strengths. They bled together and knotted, becoming heavy in my hands. When I looked down I almost couldn't tell where the net began and I left off. My skin had disappeared again, leaving me nothing but a network of power and strength, silver-blue oil-slick rainbows.

I wanted to stay like this forever. I could feel everything in Babylon: the healing, the fear, the confidence that I would make good my promise and take Cernunnos and his riders away from this place. Beyond that, between the blackness of the stars, I could feel other life, a tremendously deep hum that spread from one end of eternity to the other. It was the void that bound all the worlds, and I knew I could step out into it, explore it, with just the impulse to do so.

But Cernunnos was rolling to his feet, graceful again, though seeming tremendously slow. His broad shoulders shifted, weight coming forward, and I could feel his intent as clearly as if it were my own. Reaching his sword was first: after that he would turn on me and crush me like the mortal fool I was. I flung the net of power out from splayed fingers, not at where Cernunnos was, but at where he'd be.

He and the net came together in glorious slow motion, the vivid green of his power smashing into the woven silver tendrils of mine. Mine collapsed, not under his assault, but as it should, just like any perfectly ordinary net, tangling around him. He stumbled and crashed to the cobblestones, rolling as he struggled to get free. He thrashed his head, antlers ripping the net apart, but it wove back together as I clung to the idea of it.

"You won't yield, I know that," I whispered. "So I'll drag you back, just like you'd have had to have done to me." I pulled the rapier out of the stones with a whimper and forced myself upright without it. I was breathing through my teeth, every motion a jab of pain through my middle, but I felt absurdly attached to the need to do this without the pretense of physical support. I pulled the net in to myself, hand over fist, tightening it around Cernunnos until he was caught in an embrace tight as a lover's.

I dragged him across the cobblestones, taking stumbling, half-running steps, afraid that if I stopped I would never be able to start again. I used my shoddy momentum and the borrowed strength of my friends to fling him over the haunches of his magnificent stallion. Then, with all the grace and arrogance I could manage, I swung up onto the stallion's back myself. The sword hole running through me screamed. Cernunnos screamed.

The stallion held very still, his ears pinned back and tail snapping with disapproval, his teeth bared. I leaned forward, because sitting up hurt too much, and put my forehead against the crest of his mane. "Just bring me home, beautiful," I whispered into the liquid silver hair. I stroked his neck, and lifted my head very slowly. Cernunnos's fury was palpable, a living green thing that drove spikes out at me as he tried to free himself from the net. My head swam suddenly, blood loss and exhaustion crashing over me. I stretched one hand forward, whispering, "By candlelight, and back again."

The candle flickered into being, a light to guide me out of Babylon with the Wild Hunt riding behind me.

I opened my eyes to a different sort of chaos. Three or four of the cops had collapsed and lay where they'd fallen. My shoulders slumped in dismay; I'd been trying not to hurt anyone. Voices were lifted all around, not quite shouting as paramedics swept in to examine the people who'd fallen.

Most of the group were still standing around me, with expressions ranging from surprise to fear. I could barely bring myself to look from one face to another, afraid to learn what people thought of me now. Billy looked tired but not frightened. That was something. Gary watched me with curious respect. He wasn't beating the drum anymore.

And the Hunt swarmed around the mortals in the room, half-visible, like ghosts. I wasn't the only one who could see them: Jen and Billy kept flinching as enormous horses and hounds slid through them.

Cernunnos, looking nearly as bad as I felt, was mounted on his stallion, forthright fury in the beautiful eyes. "I won, my lord master of the Hunt," I croaked. Gary sat up straighter, looking to see to whom I was speaking.

"You won," the god growled, "but this is not over yet, little shaman." I wasn't sure if I heard the words in my mind or my ears. The ease of speech in Babylon was already slipping from me.

I grinned very wearily. My body hurt from the fight, but the ache in my head had died away some. I couldn't remember if I'd managed to heal myself while in Babylon, but maybe being a conduit for the kind of power I'd been using had some kind of positive effect. It was equally possible that I was horribly deluding myself, but I didn't want to think too hard about it, for fear of making the pain start again. "Not quite yet," I said to Cernunnos. "Who do you think will make it to your son first, me or you?"

"For the sake of thy world and thy soul," Cernunnos said through fixed teeth, "thou hast best hope it is thyself. I would not wager on it, little shaman."

"Not so little," I protested. By now nearly everyone was staring at me, the bustle of moments earlier dissipated into expectant waiting. "I defeated a god in fair combat." Was I out of my mind? Throwing his loss into his face? I wasn't *that* good.

No: as I said the words, Cernunnos became a solid thing, every bit as real as the cops who'd been more prosaically visible all along. Thor the Thunder God said, "Holy *shit,*" and everyone still on their feet backed up against the walls.

Cernunnos filled the room. Had it not had the garage's high roof, he'd never have fit. As it was, he took up all the air again, just as he had at the diner, his emerald eyes burning with anger so hot I thought I would burn. "Defeated, Siobhán Walkingstick," he said in his velvet voice. I wondered if everyone else could understand him. "Defeated, but not dead. Your soul will be mine to collect before the midnight hour, *gwyld.*"

Gwyld. It was the word Marie had used. It meant shaman, or wise man, in Gaelic. That knowledge came to me, so I knew I was hearing Cernunnos in my mind again, his gift for breaching languages as strong a thing as Babylon had.

"Open the doors," I whispered, turning my head toward Billy. "Open the garage doors. Let them go without the steel and concrete to harm them."

The big cop frowned down at me. "You sure, Joanie?"

"I'm sure." I didn't dare take my eyes off Cernunnos. "He's

not—*they're* not—meant to be bound by people like us. Let the Hunt go. Tonight they'll be sent back home, anyway."

There was, for a moment, respect in Cernunnos's alien eyes. "You are a fool, *gwyld,*" he said.

"Everybody's got problems," I said with a tiny shrug. "Tonight, my lord master of the Hunt."

"Tonight." Cernunnos turned his massive stallion in the small confines of the room. He ducked as he left through the door. The host followed him, the sound of hooves ringing loud on the concrete floor as they faded away, leaving a silent and awestruck police force behind.

CHAPTER TWENTY-SEVEN

It took a minute to trust that I could get up. Gary took the rapier away from me and slung it over his shoulder, then offered me a hand. "You're gonna poke somebody's eye out with that thing," I said as he pulled me to my feet. He glanced at the blade, bushy eyebrows lifted, and lowered it to lean against his leg instead.

"Just helping Darwin along. Now what, boss?" He tilted his head at the dispersing cops. Few of them wanted to look at me. Part of me wanted to be a fly on the wall to hear the gossip for the next few hours. More of me wished my life was still normal, like it had been a mere seventy-two hours earlier. Yeah, well, if wishes were horses, beggars would ride. I patted myself down, seeing if there was any part of me that hurt too much to ignore. There wasn't, although I could feel the ball of energy inside me fizzling out. You want your car analogies. Talk about running on empty. I exhaled, puffing my cheeks. "'Boss', huh? I kind of like that. We're going to go look for a pretty teenage girl."

Gary grinned, cheerfully wicked. "Sounds like my kind of plan."

"You're an old pervert."

We left the office a few steps behind the mechanics. Nick, my former supervisor, averted his eyes when I offered him a weary smile. It felt like a gut-punch. Gary saw it and nudged my shoulder as we went by.

"Hey, it's a tough job, being a dirty old man. Who's the girl?"

My head swam. It didn't seem possible Gary didn't know what had happened, but telling him distracted me from Nick's carefully blank expression. Gary herded me into the front seat of his cab and I spent most of the drive to Suzy's address to get all the details in more or less the right order. When I was done talking, I looked around for the first time, realizing we'd driven into one of the precinct's posher neighborhoods while I'd been concentrating. "Suzy Q's a rich girl," I murmured.

"Poor kids don't go to Blanchet High, Jo," Gary said. I shrugged.

"Never paid attention." I remembered how clean and big the school was, though, and tried not to compare it to my high school. That led, inevitably, to trying not to remember old scabs Cernunnos had ripped the tops off. I hunched my shoulders and stared resolutely out the window, not thinking about it.

The problem with not thinking about a specific topic is that it eats at your brain and won't let you think about anything else until you're distracted by an outside influence. I was grateful when Gary pulled up beside an imposing, dark-windowed house, and said, "Here we go. Doesn't look like anybody's home."

I leaned forward to peer out the windshield at the house. It was painted in cream with brown trim and had enormous, imposing pillars holding up a front porch. "Abandon hope, all ye who enter here."

"Abandon all hope, ye who enter," Gary corrected. I glared sideways at him and got out of the cab. Most of the muscles in my body groaned in protest, and the bruise from Cernunnos's sword reminded me it was there. I rubbed it gingerly as I climbed the steps to the front door. A neat little red-and-gold sign greeted me: No Solicitors.

"Wonder what they've got against lawyers." I cast a wary glance over my shoulder. Gary was still in the cab, from whence he couldn't hear me making smart-ass remarks to myself. Satisfied, I located the doorbell, which was irritatingly hidden in an intricate carving of leaves framing the door, and rang it.

There was no answer. I stood there a minute, then rang the doorbell again, more than half-expecting a tuxedo-clad butler to appear, looking irritated and aloof. When, after another minute, one didn't appear, I idly tested the doorknob.

Which turned, and the door swung open. I jumped back with a yelp and stared into the foyer. The floor had the ugliest tile pattern I'd ever seen, fleur de lis of thick blocky lines. I imagined it was very expensive.

"Well, now what?" Gary asked from behind me. I yelped, turning to scowl at him.

"I didn't hear you."

He looked like a pleased five-year-old. "I know. I snuck up on you."

"Well, don't!" He might've looked like a pleased five-year-old, but I sounded like a petulant one. "Oh, be quiet," I muttered, and turned around to look into the foyer again. "Now what?"

"I asked you first."

Damn. I'd been hoping he wouldn't remember that.

"Front door's open," I said. "Isn't that an invitation for cops to sneak in, in the movies? As long as you don't touch anything? To, um, make sure everything's okay?"

"This isn't a movie," Gary pointed out, "and the door wasn't *open*."

"It was unlocked. That's like open." I leaned forward and stuck my head into the foyer, shouting, "Hello?"

It echoed, but no one answered. I looked at Gary. He shrugged. "This is the police!" I shouted, and then burst into a fit of giggling. Gary grinned. "Sorry," I said when I got my breath back. "That was just fun to say." In fact, I said it again. "This is the police! Is anybody home? Suzanne? Mrs. Quinley? Mr. Quinley?" The foyer smelled faintly of chocolate, like someone had been baking.

Still no one answered. Gary shrugged again when I looked back at him. "Got any gut feelings on it?"

One very small part of me announced, *I don't do gut feelings,* but by this time not even I believed that, so I didn't say it out loud. Instead I took a step back, crowding into Gary. He muttered and moved back while I closed my eyes and tried to ignore the aches and pains and goldfish that kept distracting me from focusing my power. Every time I opened myself to it, it collapsed around me like a misty waterfall: there, but intangible. Distantly, I recognized what the shamans might have considered to be rudimentary shields causing that collapse. My mind and body knew when I'd pushed them too far, even if I didn't want to acknowledge it. I couldn't afford to burn out yet.

"Jo?"

I became aware I'd been standing with my eyes closed for over a minute. "Just a little tired." The words came out thick, like syrup. I rubbed my breastbone, above the bruise, and dropped my chin to my chest. If I couldn't control it, I'd try for the other way. "C'mon," I said out loud, to the city. "Hit me with everything you got."

In the future, remind me not to ask a city to hit me with everything it's got. Cernunnos had nothing on the influx of power that slammed through me as my pathetic shields disintegrated. I staggered back, my back foot catching the edge of the top step. I held my balance there, weight off-center, the city revitalizing me like fresh strong blood in my veins. Inside a breath I was a mugger, a fireman, a newborn, a dying man. The impatient roar of vehicles filled my ears, the city's lifeblood flowing from one place to another. Even the air was charged, electricity carried in the molecules along with particles of smog and dust. If I could carry this in me all the time, I would never be tired, never need to eat or breathe. It was exhilarating, every life in the city my own, and mine a part of everyone's. Had this once been shared by all humanity, as Eve had implied? A long time ago, when there were far fewer of us? I couldn't imagine anyone being willing to give up something this good, being so connected.

There was a storm building off the coast. It was only a change in the wind now. In a few days, it would gather, and late next week it would dump eight inches of snow on the city. I knew it as clearly as if I were already in the midst of it.

"Jo?" Gary said again. I opened my eyes. He was brilliant again, the thrumming V-8 engine, his colors surrounding him in curious pulses. Unable to resist, I reached for him specifically, out of the millions of lives in Seattle. His was a joyous one to touch, tempered with pain. In his memory, I sat by Annie's deathbed, holding her hand. She was delicate and pretty, thin hair neatly coiled. Her grip was firm even though she was dying. She spoke quietly, smiling, not about regrets, but about all the beautiful things in her life. Stories about me, about us, making me laugh, even knowing the conversation was her last. Leaving a good memory, for the last one.

And the first one. A tiny elegant young woman, in an evening gown the color of peaches, the back swept down low and her golden hair in permanent waves, Veronica Lake-style. I was a soldier on leave. I asked her to dance, knowing from the very beginning that I wanted to spend my life with her. Daring and confident,

I kissed her at the end of the evening. What a lifetime it was going to be, with Annie at my side.

Scarlet fever, terrifying. Annie, never robust but always strong, so fragile I counted her breaths to make sure she still lived. The doctor, apologetic. There would be no children. It didn't matter: my Annie was still alive. The fights, oh, the fights over that, when she wouldn't believe that I still wanted her, when she saw herself as only half a woman. I held on and waited it out. There was nothing else I could do. In time the pain faded.

I drew back from Gary's memories with a shiver. He watched me with a frown, tilting his head toward the house. "Anything?"

I remembered what I was supposed to be doing. With the strength of the city energizing me, I left my body behind and stepped into the foyer.

The house was eerily cold. I hadn't noticed temperatures before, except in the desert where Coyote met me in the first place. It had been, well, desertlike, but not even the void between the stars had been cold like the Quinley's house was. Even with the force of the city running through me, I couldn't feel any life in the austere building.

I walked across the ugly tiles silently, then up a sweeping Cinderella staircase, perfect for making an entrance. Glittering above the stairway was a silver Mylar sign, block letters spelling out Happy Birthday, Sweetie!

The hall the stairs led to was marble, too, the same ugly tile as the foyer, though the stairs themselves were white. This was a house for sneaking around in barefoot. Woe betide anyone in hard-soled shoes trying to make a silent getaway.

Upstairs was more oppressive than the foyer, the cold deeper. I stood in the hallway, trying to analyze the chill. Was it just that the house had never seen much love between its walls? That seemed so corny I rejected it, despite my crash course in the strange and unusual. It felt more complicated than that, and I was supposed to be paying attention to how things felt.

I exhaled, nevermind that my body was somewhere else. The sound was muffled, like I'd breathed into a blanket. That was it: the heavy lifelessness lay over the house like a blanket, like something someone else had put there.

Like something Herne had put there. I recognized the touch with a shock, the dark taint of the god's son settled over Suzanne Quinley's home.

"Call the police," I said out loud. A small part of me was aware of Gary startling, and hurrying for the cab. I waited until I heard the static of the CB before steeling myself to walk forward. Past two doors on the right—linen closet, bathroom, my superconscious told me—and turned to the left, into a bedroom. Fear hit me like a wall as I stepped over the threshold. I squeezed my eyes shut.

Unfortunately, although screwing my metaphysical eyes shut had the peculiar effect of rendering me unable to see, it had no effect at all on the shattering agony that stained the room. Far more clearly than I could see with my eyes, I watched and felt everything that had happened here in history so recent it hadn't really ended yet.

Rachel Quinley worked part-time as a lawyer, her mornings tied up in legalese. She was always home by midafternoon, though, so Suzanne wouldn't come home to an empty house. She hadn't gone to work today for a hundred reasons. First, it was Suzy's birthday, though the Mylar sign seemed tacky in the face of yesterday's horror at the school. Then there was that thing itself, so many of Suzy's friends brutally murdered. Rachel had wanted Suzy to stay home today, but the girl—young woman, her mother thought with a combination of regret and pride—insisted on going. There were to be no classes. It was going to be a day of counseling and healing and talking. Suzy still wanted the cake for after dinner, too: she'd said it would make her feel more normal. How anyone could feel normal after yesterday—but Suzy'd been strange for months already. It was part of growing up. Rachel remembered the alienation she'd felt in high school, for all that she'd been popular. It was a universal feeling, she thought.

But she'd stayed home. To make the cake—chocolate with raspberry swirls, Suzy's favorite—and to wait to see if Suzanne needed to come home early. She wanted to be home, so her daughter wouldn't feel any distress over interrupting Mom at work. Just in case, she'd told herself. Just in case.

David Quinley came home at lunch, just in time to lick a cake beater. He was taking a half day off from his own law firm, to be home when Suzy got in. But she wasn't home yet, and they both were...

I blushed my way through the next eternity. I really thought people only used kitchen counters for that in the movies. This being a shaman thing was very enlightening, in an embarrassing way. When the cake was done baking, they moved upstairs to the bedroom, and that's where Herne found them.

I didn't envy them what happened next. I stood there, eyes shut, a silent, screaming observer of a thing I was too late to stop. It was not as fast or as comparatively easy a death as Marie had suffered, or the Blanchet High students, or Mrs. Potter. I understood *what* he was doing, if not *how:* Herne was harnessing the last of the power he needed to complete his night's task, and that took ritual.

I could feel him drawing in power in a way that felt like what I'd done with the police officers at the station. Where they'd offered goodwill and hope, though, Herne seemed to be taking from the darker things that man had to offer: lust and pain and greed. The coil of energy inside my belly spat and bubbled so fiercely my insides cramped, reacting physically to the dark power Herne called up.

The horrifying thing was how *close* it felt to the power inside me. The other side of the coin, a razor's edge away. Yeah, so I was mixing metaphors again, but that's how it felt: clearly the other side of the power I could access, so close it would be terribly easy to slip over the edge and call on it. It was a difference of motivation, the slender line between compassion and vengeance.

Even what he was doing wasn't so far from what I'd done with Cernunnos. I'd bound the god to drag him back to a world he could be controlled in. Herne bound Suzanne's parents in the same way, weaving a net of power. The difference was that he intended to take them all the way into himself, subsume them and use their power to strengthen himself without leaving anything for them to return to. They were the last piece of his power source, made a part of him, where I'd only held Cernunnos captive a brief while.

I couldn't help but wonder if it would have been easier with more bodies, creating the same kind of power circle Henrietta Potter had disrupted in the classroom. I watched him—no longer obscured, at least for this task, although I could feel a gray blankness within the city where he was out there *now*—as he opened veins and drew a bloody circle, himself and the Quinleys inside. The gift of Babylon had left me, and he made no effort, as Cernunnos had done, to be understood. His invocation was in an old language, but not, I thought, the Gaelic Cernunnos spoke. It wasn't Latin, either, but something harsher and uglier: a dead language, but more to the point, a death language. In the same way that I'd seen the energy offered up by the cops, I could see the life forces that Herne stole from the Quinleys. Where what I'd been given had been free and without fear, the Quinley's spirits were streaked with pain and terror, the brightness of their lives swallowed whole by the darkness Herne carried within himself.

I realized I was throwing everything I had at the memories the room held, trying desperately to stop what was happening in front of me. Waves of silver power rolled off me, splashing uselessly into the apparitions. Had I been here earlier, I could have stopped this. I watched brilliance slowly rise up from the dying Quinleys, blackening like burning paper as Herne stole their life force for his own purposes.

A purpose you still don't understand! a little panicked part of me screamed. How could I stop the child of a god when I didn't know what he intended? How did he mean to protect himself against hurt?

By taking Cernunnos's place in the Hunt. The thought struck me so hard I literally staggered. I didn't know if I'd come on it myself or if it had slipped away from Herne in the midst of his intake of power, but that was it.

Holy God. Cernunnos might have been better off if I'd left him in Babylon. I shuddered. Herne, his head held triumphant, closed his fists in the memory of the room. The last of what had been David and Rachel Quinley became his, swallowed whole by his hatred. He smiled, thin and mocking, and looked directly at me. I clamped down on a useless scream as he crouched and dipped a hand into blood, then stepped to a wall.

Against my will, I opened my eyes to read the message he'd left me.

Too late, gwyld.

CHAPTER TWENTY-EIGHT

When I opened my eyes—the physical ones—I was lying flat on my back with my heels still on one of the cement steps leading up to the porch. My head hurt again. More. Gary came hurrying up the driveway and crouched beside me.

"Cops are coming," he said.

"What am I doing on the ground?"

He frowned at me. "You fell over as soon as I asked if you sensed anything in the house."

"Uh-huh. Has me falling over gotten to be such old hat that you figured you'd just leave me here?" I, personally, was all for leaving me here. My head hurt, but nothing like as badly as I suspected it would when I stood up and blood started changing directions.

The big cabby looked offended. "'Course not. I was coming to pick you up when you told me to call the cops. I figured if you could talk in my head you weren't hurt too bad."

That was irritatingly logical. Except for one thing: "In your head?"

"Don't tell me you think *that's* weird, after alla this," Gary said.

I shrugged my eyebrows. He had a point. I pinched the bridge of my nose, as much movement as I could convince myself to make. "Suzanne Quinley's parents are dead."

Gary let out a puff of breath that steamed in the air. "What about her?"

"Not here. I don't think she even came home from school."

Gary nodded. "What next?"

I couldn't decide if I liked him assuming I knew what to do next, or if the idea of being in charge terrified me out of my mind. "Next I see if I can sit up without puking." I gingerly slid my hand under my head. There was water from melted snow and rain, but there didn't seem to be any mushy bits that would indicate my brains were leaking. Gary offered me a hand and I took it with my free one, letting him pull me up slowly while I kept my hand clamped to the back of my head.

"Y'know." I tried to imagine the pain away. "I used to think people who believed in all this crap were soft in the head. If they all get into messes like I'm in, they really *are*. If I get hit in the head one more time, I'll be..." My imagination failed me, both in terms of what I'd be and in making my head stop hurting.

"A monkey's uncle," Gary supplied. I winced.

"Don't say that. The way things are going around here, anything is possible."

"Got any brothers or sisters?"

"No, and I'm a girl, too, but at the moment I'm not willing to discount any absurdities. Okay, help me stand up." I clung to Gary's arm rather more than I wanted to, trying to keep my balance. "I don't feel very good," I reported, once I was on my feet.

"Gee," Gary said dryly, "I wonder why."

"I think it's all the caffeine," I said seriously, and spread one hand when Gary looked at me. "I should eat some real food. I read something saying you should eat and drink after you've been running around out of body. To ground yourself again."

"There's a pastrami sandwich in the car."

I looked up at him gratefully. "I would worship at your toes for..." I was having a hard time completing thoughts. "For as long as I could stay awake," I finished, feeling it was something of a triumph to manage to get through the sentence. Gary laughed.

"I don't figure I'm in for much worshipping, then. Can you stay up?"

I spread my hands a little more, judging my balance. "Yeah, I think so." He stepped away, toward the car. I maintained an upright position for about five seconds, then decided the stairs would be nice to sit on. My butt was already cold and wet anyway from the spill I'd just taken. "How long was I out, Gary?"

"I dunno. Two minutes, maybe."

"Oh." I wondered if you actually had to travel to fairyland to experience the more-time-passes-here-than-there phenomenon. Thus far, all my experiences had seemed much longer to me than to the mundane world around me. Gary handed me the sandwich and an unopened bottle of water. I gobbled the sandwich down so fast I almost didn't taste it, and drank most of the water before I even thought to thank him.

Right about then the cops showed up. Under normal circumstances—which is to say, in any case I wasn't involved with—Morrison would not have been heading the pack. As it was, I wavered on how to feel about it, but ended up just going with tired. I didn't try to stand up. He could yell at me while I was sitting down just as well. "Two bodies upstairs in the master bedroom," I said to his knees. "Suzanne Quinley's parents."

"You went in there?"

"Not physically." I sounded like my voice was coming from somewhere a very long way away from me. I wished the high I'd gotten from my first attempt at a trance was with me now. Right now anything I did took everything out of me. Borrowing power from the city and from the people around me was the only thing that was letting me function as a seminormal human being.

"Not *physically?*"

I stood up, half-concussed or no. I was on a higher step and stood four inches taller than my boss. "Don't," I said flatly. "Just don't. Okay? Can we not do this, this time?"

Morrison pressed his lips together, staring up at me. I admired him: he didn't climb the step to put himself on an even keel with me. I doubted I'd have been able to resist. Morrison was a better man than I.

Well, duh.

"What happened," he said after a long few moments.

I stared at him, then looked away. "I got here too late. I don't know if I could've gotten here on *time*. Maybe——" My voice sounded hollow. Maybe if I hadn't fallen for Cernunnos's little seduction, if I hadn't fallen on the steps, if I hadn't gone to lunch with Kevin——

Truth was, I hadn't had the information on who Suzy was in time to have done any good at all, and if I hadn't fallen on the steps, I'd have gone to Suzy's school anyway. I simply wouldn't have been here to stop Herne. Somehow the thought didn't really help.

"They're dead. I'm sorry." It was the only thing I had left to say. Morrison kept looking up at me, a scowl written around the edges of his mouth. Then he let out a quiet sigh and shook his head.

"All right. What's next?"

I looked at him without comprehension for what felt like a long time. "I already know what happened here. I don't understand a lot of it, but I need to find Suzy. She's——she's okay still." God, I hoped I was telling the truth. "I need to get ahold of Jen and ask her some stuff, and I need to find Herne."

"You don't know where he is?"

I gestured to the southeast. "That way." I couldn't even feel his wall obscuring the city right now. I was as ordinary as I'd been a week ago. Less than an hour ago, that'd been all I ever wanted. Why didn't it make me happier?

"You're not filling me with confidence, Walker."

"Great. That's two of us." I moved cautiously onto his step. "Do you have a cell phone I can call Jen with?"

"Use the radio."

Oh. "Right. Thanks." I wobbled down the last step. Gary offered me his arm. I leaned. Morrison turned to watch us.

"Walker."

I didn't want to stop. I didn't want to look over my shoulder and see censure in the captain's eyes. Anything was better; our endlessly antagonistic relationship was *much* better. My shoulders tensed up as I looked back at him.

"Be careful." Morrison inclined his head, then took the steps up to the Quinley house two at a time, leaving me gaping at his broad shoulders.

"Toldja," Gary said. "He likes you."

"Oh, for God's sake, Gary." I groaned and staggered down to Morrison's car, flopping across the front seat and picked the radio up. "This is Car 187, over."

"Your voice sure has changed, Captain. Over."

I grinned wearily. "Hi, Bruce. What're you doing on dispatch? Is Jen still there?" He sounded as if everything were completely normal. I wanted to hug him.

"Amber's on a potty break and Jules called in sick. Yeah, she's here, hang on."

A minute later Jen's faint accent came through the radio. "What's up, Joanne?"

"That kid who has a crush on Suzy."

"Yeah?"

"Got his name? Number? Anything?"

"You ask for the damnedest things."

"Part of my charm."

Gary, leaning on the door, snorted. "That's my line, lady."

I cackled over the sound of my stomach rumbling. It had noticed the sandwich and was now on the warpath for more. I rubbed my hand over it, whimpered when I hit the bruise, and sat on my hand.

"All right, give me a few."

I closed my eyes and let the radio fall on the floor. I'm pretty sure I fell asleep in the three minutes before the radio let out a burst of static. "Joanne?"

I flinched up. "Yeah?"

"His name's Stuart. Damned if the kid didn't put down his number in case we needed anything else. Got something to write with?"

"I'm in a cop car, Jen."

She laughed. "Yeah, sorry." She read off the number and I scribbled it down on the notepad on the dashboard.

"—wait! Jen?

"What?"

I put my teeth together. "That file on Suzy. Does she have any other family?"

Dismayed silence answered me before Jen's voice came through, low. "I can check. Bad news?"

"About as bad as it gets. Her parents are dead."

"Jesus." And a silence in which I could all but hear her nod. "I'll find out."

"Thanks Jen."

"You owe me."

"I'll fix your car for a year. Thanks again." I clipped the radio back in place and tore the paper off the pad. Great. Now I had to stand up again. I wasn't so crazy about that part right now. The car was comparatively warm and smelled strangely familiar. Like worn leather and cloves and a little bit of Old Spice. Like Morrison. Great, twice. Why did I know what Morrison smelled like?

Sliding out of the car was easier than pursuing that particular train of thought. "Cell phone," I said generally, and one of the cops nearby tossed me one. I punched out Stuart's number without really thinking about what I was going to say.

"Ssturrit."

I frowned. "What?" I hadn't thought about what I was going to say, but I had expected words I understood on the other end of the phone.

Infinite patience: "This is Stuart."

"Oh. Oh! Stuart, hi, this is Joanne Walker with the police."

"Oh, shit," the kid on the other end of the line said. "Is Suzy okay?"

"I was hoping you could tell me. Do you know if she came home after school tonight?"

"Naw, her dad picked her up."

I turned around and stared at the house. "What? Mr. Quinley?"

"No, her other dad." Usually a sentence like that would be delivered with sarcasm, but Stuart appeared to be perfectly sincere. "She's adopted, you know? She looked up her blood parents when we were in sixth grade. Turns out her sperm dad lived in Seattle."

I choked. "Sperm dad?"

I could hear Stuart's grin. "That's what she called him. Anyway, it's her birthday, so they were going out to the carousel at the Seattle Center before she went home."

I felt like I was about two laps behind. "Carousel?"

"Yeah, the carousel. She likes carousels. I guess I didn't send any pictures of her on it." Worry came into the boy's voice. "Is she okay, Miss Walker? She's been acting funny."

"Funny how?"

"She's always been kinda artsy and weird, y'know? But she's been even weirder for about, I dunno, the last year. I remember 'cuz she completely zoned out during her birthday party last year. And since, like, Halloween, it's like she's practically forgotten how to talk."

"Since *when?*"

"Since like Halloween. I remember 'cuz she passed out at the Halloween dance. I never saw anybody faint before. It's freaky. She just fell over and nobody caught her like they do on TV. She hit her head on a table and bled for about six years. She had to go to the E.R."

"Jesus. Halloween? Halloween doesn't make any se—oh! Oh, crap, yeah, of course. Halloween. Sam-haine." I was more than a little slow on the uptake. "The Hunt starts then."

"What?" Poor Stuart sounded completely bewildered.

"Sam..." No, that wasn't how they'd said it. "Sow...it doesn't matter. The Hun...it doesn't matter. Look, you've been very helpful, thanks, Stuart."

"Is she gonna be okay, Miss Walker?" Stuart was scared, and I didn't have a reassuring answer for him.

"I hope so. I'm going to do everything I can to make sure she is. You've been a lot of help."

"Thanks." The boy's voice was nothing more than a whisper. "Will you call me if anything bad happens?"

Morrison would kill me. "Yeah," I said without hesitation. "Yeah, I will, Stuart, I promise. Just hang tight. And Stuart?"

"Yeah?"

"Think good thoughts for her."

"You mean pray?"

"If that's how you want to do it. It makes a difference." I hung up, hoping I hadn't just warped the boy for life. If I didn't get Suzy out of her predicament, the poor kid might blame himself for not thinking good enough thoughts. Why didn't I ever think of these things before I said anything?

I tossed the phone back to its owner with a nod of thanks, and tucked Stuart's phone number in my back pocket. "Somebody tell Morrison I'm going to the Space Needle." I grabbed Gary and we went before anybody actually had time to tell Morrison. It seemed like the best route. Easier to get forgiveness, and all that, although I thought I had tacit permission to go off chasing wild hares. Or Wild Hunts, more accurately. I took another catnap in the cab, unable to stay awake with the quiet thrum of the engine sounding in my ears and the car's vibrations relaxing my muscles.

It was dark when I opened my eyes again, city lights reflecting off low gray clouds, the top of the Space Needle wisped with fog. Gary pulled into the 1st Avenue North Garage, crawling up to the roof parking. We sat under the off-colored light for a few moments, staring around the empty lot.

"I ain't never seen this place empty," Gary announced.

"Me either," I said nervously. "Especially not at six at night."

"Is there some kinda construction going on?" Gary shifted his shoulders. I shook my head, climbing out of the cab. Hairs on my arms stood up, even under my jacket, and I rubbed them briskly.

"This isn't natural."

"No kidding." Gary closed his door behind him, eyeing me. "This is prime parking. The monorail stops here."

"Yeah, I know. Well, hell." I leaned on the hood of the car, puffing my cheeks out. "Faint heart never won fair lady, right?"

I stepped out of my body, all my rudimentary shields collapsing. Grayness rushed over me like a tidal wave, drowning me with its weight. I could barely breathe in the thickness, my lungs filling like it was poisoned air. It had a purpose, that grayness. It was meant to obscure. I took a few steps away from the car, toward the doors that led down to the Center. "Jesus, we're right on top of him."

"Jo?" Gary asked nervously. I turned around to find my body slumped over the hood of the car, the unnerved cab driver staring at it.

"I'm over here," I said, half to see if he could hear me. He twitched and straightened, looking around warily. I waved. He didn't react. "To your left," I volunteered. He jerked to the right.

"Stop that," he demanded, not looking quite at either my unconscious body or my spirit self. "I can't see where your voice is coming from."

I grinned. My body did, too. I squinted at it. I wasn't really keen on the idea of leaving it lying around. It seemed sloppy, not to mention dangerous. "Okay," I said under my breath. "I did this earlier, right? Saw in two worlds while operating the flesh. I can do this."

I edged back toward myself and folded down over myself, which felt tremendously weird. I settled in again, remembering the idea of breathing while hanging on to the deep sense of the world around me, and then, tentatively, opened my eyes.

The world shifted, 3-D afterimages playing with my vision as I refocused with my physical eyes without losing the peculiar vision that let me see the colors and shapes of the spiritual world. Gray settled over the amber-lit parking lot as the two worlds resolved into one. I was going to have to learn to turn this second sight thing on and off with fewer dramatics. Right now I had all the grace of a bull in a china shop.

Right now, that didn't really matter. I straightened up, no longer afraid that the slightest movement would jostle myself out of alignment again. "Sorry. They're in there. *He's* in there, at least." I could see a center to the grayness now. Either I was getting better, or Herne was distracted enough that his shield was failing. I could even follow the slender line of truth that had tied me to him in the first place.

I opened the back of the cab and took out Cernunnos's sword. It shivered a vibrant blue, stronger than the gray of Herne's obscurity. It had a purpose, too. It was meant to end things.

I spun the hilt in my hand, watching the blue glitter, then grinned faintly at Gary as I headed for the door. "Coming?"

"Lady, I wouldn't miss it for the world."

CHAPTER TWENTY-NINE

The Space Needle is only the most famous structure in the Seattle Center. The whole Center covers something like seventy acres and has everything you can think of except a way to prevent people from wandering the grounds at any hour, day or night.

It was entirely empty. No bums, no skateboarding teens, no businessmen coming down from the monorail to catch a bus or to go to their cars. Coming out of the parking garage was like walking into a barbed wire fence: every step forward bit and nipped at me, trying to push me back. Gary, a step or two behind me, grunted. "It's all in your mind," I muttered.

Streetlamps discolored patches of snow into unhealthy yellows and lilacs. Bits of paper debris scattered across stretches of concrete, their rattling surprisingly loud without the sounds of people to muffle them. The desolation was uncomfortable, and that was just on the obvious side of things. With the brilliant colors of my other Sight distorted with gray, the Center looked a carnie's particular view of Hell.

"Where we going, Jo?" Gary asked very quietly. He was spooked, his big shoulders hunched and his colors muted in a way that had nothing to do with Herne's obscurement.

"It's all right," I said. "You don't have to be here, you know."

Gary straightened, offended. "You think I'm backin' out now? After being along for the whole ride?"

I shifted my shoulders uncomfortably, but didn't slow my pace. The thread between Herne and myself was contracting, drawing us closer together and getting stronger. I couldn't see him yet, but I felt him. I wondered if he felt me. "You could get killed," I said. "So far everybody else has."

"Nah," the cabby said. "I'm your good-luck charm."

I laughed, the sound unexpectedly bright in the gray light and the frozen walls. "You're a little big to put in my pocket."

"Guess I better just tag along, then." He straightened his shoulders again. I smiled.

"Gary?"

"Yeah?"

"Thanks."

"Sure. Now, what's the plan?"

"The plan? I'm supposed to have a plan?" The cord contracted again, a physical pull, and I stumbled. Gary put a hand out to steady me. "The plan is to rescue the princess, slay the dragon, kick some booty and be home in time for dinner. What time is it, anyway?"

"Couple minutes to six. You need a watch."

"I have one." I put out my wrist and discovered I was still wearing the bracelet, my watch abandoned at home where it presumably continued to tell the time in Moscow. "Nevermind."

The cord contracted a third time. For a moment, the careful realignment I'd done of body to soul was pulled askew and I flashed forward through the park to the carousel.

It spun, its music turned down, not needing to compete with

the sounds of other rides or people calling back and forth. On the outer ring, a slender blond girl rode a beautifully carved wooden horse, painted golden as sunlight. She stood up in the stirrups as I watched, leaning to make a laughing snatch at a brass ring.

"Almost," Herne said, full of amusement. I looked past Suzanne to the inner ring of the carousel. The god's son leaned against an intricate red dragon, watching the child of his blood settle back down into her saddle.

Kevin Sadler leaned against the red dragon, watching his daughter pout with laughter and get ready for another try.

I snapped back into my body, stumbling from shock. "Oh, my God, I am so stupid." I spat bile and began to run. Gary startled, then fell into a run behind me.

We skidded over the threshold of the carousel together, just in time to see Suzy make another grab for the ring, and, with a triumphant shout, come away with it clenched in her fist.

With it came down the walls that separated one world from another. Cernunnos's stallion screamed, the deep primal sound that kept making me want to scream in return. Suzanne *did* scream in response, clutching at the wooden horse's spiral pole as the Wild Hunt burst from the sky to ride down at her, twelve riders strong and one lonely mare. Even as she screamed, Suzanne's eyes went to the mare, longing. Cernunnos shifted in his saddle, leaning toward her like a hero in an old western, about to scoop up his beloved.

Herne stepped in front of her, the vestiges of his assumed human form shedding away.

I should have seen it before. Everything was there, the green eyes, the long jaw and high cheekbones. The man was slight where the demigod was broad, but the hair was the same ash-brown, albeit in different quantities. And I had known almost from the start that Herne wasn't trapped in just one shape.

"Stop," the god's son said, really very softly. The host parted and swept around them like waves, galloping ethereally through the carousel. Only Cernunnos reined up with easy strength, no sign of the injury I'd done him a few days earlier. The stallion reared back to kick at Herne before prancing nervously to the ground again. In moments, the riders swung back around and gathered behind Cernunnos, stilling their horses. The red-eared hounds slunk under the horses and leaned against their forelegs, glaring toward Herne with angry red eyes.

Suzanne hung onto the wooden horse, crouched small, too frightened to make a sound. Now that I was closer, looking at her was difficult. The slender body seemed overfull, and my eyes slid off her like I was trying to follow the shape of a second person occupying her space.

"You're much too late, Father," Herne whispered. His voice carried across the silent grounds with the clarity of a sound studio, words clipped and edged. "I've worked for this. Can't you feel it? The Rider's almost lost to you. Only a few more minutes."

Cernunnos looked beyond Herne to Suzanne. "Take her," he murmured. "I have one to replace her." He smiled, curved teeth bright in the ugly light, and looked from Suzanne to me. Herne turned, surprise filtering through his eyes. Greener eyes than they were as Kevin Sadler, but still unmistakably the same. How could I have missed it?

"You didn't check your messages, Jo," he said affably. Herne's faint English accent was gone, replaced by Kevin's Anywhere America accent. "You'd be halfway to Portland by now. I'm disappointed."

"I didn't have time," I admitted. There didn't seem much point in lying. "Lucky for me, I guess." I wondered if they made dunce caps big enough to hide under. Forever. I shifted my gaze from Herne to Cernunnos, and added, "I beat you once already, my lord master of the Hunt. I don't owe you anything."

"I lost one challenge," Cernunnos agreed, "and my word keeps me from Babylon forever. There was no caveat against a second reckoning, little shaman."

Oops. Oh well. I'd deal with that later. Assuming there was a later. "What have you done to her, Herne?"

"Can't you tell?" The touch of England was back in his voice. "Really, I knew you were a novice, but I thought it would be obvious even to you. Look closer, Joanne Walker. Siobhán Walkingstick. *Gwyld.*"

I didn't want to. Looking at Suzanne with the second sight made my head hurt. Herne's voice, though, was terrifyingly compelling. I shuddered, trying not to look, but against my own wishes, my head turned and I Saw.

Suzanne Quinley *was* overflowing, two bright souls battling for dominance in her slender body. One was so old I didn't dare look at it for long, feeling the pull of its power even at a glance. I could drown in its strength, every bit as easily as I could drown in Cernunnos's. That soul's ties ran in bright silver threads to each of the riders and to Herne, and strongest of all to Cernunnos. It was also bound, by blood and darkness, to the far more fragile soul that was Suzanne's, a mortal child buried under the weight of eternity. With every moment that passed, the immortal Rider's soul became more firmly a part of Suzanne. It was a matter of minutes before the girl herself was gone forever.

The most terrible thing was that the Rider's soul held no evil in it. It had been siphoned from its true host in fragments, stretched thin over many years, until there was so little left binding soul to body that the body could no longer keep its hold, and the soul abandoned it entirely, in need of a place to continue. And Suzanne Quinley had been primed as the new body.

"Her birthday's in a few minutes." I said softly. "I mean, the time of her birth. How did you lose her, Herne? Your own daughter. You must have tried for a very long time to father the perfect child.

Was Adina her mother?" How had he hidden himself from Adina? Had she chosen not to see, or was his strength so much greater than hers that she never stood a chance? All I knew about her was that she'd tried to help me.

"Of course not. Her mother's dead. It's easy to lose children when you've fathered as many as I have. I only found her a few years ago."

Memory, sharp and searing, cut through my mind, something I'd written off as a dream. A brick red boy, a few years older than I was, lifting startled golden eyes, to smile at me. *Welcome, Siobhán,* he'd said, offering me a hand. *This is where it begins. Brightness of body, brightness of soul.* I'd woken up with my first period staining my panties.

"When she hit puberty," I said stupidly. I remembered the brick red boy from other dreams, here and there, until I was fifteen. I even remembered thinking that it seemed like he was visiting me on purpose. They stopped very suddenly. I hadn't had one in twelve years. I was going to have to ask Coyote about that.

Later. Now there was too much to do. Herne looked ever so slightly impressed. Not, unfortunately, impressed enough to lie down and roll over for me, but a little impressed. "Very good. There were so many factors. Most important—"

"Was the birthday. Twelve days after Christmas. So that when you defeated Cernunnos, it was at the height of his power, and it was all yours. *That* much," I said bitterly, "I figured out."

"But too late." Herne turned his back on me. Nice to know I was such a threat. Cernunnos watched Suzanne calculatingly and a bad feeling came into the pit of my stomach.

"Gary?"

"Yeah?"

"You still any good at the whole linebacker gig?"

The big man chuckled. "Not quite as limber as I used to be, but I can make do in a pinch."

"Cernunnos is going to kill Suzanne at six-oh-seven. I may be busy. Stop him."

Gary lifted a bushy eyebrow at me. "At six-oh-seven?"

"It's when she was born," I said softly. "Her soul and the Rider's will be irrevocably bound at that moment. If he destroys her, he destroys the thing that keeps him from riding free."

"'M I supposed to understand what you're talkin' about?"

I shot him a dirty look. The other sight flashed red into the look, physical effect of a glare. I bet there were some people out there who could really kill with that kind of look. "Just be ready to play ball."

Gary grinned, bright white. I jerked my head around, startled. While I'd been talking to Herne, the obscurity had failed. I wished I thought it was a sign of his power weakening. It was more likely it just wasn't worth the bother, now that I'd found him and his moment was at hand.

"You have her," Cernunnos said, "but you still have me to defeat, my son."

I muttered, "I am your father, Luke," and moved forward, stepping up onto the carousel platform. Suzanne was slumped over her carousel horse. The pale mare stood beside her, between worlds, her tail flickering through the red dragon Herne had leaned against. She nosed at Suzy's sleeve, less than the wind in effect.

Just ahead of them, Herne drew a sword nearly identical to his father's, and bowed without half the grace that Cernunnos returned the acknowledgment with. I could see why he was jealous.

The clash of swords had nothing on the roar of power that was released as the two came together. Unshielded either physically or psychically, I staggered under the onslaught of strength, green and brown and impossibly potent. Lightning slammed down from the sky, into both opponents. Neither flinched. Nor did Suzanne. This close, I felt her heartbeat faltering, uncertain under the insistent pressure of the Rider. Out of the corner of my eye, I saw Gary edging closer, watching Herne and Cernunnos intently. I nodded, relieved, and stepped behind a winged swan, coming up behind Suzanne to pull her off the carousel horse and into my arms.

Electricity slammed through me, endless painful voltage. My muscles locked up hard enough to make me tremble, and I dropped to my knees, but I kept Suzanne in my arms. The bright soul of the Rider swept over me without malice, only the simple determination to survive. Entangled with it, I felt the faintest slender thread back to the body it had once owned, fey and green-eyed and boyish. And dying.

Ironic, the Rider said, less words or coherent thought than a fleeting feeling. The child who housed the soul of Death itself was finally dying in turn. Hour by hour he had slipped away from his fragile body, guided by the only thing that could compel him: demands made by another of his bloodline. Herne called the young Rider's spirit to him, binding it with blood and death, weakening him as Herne bided his own time.

Until now. Until this most recent of Rides, on All Hallow's Eve, when the world walls were thinnest. The Rider had led the Hunt forth into the void between worlds, and Herne had struck a telling blow. Taking power stored from centuries of sacrifices, he smashed the link betwixt body and soul, sending the boy Rider's body tumbling back through blackness to the world he called home. Binding the freed soul to a girl. His daughter. Suzy. Only the most tenuous connection still held the Rider's soul to the body he'd once owned.

More than just sacrifices, the Rider murmured to me. *Like*

Suzanne, those he killed to gain his power were blood of his blood. Little is as strong as blood magic.

"Blood—" I shook my head, confused, then understood: how many children *had* Herne fathered over the years? Half the world could share his bloodline by now. Hell, I could.

Except the Old Man had apparently made me from scratch, and it seemed like if you were going to bother to do that, you'd make sure you weren't getting anybody else's magic tangled up in your recipe.

Which was *so* not what I needed to be thinking about right now. I could still feel the Rider's thoughts and memories, dispassionately shared with me. He'd been caught in my world, separated from the host body and terribly vulnerable. With Herne's direction, he sought a new host. The child in—where was it? It was the silver misted world whose loss I had felt so keenly outside of Babylon, but what was it named?

Tir na nOg, the Rider replied, and for the first time there was longing in his thoughts. Herne's bindings hadn't yet wiped the need for home out of the Rider's soul. *Anwyn, Avalon, fairyland, Islands of the West, name it what you will. It is older by far than mankind and will continue when you and your names are ancient dust.* There was no apology or sympathy in the telling, the Rider's concerns too remote to be even neutral.

The dying body, the boy Rider in Tir na nOg, was Cernunnos's first child, half-mortal and half-god. He no longer knew, if he ever had, who his mother was. Blood of the god's blood, he'd taken a piece of the god's power with his birth, and with it tied the Horned God to the mortal cycle of death and life. He rode with Cernunnos of his own free will, and doing so rendered himself immortal, untouchable by the god who might otherwise sacrifice his first-born child in favor of riding free. In all his terribly long life, no one had ever compelled him against his will.

Until Herne. Blood of the god's blood, once more. Brother to the ancient Rider, but a lesser creature. There was no remorse in the Rider's thoughts: for him there was, and there was not. Neither had any reason to carry emotion. *Our father learned from me. To be cautious of what he gave the women he lay with. No other son of Cernunnos can bind him as I do; no other child has such power.*

"But Suzy," I whispered. I couldn't tell if it was out loud or not, but it didn't seem to matter. The Rider responded with the vast indifference of an immortal shrug.

She will change the bond. Blood magic is strong, and my brother has chosen well. He has sacrificed the one he loved.

Adina, I thought in despair. Had the other shamans been her friends before death? Had Herne gained his blood power through killing everyone closest to the ones closest to him?

The girl's parents. Her friends. The Rider's answer was an agreement. *It changes the balance of power. My loyalty is Herne's.*

"But that's *wrong!*"

I felt the surprise of the Rider's soul as it seemed to turn and look at me for the first time, leaving off in its quest to take over Suzy's body.

Human fallacies, he said. *Right and wrong do not matter to me.*

"What does?"

Suzanne herself turned her head to look for the pale mare. "Riding," she whispered, the desire in her voice clear and pure. She was a fourteen-year-old girl. She didn't even need the Rider's soul to want that horse with everything she had, but the power of the immortal soul within her gave the single word such an ache that I felt tightness in my throat, tears stinging my eyes. It would be Herne whom the Rider would follow, and with this child's innocent strength behind him, Herne would defeat Cernunnos and take his place. It made no difference at all to the Rider. His power and purpose were enough to rein in any god, and he would do so gladly until the end of time.

I wondered, very briefly, if Herne realized he wasn't going to be obtaining ultimate power if he won the battle. Then the electricity of the Rider's power left me and there was no time left at all in which to think.

I heard it like a chime, the clear moment of Suzanne Quinley's birth, resonating down through fourteen years. I dove to the side, dragging Suzy with me. Cernunnos vaulted the wooden carousel horse, leaving a surprised and furious Herne behind. Gary bellowed a war-cry and flung himself at Cernunnos, crashing into the god with a braced shoulder. The Rider howled in delight and dove deep into Suzanne's body, while the remaining fragments of the girl's soul shrieked in desperation and fled.

I'd caught Cernunnos with a net, in Babylon. There was so little of Suzy left that she'd slip right through a net. Instead I reached inside myself for the weary coil of energy and shaped it into a ball, fragile and pearlescent as a soap bubble. There wasn't enough time!

Except inside the little bubble of my shield, there was. The music of the chime held, a long thin sound vibrating the air. Nothing stopped, but what had been chaos almost too fast to see played out in elegant slow motion.

Cernunnos jolted to the side as Gary impacted him. His sword dragged a thin line of red across my shoulder blade as I rolled with Suzanne. I felt skin parting, and waited for it to hurt, but the pain came even more slowly than the attack. Stumbling, his features contorting with rage, Cernunnos drew the broadsword back as he turned to face Gary, the motions so precise it could have been a choreographed ballet.

No ballet I had ever seen, though, had the bad guy stick a real live four-foot long sword through the good guy's rib cage. Surprise widened Gary's eyes as he doubled and staggered back, sliding off the sword and crashing hard into the wooden horse. As easily as that, Cernunnos dismissed him, turning in slow motion back to Suzanne and myself.

My roll brought us up against the red dragon's pole, my back to Cernunnos, protecting the girl as best I could. The chime that sounded her birth hour in my head was still loud and strong, her fragmented soul caught against the bubble of slow time. Knowing it was going to get me killed, I contracted the bubble, bringing the slowness and the shards of Suzanne's soul closer and smaller until it was within her entirely, and time outside it sped back up.

I followed the bubble in.

The Rider's soul was a parasite, rust on a car, captured in the last seconds before it destroyed its host entirely, no more able to free itself from the slow time bubble than Suzanne's soul was able to wrest free from the Rider's. In here, I had all the time in the world to do repairs. Out there, if I wasn't careful and quick, I wouldn't have a body to go home to.

Just like the Rider didn't.

Your world, Cernunnos had said, and made one fist. *My world.* Another fist, not quite touching the first. *And we are here.* The blackness between the worlds. I could reach that. Could I take down the walls that held the two worlds apart?

I closed my fist around the bubble of slow time, reached for power, and threw myself into the void, dragging the Rider and Suzanne along. I didn't know where the strength to do it came from: I was afraid to wonder, just then. It flooded through me, though, once more washing away all the exhaustion and pain of the past three days. I felt, quite literally, as if I were flying.

Flashes of other worlds, closer to mine, came and went in bright colors that moved too fast to imprint. For a painfully long moment there was nothing, not even the starscape, just an ago-nizing emptiness. I held on to the sound of the chime and dredged up my own memories of the silver mist world. I flung both those things into the emptiness, like sonar, hoping for them to be rec-ognized and draw me to the right place.

Home. The longing in the Rider's voice was so intent it hurt. Inside of an instant, I was the tagalong, no longer in con-trol. The binding wound around the Rider shattered, my power replacing Herne's as the Rider and I reached for a com-mon goal.

My power replacing Herne's. This would be a good time to instigate some control. The last thing I wanted was for the youth-ful Rider to leave Cernunnos behind on Earth, where he could wreak all the havoc he wanted without the controlling influence of the child.

Unfortunately, I didn't have a single goddamned clue how to do that. *Stop! Or I'll say stop again!*

The Rider laughed at me, a sharp, bitter sound, and darkness ex-ploded into a haven of deep green leaves and silver trees, wreathed by gentle cooling mists. *Home,* the Rider thought, and I echoed it, his need for refuge resonating deep in my own soul. His need over-rode my purpose, and for a deadly moment I relaxed. Triumph, as palpable as with Cernunnos, leaped through the link we shared and I knew I was lost, unable to control the son of a god. Tir na nOg would be peace; it would be rest, after a very long journey. It was enough. I followed the Rider's lead, content to have done with it.

Home, Suzanne whispered, like a memory. It stung me into re-membering her, remembering the world we were leaving behind, and I groaned. "No." My own voice was a whisper, too little power behind it to make the Rider take pause. I closed my eyes against the green misty world and said something I'd told Gary not to, about a million years earlier: "In Cernunnos's name I set my geas."

The Rider stopped so abruptly I flew ahead of him, my own journey not yet finished.

A boy slept in the silver woods, fey and slender and so pale it seemed like death must have already visited him. I knelt beside him, putting my hand on his chest. There was a heartbeat, so faint and irregular I might have imagined it, and his chest rose and fell very slowly, the last breaths of a dying child. I couldn't remember the words to the spell I'd found on the Internet, but it hardly mattered. I had the idea of them in the back of my mind, and I bent over the child, whispering them.

"I call down the walls of the world to help free you. I call on the god who must listen to me. I call on wind and earth and sea. I call on fire to help free you. In Cernunnos's name I set this geas. By my will and by these words I bind you to ride eternity."

The coil of energy unleashed inside me as I spoke, weaving a net of silver mist and green power that wrapped itself around the boy's sleeping body. I pulled it into my arms as I'd done with Cernunnos and stood, cradling the child. He weighed almost nothing, as if he were spun from air. I could feel the resistance from his soul, which wanted nothing more than to stay in Tir na nOg, in the silence and safety that had been torn from it. He struggled against the binding I'd wrought, but he'd told me himself: blood magic was strong, and I'd invoked the strongest blood link of all, that of the father and son.

"I'm sorry," I whispered. "I need you to send Cernunnos home. Just a few more hours and the ride will be done until next year. You'll be able to go home. I'm sorry."

I fled the compelling world of Tir na nOg, bringing the boy's body back as a physical thing.

CHAPTER THIRTY

We surged out of the void into a blackness unlike anything I'd ever seen in a city, split by lightning from a storm that hadn't been there when I went under. The wind was colder than death, cutting through me and yanking at my hair like it was trying to pull it out. Pellets of snow and water struck my hands and face.

There was an extraordinary line of fire stretched over my back. When I tried to roll over the movement made me scream, a hoarse guttural sound that I was growing all too familiar with. For a moment I just lay there, trying to breathe.

Then, because there wasn't really time to lie around feeling sorry for myself, I forced my head up. As obvious as it was that I had something desperately wrong with me, it was equally obvious that Suzanne hadn't been struck by Cernunnos's blade. Her eyes were closed, but there was color in her cheeks that even the flashes of lightning couldn't bleach out, and her breathing was steady.

Which meant either I'd succeeded utterly or failed completely.

There was no boy in my arms. Wasn't that a Scottish fairy tale? I laughed, a high-pitched sound of panic, and rolled over just in time to miss being stabbed in the back a second time by an extremely unhappy god. The sword stuck into the wooden carousel floor. Cernunnos snarled. I smiled up at him and looked through his legs to see what was going on.

In the flashes of light, Gary slid down the carousel horse, dark blood seeping through his coat to stain it black. Behind him, a spark with the same unearthly luminescence as the Hunt appeared, whirling in unexpected directions as the wind snatched it back and forth. The Hunt came forward through the storm, gathering around the rapidly growing spark.

Cernunnos yanked his sword from the floor as the pale mare let out a nicker of pleasure and shadowed through both Gary and the carousel horse. The Hunt parted their circle for her, and I realized I was still seeing through solid objects.

"Stupid shaman," I mumbled, and closed my eyes. The darkness went away, replaced by the brilliance of pure spirit in everything from the carved carousel animals to the god of the Hunt himself. When I opened my eyes again it was easier to see, physical forms faded to lesser importance.

Gary was dying. Every heartbeat drove thick blood out, more slowly now than a few moments ago. Suzanne—I didn't even need to turn my head to see her—was growing stronger, her breathing deeper. Cernunnos swept his sword up and I flinched, too badly hurt to move more, waiting for the next blow.

Instead the god parried a blow he couldn't have seen, sword braced over his shoulder as Herne drove his own sword down from behind Cernunnos. Metal sang as they smashed together, then scraped as Cernunnos whirled, drawing his blade along the length of Herne's. It was perfect: Herne's sword was pushed wide, and Cernunnos opened his son's ribs from side to side in one long sweep. Herne dropped to his knees, sword falling from numb fingers, the emeralds and browns of his colors suddenly bleaching.

Cernunnos drew back his sword for the final blow, and a child's voice rang out: "Stop!"

Cernunnos dropped his sword like a marionette released from its strings, turning in shocked rage to face the young Rider. He stood fey and slender and stunningly beautiful, with a look of deep resolve in his brilliant emerald eyes. He sat astride his pale mare, one palm reassuringly against her neck, his other hand easy on the reins. Behind him, the Hunt were gathered, the hounds sitting and lying at the horses' hooves rather than slinking around.

"This one is not yours, Father," the boy said, almost apologetically. "I would that he were, for the Hell that has been visited on me. But of your blood, none is less meant for you than he but I myself."

Cernunnos's mouth curled in a snarl. "Thou wouldst have mercy on the one who stole your power and would have usurped mine?"

The boy shrugged, as painfully graceful as Cernunnos. "It is not mine to say. There is no mark on his soul that gives him to you. He is your child, Father. You cannot have him. It is the way of things."

Behind me, Suzanne whimpered and shifted, the warmth of her body moving away. Cernunnos turned, eyes bright with anger, and lifted his sword again. I felt a peculiar kind of relief, knowing that I was his target, rather than the young woman sprawled on the carousel floor.

"Father," the boy said, apologetic and warning.

"*I* can see the mark on this one," Cernunnos growled. The boy inclined his head.

"So can we all, Father, but not yet. She has a long journey before she comes to the Shadowlands."

That didn't relieve me as much as it should have. "Nor are you done here, *gwyld,*" the boy said. "Get up. Finish your tasks. We have a long Hunt before us tonight, and I will not ride until I see this thing finished."

"You're welcome too," I croaked. Ungrateful little bastard.

"Make right what has been put asunder," the boy said sharply. The mare pranced, a few nervous steps, and he stroked her neck again.

"Make right," I mumbled. "Make what right?" I closed my eyes again and sank into myself, reaching out toward everyone who stood or lay around the carousel, looking for something that was obviously wrong, knowing better than to expect the superficial physical wounds to be the problem.

Big fat sword holes are superficial? a little part of my brain asked. I told it to shut up and go away. To my surprise, it did.

Nor were my own flaws the problem. I knew that without bothering to look to myself. I touched the others only fleetingly; it was Herne, I knew that, much as I didn't want to face another encounter with him. A schism ran through his soul, a chasm of pure blackness, holding apart the thing that he was from the thing he was meant to be.

Green Man. Protector. Healer. Godling. Those things lay on the wrong side of the gap, torn and distorted by a terrible jealousy, by anger and bitterness at a mortal lifetime gone wrong, hundreds of years ago. Herne had turned his back on a shaman's path, and his immortal blood had granted him no peace since then. He'd buried pain in the pursuit of power.

Would this have happened to me? I could see the potential in myself, the buried anger from a dozen years ago, never acknowledged, never dealt with. Nor was I ready to deal with them now.

But I could acknowledge. I swallowed hard and laid myself open to Herne, soul to soul, matching wound for wound, fissure for fissure. His were deeper, more plentiful than mine, but this wasn't a popularity contest. Shared pain was pain eased. The elder who'd given me my drum had told me that after Ayita died. I'd turned away.

As Herne tried to turn away now. I caught him in a web of silver rainbows, wondering where I was getting the power to maintain my own strength, when I'd started out the evening exhausted already.

Soul to soul, we met, and Herne screamed out the unfairness of his death six hundred years before.

You're right, I said without thinking. *It sucks.*

On some microcosmic level, he stopped shouting and stared at me in astonishment. I shrugged. *It sucks,* I repeated. *It wasn't fair. But nobody said life is fair, and you've been behaving like a three-year-old long enough.*

Herne gaped at me.

Look, I'm calling the kettle black here, okay? Except I've only been sulking for twelve years, not six centuries. You're the soul of the forests, you idiot. You've been ignoring them for half a millennium. Look what's happening to them. Look what's happening to you. Green Man. I poked him in the chest with two fingers. He stumbled back a step, looking down at himself.

It still lay within him, the depths of the great woods, buried beneath centuries of pain. Once noticed, the ancient strength of growing things flared up like a challenge. It lit him from the inside, showing all the cracks and flaws in his character, just as my own spiderweb of broken glass did to me. Herne howled and flung his arms up, an action of denial even as his hands curved as if to pull all the power and strength of the woods into himself. He stood frozen like that for what seemed a brief eternity, and then the lure of power was too great for him to resist. He grasped at it, and something fundamental changed in the world.

A roar surfaced, so loud it threatened my eardrums, so loud it seemed impossible that everyone could not hear it. It was the sound of welcome, of green things recognizing the touch of their protector, and it went on and on.

Even with the onslaught of power and welcome from the earth, it took a terribly long time to delve into Herne's dearly held grievances and draw them out. But I had made him listen, for one brief moment. Long enough to begin a change somewhere deep within him, and once begun, I neither could nor would stop until the healing was complete. The power within me exulted, shooting sparks through my body that kept me on my feet much longer than I thought I could manage. There was joy in the healing, empty places inside me filling with relief and purpose that I'd never known I was missing.

I went at Herne mindlessly, stripping away lies: Richard had not betrayed him; Cernunnos had not abandoned him. Herne shrieked with rage and pain, fighting to cling to the lies and the life he'd built around them.

Adina. The essence of the woman rolled over me, through us, and for a moment it seemed like she stood with us at the carousel, expression sad. She had known, of course, that her husband had power, and more, that he had been in great pain. But she was no more able to see through the veil Herne constructed than I had been. I was grateful, very briefly, that I wasn't the only one who couldn't recognize Herne and his power instantly, even if I'd been convinced I could. Adina seemed to share a sad, wry smile with me, and then she was gone.

With her departure went the tangled remains of Herne's pain. I realized with a shock that we were tearing down even the links that held soul to body, and drew back, alarmed.

"Let it go." As with Cernunnos, I wasn't sure if the words were spoken aloud or inside my head, but they were said with tired confidence. I hesitated, and Herne repeated himself more insistently: "Let it go."

He stood in front of me, hands spread a little. The pale-skinned half god was gone. In his place was a woodling god, skin dark and gnarled as an oak tree, fingers knotty and a little too long. Looking at his face was difficult, like finding faces in tree trunks. The pale brown hair had thickened, darkened, flowing back from his face in knots and tangles. Even his colors, the otherworldly light from within, had deepened, into rich browns and dark greens, the color of good soil and summer leaves. In the half-light, only his eyes were the same, brilliant emerald-green. The betrayal in those eyes had been replaced by loss and an ancient sadness.

"Did you have the right to do this?" he asked, and his voice scraped, like rough bark being torn.

"Yes," I said without hesitation. "I couldn't have if you hadn't agreed. Hadn't helped me. All I did was make you see."

"I feel no peace," the Green Man said. I tilted my head.

"I don't think it comes that easily. Still, you've got all the time in the world."

Herne laughed, wind through leaves. "Sever the last bonds, *gwyld*. Let me go."

I looked down at the shallowly breathing body. Only a few threads still held the tree spirit to the physical form. I put my hand on Herne's chest and looked up at the godling one more time to be certain. He nodded.

I drew the rapier and swung it in a low phantom loop just above Kevin Sadler's body. The threads leaped free, coiling up into Herne as fast as released springs.

A ball of pure light erupted, expanded beyond the carousel in a flare of shocking brilliance, as white as a nuclear bomb. It collapsed back in on itself in the same instant, and the Green Man was gone.

* * *

I woke up a little while later with Gary crouching over me. The Center was dark, the lights on the Space Needle blacked out. I wasn't seeing in two worlds anymore, but the Wild Hunt still milled around, bearing with them their own unearthly light. "You're dying," I accused. Gary grinned.

"Not anymore."

"Oh, good," I said faintly. "How'd that happen?" I shifted a shoulder tentatively. The line of fire in my back had disappeared. "I missed something, didn't I? What happened to the lights?"

"They went out when you grabbed Suzanne," Gary answered, taking the questions in the opposite order. "All over the place."

Oh. That maybe explained how I'd kept on my feet, metaphysically speaking. I'd borrowed the whole city's power. I hoped I hadn't hurt anybody. "And you're not dead because...?"

"Big ball of light," Gary reported. "Weirdest damned thing I ever saw. I could see you lying down on the job over here and standing nose to nose with Herne at the same time. You swung the sword and he lit up and you faded away. Thought you were dead. Then the light faded and everybody was patched up. Was that you or him?"

"I dunno." I sat up carefully. Suzanne Quinley was kneeling by the extraordinarily ordinary body of Kevin Sadler, sightlessly rocking forward and back. I glanced at Gary, then climbed to my feet and walked to the girl in an almost straight line. "Suzanne?"

"My parents are dead, aren't they," she said in the same thin soprano I remembered from the theatre.

"Yeah," I said quietly. "I'm sorry."

"He killed them. My sperm dad killed them."

"Yeah," I said again, because I didn't know what else to say.

"Why?"

God. What a question. "Someone hurt him a long time ago," I

said slowly. "I think maybe it drove him insane. He was trying to protect himself from being hurt again."

Suzanne swallowed and looked up at me, then climbed to her feet. "He was trying to steal my soul, wasn't he? Could he do that? What was he?"

I rubbed my breastbone. "Do you really want the answer to that?"

She gave me a scornful look. "I saw what happened. He turned into a...spirit-thing. What was he?"

"A demigod," Cernunnos said from a few yards away. His stallion stood stone still, radiating impatience to be off. "His name was Herne, and he was my son."

"He still is your son," I mumbled. "Just a little less corporeal."

"So you're my grandfather." Suzanne ignored me. Cernunnos blinked, taken aback.

"We must go, Father," the youngest Rider said quietly. Cernunnos glanced at the boy, then back at Suzanne.

"I am," he agreed, and shot me a look of venom. "But I am bound to another world, granddaughter, and I cannot stay."

"Will I ever see you again?" Suzanne sounded very young and alone. I bit my lower lip. Cernunnos looked back at the young Rider, who smiled.

"At the hour of your birth, each and every year until your mortal life ends, we will greet you, if only for a moment, niece. I will lead the Hunt to you. Only do not fear us, and all will be well."

Suzanne lifted her chin and nodded, green eyes wide. "I'll see you next year, then," she whispered, and looked down at the body at her feet. Anger set her jaw, and she drew one foot back and kicked Kevin Sadler's body in the ribs, hard. Then, chin lifted again, she stepped over the body with immense dignity and walked away from the carousel, pausing for one moment to put her hand on the nose of the pale horse she'd ridden. Then she stepped down and began walking across the Center grounds back toward the parking lot. It was only then that I noticed red-and-blue flashes of light and the approaching sound of sirens, and closed my eyes. It was all over but the yelling.

"Not quite yet, *gwyld*," Cernunnos murmured.

"Oh, no," I said out loud, and opened my eyes again. Standing on the carousel, I wasn't at eye level with the god, but at least I didn't have to crane my neck too badly to meet his eye. "Go away," I said, and flapped a hand. "I won. Go ride. You don't have a lot of time."

"More than you think," the young Rider said. "We count the days from dusk to dusk. Still, waste no more time than you must, Father." He shifted his weight to the side, not using the reins at all. The pale mare turned and walked away with the rest of the Hunt following after.

"I will see thee again, Siobhán Walkingstick," the horned god said to me. I ducked my head and smiled.

"Will you visit me like you'll visit Suzanne? I may be marked for you, Cernunnos, but not yet. I've got a few things to do, first."

He reached down and slid gloved fingers under my chin, tilting it up so I met his eye again. "Not yet," he agreed, emerald eyes full of things unfamiliar: respect, admiration, even affection. "Thou art a worthy opponent, *gwyld*. I think I will leave you a gift. It amuses me."

He bent with all his customary grace, and even though I knew what was coming, the compulsion of his brilliant eyes held me where I was. Or maybe I just didn't really *want* to move. In the distance, Morrison bellowed, "Walker!", and Cernunnos kissed me, a horrifyingly good kiss that would have weakened the knees of a lesser woman.

Oh, all right, a horrifyingly good kiss that weakened *my* knees. Gary, the helpful son of a bitch, let out a piercing wolf whistle, and I colored from my collarbones to my hairline. Cernunnos released me, chuckling. "Until later, Siobhán Walkingstick."

I had just enough presence of mind to sketch a half bow, and reply, "Until later, my lord master of the Hunt."

Cernunnos returned the bow, then whirled the stallion about and, with a shout, led the Wild Hunt in a gallop up over the heads of the arriving cops. Even Morrison ducked, then glared at me through the distance like it was my fault. The lights were coming back on, slowly.

"Consorting with the enemy, Walker?" he demanded as soon as he was close enough to speak.

"That's not the enemy. The enemy's over there." I jerked my head toward the carousel, still watching the Hunt disappear up into the stars. Morrison climbed up onto the carousel and went to look at the body, eyebrows drawn down.

"That's a demigod?"

"Not anymore," I admitted. Morrison scowled at the body.

"What happened?"

I groaned. "I'll put it in my report. That's what I'm supposed to say, right? I'll put it in my report?"

Morrison frowned magnificently at me. "You're sure that's him?"

"Oh, yeah," I said in a chorus with Gary. We exchanged weary grins that nearly turned into exhausted giggles before I pulled myself back together. "Suzanne Quinley just walked away on her own." I had to stare hard at Morrison to keep my thoughts in order. "Her whole family's dead. Somebody should get her."

Morrison's mouth thinned as he looked to where I gestured, then turned away briefly, calling, "Gonzalez! She's that way."

Jen Gonzalez came out of the dark and jogged across the Center grounds after Suzy. Morrison and I both watched her, before he looked back at me. "Her aunt lives in Olympia. Gonzalez called her. She's on her way." He hesitated a moment before adding, "Suzy'll be okay."

I dropped my chin to my chest. Jen'd come through for a girl who wasn't missing and Morrison was enough on top of the details to be able to reassure me. I was wary of saying thanks, out of fear I might fall apart. Instead I swallowed and nodded. "Can we go back to the station so I can fill out whatever paperwork I need to fill out, and go sleep for a week?"

Morrison thrust his chin out. "Is it your fault all the lights went out?"

"…probably."

"Care to tell me how you managed to keep power going at hospitals and emergency services and nowhere else?"

I lifted my head and stared at him for a tremendously long time. "No," I finally said, but I smiled. "No, I don't care to tell you that at all. Neat trick, though, huh?"

Morrison scowled some more. "Yeah. It was." He struggled with the next words for a few moments, looking as if he was trying to find a way not to say them: "Good job." He gave me one sharp little nod, then flared his nostrils. "Get your ass in the car, Walker, and get back to the station. I want to know what happened here."

I took a couple steps, then paused and looked back at him. "Isn't that, 'Get your ass in the car, Officer Walker'?"

Morrison glared hard enough to set my hair on fire. Thank heavens he didn't have my exciting new power set. "Get your ass in the car, *Officer* Walker, you…" He trailed off, unable to come up with sufficient invective to describe me.

Grinning, I got my ass in the car, and fell asleep on the way back to the station. There was a hell of a lot waiting for me just on the other side of sleep, but I pushed it away. For a few minutes, at least, I figured I deserved to be satisfied with saving the girl and stymieing Morrison. The rest of the world could wait until tomorrow.

I was pretty sure it would.

* * * * *

Made in the USA
Lexington, KY
09 March 2016